Maggie Mason is a pseudonym of author Mary Wood. Mary began her career by self-publishing on Kindle, where many of her sagas reached number one in genre. She was spotted by Pan Macmillan and to date has written many books for them under her own name.

Mary continues to be proud to write for Pan Macmillan, but is now equally proud and thrilled to take up a second career with Sphere under the name of Maggie Mason.

Born the thirteenth child of fifteen children, Mary describes her childhood as poor, but rich in love. She was educated at St Peter's RC School in Hinckley and at Hinckley College for Further Education, where she was taught shorthand and typing.

Mary retired from working for the National Probation Service in 2009, when she took up full time writing, something she'd always dreamed of doing. She follows in the footsteps of her great-grandmother, Dora Langlois, who was an acclaimed author, playwright and actress in the late nineteenth–early twentieth century.

It was her work with the Probation Service that gives Mary's writing its grittiness, her need to tell it how it is, which takes her readers on an emotional journey to the heart of issues.

Also by Maggie Mason

Blackpool Lass
Blackpool's Daughter
Blackpool's Angel
Blackpool Sisters
A Blackpool Christmas
The Halfpenny Girls
The Halfpenny Girls at Christmas
The Halfpenny Girls at War
The Fortune Tellers
The Fortune Tellers' Secret
The Fortune Tellers' Daughters
A Mother's Hope

As Mary Wood

An Unbreakable Bond
To Catch a Dream
Tomorrow Brings Sorrow
Time Passes Time
Proud of You
All I Have to Give
In Their Mother's Footsteps
Brighter Days Ahead
The Street Orphans
The Forgotten Daughter
The Abandoned Daughter
The Wronged Daughter
The Brave Daughters
The Jam Factory Girls
The Orphanage Girls
The Orphanage Girls Reunited
The Orphanage Girls Come Home
The Guernsey Girls
The Guernsey Girls Go to War
The Guernsey Girls Find Peace

A Daughter's Dream

MAGGIE MASON

SPHERE

SPHERE

First published in Great Britain in 2026 by Sphere

1 3 5 7 9 10 8 6 4 2

Copyright © Maggie Mason Ltd 2026

The moral right of the author has been asserted.

All characters and events in this publication, other than those clearly in the public domain, are fictitious and any resemblance to real persons, living or dead, is purely coincidental.

All rights reserved. No part of this publication may be reproduced, stored in a retrieval system, or transmitted, in any form or by any means, without the prior permission in writing of the publisher, nor be otherwise circulated in any form of binding or cover other than that in which it is published and without a similar condition including this condition being imposed on the subsequent purchaser.

A CIP catalogue record for this book is available from the British Library.

ISBN 978-1-4087-3214-4

Typeset in Bembo by Hewer Text UK Ltd, Edinburgh
Printed and bound in Great Britain by Clays Ltd, Elcograf S.p.A.

Papers used by Sphere are from well-managed forests
and other responsible sources.

Sphere
An imprint of
Little, Brown Book Group
Carmelite House
50 Victoria Embankment
London
EC4Y 0DZ

The authorised representative
in the EEA is
Hachette Ireland
8 Castlecourt Centre
Dublin 15, D15 XTP3, Ireland
(email: info@hbgi.ie)

An Hachette UK Company
www.hachette.co.uk

www.littlebrown.co.uk

To all who are caring for a loved one and to those who offer them love and support. Especially the wonderful team of volunteers who run the uplifting Forget Me Not Dementia Café in Blackpool. Thank you for all your hard work, joyfulness and support. You give hope when there is despair.

PART ONE

Hope of Change
1903

CHAPTER ONE

Sixteen-year-old Elisha put the heavy tub of wet washing on the ground, straightened and looked back towards Primula Cottage, which stood back from Common Edge Road, Blackpool. Ram-shackled, with its thatched roof needing to be repaired after the winter storms, its paintwork peeling and its long garden overgrown, it had once been a home that held happiness. Now, its walls were permeated with fear and drudgery.

But despite this, Elisha only had to close her eyes to feel the love that had once been woven into its fabric by her Grandma Millicent, and her ma and da. Doing so now, she imagined she could hear her grandma's lovely gentle voice, and the sound rolled back the years like clouds floating on an endless journey.

'Oh, Elisha, look at you. Your ma will have me guts for garters!'

'Sorry, Grandma, I wanted to help.'

Grandma brushed some of the dirt from Elisha's frock, 'I knaw, lass. You take after me for loving the garden. It's what saved us, you knaw.'

Elisha smiled to herself as she came back to the present and remembered how Grandma had gone on to tell her for the umpteenth time how devastated she'd been when she'd been left a widow.

She, and the granddad Elisha never met, had been living in Lancaster when Granddad had died from TB. Elisha had never known what that was until three years ago when her best and only friend died of the dreaded disease. It was then she'd learnt that its proper name was tuberculosis.

Destitute, Grandma had seen an advert for a housekeeper/nurse to wheelchair-bound Raymond, the then owner of the cottage.

Wanting to hear Grandma's voice in her head again, Elisha bent to lift the heavy, dripping wet sheet onto the line and allowed herself to go back to that day in this very garden with Grandma and listen to her reminiscing.

'I used me last pennies to get on the train! By, that was an anguished journey – me wondering if I'd be accepted with me two lads, while all around me excited holidaymakers chatted about the time they were going to have in Blackpool!'

Grandma was silent for a moment, but then said, 'Eeh, lass, you don't knaw you were born, you have a good life, and it's what I strove for. Help me pick these peas – mind, no eating them! I've seen you chomping away on a pod afore now!'

The child Elisha was then had giggled.

'The journey here were a lifesaving mission, Elisha, lass. If Raymond refused me, then it were the workhouse for me!'

But Raymond hadn't refused her. Desperate for help, he'd accepted her two young boys.

'We settled in well, lass. Me and me lads – your da and your Uncle Joe. Though Joe were never happy, and that's why the moment he reached sixteen he went back to Lancaster.'

Remembering her deep sigh and knowing Grandma's expression was of a mother missing her son, Elisha was glad that Grandma never knew how Joe had turned out. As now he was the object of Elisha's fear.

Glancing back at the cottage sent a shudder through her. The curtain was pulled back and Uncle Joe stood there watching her. He moved away at seeing her look up at him.

To block out her fear, Elisha desperately brought the memory back and let herself listen again to Grandma telling how she'd fallen in love with Raymond and how, when he died and left her the cottage, she'd worked hard to build a market garden business on the land surrounding it.

'I couldn't have done it without your ma and da. Eeh, your da has such wonderful dreams for this place, lass. So, the quicker we get these peas picked, the quicker they can go to market and help him to realise the ambitions he has.'

The lovely fresh smell of the young peas assailed Elisha now – but only in her memory, for all around her were tangled weeds and overgrown paths in this vast neglected garden, once loved, once productive and once filled with laughter.

Elisha brushed away her tears. Tears of grief for her grandma, her da and her ma, and for her da's dream. All gone in an instant. An instant of laughter and anticipation, two years earlier. But the act of drying her eyes didn't stop that time coming to life again, as she once more heard that laughter as Grandma had an argument with Grundy, their beloved donkey.

'It's naw good you being stubborn today, Grundy!' she'd said. 'You're going to market and that's that!'

Grundy had opened his mouth and let out what sounded like a laugh. They'd all fallen about giggling. But at last Grundy had decided he couldn't win and had trotted off pulling a cart full of veg, with Ma, Da and Grandma sitting on the bench behind him.

Elisha could see them waving and smiling. But then she covered her ears as the sound of screeching brakes and skidding tyres came to her and she saw a lorry pile into the cart.

Only Grundy had survived, as the impact had sheared the cart from his harness.

Putting both hands over her mouth, Elisha only just stopped her screams of that day releasing once again. She had to, or she would scream for ever and ever.

What had followed that dreadful carnage was the blur of a triple funeral and the coming back into her life of the uncle she'd rarely seen, as Joe claimed the cottage and the land as his.

Trembling with the sadness that weighted her heart as pain seared her afresh, Elisha was once more aware of Joe watching her as the curtain twitched, alerting every sinew of her body and sending her emotions from grieving the past to the fear and disgust of now.

This heightened as the sun glinted on the jug of brown ale Joe swigged – always when in drink he forgot she was his niece and used her as if she was a whore.

The tears came back at this thought as she bent and picked up the empty wash basket, brushed away the dripping wet sheet caught in the breeze as it tried to wrap around her, and prayed her uncle wouldn't shout out for her to hurry as he wanted her to do that thing to him that sickened her stomach.

A clever girl, Elisha had been at the top of her class in the church school and constantly told she was destined to make something of herself. And whilst growing up, she'd been encouraged and allowed to study, and had begun to have ambitions of becoming a teacher.

To accommodate this, she'd only been called on to help with the market gardening at very busy times – picking the gooseberries or cutting the sprouts from their stalks and weighing them into bags. Always, she'd been told that she would never work the land but was to realise her ambitions.

That had changed.

Now she was at the beck and call of her hated uncle. Made to cook and clean amidst constant complaining, slaps with the back of his hand and often the snide remarks that he should never have been saddled with her. But worse than his violent outbursts were his sexual demands. He'd never taken her down but made her use her hand to pleasure him – an act that made her skin crawl and brought the bile to her throat.

* * *

A sudden banging on the window compounded her fear. Elisha drew in her breath, vowed to herself that she wouldn't touch him or allow him to touch her, but then tripped on a loose brick in the path and winced with the smarting of her back and the cheeks of her bottom, still sore from the strapping Joe had given her when she'd refused to do his bidding last time.

But then, wasn't that a better alternative? she asked herself. Hadn't it had the effect that Joe desired, as he'd suddenly stopped hitting her and bent double? His knees had buckled as he'd cried out in the same ecstasy he did when he reached that point when she did as he asked. Could she take that punishment again to achieve his desire without touching him?

At this moment, she didn't think she could.

Elisha closed her eyes. *Please God, help me.*

Opening the door and hearing his husky, 'At last. What've you been playing at, lass, you knaws what I want!', she hesitated. Wanted to run and never stop running.

'Come in then and get on with it!'

Elisha's throat tightened, but then the sound of the garden gate's latch saved her. She turned to see a young man, not much older than herself, enter the garden. He had a heavy-looking bag slung over his shoulder.

Taller than her, he had a cheeky grin as he sauntered up the path.

'Tell him to get out of 'ere and come back another day ... Go on! And get back here quick!'

Blinking away her tears, Elisha turned. The young

man spotted her and called out, 'Is this where Joe Finley lives?'

'Aye, it is.'

He looked around the garden, pushed his dirty tweed cap back off his head revealing a shock of jet black, curly hair, and let out a long, slow whistle. 'By, it's in need of more than a bit of seeing to.'

He was closer to her now and she could see his twinkly dark eyes that gave him the look of someone amused.

'I'm Jack Randal. I'm a stranger to Blackpool. I've come from Blackburn looking for work. Walked it, I did, and I've spent the last couple of weeks on the step of the pub asking folk for a job ... and for a bit of spare change to get sommat to eat ... Anyroad, Joe told me he had a small holding and might be able to set me on, though he could only offer me one meal a day and a bed to kip in. So, here I am.'

Yes, here he was – a beacon of hope, as surely her uncle wouldn't do anything to her with him around?

Though mystified at this turn of events, Elisha could only think that Grandma's money must be nearly gone and that her uncle had decided it was time to try to restore the market garden and make it earn some badly needed cash for them.

'Cat got your tongue, or sommat?'

'Naw. I'm sorry. You took me by surprise. I'm Elisha. Me Uncle Joe hadn't said owt about hiring anyone. But he said you were to go away and come back another time.'

Hoping he wouldn't and trying to stop him doing so, she added, 'He's indoors if you want to ask if he's still of the same mind to take you on ... Are you a gardener, then?'

'I like gardening, and knaw a thing or two about it. Me da had an allotment. Only, he died and I were put out of our cottage. They wouldn't let me take on the renting of it . . . me ma died two years back you see. She had a bad chest.'

'I'm sorry. I knaw what that feels like. Joe's me uncle. And me only relative.' As she told him of the accident that had taken the rest of her family, she felt like adding that she would be so glad of him coming and living in the shed – a huge potting shed that needed a good clean out – as he may stop things from happening.

But as she thought this her uncle opened the window and bellowed, 'Oi! Scarper you! I told you to come on Friday!'

A shiver shook Elisha's body. Without thinking she said, 'Don't go!'

Jack's expression changed from embarrassment to concern. 'Is owt wrong, lass?'

Afraid for him now, Elisha shook her head. 'Naw . . . I – I just thought that one day won't make a difference, you can sleep in the shed, he won't knaw. Go out of the gate and turn left. There's a jitty there. You'll see the shed. Climb the fence and you'll see a loose panel. Slip in through there. I'll get sommat to you – a blanket and some of the stew I've got cooking. Mind, I can't say what time.'

'What're you two talking about, eh? Bugger off, lad. I've business to see to. Come back when I told you to . . . And you, Elisha. Get yourself in here, now!'

Elisha couldn't stop the tremble of her lips.

Jack didn't comment. But then, he'd have no idea what she faced.

He straightened his cap. 'Ta, Elisha, I'll see you later, lass.'

He lifted his hand in a wave and slipped out of the broken gate onto Common Edge Road.

Elisha watched him go, trying to delay going inside, hoping Jack would get into the shed where he would hear any loud noise from the cottage, but her uncle's urgent, 'Come here, now!' made her hurry towards the house.

When she got to the door, the sound of creaking wood told her that Jack was entering the shed. The thought gave her comfort. Though it was crowded out by her uncle's urgent, hoarse whisper, 'Hurry, I want it now!'

Elisha's heart sank to see him stood with his trousers around his ankles and his need exposed to her.

'Get on with it, you knaw what to do. And you do it well, an' all.'

'Naw. Naw. I ain't doing it. It's disgusting!'

His smarmy expression changed.

'Get on with it . . . And hurry. I told you; I could do a lot worse to you, but I don't. I just ask you to do this for me.'

Not sure if knowing Jack was nearby fuelled her defiance, Elisha spat out, 'I hate you. You're vile!'

Joe lunged forward. Stumbled and fell as his trousers tripped him up.

Elisha ran for the stairs, her footsteps resounding on the threadbare carpet.

Getting to her room, she thanked God for her da having put a bolt on her door to give her privacy.

It ground into place.

His banging and kicking on the door had her praying, *Please don't let him get in to me!*

At last, all went quiet.

Elisha waited.

'You'll pay for this; you can't stay in there for ever!'

The sound of his footsteps going down the stairs gave her a chance to breathe again. But with the relief came the desperate tears. Yes, she'd dodged touching him this time, but what of the next time?

Despair clothed her.

The times that she had done as he'd shown her, to save him beating her any more, she'd been physically sick the moment he'd told her to stop. Running outside, she'd held her ears against his cries. Knew he was experiencing a good feeling by the sounds he made – she hadn't wanted to be part of that. He was her uncle. He shouldn't make her do such things.

Hearing the door slam, she went to the window. Uncle Joe was walking down the path, his stride telling of his anger. Once through the gate he turned towards the Shovels Inn. She prayed he would get blind drunk and be carried home on a handcart as happened at regular intervals, for then he would sleep for a night and day, wake with a sore head and not remember anything, or have those feelings for days that meant he wanted her to relieve him.

Dropping to her knees, she asked, 'Take me away from here. Please let me never have to do that thing again!'

CHAPTER TWO

Calming herself, Elisha remembered her promise to Jack.

Getting up, she poured some of the cold water from the jug on her washstand into the bowl next to it and swilled her face. This done, she went back down the stairs, relieved of that feeling of fear and dread.

The delicious smell coming from the kitchen met her, as did the sound of the lid of the huge iron pan bobbing up and down. She needed to attend to the stew before it burnt to the bottom.

Torn between saving the stew and going to check that Jack was still there, Elisha hesitated. Jack seemed like a saviour to her. But she reminded herself that besides being twinkly, his eyes had reflected his hunger. With this thought she lifted the lid of the stew.

Relief entered her on finding it just how it should be, with meat and veg tender, and a sip from the large ladle told of the gravy being thick and delicious.

Drawing the pan onto the cooler side of the hotplate, she wiped her brow as the embers from the fire heating the stove wafted up. But as hot as they were, she needed to top up the flames to keep the stove and ovens warm.

This done from the wood basket that stood in the corner by the back door, Elisha turned and went over to the sink. Leaning on it, she looked around the kitchen. *How can this room, that had been the hub of our life, look the same – lovely, inviting and as bright as the days when all those I loved were still here?*

The scrubbed wooden table still straddled the middle of the kitchen – how many laughs they'd had as they sat around it and enjoyed a hearty dinner. And the curtains still hung, fresh and cheery, as their pattern of yellows and blues brightened what could be a dark space at the back of the cottage, letting in light but shielding the rays of the sun. The deep pot sink, where they had stood washing clothes and pots and filling buckets to swill the stone floor, still gleamed as if life hadn't changed. *But oh, it had!*

Taking a deep breath, Elisha looked into the mirror hanging above the sink. A girl with no sparkle looked back at her through puffy eyes. A girl who had always been laughing but now showed the scars of bruising on her cheeks.

Telling herself that things could be better for a couple of days, she managed a smile – saw remnants of the girl she used to be . . . Beautiful, her da had called her, 'Just like your ma!' That showed through now, as she did have her ma's long chestnut-coloured, wispy hair and large blue eyes framed by black eyelashes that curled upwards.

This appraisal gave her a warm feeling as she opened the door, smiled at how it creaked and stepped outside.

* * *

Knocking on the shed door, Elisha called out, 'Are you still there, Jack?'

'Aye, I am. Is the coast clear?'

'It is. Me uncle's gone to the pub.'

The shed door creaked louder than the kitchen door had as Jack poked his head around it. His eyes showed signs that he'd been asleep. But as he looked at her, his face lit up as it had earlier, and his eyes sparkled, though instantly his expression changed to concern.

'Are you all right, lass?'

Lowering her head to hide her blush, Elisha nodded. 'Aye, I'm fine ... I – I wanted to get you settled afore me uncle comes back. What do you need?'

'A blanket, maybe, and a pillow if you can spare one. Oh, and a bite to eat, as me stomach's dropping out.'

Knowing she was taking a chance, but not caring, Elisha said, 'Come up to the cottage and we'll get all you need and carry it out together.'

As they stepped inside the cottage, Jack looked around the living room. 'Well, I didn't expect this, it's lovely.'

A pride entered Elisha as she followed his gaze. Yes, it was lovely. Made so by her ma and her grandma, and she'd kept up the caring of it.

The mahogany dresser displaying the best china stood proudly against one wall beneath, and almost touching, the low-beamed ceiling. And in the centre, around the huge fireplace that was set into the opposite wall, stood a sofa with a flowery loose cover draped over it and two matching armchairs. All had shiny mahogany arms.

In front of the hearth lay a beautiful rag rug of many colours, made by herself, Ma and Grandma. And, on the walls, pictures of Ma and Da's wedding, and of her grandma and herself – a room that had only known love in the past.

Elisha could be transported back to that love just by looking around, if her fear left her, like now.

Jack muttering, 'Mmm, sommat smells good an' all', brought her back to the present.

'Aye, I've a stew on the stove. Come into the kitchen and have a bowl of it. I've some fresh bread I baked earlier for you to dip into it.'

Jack didn't speak for a while as he tucked into the stew, but after a few mouthfuls and appreciative mumbles, he looked across the table at her. 'Sommat ain't right here, Elisha, I can feel it. It's like you're a prisoner. And how did you get those bruises, lass?'

Afraid to say anything, Elisha gave a nervous laugh, 'I'm just clumsy. I can trip over sommat that ain't there!'

Jack giggled, but his eyes held an intensity as he looked at her. 'It's your uncle, ain't it? I can sense you're afraid of him. Well, don't let him intimidate you, Elisha. Stand up for yourself.'

If only he knew how much she tried to do that, had done today, but knew she would pay for it one way or another.

Changing the subject, she asked, 'So, what did me uncle ask of you, is he thinking of getting the market garden business up and running again? It thrived once and brought in a good income that kept me and me ma and da and grandma going.'

'Aye, that's what he talked about. He said he didn't knaw owt about gardening and veg growing, and was looking for someone who did. That he couldn't pay much but could offer a bed and board. I didn't realise that would be in a potting shed and me sleeping on a pile of sacks!'

Afraid that he was going to say that he wasn't going to stay and take the conditions offered, Elisha thought quickly.

'It's bigger than most potting sheds though, and has a window and a stove. We could clear one end, and you could take the armchair and the spare bed from my room ... me grandma used to sleep in it as we only have two bedrooms and Ma and Da had the other bedroom.'

'I'm sorry about what happened, Elisha, it must have been hard for you to get over all of that.'

Elisha bowed her head.

'We're in the same boat, you and me. We've both lost them that were dear to us. We can help each other. I already feel I've met someone who understands.'

'Ta, Jack, I do an' all. It's sometimes like they didn't exist. Me uncle cares nowt for their memory. Nor does he care about me. I – I was working towards being a teacher but if I pick up a book and pen, he ridicules me. Mind, he don't see what I do in me own room. I often get me books out and study late into the night.'

'That ain't right. You should be free to do what you want to do. I like to read – maybe I can borrow a book or two from you ... I mean, if you don't mind.'

'You read!'

'Aye, I do. Me da said that if you can work with what you know instead of what you do, you can be a rich man ...

he was thinking about solicitors and the like – not that I'm clever enough for that, but I like working with numbers and he said if things were different, I'd have made it to being an accountant or sommat of that nature.'

'Me grandma said that we can all make of ourselves what we want to with a bit of determination and hard work.' She told him her grandma's story.

'She sounds like my kind of lady. And me da would have loved her as that was his way of thinking. Anyroad, if we're to sort things for me, we'd better get on and do it as your uncle could come back at any minute and chuck me out.'

'You want to stay then?'

'Aye, I do. I can make sommat of that garden, like your grandma did, and we can approach the customers she had and hopefully start to supply them again besides stand market as she did an' all.'

An hour later, they had the chair and the bed set up in the shed, and Jack had a fire going in the cast iron stove that stood in the corner.

'Home from home! All I need now is a kettle, teapot and a mug and I'll be well away.'

'I ain't got a spare kettle, but I can let you have a saucepan, and there's a tap just outside the door. The tea, cup and a drop of milk are easy to do though.'

'Ta, Elisha, I feel as though I have landed on me feet. I just hope that Joe's all right with it all. He seems to blow hot and cold.'

'He's never in a good mood with me, but I expect he's different in the pub. He lives for a drink.'

'Ain't he ever married?'

'I don't knaw, he wasn't in our lives really. Grandma used to fret about him and want to hear from him, but she rarely did unless he wanted money.'

'Well, that ain't right. Anyroad, we'll see how things pan out.'

Wanting to know more about him, Elisha asked, 'How old are you, Jack? Did you have a job in Blackburn?'

'I'm nineteen turned, and aye, me da were a carpenter and taught me his trade. We had a good thing going between us, but then me da became ill and I had to care for him. We fell behind with the rent, had little food, and, well, here I am.'

Elisha had the urge to take him in her arms and make his world better, as she knew he would hers. With this came a feeling she'd never known before, but it seemed to bind her and Jack together.

In the silence that followed this revelation, they gazed at one another. Jack suddenly turned away. 'What about you, how old are you?'

'I'm sixteen turned.'

'Have you any friends? What do you do besides keep this place going and cooking for your uncle?'

'Nowt, other than read and study like I told you. I used to help a bit with the family business, but mostly I studied. Me grandma paid for a tutor for me. But I've naw friends to speak of . . . I – I lost me best friend to TB. I knaw a few others from school days, but I weren't close to any of them.'

'Strikes me you must have been a bit lonely.'

'Naw, never that until . . . well, until the accident.'

'You've had a rough time of it, Elisha, I hope things turn around for you soon.'

She wanted to say they already had with him coming into her life, but she turned to go, telling him that she was to tidy up the kitchen before her uncle returned. Truth was, she wanted to be done with all her chores and upstairs locked in her own room before he did.

'I'll come with you and get that saucepan and stuff, oh, and if you could lend me a book, Elisha, that'd be good. I couldn't carry owt other than a change of clothes in me bag. And the landlord took everything that was left in our cottage as payment for the back rent.'

As they walked back to the cottage, Elisha told him, 'I have a few Charles Dickens novels, I think you'd like them. Me others are Jane Austen, and I still have a couple from me childhood. They're by Rudyard Kipling.'

'Eeh, I didn't expect owt so highbrow, but I'll give Charles Dickens a go.'

'They ain't highbrow, they're about folk like you, homeless, and how they survive, though in London, which is different to doing it here in Blackpool.'

'What? Charles Dickens writes about folk like me?'

'He does. What have you been reading up to now then?'

Jack looked a bit shamefaced. 'Comics mainly. And books about maths. I got them from the library and did the arithmetic problems in them.'

'Well, that's more highbrow than what I'm offering you – at least the maths books are. But I reckon that it doesn't always matter about what you read, as long as you do.'

Jack grinned. 'Now, that sounded very much like a

teacher. I reckon you've found your calling, lass...Anyroad, I'll take the book and run, as your uncle could be back at any moment.'

Jack left a few minutes later with what he needed to make himself a hot drink and clutching a copy of *Oliver Twist*. Grandma had bought that book for her as a present and had written a little message inside of love and her hopes for Elisha's future.

Feeling bereft of Jack's company, Elisha went outside to retrieve the sheets. For the first time in a long time, she enjoyed seeing them billowing out in the wind. But before taking on the battle of gathering them in, she took a moment to lean on the gate and look down the street. With no one in sight, she sighed a contented sigh. It seemed the landlord of the pub hadn't chucked the drinkers out, which meant they would be locked in and drinking until probably midnight.

Uncle Joe was bound to drink the most and be helped home and to bed. He wouldn't bother with the stew. She could safely put the pan on the cold shelf for tomorrow.

As she turned back to face the garden, a thin curl of smoke came from the chimney of the potting shed. Elisha smiled. Joe wouldn't notice that, and as the September evenings drew in, it could be cold after dark, so she felt happy that Jack would be warm and had been fed well too.

She watched for a while, finding comfort in having him so close. His face and his cheeky grin came to her mind, making her heart flutter. Her hand went to her hair and idly twirled the few curly strands that had escaped the scarf she had tied around it. But then, blushing at her thoughts, she grabbed at the sheets and stumbled back to the cottage with them rolled into a huge ball.

By the time Eliza climbed into bed half an hour later, making sure to bolt her bedroom door, the feelings she'd tapped into had grown to a warm longing. Lying back, she tried to imagine Jack kissing her and holding her in his arms.

But then, what would he think of what she'd been forced to do? Would he be disgusted that she'd even done it, despite her being afraid of a beating if she hadn't? Did all men like women to do that to them? From what she'd read there was a lot more to making love. There were caresses, kisses and touching of private parts, but there was also the act of a man entering you to give you a baby. The thought of Jack one day doing that to her tightened Elisha's tummy muscles and gave her a strange but nice feeling.

This once more went into the disgust of what her uncle demanded from her. Turning over, Elisha allowed the pain she'd held at bay to manifest itself in huge sobs. Someone as beautiful as Jack wouldn't want her. She was soiled, had taken part in a vile act to satisfy her own uncle – no matter what she faced if she didn't, she should have stood out against him. *Why didn't I? Oh, God, why didn't I?*

CHAPTER THREE

As weeks went by without any demands from her uncle, Elisha began to feel less afraid. Especially as he'd taken to going off for hours, leaving her wondering if he'd found himself a lady friend.

A happiness she hadn't known for a long time clothed Elisha with the relief of this thought and with the joy of working alongside Jack in the garden as soon as she'd finished the chores. Chores that used to take her twice as long, as her heart wasn't in them, but now were done in such haste, they took no time at all.

Together, they'd cleared all the weeds and twitch from the soil, given it a good turn over with garden forks, and by the end of October had planted peas and onions, and organised where the spring planting was going to happen.

Elisha looked over at Grundy. As always while they worked, he trotted up and down or stood grazing on a patch of rough grass they'd left for him. Jack had tended to and groomed him regularly, and had bonded with him. Grundy loved the attention and being let out of the stable to be alongside them in the garden as he was now.

On rainy days, Jack had worked in the shed behind the stable repairing an old cart, saying they would need it once they had their first harvest.

'You knaw, there ain't much more we can do today, let's harness Grundy and go for a short ride along Common Edge Road, eh? We can head towards St Anne's.'

Elisha grinned. The thought of escaping the perimeter of the cottage filled her with excitement. 'Eeh, yes, let's!'

A tiny twinge of doubt entered her at the thought of Joe returning and finding them gone, but she brushed it aside. She so wanted to be free for just a little time.

Jack's face lit up. 'It'll be a chance to make sure the cart'll stand up to being used.'

'It better had! I ain't going if there's a risk of it dropping to bits under us!'

They both laughed like excited kids.

'I'll tell you what, while I harness Grundy, why don't you fill a bottle with tea and pack a couple of them cakes you baked yesterday, we could have a picnic!'

'On the beach, you mean? That's a long way ... what if ...'

'Don't worry about Joe, he's allus three sheets to the wind when he comes home. All he wants to do is flop in the chair and sleep it off ... but naw, I think the beach is a little far for Grundy. He ain't pulled a cart for a while. I was thinking of us going into one of the fields. He can graze on some nice fresh grass while we sit in the sunshine.' Jack looked up at the sky. 'Mind, we might need a blanket, there's not that much warmth and the breeze is chilling.'

Though nervous about going, Elisha didn't want Jack to talk himself out of it. 'It's grand for autumn. You wait till the winter comes! We don't get the snow much, but the winds coming off the sea can cut you in two!'

'Ha, naw snow! In Blackburn it'd be almost up to your shins in winter!'

'Well, we sometimes get some, but it don't hang around. I reckon the salt in the air gets rid of it. Grandma used to say we were protected by the mountains surrounding us – the Lake District to one side and the Pennines to the other ... I've never seen a mountain.'

Jack turned towards her, 'What! By, you're missing sommat, lass. One day I'll take you to Blackburn. You're only a short distance from the Pennines there – and I'll show you Pendle Hill where they hung them poor women as they thought they were witches.'

'I've heard of that ... A tragedy.' But sadness for the women this happened to was soon swept aside by the feeling in her that there was so much in the world to see, and she wanted to see it all. 'Eeh, Jack, I'd love to travel!'

'Well, look lively as you can start with us going down the road, but we have to get going soon as the light fades earlier every evening!'

Elisha giggled as she ran to the cottage.

It took no time to make the tea as the kettle, always simmering on the side of the hob, soon came to the boil. The cakes – raspberry buns she'd made the day before – looked delicious. Pride filled her as she wrapped them in greaseproof paper, as even the jam filling them was from the batch she'd made herself some time ago.

This made her think of Christmas.

Jack had already begun to carve Christmas figures from scraps of wood, and planned on painting them to sell, and Elisha had the idea of making Christmas-themed cakes. The whole project had been a journey to work on together.

With everything ready for their picnic, Elisha grabbed her bonnet and a shawl from the back of the kitchen door. Then, having to stop herself from skipping with joy and excitement, went outside to where Jack stood with Grundy, both looking impatiently patient!

'He's chomping at the bit, lass, and so am I.'

Elisha climbed up onto the bench seat of the cart. Jack patted the space between them. Shuffling along into it heightened Elisha's senses as their thighs touched. The look Jack gave her enhanced this further. Smiling at him to try to get some normality back into the situation, she was glad when Jack grinned and winked in response, then turned away from her and gave his attention to guiding Grundy through the open gates as he said, 'Giddy up, Grundy, let's see what you're made of, lad.'

Once through, Jack stopped and jumped down to close the gates, giving Elisha a sense of loss for a moment, until he climbed back into the bench beside her and slid along.

Neither of them spoke as Grundy moved off and settled into a rhythm of almost trotting, though she knew from old that Grundy had only one pace and that was slow! But it didn't matter. To Elisha, she was escaping into the big wide world beyond her gate, something she hadn't done for two years, even the shopping they needed had been done by Joe dropping off a list and the delivery lad bringing their needs in a basket on the front of his bike.

'This is wonderful! Ta, Jack.'

'It's a pleasure, madam!'

This took them into a fit of giggles, leaving Elisha feeling a happiness she hadn't truly felt for a long time.

But then thoughts of what her life had been like in the abyss of loss, and of the depression she'd sunk into – the awful things that had happened, the dirty, filthy things that had soiled her young life – blotted her happiness and she looked away.

'What troubles you, Elisha? There're times I think you've a great burden on your shoulders. You can tell me, lass.'

Elisha shook her head, not just to say no, but in an attempt to banish the thought of it all and stop it from spoiling what had started as an exciting adventure.

Jack didn't say any more as they travelled along, the motion of the cart swaying them this way and that. It wasn't until he spotted a gateway to a field after they had travelled about half a mile that he spoke. 'I think this will do nicely. I can't see a farmhouse, so we're unlikely to be spotted and shooed off.'

Once they were through the gate he offered her his hand. His grin told her he wasn't going to pursue his questioning. This helped to lighten her mood. She grinned back. 'I feel like a naughty schoolgirl playing truant.'

'It shouldn't be like that . . . And one day it won't be . . .'

Jack looked away, then, letting go of her hand, went to unharness Grundy. Slapping the donkey's bottom he said,

'Go on, lad, fill your boots. This grass is sweeter than any we have back at the cottage.'

With this, the tension passed as they both laughed at Grundy's antics as he kicked his hind legs up in the air, then arched his back and seemed to do a little dance!

'Well, he's happy. And so will I be if you get that tea poured and give me one of your delicious cakes!'

This further lightened the mood and Elisha felt she could put all the badness behind her for now and enjoy this rare treat.

The tea and buns tasted a million times better than they did when they sat outside at home. Though she loved the garden and the wonderful memories she had of it, it had become like a prison to her. But now she was free, and the thought made her smile as she looked up at the dancing clouds and allowed her happiness to blot everything else out.

Jack saying, 'By, Elisha, I'm glad to have made you happy', drew her eyes towards him. Their gaze locked. Sensations tingled through her. She longed for him to take her in his arms, but suddenly he looked away, made a pretence of wanting to check on Grundy, rolled away from her and stood up. As he did, the feelings Elisha had experienced crashed into ones of disappointment and loss.

Brushing crumbs from her skirt, she too rose. 'I suppose we'd better get back. If Uncle Joe returns before us, there could be hell to pay!'

They arrived back at the cottage having only made a little conversation on the way. The air between them wasn't uncomfortable, but different. Jack seemed pensive, and Elisha felt suddenly shy of him. She was glad of the distraction of working together to free Grundy from the load of the cart and bed him down in his stable at the back of the cottage.

'I'd better go in and get the meal ready, Jack.'

Trying to lighten the moment, she told him, 'It's your favourite, liver and onions.'

As there was no response, Elisha made another attempt, 'Mind, I only just afforded that! Uncle Joe hasn't upped my housekeeping allowance and food prices are rising all the time!'

'I'm putting an extra burden on your shoulders ...'

'Naw! I – I didn't mean ... I was just making conversation. You're very quiet, Jack.'

'Sorry. It's just ... well, anyroad, while you're busy in the kitchen, I'll get back to spreading more of the compost on the garden, then we can dig it in tomorrow. I've some carrot seedlings we can plant.'

With this he turned away and strode towards the potting shed.

By the time Elisha served the dinner, Joe had returned and, drunk as usual, had slumped into the armchair next to the fire. He was soon snoring loudly.

Not wanting to wake him, Elisha shut the door to the living room, put his plated meal into the warming oven and opened the back door to look out for Jack. She hoped they would be back to normal as they ate, as it troubled her to have this gulf of emotions hanging between them. In such a short time, everything had changed. The carefree relationship they'd enjoyed seemed to have turned into a feeling of tension.

To her relief, when Jack reappeared he was his old self and as if nothing had been silently exchanged between them, as he came bounding in with his usual grin on his face.

'By, that looks good. I could eat a horse!'

Elisha laughed. 'You haven't long had a raspberry bun, lad – by, there's naw filling you!'

Their chat was easy as they ate. Jack had brought a couple of pieces of his artwork with him to show her.

The figurines of the Virgin Mary and Joseph were exquisite. 'Oh, Jack, I love them so much. You'll need to make a lot of them though, as they'll fly off our table at the fayre!'

'That's where you come in. I wondered if I carved them, if you could paint them? I found pots of paint in the old lean-to, there's blues and reds, and I mixed a yellow with some of them to get the brown for Joseph's shepherd's crook, and then I found a white paint for Mary's veil. Mind, I did wonder why there's so many paint pots out there?'

'That was Ma. She used the blue in their bedroom, the white down here, and the red for the front and back doors. The yellow she used in my bedroom. She loved painting – not how the artists do, but decorating and making the home nice, though Da used to stop her going up ladders and did the high bits.'

'Well, she did a lovely job, I'm always admiring this cottage, and unbeknown to her, she's helping us towards making our first income!'

'Ooh, we might make enough to buy a cockerel for Christmas dinner!'

'Naw, we're not going to eat our profits, better to invest. I was thinking of a chicken run, and yes, buy a cockerel – not to eat, but to secure the future of our own egg business!'

'That's a brilliant idea. It's sommat me da talked about doing, he had such dreams for this place. He wanted to buy the field at the back and expand into keeping animals.'

'A regular farm then, eh?'

'Sommat like that. Though me grandma didn't think big like me da, but never thwarted his dreams and allus wanted to fulfil them for him. So she threw herself into them, keeping chickens, and even bought a roll of barbed wire in preparation for it being done the following spring ... You knaw, Jack, one day, I'd like to carry that dream on for me da.'

'That's good, lass. But what happened to your grandma's plan to build a chicken run for him?'

'It never did materialise as ... well ... the accident ...'

'Then let's make it happen for her and your da, eh? We can call our cockerel after your grandma, then it'll be as productive as she was!'

Elisha laughed out loud, 'You can't call a cockerel Millicent!'

'No, but we can call it Millifred!'

They both laughed then.

When they calmed, Elisha said, 'The problem is, we need the funds from Uncle Joe, and he's complaining all the time about what we're spending as it is.'

'I'll talk to him, make him see how much money can be made from an egg business.'

To Elisha, at that moment, it seemed that their future was bright, and they would share it here for ever. This cheered her and banished her feelings that everything had changed between them. They once more seemed to be on a good friendship footing, though Elisha hoped there would more between them one day, as she tried to quieten the doubts inside her that warned that everything could be spoilt on the whim of her uncle.

She fell silent as she prayed that he wouldn't put obstacles in the way of their plans and that he'd never, ever return to his old ways. This last thought made her body shudder and brought back the feeling of being unclean – could she ever rid herself of that? Would Jack judge her on it? She hoped with all her heart that he never found out.

The next day Elisha felt full of hope again, not having given much attention to dark thoughts and allowing only the notion of how it seemed that the sun had come back into her life with Jack by her side. She was confident, too, that he felt the same for her. For despite his reactions the day before, there was no denying the odd glance that had held their eyes locked on one another, or the times when their hands accidently brushed and released a sensation of electricity passing between them. And now, the gentle companionship she felt as they cut back the hedges together, Jack wielding the scythe as she gathered the clippings and small branches, and stacked them in a heap to burn once they had dried out.

When Jack broke the silence between them by saying, 'You're quiet.' Elisha jumped.

'I was just thinking how me life's changed so much.'

'Mine too ... Elisha, can I ask you sommat?'

'Aye, of course.'

'Let's sit on our buckets.'

Elisha giggled at this. Jack had spoken of wanting to repair the bench that stood under a large tree in the corner of the garden, but hadn't found the time to do it. And so, two upturned buckets had become their resting place between chores.

Once sat, Jack became serious. 'I think you know how I feel about you, Elisha ... yesterday I almost said, but ... well, I wondered if you feel the same?'

He turned to look at her, taking one of her hands in his. Elisha felt a beam of light warm her through. Happiness clothed every part of her. Her smile widened as she looked into his eyes.

'You're so beautiful, Elisha ... I – I wanted you to knaw that I love you and want us to be together.'

'Oh, Jack ... I love you too. More than I can say.'

Slipping onto one knee in front of her, Jack said, 'I've nowt to offer you, me little lass, but I'll work hard and build this business up and then ask Joe for a wage. If he agrees, we can look for a place to rent. I want you to be me wife, Elisha.'

He rose, pulling her up with him. Their eyes held. His lips came closer, till they covered hers, bursting her world into a million stars as she drank in the sensation of his touch, his arms around her holding her tightly to him, the contour of his body, and yes, the feel of his need for her.

This didn't repulse her in the way it had done when Joe presented like this, but lit a fire in her that she could hardly control. But, as quickly as it was realised, her dream was shattered by the sound of Joe's angry voice: 'What d'you think you're up to, the pair of you? Get off her! I'll whip you to kingdom come, you thieving bastard!'

Elisha's body jerked away from Jack's.

Joe stood unsteadily, hanging on to the gate. His lips sagged in a drunken, uncontrolled way. 'Pack your bag and get gone! You're a no good. How dare you put your filthy hands on what is my property!'

Jack's eyes held a question as he glanced down at her. Elisha willed her uncle not to say any more.

'Get inside, you. Go on. And you, bugger off sharpish!'

Jack held her closer. 'If I go, Elisha comes with me!'

'Oh, naw she don't!'

As if propelled, Joe was by their side. Elisha felt a painful grip on her arm, then, unable to beat the power of the tug that pulled at her shoulder socket, found herself dragged towards the cottage.

'Let me go, I love Jack, we're going together away from here!'

'Ha! Never in a million years.'

With one violent movement, Joe flung her towards the open door.

Jack lunged forward but a ready fist caught him on the chin and sent him reeling backwards.

Taking his chance, Joe lifted her feet off the floor and

propelled her forward. Once inside, he flung her to the ground, slammed the door shut with his foot, and shoved the bolt into place.

Turning, he looked down at her. 'Get up! You're going to give me what Lizzie didn't today.'

Not knowing who Lizzie was, Elisha cowed away. She could only guess what this Lizzie did for Joe, and in doing so now knew why he'd left her alone for so long.

'I told you to get up!'

As he said this, he unbuckled his belt. Elisha couldn't move. Her lips mouthed, 'No ... no, don't!'

'Right, if you won't get up ...'

Pushing his trousers and undergarments down, revealing what Elisha hated most in all the world, Joe dropped to his knees and grabbed her.

To her horror, in the tussle that followed, Elisha came to realise that he didn't intend for her to give him pleasure in the usual way but was going to rape her!

Her scream shocked him. He hesitated, but then grabbed her skirt, holding her still from the backward crawl she'd used in an attempt to get away from him.

Getting himself positioned on top of her, he held one of her hands whilst his other found her knickers and ripped them from her.

His weight crushed her as he repositioned himself between her open legs. 'Naw, naw, please, naw ... you're me uncle, please stop!'

A crashing sound made him hesitate once more. And then, as if her saviour, Jack came from the direction of the kitchen and stood over them.

He kicked out at Joe, catching him in his side.

Winded, Joe rolled onto his back.

Elisha took Jack's outstretched hand and, with his help, managed to stand.

'Oh, Jack, he was going to—'

'Hurry, Elisha, we have to get the police!'

When they reached the door, Joe's foot moved and tripped Elisha over. She landed near enough to him to gasp in his smelly, beery breath. His eyes glared at her as he put himself between her and Jack and grabbed Jack's legs. Jack fell backwards.

'Think you can mess with me, do you? Well, I'm telling you, you can't! I'd kill you first!'

Joe snarled as he rose and went towards Jack. Elisha's heart sank. Jack looked in a helpless position as Joe's huge bulk bent over him, lifted him as if he were a child, before landing a punch that jolted Jack's body and rendered him unconscious in a heap on the floor.

Elisha's scream of 'No, no!' had Joe turning towards her.

Defenceless, Elisha's body shook with shock, fear for Jack and what she thought was about to happen to her.

But as she stared at Joe, and faced the unbearable nightmare she thought was unfolding, she saw him stagger, clutch at an armchair, saw the chair topple, and cringed at the loud crash that filled the space around her as it hit the ground. Then, almost in slow motion, Joe went with it, his arms flailing as he tried to grab something solid to save him but then fell heavily to the floor. His head cracked the hearth. His body slumped.

Not able to move, Elisha stared at Joe's still body as a pool of blood seeped from under his head.

The room spun around her. A black hole beckoned her, but Elisha could not let herself go into it as her thoughts screamed at her that she must help Jack!

CHAPTER FOUR

Finding Jack unresponsive, panic gripped Elisha. She stood and looked around her. Couldn't take the scene in. Wanted to scream and scream, but found herself propelled to the door, tugging at the bolt, then running like the wind towards the pub.

Not thinking of the rules of no women allowed in the bar, she opened the door, gasped at the smell of smoke and alcohol, took in the sudden silence, and begged, 'Help me, help me ...', before seeing the floor swirl around her and falling into strong arms.

'Eeh, lass, what's to do, eh?'

'Jack ... me uncle ... he was going to ... he had me on the floor ... Jack tried to save me ... me uncle ...' This babbling seemed to go on and on as Elisha found it impossible to control the outpouring of all that had happened.

The landlord took charge. 'Dan, run and get Mick, tell him we'll need an ambulance. Go on, I saw him come off duty a while back. He's at home now.'

On hearing this, Elisha felt comfort. They were going to help her. Mick Elliot, their local bobby, a widow and father of two little girls, lived with his ma in the first in a row of cottages that were accessed by a path leading off Common Edge Lane. It wouldn't take long to get to him – she should have thought to go there first!

Someone put a drink of water in her hand. 'Drink this, lass, everything will be right, you'll see ... By, that Joe, I knaw he's your uncle, but he's a bad 'un. You say he were trying to take you down?'

Elisha could only nod.

'He didn't, did he?'

It was as if she was in a stupor, as no words would come, but she managed to shake her head.

'Leave it, Bob, let Mick sort it out.'

This from another customer in the pub, who Elisha didn't know, stopped the questions. But half an hour later, with her uncle declared dead – a word that brought relief to her instead of grief – and Jack taken to hospital, Elisha sat in the now righted chair and looked at Mick, as he questioned her on what had happened.

'It ... it was all so quick ... we were in the garden ...'

The whole sordid tale tumbled from her, shocked her at how easily she told of her uncle demanding horrible things of her, how she had no one to turn to and how when Jack came on the scene her life changed.

When she finished, Mick wiped a tear from his eyes and blew his nose loudly. 'I were only just along the road, lass, why didn't you come to me?'

'I – I was ashamed. I didn't think anyone would believe me ... I did try to fight him off, I ran a few times and got to me room and locked the door, but ... he – he beat me with his belt ... only lately he ain't touched me until today.' She put her head in her hands, trying to shield herself from the shame and horror.

'It's all over now, lass ... You say you and Jack love one another?'

Elisha nodded, afraid now that even that sounded sordid, but Mick smiled at her. 'Well, he's a good lad, and I'm pleased for you. Like I say, the bad stuff is over for you, Elisha, you must start believing that ... well, there will be a hearing at the court, but it'll all be cut and dried, I'll see to that. Let's get you to the hospital to get you checked over and to be with Jack, he's going to need you to be strong. Can you do that for him?'

Nodding her head made tears plop onto her cheeks as a mixture of emotions assailed her. Her Jack was hurt, she didn't want him to die, but then her heart sang in contradiction, as she knew Joe was gone for ever. Never again would she have to do that filthy thing to him – smell the sour smell of him, be beaten by him with his leather strap, and for this she wanted to laugh out loud.

After treatment for her many bruises and open scrapes of her skin, and having been given a hot cup of tea laced with sugar, Elisha made her way to the ward where Jack was being treated.

Shock zinged through her, making her gasp and hold her hands over her mouth as she stared at Jack's pale and bruised face, at the bandages around his head and how his closed eyes had sunk into their red, swollen sockets.

'Jack ... Jack. Eeh, me Jack!' Kneeling on the floor so that her head was level with his, she stroked his hand. 'Jack, it's me, Elisha. Please don't die, Jack, please don't die. I love you. I love you with all me heart.'

Jack didn't move.

A nurse came over. She had a lovely face, with a smile that sunk dimples into her cheeks. Her hair – the bit that could be seen around her cap – was dark and pulled back tightly from her face. Her eyes were dark too. Elisha felt drawn to her as she asked in a gentle voice, 'Are you a relative?'

'Naw, but me and Jack are going to be married.'

'Do you knaw if he has any relatives?'

'None.'

'Aw, poor lad. From what I've been told you've both been through sommat that should never happen to anyone, and that you lost your uncle!'

'I'm not sorry about losing him!'

'Aye, I can understand that ... I'm Janet, but everyone calls me Jan.'

'I'm Elisha ... Will me Jack get better, Jan?'

'He will, I promise. He has concussion, so will sleep for a while, and a few nasty bruises, but nowt's broken ... You knaw, if you need to talk, I'm a good listener and I'm on me dinner break in ten minutes.'

Not asking how it was that Jan was due a dinner break at five in the evening, Elisha felt she was being thrown a lifeline, and though she'd always wanted to keep the sordid tale of what she'd been through a secret, she didn't any more, and she sensed that in Jan she'd find understanding.

'Ta, I'd like to chat. I – I've a lot on me plate ...'

'I can see that. You're like a rabbit in headlights, full of fear, and aye, full of sadness an' all. I'll come for you when I'm ready. I knaw a nice quiet place – it's in the garden, but shielded from the wind, and I can borrow an extra cloak to put around your shoulders.'

'Don't worry, I'm used to the outdoors. Me and Jack are working on restoring the market garden me grandma built up on Common Edge Road.'

'I reckon I knaw where you mean. Me ma used to take me there to pick veg from the barrow left outside. It had a note on saying, "Free to the needy, a penny a bagful to those who can pay." Me ma thought it the kindest thing she'd seen. She allus left a penny when she could, but mostly she had to take a free bag.'

'That was typical of me grandma, she had a kind heart and had known hard times. Me and Jack have talked about continuing that tradition.'

For some reason – Elisha didn't know why – she added, 'And we're going to buy a cockerel and name it after me grandma, as Jack says that'll make it productive like she was!' This made her giggle, and then laugh, and then go into a horrible state where she was laughing and crying, which escalated to screaming, until she felt a stinging slap across her already sore cheek.

'Eeh, lass, I'm sorry but ...'

Elisha's sobs racked her body. Jan's arms came around her and held her close. Then gently lifted her and led her out of the ward.

The ward sister, who'd let Elisha in under protest as it wasn't visiting time, bristled as she said, 'Take her out of here, Nurse Kettlewood! She's upsetting all the patients. I'd have never let her in if I'd have known she'd give such a display.'

'Yes, Sister.'

'Oh, and you may as well take your break. Use it to try to calm her. She's not to come back in here till visiting time.' She turned to Elisha. 'And not at all, young lady, if you're still in this state. I know you've been through a lot, but I have my other patients to think about!'

The sister made as if she would walk away but, still rattled, she stopped in her tracks. 'And, Nurse Kettlewood, I heard you using words like "knaw"! Again, it's "know"! And it isn't "lass" but "miss"! Or "lad" but "young man"!' She shook her head. 'How you ever got this far talking like that, I do not know. But I admire you. I am just impatient that you don't make the extra effort to speak properly. You are a professional, not the lavatory cleaner!'

'Yes, Sister. Sorry, Sister.'

'Ooh, just get out of my sight. I don't know what the world is coming to, or how you passed muster at your interview!'

Shocked, Elisha went to speak, but Jan squeezed her and shook her head.

They walked in silence along the corridor, their shoes squeaking on the polished lino, Jan's arm still protectively holding Elisha until she stopped their progress outside a closed door. As she turned to say she wouldn't be a moment, but needed to collect her bag and her sandwiches, Elisha saw tears in Jan's eyes.

'Eeh, Jan, that sister's a nasty piece of work, don't let her get you down, love.'

Jan shrugged and went through the door. When she came out, buttoning a cloak around her, she was smiling again. 'By, lass, it's me as should be comforting you! Come on, we just go through that door there and we're outside.'

The sun that hadn't given much warmth all day was now setting over the buildings that stood between them and the sea, leaving a red glow bathing the sky.

Jan shivered. 'Do your coat up, love, it's not very warm.'

They'd stepped out into the garden in front of the hospital and were facing Whitegate Lane. There was a peaceful aura that helped to calm some of the many thoughts assailing Elisha.

Jan pointed. 'We can sit on that bench near to the wall. It's a lovely spot.'

Looking at buildings, and a garden that showed signs of everything dying in the autumn massacre of greenery, didn't make Elisha see it as a lovely spot, but she followed Jan and sat down, not taking heed of the dampness of the seat.

'I'm sorry, Jan, I just don't knaw what came over me. Though I've enough on me plate to drive me insane ... Is that what happened? Did I go insane?'

'Naw. You had hysterics, and the only cure is a shock, which is why I slapped you. Ha, a good introduction, eh? We just meet and you scream, and I belt you one!'

Elisha laughed out loud at this – a proper laugh this time, not one that would consume her. Jan joined her and, as they giggled together, Elisha felt that she'd met a friend.

Their general chat soon turned to Elisha opening her heart, describing more than she'd ever told others, as somehow she knew Jan wouldn't put the blame on her as a lot would.

'By, lass, your uncle were a monster and you're well rid of him. Try to let it all be buried with him now though, or it will haunt you and ruin your life.'

'I will. Though how I'm going to find the money to bury him, and—'

'Let him have a pauper's burial. Let them take him and do what they want with him. Don't you go forking out!'

'I could do that ... though not sure I'll be allowed with him owning property.'

'A dead man can't own property. I'd say the cottage was yours now. Not that I knaw, mind, but that's how it should work ... Anyroad, I cut you off, you said you didn't knaw how you were to find the money for his burial, but you were going to say sommat else?'

'Aye. The medical fees for Jack. I don't knaw if there's any money left for me to use. Though the policeman did tell me that they'd most likely be giving me uncle's possessions to me tomorrow and that there was a wallet with some money in it. He said he'd guard it for me.'

'There you go then! From what you've told me of your uncle he must have some money. It sounds as though he's been paying a whore lately, an' all. Probably, like you say, Jack's presence had worried him that he might get caught in his wicked act.'

With this, she put out her hand and took Elisha's. 'How you got through it all, I don't knaw, lass.'

'I suppose I just had to.'

'Here, have a sandwich, love. It's cheese and me ma's homemade pickle.'

'Ta, I've just realised, I'm starving!'

After a moment, Elisha asked, 'Can I ask you sommat?'

'Not with your mouth full you can't! You're spitting crumbs everywhere!'

Again, they giggled as Elisha chomped away, trying to rid herself of the delicious bite she'd taken from the soft bread.

'Mmm, that's the best pickle ever! ... But, well, I didn't like how that sister spoke to you. How dare she? Why can't you speak the way all Lancastrians do? Who does she think she is?'

'The thing is that there ain't many nurses from my class of folk. You see, it costs money to train. Most are from rich families and speak as though they have a plum in their mouth ... Having said that, they all accept me and are good friends, it's just them who are higher up that get irritated with me.'

'I don't mean to be rude, but how did you afford to train if it costs money?'

'I had an uncle, me da's brother. He never married and went into the navy. He became a captain. I didn't see him often, but when I did he were lovely. I wrote to him and told him everything, how I got on at school, how I loved me lessons. And then I was taken into hospital as a child – the workhouse hospital in Wesham – with what they thought was polio but turned out to be an infection. Me uncle came on leave while I was there. He moved me to here. And that was the moment me life ambition took hold of me. All I talked about was becoming a nurse. Me uncle died, and in his will he left me enough money to get through me training. I was an oddball amongst all the others, but I weren't treated unfairly. I just have to put up with things like the sister puts me through, that's all. But I love me job enough to do that.'

'I had dreams once. I wanted to be a teacher. Me family wouldn't let me work a lot in the garden, but encouraged me to study, me grandma paid for a tutor for me, but it all ended when ...'

'I knaw what happened – the terrible accident. Eeh, Elisha, you've been through so much. But you can start again, lass. There's nowt stopping you now, your life will be your own. How old are you?'

'Going on seventeen.'

'Well then, you've plenty of time. Me uncle used to say, plan out what you want to do and then work through your plan, and you'll achieve your goal. You can do that. As I see it, you and Jack are in love, and I expect you want to marry. So, you have choices – you marry and carry on building up your business, or you pick up your studies again and leave Jack to build the business.'

'I can't think about it all now, but ta for listening to me, Jan. I just want Jack to get better and to find out where I stand.'

'Aye, I can understand that. I didn't mean to barrage you with sorting out your future, only to give you hope that there is a future, and you can do with it what you want.'

'You've done that, ta ... Can we stay in touch? You'll be welcome at mine any time.'

'I'd like that. I'm on late shift and finish at ten, I started at two, so I could call at yours tomorrow morning around eleven and have a cuppa with you. How would that be?'

'That'd be grand, Jan. I'll look forward to it.'

Jan looked at the watch hanging from a little chain pinned to her apron, 'Right, there's only ten minutes of me break left, and I need a pee. If I don't go, I'll have to wait until I finish work, so we'd better go in. You can sit on the bench outside the ward till the bell goes telling of visiting time. And don't worry, Jack's going to be all right, and if there's any change, I'll find a way to pop me head around the ward door and let you knaw.'

As they stood, Elisha had the urge to take Jan in her arms and hug her, but she held back, knowing that the extra comfort she would receive would undo her again.

It seemed the same had occurred to Jan as, when they were about to go inside, she turned. 'Aw, Elisha, love, I want you to knaw, I'll allus help you if you need it. Can I give you a hug?'

The hug did comfort, but didn't bring the expected tears, for as she clung on to Jan, Elisha knew that though she'd lost a lot today, she'd gained a lot too – she'd found a friend.

CHAPTER FIVE

Elisha stared at the thickness of the wallet that PC Elliot handed to her, and gasped as she opened it and saw the wad of notes inside.

'But ... I – I never dreamt ... he allus said we were broke! But how? He never worked, and Grandma's money must have run out by now!'

'Gambling. Joe were known for it and was a lucky beggar with it. Though he did have a great knowledge of the horses. The bookie barred him once, but he took to using several bookies' runners. As long as he slipped them sommat, they didn't let on the bets were from him.'

'A gambler! I never knew! There's a fortune here, and we've been living hand to mouth to get what we needed for the garden!'

'Eeh, lass, I wish you'd have come to me. I turned a blind eye to others gambling as long as I didn't see any harm being done. With how this place was taking shape I thought Joe was funding you, and I liked to see you recovering from the tragedy of losing your family.'

'I didn't knaw as I had folk I could turn to, I thought I'd

be judged, and, well, it wasn't sommat I could talk easily about.'

'I knaw, lass, but you will remember where I am in the future, won't you?'

'I will, ta, Mick.'

'Well, I'll be off. Give young Jack my regards when you see him, and I'll let you knaw when the hearing is. As you knaw from losing the others there's always an inquest of a sudden death. But don't worry – as I promised, I'll make sure everything goes all right.'

Thanking him, Elisha saw him to the door.

'By, it looks like you've another visitor ... Morning, Jan. Are you not at work at the hospital today then?'

'Aye, I am later, Mick. Only me and Elisha met there yesterday and I'm calling to see how she is.'

'That's good. Elisha needs a friend, and there's none better than you, lass. I can leave her with a lighter heart now I knaw you're here with her.'

As they waved Mick off, Jan said, 'You look as though you've had another shock, Elisha. Has sommat else happened?'

Elisha told her about the money. 'And yet, he kept us short!'

'Well, you've got the last laugh, so enjoy having at least some of your worries lifted as you'll be able to pay for Jack to stay in Blackpool Victoria and not have to send him to the workhouse hospital ... Mind, I'd still let your uncle have a pauper's funeral.'

'How can I? Our local bobby knaws I've got this.'

'Mick won't say owt. I'll have a word with him. When

they contact you to tell you they are releasing the body, you just tell them then that you can't afford to bury him and don't want a service. They'll most likely knaw the facts and just dispose of him.'

This sounded terrible to Elisha as she remembered her grandma had loved Joe, despite him not caring for her. But then, she would understand needs must!

'I'll do that, 'cos I don't even want to knaw where he lands up.'

'Good. Now, what does a girl have to do to get a cup of tea around here?'

'Eeh, I'm sorry, love. Coming up. But first, how was my Jack when you left work?'

'He was just the same, but we expected that . . . Look, if you get ready after we've had a cup of tea, we can go to the hospital together as it's visiting time half an hour after me shift starts. Have you got a bike?'

'Aye, I have, in one of the sheds. Not sure it still works though as I haven't ridden it for over two years.'

'Is the shed open? I'll go and have a mooch and find it while you make that tea!'

'I'll give you the bunch of keys, but be careful, you'll get your uniform dirty. Are you on your bike, then?'

'Yes, I allus ride to and from work. I don't live far from you; me and me ma live in a thatched cottage in Fisher's Lane.'

'By, that's only just around the corner! How come we ain't met before?'

'Well, I am two years older than you, so we wouldn't have been in the same class at school, and me ma never let me play out of our lane. Me da used to work on the farm down there, but he died five years ago. Me time as a kid was spent feeding the animals and riding on the tractor with him. I had a grand time.'

'And mine was spent here with me family, and me friend, Stella, but she died of TB when she was fourteen.'

'Aw, naw! I'm sorry to hear that, love. Look, we can chat some more over our cuppa. I'll nip out and look at this bike of yours.'

Just as Elisha was pouring the tea, Jan came back inside. 'It's in grand condition, someone cared well for it. Its tyres need pumping up, but that's not a problem as I've got a pump. I won't be a mo!'

'Have your tea first!'

'Naw, we need to knaw if the tyres will stay up, it'll be a test for it while I drink me tea. I don't like it too hot anyroad.' Ripping her high collar off, Jan disappeared out of the door.

Elisha picked the collar up and buttoned it around her own neck. She grinned as she looked in the small mirror hanging above the sink. She looked regal, but how Jan stood it for a long shift, she didn't know. Starched and sitting as high as her chin, Elisha thought she would choke.

When they finally sat down to drink their tea, Jan said, 'I need you to be prepared, Elisha. Sometimes things don't go how we want them to with patients, especially when they have concussion.'

Elisha's arms pebbled with goosebumps. 'Me Jack'll be all right, won't he?'

'He wasn't showing signs of anything, but it's one of the reasons I called, only it's taken me messing with the bike and drinking this tea to get around to approaching the subject with you. I – I just want you to be prepared, that's all.'

Elisha stared at Jan. She'd felt so confident that all would be well, but now doubts clouded her mind. However, Jan's cheerfulness as they mounted the bikes and rode down the path relieved the feelings.

'You're a bit wobbly, lass. Watching you from the back, you look like the jelly me ma made.'

Despite her worries, Elisha laughed. 'It's been a while and I think I've grown – the saddle seems really low.'

'It'll have to do, I'm no good with spanners. But you need to steady yourself once we are on the road!'

Manoeuvring through the gate, Elisha tucked her long black skirt under her as she remounted the saddle, and felt a lot more comfortable. Soon she was enjoying riding along the lane giggling as her bonnet ribbons flapped around her mouth and she blew and spat them away. But her legs tired as they reached Whitegate Lane, and she began to wonder if she could make the last five minutes of their journey.

At last, they had turned into the hospital drive. Dismounting, Elisha's legs shook and her breathing laboured.

'Eeh, love, you're not fit. We need to go for a few bike rides to get you back in shape.'

Elisha could only nod as she gasped for breath and wiped the sweat from her brow. Taking her shawl off, she flapped it to cool her down.

'By, that took it out of me, Jan, but eeh, I loved it.'

'I enjoy cycling to work as long as it's not raining ... Right, we'll put our bikes around the side. Then I'll go in and get myself ready to go on duty, but you shouldn't have too long a wait in the corridor.'

After ten minutes had passed, the ward door opened and Jan came out. She sat down next to Elisha and sought her hand. 'It's not good news, love. I'm sorry, but Jack has pneumonia.'

'Eeh, naw!'

'He's poorly, but not critical. He's in a side ward ... But I'm sorry, lass, as that room has to be kept sterile, you won't be allowed in.'

Elisha knew her mouth had dropped open as she stared at Jan, but seemed unable to control it. This couldn't be happening!

Jan's arm came around her and pulled her close. 'He'll get through this, he's a strong young man. I'll keep you updated on his progress, but I've to go now or Sister will have me guts for garters, she's allus looking out for me doing owt wrong.'

'Tell him I love him, Jan. Tell him to get better. Beg him to!'

'I will. I'll take special care of him, and I'll drop in after work. It'll be about ten thirty, mind.'

'I'll be up and waiting patiently for you.'

How she got through the next few hours, Elisha didn't know. But she kept herself busy, forcing herself to concentrate on cleaning the beautiful rag rug, which she'd been soaking ever since the horrible thing happened to stain it with the blood of the evil Joe.

In her mind, she didn't give Joe the status of being her uncle. He was just someone to hate, to rant against — the man who'd taken her to depravity. But she wouldn't let him win, she'd do as Jan had said and let him go to a pauper's grave, and she hoped he'd rot in hell.

The sight of the water, red with his blood, made her heave, but she wasn't giving up on getting the rug back to how it used to be — nor on the memory of the hours and hours of pleasure it had given to her, her grandma and ma as they'd worked, chatted and laughed during the making of it.

After rinsing the rug for the umpteenth time, Elisha filled the dolly tub with hot water and dissolved soda crystals into it before dunking the rug then working furiously with the dolly. She wasn't just washing the rug; she was beating Joe with the dolly — cursing him and trying to cleanse herself of him.

Sweat ran off her brow, stinging her eyes, her back ached and her nose ran with snot as tears fell like thunderous rain down her cheeks.

At last, she stopped, slumped over the handle of the dolly and allowed herself to sob — huge racking sobs that shook her body ... Why? Why? Why? What had she ever done to be punished like this? To suffer the loss of the three people she loved most in the world, and to be put through what no young girl should ever be put through by someone who was meant to protect her, and now to face losing her beloved Jack.

Her strength ebbed from her, drained little by little by the enormity of the emotions assailing her, and yet she knew, until the rug was back where it should be and cleansed of the story of the awful night that gave her nightmares and threatened to take her Jack from her, she would know no peace.

Gathering what little strength she had left, Elisha dragged the heavy mangle in front of the sink and, though feeling weak and drained, forced herself to lift the dripping rug to get it wedged into the rollers of the mangle.

Turning the handle pulled on the muscles in her arms but at last she had it through and could start to wring it.

How long it would take to dry, she didn't know, but the autumn winds would help.

At last, with the rug pegged securely, Elisha had a sense of being cleansed, but only partly. She was healing, but there was more she needed to do.

With the dolly tub emptied and the dolly stored against the outside wall to dry, and the heavy mangle pushed back into its place in the corner next to the sink, Elisha ignored her aching bones and made herself run upstairs and into Joe's room.

There she emptied the drawers and his wardrobe, and piled the contents onto the bed, before wrapping and tying them into many bundles and throwing each one through the small window onto the ground below.

It wasn't long until there was a huge fire sending flames high as she burnt the lot, soaked in the whisky he hadn't drunk, whilst the leftover beer she poured down the drain.

It was done. He was gone.

She would feel no compunction about selling his watch, his leather wallet or his silver cufflinks. The money she got for them she would add to the ten crisp five-pound notes she'd found in the wallet – more than a man doing a labourer's job earnt in a year! And that swine had kept them eating from hand to mouth!

Weary to the bones of her, Elisha forced herself to drag the tin bath inside. The huge pan she'd replenished with water and put back onto the stove was now boiling. It didn't take long to scoop it in the bath and cool it enough with cold water for her to get in and soak herself.

As she lay back, she felt like a different person. Jack would get better, they would marry, they would build the market garden up into something Grandma would be proud of, and, yes, they would buy a cockerel but call it Matty and not the silly names they had laughed about earlier.

PART TWO

Love Brings Hope
1905–1906

CHAPTER SIX

Jack's recovery from the pneumonia had been slow, but now, fifteen months later, he was regaining some of his strength.

Elisha had worked hard during this time keeping up the progress they'd made – doing the winter digging, turning the earth before the frost set in, and then, when spring arrived, hoeing out the weeds and planting more crops, and now – under Jack's direction and with a little help from him – building the pen around the coop for the hens and the cockerel they'd bought, which were soon to be delivered.

Sitting a moment on the buckets to catch their breath, Jack wiped the sweat from his face. 'Eeh, lass, I wouldn't be here but for you.'

'I love you, Jack, and would do owt to keep you well.'

'I knaw, and I love you with all me heart. Will you marry me . . . and soon?'

'By, Jack, I thought you'd never ask! Yes, yes, please!'

'Ha! Naw need to say it like that, I ain't much of a catch.'

'You're all I want in the world. Let's make it soon.'

'Aye, I don't want to spend another winter in that shed!'

'Is that all you're marrying me for, then, so you can move into the house?'

Jack laughed at her indignation. Then in a husky voice that thrilled her, he said, 'Naw, into your bed, lass.'

She blushed crimson, lowered her eyes, but when he shifted his bucket nearer to her and took hold of her hand, and with his other hand tilted her chin, she saw his face full of love, and she too wanted just that.

The weeks that followed centred around preparations: posting their banns, making plans for the day and, for Elisha, baking cakes and the excitement of seeing the frock she would wear take shape as Hetty, Jan's mum, who Elisha loved, cut the pattern out of the lovely roll of white satin fabric Elisha had bought off the market stall.

Hetty's talent was amazing, and her treadle sewing machine a marvel as it ate up the rows of stitching of seams and hems.

'Eeh, lass, you might have given a bit more notice! But, don't you worry, we'll get it ready ... By, you're going to look a picture!'

Elisha couldn't imagine herself in the beautiful, elegant gown that would flow to the floor from a bodice that fitted into her waist.

She fingered the smooth satin. 'It's so lovely.'

'Aye and so is the girl who will be wearing it. And that's what you are, just a girl. But, eeh, you've been made to grow into a woman afore your time. Now, lift your arm, I want to make sure I have the length from there to your waist correct, lass.'

Jan came in as this measurement was taking place. 'Aw, you're going to look so beautiful, Elisha. I'm right happy for you.'

'Ta, Jan. And so are you as me chief bridesmaid.'

'I love me lemon-coloured frock, and it was a snip with it being second-hand. It fits like a glove. Ma only has to let the hem down a little.'

'It was a grand find. Second-hand Lucy gets a lot of her stuff from them rich folk as come up for the season — their maids bring them in, and Lucy says they ask a fair price for them. I got two lovely frocks for Mick's girls, Mabel and Reen. They're a golden colour and have sailor collars ... ooh, I can't wait for the day!'

'It'll be grand. You'll look a picture, Elisha, and the sun will shine ... How's the baking coming along?'

'I've me cake made, and the landlord of the Shovels, and Hannah his wife, are putting on a wedding breakfast for us at a good price — Jack knaws them well. They were kindly to him when he arrived homeless. They didn't make him leave their pub steps, even though he was begging, and often brought him a mug of beer and a sandwich.'

'Aye, I've heard tell they are good folk ... Eeh, only a few days to go ... Carry on stitching, Ma!'

'Ha, I've done that seam whilst you two have been gossiping. It'll be done all right, don't you worry about that!'

'Ma can't wait to get her hat out. She bought it at a jumble a few years ago, thinking it'd come in handy for my wedding, but now she'll get to wear it sooner!'

Elisha giggled. Not that what Jan had said was funny, but the bubble of happiness in her just needed release. She and Jan had become such close friends, and Elisha had realised that had been missing in her life since Stella died. Always, since then, she'd had her head in a book and not bothered with others, but then had come the day her life had changed.

Her body shuddered at the memory. *Grandma, Ma and Da should be here to see me wed. How proud Da would be to give me away, and they'd love Jack, and Joe would never have got near to me.*

'Never look back, lass. Unless it's to happier times.'

'You're right, Hetty. I did let sommat in that marred me happiness.'

Jan's arms came around her. 'Let's have a hug. All that's behind you now, and only happiness awaits. Your Jack's lovely, and he'll take care of you and help you to forget, love.'

'I knaw ... Eeh, I can't wait for Saturday!'

'Flipping 'eck, I'd better get a move on. Go and make me a cuppa, the pair of you, and stop your chatter around me, I'll never have this gown done else. It's to be finished today so it can hang for a couple of days to get the creases out ... Go on, shoo!'

Elisha grabbed her long grey frock and donned it over her petticoat. It felt dull and the cotton material heavy and dowdy after the feel of the satin floating around her. Her heart thudded with excitement, dispelling the downcast thoughts she'd had and the moment of remembering her life with her uncle.

★ ★ ★

At last, the day was here! The April sun was shining, and the few floating fluffy clouds seemed to be dancing in her honour.

Jack would be waiting for her at the church. He'd borrowed a suit from Mick. It had been Mick's dad's best, and Jack had told her it fitted him a treat.

'By, you look lovely, lass, and at last going to have the happiness you deserve.'

'Ta, Mick. And for giving me away and then stepping to the side of Jack to be his best man.'

'It's an honour, lass.'

Elisha caught sight of her reflection in the long mirror that hung just inside the porch.

Tears clouded her view as she saw her ma's face in her own. She hadn't realised how like her ma she'd become. The same golden hair that hung in curls, with the odd ringlet tumbling to just below her neckline. The same porcelain skin. And her eyes, greeny-blue, sometimes looking more green than blue.

But this wasn't a day for sadness, so she smiled happily at herself, showing her even teeth that she kept white by using her ma's trick of brushing them with salt and occasionally with soot from the back of the fire breast.

The long satin gown, fitted at the bodice and flowing elegantly to the floor, made her look almost regal, and her veil contrasted with her golden curls, making them appear vibrant as the sun caught the light, gingery-coloured strands.

'Let's do this, lass. Let's get you happily married to your lovely Jack.' Mick smiled and hugged her as he said this.

★   ★   ★

When she arrived at the church, Elisha was met by Jan, looking elegant in her lemon frock, and the excited Mabel and Reen — short for Maureen — so pretty in their golden frocks.

'Aw, Elisha, lass, you look grand.'

'I've collywobbles in me belly, Jan.'

'Ha, so has every bride, so that's normal. But all will go well, and you just have a lovely day, eh?'

'I just wish ...'

'Naw, don't give time for wishes ... Your ma and da and grandma are here, I promise.'

At that moment, the blossom tree at the entrance to the church was caught by the breeze and showered them in discarded petals.

'There! I told you so. You said your grandma was mischievous, I bet she shook that tree to let you knaw of her presence!'

They both giggled as they picked the tiny petals from their frocks.

'Right, Jan, lead the way, and you, Mildred and Reen, follow Jan — and naw giggling, as I'll be right behind you taking Elisha to her Jack!' Mick told his little girls in a mock stern tone, but then smiled proudly at them.

The girls were angels as they walked in front of her, waving to folk as they passed them by. Elisha hadn't expected to see so many in the church. She spotted Nancy Barnes from the local shop and smiled at her, then there were folk who had stalls on the market, and others she recognised who passed by the cottage on their way home or to work and often called a cheery greeting to her Jack, and of course Hetty, looking lovely in her bright blue hat and navy coat. Her smile gave encouragement, but Elisha didn't miss her wiping a tear from her eye. Sitting next to Hetty was Mick's ma, her face straight as usual, though she did break into a smile when she looked down at her granddaughters, who gave her a wave.

They'd reached the altar, and Jack, whose back was all Elisha could see until then, turned. He gasped at the sight of her. His eyes filled with the love he had for her, and a smile played around his lips. At that moment, the sun shone rays of light down on him and Elisha thought him beautiful.

Happiness filled every corner of her body as the priest said, 'Who giveth this woman to this man?'

Mick presented her hand to Jack. 'I do.'

A feeling went through Elisha like none she had ever felt. It held love and hope and happiness as she gazed into Jack's eyes.

Mick stepped to Jack's other side and the ceremony began. Most of it, Elisha didn't let sink in. She couldn't, as the bubble of happiness and expectation that held her shielded her from everything. But when the priest asked them to repeat after him the vows that would bind them, Elisha gave all her attention to answering, whilst looking into Jack's eyes. To some they were just words, but to her they meant the world. Jack was consenting to love her until death do them part. The death bit had no impact on her, but him saying he would love and cherish her made her world complete.

★ ★ ★

Once again as she entered the pub, Elisha was struck by the smell of beer, and the cigarette and pipe smoke that stung her eyes a little. But none of that mattered when they walked into the snug and saw a long table laid out with what looked like a feast of sandwiches, along with the cake she'd baked and iced standing proudly in the centre.

The room filled with laughter and love as the afternoon wore on. People drifted in, wished them well, grabbed a plate of sandwiches and drifted back to the bar, all adding a jovial feeling to Elisha's happiness.

'Gatecrashers, love, take naw notice, it allus happens when we have a do on. But they sup plenty of ale, so we don't mind,' Hannah the landlady told her. 'You just enjoy yourself.'

This Elisha did, laughing with Jan over Hetty's hat, which was far too big for her but she seemed to love, and secretly at Mick's ma's expression, which hadn't changed from grim the whole of the time. But that was her, looking at the world with a constant critical eye that was usually disapproving.

Just then Elisha's attention was taken as someone put the wireless on and a song that wasn't appropriate rang out:

Hello, Central, give me heaven
For I know my mother's there
And you'll find her with the angels
Over on the golden stair . . .

Jack grabbed hold of her and everyone cleared a space. In his arms, the words seemed different. They seemed to

Elisha as if she was calling her ma up, as the jolly music that didn't go with the sadness of the lyrics took hold of her and she swayed happily with Jack.

'Our mas are with us, and our das and your grandma, darling. Let's dance with them and for them.'

Elisha had never really danced, but she found that with Jack's guidance, she did sway and step to the music, and suddenly the lyrics were appropriate as she imagined her loved ones were with them and happy for them.

All too soon the moment was on them. They were home. Brought there by a parade of folk wishing them happiness, and hugged at the gate by Jan, Hetty and Mick, with a nod from Mick's ma, and then excited hugs from Mildred and Reen. As they walked up the path holding hands, Elisha knew her happiness was only just beginning to bloom.

This was compounded as they closed the door of the cottage and Jack took her in his arms and kissed her – lightly at first but deepening to a passionate kiss. Elisha didn't object as his hands explored her breasts, as the feelings that took her reverberated thrills that clenched the muscles in her stomach and tingled her thighs.

Coming together with Jack lay to rest the happenings of the past, as they discovered the wonder and sheer, exquisite joy of giving and taking the love that they had for one another, and then fell asleep in each other's arms.

Elisha woke first. Glancing over at Jack, she marvelled at them being in bed together and thrilled at how they had made love for hours, sealing their happiness, and yet she worried too, as she listened to the rattle of his chest as he breathed. Would he ever get better?

She prayed he would, and vowed she would take the burden of them building their market garden business and take care of him – see to it that he had plenty of rest and the best food she could give him. She would make sure his health improved.

But alongside this optimism a little voice nagged at her that they had a long way to go, and the journey wouldn't be easy. But then she answered back in her mind: *Grandma did it, and so can I!* With this thought, she flung the covers back and jumped out of bed – though was careful not to make any noise and awaken Jack.

When she was downstairs and had opened the curtains, she found it wasn't such a good day as yesterday – her wedding day – had been. Those floating clouds had become heavy and looked to hold rain. But then that was good too, in its way. The plants needed both sun and rain to flourish.

Happiness could be like that, she thought – moments when the sun shone and all was wonderful, but yes, there would be times of cloud when the path they trod wasn't so easy. But they would tread it together and do their best.

Taking her cloak from behind the door, she wrapped it around her and went out to face a new day – a day as Mrs Randal, a day that would be the start of the rest of her life.

CHAPTER SEVEN

Elisha fell about laughing.

'Help! Shoo him away . . . Elisha!'

But Jack's half running, half hopping and jumping, rendered her helpless as Matty – wings flapping – crowed furiously in hot pursuit, determined to peck a piece from Jack's bottom.

Holding her bulging stomach, Elisha thought she would have her baby there and then if she didn't control her laughing. But then Jack's cries turned to a hacking cough, and he stopped, bent over and gasped for breath.

Propelled by her fear for him, Elisha grabbed the besom, which they called their witch's broom, from where it hung on a nail by the back door and shooed Matty away.

'Eeh, Jack, Jack, are you all right, me love?'

His laboured breathing told her he wasn't. Elisha's heart pounded as she put her arm around Jack's bent figure and gently rubbed his back the way Jan had taught her. This always helped him to shift the awful slime that still gathered on his lungs.

★ ★ ★

Eight months had passed since their wedding day in March – a time when she'd worked hard, weeding, planting and building the pen for the hens and Matty, their proud cockerel, around the chicken coop they'd had delivered. All under Jack's direction, whilst he agonised at not being able to help.

This time had also been a further cementing of their feelings for one another, and when Elisha missed her period and began her morning sickness, the journey of carrying their first child seemed a completion of their love.

Now she was fraught with worry once more as the rattle he'd had in his chest had worsened, and there were more and more times like this one when she recalled what the doctor at the hospital had warned when he'd discharged Jack: 'Your lungs may be scarred, Jack, leaving you with lasting problems. Rest often and be careful not to catch a cold.' And, true to that prediction, Jack's problems were getting worse and Elisha feared for their future.

'Let's get you to the bench, me love ... Aw, Jack, you don't deserve this.' Elisha steered Jack towards the bench that he had finally made, which stood where the buckets used to – now they were full of earth and had forget-me-nots planted in them, and took pride of place, one each end of the bench.

'Naw, neither do you, me little lass. I'm near useless to you.'

'Never that, Jack. Naw, never that.'

'But any exertion renders me so.' He gasped in a deep breath. 'Our crops did well, but now we only have the few sacks of spuds to sell . . . I'm worried, Elisha. Our money is running out.'

'We have enough left to see us through the winter, and the time of the birth of our child and my recovery, then I can do all that needs doing.'

'That will be too late, love. We haven't sent anything but eggs to market for a while and you're not able to stand market now!'

'I am. I'll ask Jan to help me to gather the Brussels sprouts. We've a fair crop of them, and folk love them for their Christmas dinner. And we've still some carrots and, as you say, the rest of the spuds, and besides that the hens have laid well. That lot will bring a bit in.'

'Eeh, Elisha, what would I do without you? I do love you.'

Elisha pulled her shawl further around her and lay her head on Jack's shoulder. As she did, she looked towards the gate. 'Me life changed when you walked through that gate, Jack. It's me that should ask what I'd do without you!'

They held hands.

'Don't worry, love,' she continued. 'We're not finished yet. Jan said she'd call in later. You'll see, she'll help me with all there is to do.'

It was the next day, with Jan on two days' leave, that they all three manned the market stall they'd set up.

The work of gathering so much together to sell had been hard and mostly done by Jan, who'd donned one of Jack's brown overalls to cover her uniform and got stuck in to digging like she was born to it. Elisha had gathered the spuds and carrots Jan had overturned, and then together they'd spent an hour breaking the sprouts from their stalks and bagging them in small and large bags.

Jack had recovered enough to collect the eggs, and it was these that were drawing folk to their stall, but once there, Elisha and Jan managed to sell their produce to most of them. By lunchtime they had sold out.

'Well, lasses, I reckon with what we've made we can treat ourselves to some shellfish from Roberts'. I ain't had any since coming here, but I'm allus being told you can't beat sitting with a pint and a plate of shellfish in Roberts'.'

'That'd be grand, Jack, but you'll have to fetch your beer from the Mitre around the corner. Can you stay an' all, Jan?'

Jan had been looking in the direction of the prom for the last few minutes as they'd cleared down their stall. 'Aye, but I'm looking out for me ma. She said she'd have a wander down, but ... Aw, there she is ... Ma, Ma, over here!'

Elisha looked over and saw Hetty walking towards them.

Hetty's kindness had helped them so often over the last months, often sending over a pie she'd baked for them, or coming and sitting on their bench and encouraging them on. Always she told the same story Jan had told, of how many a time what she took from the barrow at their gate had saved her. 'Your Gran was a belter. Allus working hard, but allus giving to others,' Hetty had told her.

As she came over now, wearing a long grey skirt with a twinset in blue, and dark hair speckled with grey strands tucked under her bonnet, her smile warmed Elisha's heart.

'Eeh, Ma, you're late,' Jan called out to her, 'I've been looking out for you this ten minutes since.'

'I had a wander around . . . Well, it looks as though you've had a good morning. You're sold out! I'm glad for you, Jack and Elisha – you both deserve a cuddle.'

With this she hugged them to her.

'We couldn't have done it without Jan's help, but yes, we've a fair bit of cash in our bag now. And Jack has suggested we have a rare treat and go to Roberts' Oyster Bar!'

'By, I'll join you in that. The last time I went there was years ago!'

They were soon walking down the promenade, with Jack leading Grundy, as it hadn't taken long to dismantle their stall and load it onto the cart.

'This is grand, ain't it?'

'It is, Hetty. I love being down here. The sea, and listening to it crash onto the beach, the sounds of the traders calling out their wares. The sight of the posh cabs taking the Londoners and such wherever they want to go, and all to a chorus of seagulls!'

'Aye, I do an' all, Elisha, love. Them rich folk love to come and dip in the sea even in winter, as some of them are here for Christmas. They say it has properties that are good for their health . . . Well, rather them than me – it's freezing in summer, let alone now! I've only ever dipped me toes in it!'

'Let's do that now, eh. Me feet are killing me with standing,' Elisha said.

Jan took this up. 'Aye, let's! Mine are aching an' all, so I dread to think what yours feel like, Elisha, carrying that bulk around with you.'

Elisha laughed but put her two hands on her stomach as she did. She couldn't wait for her babby to be born. Not least to feel human again, but imagining holding her little one sent her into happy dreams.

'Well, I'll give it a miss and carry on to Roberts' – I can see there's a space there to tether Grundy,' Jack told them.

'Why not order our food and bring it out here, Jack?' Elisha asked, suddenly not wanting to sit in the small space with others and breathe in the smoke they puffed from their pipes.

'Aye, all right, only I'll sit in with mine as that pint's calling me. Are you sure you'll be warm enough?'

'I won't be, but I can't leave this daft pair to their own devices,' Hetty told him.

Jack laughed and, as he did, his breath formed a cloud of mist, making Elisha realise just how cold it was. And, she thought, Jack looked tired as he stepped onto the bench of the cart to drive the rest of the way. She hoped his rest in Roberts' bar with his pint would do him good.

The three of them went towards the steps to the beach. Jan ran down them, but Hetty and Elisha took their time, Hetty clinging to the rails and Elisha waddling duck-fashion as she held on to her bulk.

Once on the sand they discarded their shoes and ran to the water's edge. The cold water tingled but soothed, and Elisha felt herself relax in a way she hadn't done for a long time.

'By, your Jack's looking well today, lass.'

'He is, Hetty. He had a bad day yesterday, but having a bit of hope allus helps him.'

'There's a lot of work being done on how stress can make folks' symptoms worse,' Jan told them, 'so that's what we must aim for for Jack – a stress-free life.'

'That'd be good, but hard to do. He worries about everything.'

'Well, he has a lot on his plate,' Hetty said. 'It'll be better when little one is born – he feels the weight of watching you work when he can't.'

'Not long now, and that should happen, but by, I'm scared of when it does. I don't knaw what to expect and lie awake thinking of how it can come out of such a small opening.'

Hetty sighed. 'Do yer want to knaw, as it ain't all good? But I'm a believer that if you have the facts you can deal with them.'

'I do, Hetty. I've asked Jan, as she knaws, but she says I'm better not knowing.'

'That's her medical training – keep folk in the dark then they don't worry about it! It's daft.'

'I knaw but, well, it's what they teach us,' Jan replied. 'Like I say, worry can escalate conditions.'

'But folk have a right to knaw what's happening to their own body. In my mind they can prepare for it and do sommat to help themselves.'

'Well, I want to knaw, Hetty, as I lie awake at night thinking about it and how it'll happen soon.'

A wave bigger than the rest ended the conversation and sent them running back up the beach. When they reached the wall, they sat down giggling and panting for breath. The beach donkeys, brought out for the Christmas season, went by at that moment, and one of them turned and gave that laugh that donkeys give.

'By, you wouldn't laugh if you'd just been soaked up to the knees, you big oaf,' Hetty told him.

This sent them into a giggling fit that made Elisha's tummy ache.

Jack came back at that moment carrying a bag of seafood. 'Here you are, lasses. Enjoy. I'm going back to me pint.'

He bent and kissed Elisha on the nose. She blushed at this public display of affection, but loved the feeling it gave her as he winked at her. 'Enjoy. I won't be long.'

With the promise in the wink, Elisha so wanted her babby born so that she and Jack could get back to the normal rough and tumble in their bed. She yearned to express her love for him, instead of the fumbling and uncomfortable lovemaking they indulged in whenever Jack felt well enough. Though she loved the cuddles they enjoyed when he didn't. Snuggling into Jack's warm body gave her comfort and a feeling of being loved and safe.

The thought came to her – was she safe? With it, a shudder trembled through her. How could she get Jack well? How long could he carry on building her da's dream with her? As that's how they looked on the market garden – to one day make it as her da had dreamt it would be.

'Eeh, you're quiet, lass. Come on, let's tuck in.'

'While we do, tell me how the birth of me young 'un'll go, Hetty. I'll feel better for knowing.'

Though, as she listened to Hetty, Elisha wasn't sure she was feeling better or more afraid.

'The thing is, lass, it has to happen. It's there and it has to come out. So, do as me ma told me to do – go with it. Let it happen, encourage the pains and work with them, as its them that will open you up and let your babby come into the world.'

Elisha didn't like the sound of 'opening up', but the last bit of Hetty's sentence filled her with joy. Aye, she would let her babby come into the world. She couldn't wait to welcome it. It was then she knew that no matter what it took she would do it and, as Hetty said, go with it.

Her curses didn't speak of this three weeks later, on Christmas Day, when after helping Jack to feed the chickens, Elisha was doubled in pain. 'Help me, Jack, help me!'

'Aw, me little lass, has your back pain got worse?'

As she clung on to him, she told him, 'Aye, it has Jack and I'm thinking that it's nowt to do with the hard work! Sommat's happening ... Eeh, naw! I've wet meself!'

'Ha! That'll be babby on the way. A mite early, but not too early. Let's get you on the bed and I'll fetch Hetty over.'

Two hours later, with sweat running off her brow, any swear word Elisha had ever heard in her life tumbled out of her mouth as she railed at Jack and Hetty.

'You swear all you like, lass. It ain't naw picnic. But remember what I said, it's how your young 'un will get into the world and that's the important bit.'

'Ain't you better to save your energy, me little lass?'

'Let her be how she wants to be, Jack. It bloody hurts, I can tell you. She'll have enough energy, Mother Nature will see to that.'

'Aye, all right, Hetty, but this ain't like Elisha.'

'I knaw. Don't worry about it, she'll be right as rain. We forget the intensity of the pain once babby is put into our arms ... Eeh, that'll be any minute now ... Push, Elisha, I can see babby's head!'

Elisha put all she had into the push. She was sure her neck would burst open with the pressure of it. But suddenly there was the feel of something sliding from her and, within seconds, the wailing cry of a newborn.

'It's a lad, aw, me little lass, you've given me a lad!'

Jack was kissing her hair and her wet face, wetting it more as his tears of joy mingled with hers and with the sweat beads that trickled from her forehead.

'By, he's a big 'un an' all,' Hetty said. 'I'd say knocking on for eight pound or more. Here, Jack, I've swaddled him. Let Elisha hold him and then while I get the afterbirth sorted and clean her up, you can take me laddie to your shed and weigh him on them big scales you have.'

Nothing could compare with the feeling that surged through Elisha as she held her little son close to her. His reddish, squashed face looked beautiful to her. He had the look of his da, and yet there was a little of her around his mouth – his shaped lips and the tiny dimple in his chin. His tuft of hair showed a golden glow, so that too he'd taken from her.

'Aw, me little lad. The sunshine of me life. I'm your ma,

and I love you with all me heart. I'll take care of you. Nowt'll ever harm you, lad.'

Bending forward, she kissed her babby's head, and as she drew back, saw and felt the love he had for her. 'It's a miracle, Hetty. A miracle.'

'Aye, lass, this is the best moment in your life. You'll never forget it.'

Looking up at Jack, she saw the love he had, for her and for his son. He gently stroked the still-bloodied brow of their babby. 'Hello, me lad. Your ma and me have a name for you. You're to be named after me da, and your ma's da. Two of the finest men ever. So, welcome Edward Alfred. But you'll be known as Ted, just like me da were ... Eeh, I wish your granddads were alive to meet you.'

'That's a lovely name. Now afore we go down the road that'll turn your joyful tears to sad ones, take little Ted, Jack, and go and get him weighed ... Right, Elisha, lass, let's get you cleaned up, then when Jack gets back we'll give babby a bath and you can put him to your breast.'

'Ta Hetty, I couldn't have done it without you.'

'Aw, lass, you'd have found a way. Though you're still a young 'un yourself, you'd have got on with it. It's a natural process for us women. I wish that I could have had more babbies, but it weren't to be.'

As Hetty chatted on, Elisha wondered why – what stopped a woman having babbies – but she didn't ask, she'd heard the pain in Hetty's voice. For herself, she never wanted to go through the birth process again, and yet she so wanted a few children, so she supposed she would. She hadn't liked being an only child. It had been lonely at times.

She and Jan discussed this once and Jan had said the same, so they decided to look on each other as sisters, and the feeling of love she'd felt when they'd hugged on the deal had warmed Elisha's heart.

With little Ted being declared a whopping eight pounds eight ounces, and a big grin lighting up Jack's face, Elisha giggled as she thought that anyone would think that he'd been the one to nurture him in his belly and to give birth. His pride shone from him.

His kiss gave her every ounce of his love for her, and while Hetty worked away bathing Ted, they sat holding hands, talking of dreams for their little one – how strong he was going to be, how she would teach him to read and write, and Jack would make him wooden toys to play with. Their happiness knew no bounds. All cares left them in this magic moment of planning for their son's future.

With Ted cleaned and now being put to her breast, Elisha held her breath wondering what it would feel like, but was then flooded with even more happiness and love for her child, as he began to suckle and his eyes held hers. His seemed full of wonder, as if he knew instinctively that she was special to him. His little fingers curled around hers, making her heart want to burst with the love she held for him. She looked up at Jack, saw his grin almost reaching ear to ear, and – though she'd thought it many times before – this time, she knew her world to be complete.

CHAPTER EIGHT

When Jan arrived, it was with Mick, which was no surprise, as the two of them always seemed to be in each other's company these days. They wished everyone a happy Christmas and then cooed over little Ted, before holding hands and Jan saying, 'We have news.'

'Ha, we can see that, lass. You're both beaming like a lighthouse.' Jack grinned as he said this. He'd been speculating for a while about the growing relationship between Jan and Mick. Elisha had seen it too, but didn't think that they had, and hadn't wanted to mention it in case she pushed things that maybe weren't meant to be, though she hoped with all her heart they were.

'We're walking out together!'

'Aw, Jan, you've been doing that for a good while, though I'm not sure either of you knew it. I'm so happy for you both.'

Elisha opened her arms and Jan came into them. 'You knew?'

'Aye, we just waited for you two to realise it.'

'Ha! Well, we have now. I can't say how happy I am, Elisha.'

'I knaw the feeling, love. And congratulations. So, what's your plans?'

'My plan is to have a hug like you just gave to Jan, Elisha,' Mick broke in.

Elisha laughed as she extended her arms to Mick. He'd become like an older brother, always looking out for her. His hug was full of love for her – a different love, but one that gave her a sense of having a family, as that was what Jan, Mick and Hetty had become to her and Jack.

'Let's celebrate us having a son and you two being in love. I've still got some bottles of me ma and grandma's elderberry wine in the cellar. They haven't been touched since our wedding night when me and Jack had a sup each to give us courage.'

They all laughed at this and them doing so showed the easy rapport they had on all subjects – though they only hinted at some, as she had done then.

When Jack and Mick left the bedroom to get the drinks, Jan surprised Elisha by saying, 'We won't need such courage, as it's already happened!'

'Eeh, Jan, I knew you had a glow about you recently. But by, that's risky, ain't it?'

'Naw, Mick takes care. But in any case, we ain't waiting long to marry ... I've other news, Elisha ... I – well, me and Mick – are moving away once we're wed.'

'Naw ... Where? When? You never said owt!'

Jan took hold of her hand. 'I – I couldn't say 'cos, I didn't knaw until yesterday – that's when it happened, all of it. Mick met me out of work, sommat he's done a lot lately. And as we were cycling home, he asked if we could stop a moment. We got off our bikes and sat on the verge ... It were like sitting on ice!'

Jan grinned. 'But that didn't matter as it was then that he told me how he felt about me. Me world brightened, Elisha, as all I had been feeling suddenly made sense. Anyroad, before I knew where I were, I was in his arms, and ... Well, we went back to his. His ma was in bed. Mick made me a cuppa and then told me that he was moving away. That his uncle, who lived in Sussex, had died and left his farm to him ... He proposed then, and well ... It just happened.'

'You're ... you're leaving? Naw! I couldn't bear that ... Aw, Jan, I ...'

'I'm sorry ... I love Mick with all me heart, I have to go with him.'

They were crying and clinging to one another when Jack and Mick entered the bedroom. Jack hurried to her and sat on the bed next to her. 'Aw, I'm sorry, love, Jan's told you then?'

'You knew, Jack?'

'Naw, well, not till just now. Mick's just told me ... Eeh, I came back up to you as soon as he did.'

Jack took her into his arms. 'It'll be all right, love, they'll visit Mick's ma often, and we'll see them when they do.'

But for Elisha it seemed her world had collapsed, as she clung on to Jack's neck as if it was a lifeline. Her sobs were uncontrollable now, racking her body and releasing so much pain that had been shielded by her love for Jack and her excitement at carrying their child. All she'd been through attacked her and flooded from her.

'Eeh, don't take on so, me little lass ... Elisha, naw ...'

'Let her cry, Jack. This is a combination. It's a release of the shock the body feels at the birth and of things she has pent up inside her. Me going away was just a trigger.'

With this Jan went around to the other side of the bed and climbed onto it. Elisha felt her arm come around her from behind, and there, encased in the love these two had for her, allowed her heart to weep.

It was Mick coming in with a cuppa, followed by Hetty, that helped to calm Elisha. What happened to the wine she didn't ask, but took a sip of the hot liquid, hoping to get help from it.

'Eeh, lass, I wondered when this would happen. It allus does, but usually on the third day, not as soon after the birth as this, but Mick tells me you knaw of them leaving. By, I could cry with you, as it's broken me heart.'

'I told you, Hetty, as I told me ma, you can come with us. You get on well together and there's a cottage you can share.'

'Aw, I don't knaw, lad, I ain't known nowt but life in Blackpool. How does Vera feel about it all?'

Elisha's hand shook as she handed her mug to Jack. She wanted to shout out, 'Naw! Naw, don't all go!', but she kept quiet. She knew how heartbreaking it would be for Hetty to be away from Jan.

'She said she'd wait to see what you say, so maybe you'd better get together and have a chinwag and sort it out, eh?'

'Aye, we will, Mick, love.'

To Elisha, it was if her world was being sliced in half, as these folk were a huge part of her happiness. They were there when she needed them – when Jack needed them

– and now they were talking about going far away, to a distant county that would be impossible for her, Jack and their little Ted to get to! How was she to bear it?

'If you didn't own this place, Elisha, but only rented it, I'd say you two come an' all, but you've a lot at stake here. Why don't you get a lad to help you, eh? Someone who'll work for a good square meal a day and a small wage. It'd make a difference to what you can produce and therefore increase your income, and take the pressure off you, Jack.'

Jack answered, 'Aye, that's a good idea. We can do that, Elisha. There's a lot out of work ... We'll be all right, lass. We've to be happy for Jan and Mick, and encourage Hetty to go an' all. They've done their best for us these past months. This is a grand opportunity for them.'

Elisha felt her own selfishness, and the shame of it. She looked up at Jan.

'Aw, lass, I am happy for you. It just all overwhelmed me at first. I'm sorry.'

'Naw! I wouldn't have thought much of you if you'd have smiled and said, "Off you go then!" ... I'm heartbroken at leaving you, but you knaw the saying, "Wherever you make your bed, I make mine"? Well, that's just part of it, but the huge part is that now I've awoken to me feelings for Mick, I can't not be by his side.'

'Naw, of course not. I wouldn't ask that of you, Jan. It's just such a shock and felt as if the bottom was falling out of me world.'

'It's not. Your world is you, Jack and your little one, and this lovely cottage and the business that goes with it. Once you recover from the birth, you'll go from strength to strength. Write to me every week, lass, and I'll write to you, eh?'

'By, that'd be sommat to look forward to – mind, me letters might be like books, I've not kept up me studying, but having letters to write will be part of me getting back to that again.'

'That'd be grand, 'cos you should never lose sight of what your dream used to be. Aye, I knaw that now it's to make this place how your da wanted it, but your real dream was to become a teacher.'

Jan tightened the grip she had on Elisha's hand and gave it a little shake. 'Do that someday, lass. Realise your own dream, eh?'

Elisha didn't ever see a time that would be possible, but she nodded, an action that plopped the last of her tears onto her cheeks. Jan gently wiped them away with her thumb, then took Elisha into her arms. Jan was the strongest person Elisha knew, so to feel her body shake in a silent sob gave the knowledge that Jan truly was torn.

Not wanting this for her lovely friend, Elisha drew on inner strength. 'Eeh, now we've got the shock out of the way, it's all so exciting – you getting married, and going to live on a farm! It'll be following in your da's footsteps. He'd be so proud of you, Jan.'

Jan pulled away from her and smiled. 'It will. I allus loved working with me da. And I'll be fulfilling his dream, as he used to take me hand and look across the fields and say, "One day, I'd love me own farm."'

The strength Elisha had found grew. 'There you go then! We're both doing our das proud. I can't wait to have me "stay in bed" days behind me and get tackling the land and getting it as me da wanted it.'

'Right! With that settled, it's time you were in the Land of Nod, Elisha, lass,' Hetty said.

And as Jan slid off the bed, she continued, 'Your body needs to recover. Ted's sleeping peacefully, but it won't be long afore he's yelling for your attention, so let's all leave now, except Jack. You stay and help Elisha to relax, and the pair of you enjoy being a ma and da for the first time. I'll be back later with a Christmas dinner for you both.'

'Ta, Hetty, love, and for all you've done an' all.'

'It were nowt, lass.'

Jan kissed Elisha's cheek and smiled down at her. 'When you're up and about, we'll have a glass of that wine and talk weddings, eh?'

'By, that'd be good. I can't wait.'

'Eeh, get yourself out of here, Jan, or you'll be off talking about your plans now and Elisha's had enough to contend with.' Hetty shooed them out and, following them, closed the door behind her.

Jack climbed onto the bed. His arm came around Elisha's waist. She snuggled into him. Feeling her eyes close, she thought, *I have my world here – my lovely Jack and my adored son, Ted. We're going to be all right.*

Her heavy, swollen eyes drooped and she let herself drift off into a peaceful sleep.

A cry awakened her – not a demanding sound but a gentle whimper. Jack stirred. 'Eeh, lass, I went right off to sleep with you.'

'It's not a wonder; it was hard work bringing our lad into the world.'

'By, I did nowt.'

'Aw, you did, me darling, you did everything alongside me. Though don't be shouting about it as from what I've heard, most men go down the pub while it happens, saying it's women's work and they need to be out of the way.'

'I couldn't do that, love.'

'I knaw, and that's part of what makes you special. And by the sound of our little chap, he's hungry, but he's going to be just like you – undemanding, patient and kind. He's thinking he'll cry quietly as, though his belly's rumbling, he wouldn't want to disturb his ma and da.'

'Aw, that's a lovely thing to say, when what we did – I did – has caused you so much pain.'

'Jack! Don't you dare think like that! We loved one another and made our son together. A beautiful thing to do.'

Jack held her close. 'I love you so much, Elisha, lass. You're me world.'

'And you're mine, though it now includes Ted an' all. Lift him up to me, love.'

'Let's get you propped up first. I'll put my pillow behind you, it'll support you as you sit up.'

'Ta, that's comfy.'

As Jack took Ted out of his cradle, he said to him, 'By, lad, you've been sleeping in the cradle your ma slept in and made by your granddad, and now you're going to your ma's breast; was there ever a luckier lad in the world than you, eh?'

Ted made a gurgling sound.

'There you are, you knaw you've got your bread buttered on both sides, don't you?'

Ted gurgled again.

'Ha! I'm having me first conversation with me son! The best Christmas present ever!'

Elisha giggled. Her happiness as she watched her Jack and her Ted together far outweighed her sadness at losing Jan. She'd find a way to cope with that. She'd have to. As Grandma Millicent used to say, 'Nowt ever stays the same in this world, we just have to adapt and get on with it.'

She would do that. She would get on with building the market garden up, but more than that, find a way of getting her Jack back to full health.

As this thought came it was thrust away by Jack's hacking cough, as he unsteadily handed Ted to her. Just the small exertion of lifting his newborn son and chatting to him had made him breathless. With a heavy heart, Elisha wondered if she could ever achieve making him well.

She would never give up trying. Never!

CHAPTER NINE

The sun shone the day of Jan's wedding, three months later, though frost still lay on the ground.

The time waiting for this day had seen Elisha working her fingers to the bone getting the early plants sown, keeping the chickens fed and using their droppings to make a valuable, if smelly, compost, which she'd dug into the ground – hard going, as it was often frozen and difficult to turn.

Between them, she and Jack, with help from Jan and Mick, had managed to repair the old lean-to greenhouse with money Elisha didn't know they had, but Jack produced, saying he'd managed to save a little. And what an asset it was turning out to be! Seedlings were brought quickly to tiny plants, making them much hardier to face the rigours of Blackpool weather when she planted them out.

But there was no heavy work today, just happiness for Jan and Mick, tinged with a little sadness at them leaving later – and not just them but Hetty and Mick's ma too, who had decided they would go to live in the cottage Mick had been getting ready for them.

Both Mick and Jan had spent a lot of time in Surrey after

Jan quit her job — a time that had helped Elisha get used to them not being around every day.

'By, me little lass, you look grand!'

Elisha turned from where she'd stood rocking Ted's pram. Jack was ready at last and looked handsome in his best suit. Only the telltale red blotches high on his cheeks told of him not being well.

Doing a twirl to show off her maid of honour gown in a soft cream satin, Elisha breathed in, 'Eeh, Jack, me belly still sticks out a bit.'

'Naw. That's normal after having a babby and doesn't take owt from your beauty. You're going to outshine the bride, me darling.'

Bending over the pram, Jack went to pull the cover back. Elisha stopped him, 'Naw! He's asleep, and I hope he stays so till after the service. He's been a bit tetchy.'

'He ain't ill, is he?'

'Naw, it's wind, I've given him some Dinneford's. Anyroad, let's get going. We can't have the best man and the chief bridesmaid being late!'

The service was beautiful, and yet poignant, as although it joined together two of the loveliest people in her life, Elisha was aware that the hour of saying goodbye to them was on them.

All too soon after tea and cakes, they were at the station.

Hetty held Elisha's hand, as she gazed down at Ted snuggled in a blanket in his pram. 'Eeh, lass. I thought I'd be watching him grow and achieving his little steps in life. You will write, won't you? Tell us all he gets up to.'

'I will, love ... Oh, Hetty, what am I to do without you all?'

'You'll cope, lass. You're like your grandma, one of life's copers.' With this, she kissed Elisha's cheek, wiped away her tears and stepped back so that an impatient Mick could say his goodbyes. He did so with a hug. 'You're welcome to come and stay with us any time, lass. Any time.'

Seeing how choked up he was, Elisha smiled through her own tears. 'Hey, this is a happy day for you – don't worry about me, I'll be fine.'

Mick managed a grin. 'You allus are, lass.'

His ma, who Elisha had known all her life but never really known, kissed her cheek and shook her head. Elisha could see her emotions at leaving her home were choking her, so just nodded her head and said, 'Everything will be all right.'

Before Mick's ma could react to this, Jan stepped forward. Their gaze held for a second and then they fell into each other's arms and clung on as if they would change everything back to how it was.

'Eeh, Elisha, I've dreaded this moment.'

'I knaw.' Drawing on everything she'd rehearsed but didn't feel, Elisha took a deep breath. 'But, eeh, lass, this is your wedding day. The happiest day of your life, so naw tears, eh?'

Jan smiled through watery eyes. 'Come soon to visit, eh? Maybe in the autumn when there's not so much work to do. You'll have made your fortune by then, lass, with all that's been achieved.'

Though she nodded, wanting to give herself and Jan

hope, Elisha knew that she'd never find the money to do that. Not with how things were. But her words denied this. 'We'd love that, eeh, that'd be grand.'

The happy smile Jan had worn all day came back to light up her face. 'Eeh, lass, I'll count the days.'

'Ha, you'll be too busy, milking cows and collecting eggs and . . . making babbies!'

They both laughed, making the moment one of their fun times and lifting everybody's mood, as the excitement of the day came back amidst the four of them getting their luggage and themselves settled for their journey.

But, as the train pulled out, Elisha's sadness and a sense of being alone overwhelmed her. A feeling she hadn't had since Jan came into her life. Somehow, she told herself, she had to cope.

Jack's hand came into hers, but neither of them spoke as they watched the last of the smoke from the departing train break up and disappear, with Elisha's thoughts telling her that, somehow, she had to find a way of being strong. But as she looked up at Jack's tired and hollow-looking beloved face, she wondered how.

And with that question, the worries she'd refused to think about all day re-entered her. Her lovely Jack was poorly more days than he was well, and on top of that he'd confessed last week to having taken a loan out from the bank a few weeks before Christmas. The repayment amount they had to find each month shocked her, filling her with horror, and fear for their future.

That fear was compounded now as they arrived home, where a letter awaited them – a brown envelope that seemed to be a prophet of doom. It was from the bank, demanding money they didn't have.

Elisha wanted to scream out her frustration. 'Have we missed a payment already, Jack?'

'Aye, but only the one. Everything will be all right, lass, I promise. The money made it possible for us to repair the greenhouse and fill it with seeds, and they promise to bring in more income over time.'

'But that isn't now, Jack.'

'I'll sort it, love . . . Anyroad, forget that for now. Have you had a nice day?'

'Aye, Jack. But I can't help but worry. And I can't think how life will be for us without their support.'

'I knaw. Let's make a plan, eh?'

But with saying this, Jack gasped for air. He'd pushed the pram for most of the way home just to have something to cling on to. His cheeks had a blueish hue amongst the red blotches that always seemed to be there since his illness. Putting the letter out of her mind, Elisha helped him to a chair, then quickly got the kettle boiling and poured hot water onto some friar's balsam.

Tears ran down her face as she cradled Ted to her and watched as Jack sat at the table, bent over the bowl of steaming friar's balsam with a towel draped over his head. How, she asked herself for the umpteenth time, were they to get out of the mess they were in?

When Jack fell asleep in the chair, breathing more easily now, but exhausted, Elisha crept across the room and into the kitchen. There she opened the table drawer where Jack kept what he termed his office work – bills, records of sales and the papers he'd signed at the bank to do with the loan. Elisha had never seen these but was curious as to how they – a struggling couple with a babby on the way at the time – were ever granted a loan.

Shock held her rigid when she read that the money had been secured against the cottage – their home. Plonking down on a chair she'd pulled from under the table, the seriousness of their situation hit her – if they couldn't pay, they would lose their home! How could Jack have thought this was the right thing to do? How?

But then, when she looked back at the last winter and how they'd had to make do with meatless potato stew most of the time, she realised that maybe he'd had no choice. Taking a deep breath, she told herself that it was all down to her now. And she wouldn't let Ted or Jack down. She would tap into the same spirit her grandma had shown, and fight for them both. With this she began to explore the possibilities of how she could turn their fortunes around, and rehearse how she would put it to Jack.

By the time he awoke, she had a plan – and with making it, strength had seeped back into her, giving her the determination she'd need and the confidence that she could do this. Handing him a cup of tea, Elisha sat down beside him, glad to see how much better he looked, as this made it easier for her to keep her resolve to the fore.

'I've sommat to say, Jack.'

'Eeh, lass, I can see that. You have that look on your face that says, "I'm not to be messed with."' He grinned at her.

But Elisha remained serious. 'From now on, Jack, we'll have to reverse roles, love. You take charge of the home, and I'll work outside just as me grandma did. If she can do it, I can. We have naw choice in the matter, we just have to do what we can to save our home and feed us and our child.'

'Eeh, Elisha, lass. It breaks me heart to agree, but I've been having the same thoughts. I'm just not the man I was before the pneumonia took me, but whether I can bake a cake is another thing!'

'Ha, you'll soon learn, lad.'

'I'll give it me best shot. So, this is to be the plan, is it?'

'Aye, and the first thing we must do is go to the bank and talk to the manager about helping us manage our debt. We've only the eggs to sell at the moment, but I've been thinking, and what you just said about baking a cake fits into me thoughts. Why don't we turn what we do have into profit?'

The look on Jack's face showed how mystified he was.

'Well, you remember how well our produce went at the Christmas fayre of our first year? We'll do that again. We have blackberry bushes that are laden and will ripen soon as the warmer weather comes, and the gooseberry bushes look promising as they are sprouting buds, not to mention the rhubarb at the bottom of the garden near to the hedge being ripe an' all. We've plenty of jars for jams, and I've still got some of the last batch I made afore. And I've plenty of flour and lard for making pastry. So, while we wait for our crops, let's get busy!'

'By, me lass, you're a wonder ... I tell you what I could do an' all. You knaw how you cut labels and stick them to the jars with flour paste? Well, I could make them. I can get me paints out and paint our own name on them – sommat like Cottage Jam Company.'

'Aw, Jack, that'd be grand! And I've just remembered, we lay all those apples in straw in the attic of the potting shed. I'll check on them an' all. We could make apple and rhubarb tarts and crumbles, and with Matty having been busy, we've the chicks to hatch soon, so we may have a few of them to sell, not to mention the abundance of eggs. We're going to be rich, Jack!'

With this they both laughed, and to Elisha it was as if the light that had seemed to go out in their lives had been switched on again, as hope came back into her. She went to go out of the door with a determined stride. Jack laughed louder than he had before. 'You're not going Millicenting in that get-up are you, lass?'

Remembering she was still in her bridesmaid's dress, Elisha joined in with his laughter – Millicenting was what they called getting busy, as this was what she'd told Jack her grandma did all the time. It was a standing joke with them, though their laughter stopped when Jack's turned to a fit of coughing. Not wanting to draw too much attention to this, she said, 'Eeh, I'm a daft ha'peth, I was all ready to take the world on then, and in me finery an' all.'

When he calmed, Jack said, 'I'll come and help you out of it, lass.'

His tone thrilled her, though she worried how he would do what his eyes told her he longed to.

Ted saved the day. His yell filled the cottage.

Jack shook his head. 'Later, lass, I promise. I've been neglecting you.'

'Naw, Jack. A lass can't do such things until everything settles down after the birth. So don't be worrying.'

'Aye, but that time has long passed.' His smile showed his promise. And as Elisha hurried up the stairs, she hoped that later really did happen for them.

The next two weeks flew by, and now here they were looking at the crates that they had ready for the market.

'Not a bad load at all, lass. Should bring us in a couple of quid!'

'As much as that! Oh, Jack, it'll all be worth it if it does.'

'Well, you can sell the jam at sixpence a jar, and you've got twenty of them, so that's ten bob, and then you've ten pies you can sell at a bob each, so there's a quid. Then we've got the eggs, and the loose apples you didn't use in pies!'

'Eeh, Jack, let's hope we sell out, then we can go to the bank with a pound and promise more to come.'

'Well, we ain't got bottomless fruit, though, love.'

'Naw, but some of the veg is nearly ready and, well, a couple of the hens have seen their last days – we could sell them for meat or do the job ourselves and make chicken pies.'

'What! Well, I never thought of owt like that.'

'And you can get that gun out that was Grandma's and clean it, and then take a pot at them rabbits that hound us and bag a few pigeons an' all. Rabbit stew or pie, and pigeon pies, will fetch in a good revenue, Jack.'

'I'd feel like a murderer!'

'Ha, God gave them to us to feed us. We'll only be doing His will!'

Not looking at all sure, Jack picked up one of the crates.

'I've another idea an' all, Jack. If I get a minute, I'll nip around the cafés and ask if I could supply them with jams and pies, and fruit and veg, in between market days. They must buy them from somewhere – well, I'll undercut whatever they're paying!'

'By, you should be called Millicent. I bet she's right proud of you, lass. I knaw I am. You've given us hope of a future when I thought I'd ruined it with taking that loan.'

'It didn't help matters, love, but all we can do now is to work hard and get back to a place where we're out of debt and have enough to give our lad a good life.'

Jack grinned and winked, 'And not just our lad, the others I'm planning we'll have an' all.'

Although she grinned, Elisha thought that when Jack next approached her to make love – something she hoped would happen soon – she'd gently tell him that he had to take care in the way that Jan had told her you could. She couldn't be out of action while she carried another babby – not yet, and not for a good while.

By mid-afternoon they'd sold out, with compliments flying over the pretty-looking jars. Jack had painted their cottage on each label and printed the name of their new venture: 'Cottage Jams'. And Elisha had secured two orders from cafés for pies and veg supplies.

'Phew, two pounds, two shillings and sixpence, lass. Well done! That's the most we've ever earnt!'

'It's just the start Jack, just the start.' Hope filled Elisha, when just a short while ago she'd been filled with despair. 'You go over to the bank while I tidy up. Only hurry, as Ted'll want feeding soon.'

As she watched him go, with pride in his step, Elisha thought of how their new-found hope had helped his health. She turned to see one of his labels on the floor and her first thought was that they'd have to find a better way of gluing them on, but then she stopped and for the first time took in the beauty of the intricate painting, and gasped.

How had she taken Jack's liking for painting so lightly? She'd only glanced at the labels as she'd left Jack to stick them to the jars! Now she could see that his talent was amazing. Every detail of their cottage – still showing signs of disrepair, due to lack of money and all effort going into the market garden – was there to see! And the signwriting of the name was exquisite! *Eeh, me Jack, why didn't I realise?*

Looking up, she saw him disappear into the bank, and whilst praying all would be well for them, an idea came to her – she'd invest some of the money they had left over in a canvas for him. He already had paints and brushes. She'd get him to sit and paint a real painting. One as folk would like to hang on their wall. The rich folk that was, who owned property that they only came to for a few months in summer to take the waters, as they called dipping into the sea.

An excitement gripped her. It wasn't just that the paintings could add another string to their bow, but that her Jack would have a purpose in life again. He'd feel that he was providing for his wife and family – every man needed that.

Setting about the task of clearing up, Elisha's heart pounded as she stacked the crates ready to be loaded onto their cart, leaving one upturned to rest on when she'd finished the task. It was a mixture of hope and despair that was causing it – the hope coming with her thoughts about there being a future for Jack, but the despair nudged hard at that as she feared the outcome of his talk with the bank manager. *Please, please, let him accept the new terms we're offering!*

CHAPTER TEN

When the last of their stall was ready for loading onto Grundy's cart, Elisha thought she'd sit a while, but looking into the pram she could see that Ted, who'd slept peacefully through all the yelling of the market stallholders touting their wares, was now stirring.

As if he sensed her nearness, Ted suddenly opened his eyes and let out a demanding yell. Elisha looked around, hoping to see Jack coming back to them, praying now not for acceptance of their terms, but that they could get home before Ted needed to be fed.

Lifting him from his pram, she cradled him to her, rocking him and whispering her love for him, hoping to soothe him. But as always, it was only her milk that would quieten him when he was hungry. She felt unsure about trying to feed him as, like always, there were folk milling around – some enjoying a walk on the prom in the sunshine, kids looking for anything amongst the rubble on the ground that they could salvage, and tradesmen clearing away whilst still making the odd sale.

Ted took no notice of all of this as his persistence gave

his lungs strength and his yells got louder and more distressing. Making her mind up that his needs were more important than her dignity, Elisha sat down on the upturned crate, pulled her shawl around to shield her and undid the front of her frock. Ted latched on greedily as soon as he felt her nipple close to his cheek.

Looking around, she felt sure she was being discreet enough, as nothing could be seen but a mother holding her babby with a shawl around them both. Relaxing, she leant back against the wooden strut holding up the canvas roof of their stall.

An angry voice made her jump. 'Disgusting! Young lady, how can you make such an exhibition of yourself!'

Elisha glanced down thinking she was showing all, but no, she was covered up. Looking up into the face of a very poshly dressed gentleman, she said, 'Sir, I'm merely feeding my babby.'

'In the street!' His walking stick poked her painfully in the rib.

Keeping her temper, Elisha said, 'I'm sorry, if you're offended. My child was hungry.'

This had no effect on him. He turned and yelled loudly, 'Someone tell that policeman over there to come quickly, I've never seen such lewd behaviour in all my life!'

Shocked, Elisha protested, 'I'm not acting in a lewd way, I . . .'

From the crowd that had gathered a woman stepped forward. 'You don't knaw you're born, man! You've naw idea what we women go through! How do you think your ma went on when you yelled for food, eh? This young woman has stood market with her own produce – produce that must have taken her hours of sweat and tears to make. She ain't doing nowt wrong in my eyes and if you call the bobby, I'll tell him that you're a dirty old man peeping at a mother's breasts when she's doing what God intended for her to do!'

The crowd murmured their assent, leaving the gentleman looking afraid. He turned on his heels and walked away without another word.

'There you go, love, I got rid of him for you. Bloody stuck-up bugger!'

As her nerves left her, Elisha laughed out loud.

'But a word in your ear, love,' the woman now said, 'Don't put yourself in this position again, lass. I live just around the corner from here, number 14 Bank Street. When you're next working market, you can pop in to mine to feed your babby. I'll make you a cuppa, an' all. Me name's Jean. What's yours?'

'I'm Elisha, and ta ever so much, Jean. That'd be a help, I got caught out today.'

'Aye, well it happens. Now, I've to get going.' She turned to the others around her. 'And you lot can an' all. Leave the lass in peace! Go on!'

Everyone hurried away, no one argued with Jean. A big woman, with a hard-looking face covering a loving interior, she was formidable. 'Now, don't you forget, love. It's the third house along, with a brass doorknob.' This she said with pride. 'I'd be glad to help you out.'

'You have already, ta, Jean. I'll see you in a couple of weeks when we stand market next.'

As Jean left, Elisha couldn't quite believe what had happened, but she smiled to herself as she tucked her clothing back in place and put Jack over her shoulder. Contented now, he slept rather than giving the customary burp.

'Eeh, lad, you caused some trouble then. But you've made me a friend, and one I'm going to love an' all, I just knaw it.'

When Jack returned, the beam on his face filled Elisha with hope.

'Everything's all right, me little lass, I've agreed new terms with the bank, and as long as we keep to them, they won't foreclose on us.'

Relief was tinged with trepidation for Elisha, but she made herself smile. 'That's good to hear, Jack, as long as the terms are doable for us.'

'They are if we can keep up what we did this last two weeks and today, as we have to find two pound a month to make repayments.'

Elisha had a moment of shock. She turned away and put Ted into his pram while she drew breath. That was an enormous sum! But then her determination took over. She straightened, forced her smile back onto her face and nodded her head. 'We can do that. We can make savings on our costs . . . one thing we can do is to scrub the crates out and reuse them instead of keeping the stove going with them, as we can cut up that old fallen tree and use that to heat the oven, it'll be dry enough now.'

'That's the spirit, love.'

'And, Jack, you can contribute more – much more . . .'

'By, lass, I wish that I could; I feel I'm letting you down, but . . .'

'Not by upping your effort in owt we do, love, but by painting beautiful pictures for us to sell!'

'What? Well ... I suppose ... Eeh, I could thou knaws, lass, I could! I only need canvas. I could make frames easily enough for me work, and an easel to stand me canvas on, as I've some board I can stretch the canvas over ... I ...' Tears brimmed his eyes as he looked at her. 'I can make money at it, I'm sure I could ... maybe enough to hire a lad to help you ...'

Jack drew her into his arms. 'Aw, Elisha, you're the saviour of us.'

'Naw, love. We're in this together ... Now, let go of me, I've already been involved in a scene, and folk are looking. Honestly, the men in this family are troublemakers!'

His laughter resounded around her, bringing a smile to many a passer-by's face.

Elisha loved to make him laugh, and to fill him with hope as he was now and as she felt too. Excitement gripped her, for suddenly she knew they could do this – they could pay the loan back, and maybe even hire a lad. Like Grandma said, 'Everything's doable, it's just the will to do it as you need, lass.' Well, she had that, and at this moment she wanted to do something that wasn't like anything she'd ever done before.

'Let's get Grundy and load up, and then drive him along the promenade to Fleetwood. Everyone's talking about the delicious fish and chip meal they serve at the Dolphin chippy on the corner of Blakiston Street.'

'By, that'd be a treat, but it's a fair way, lass. Let's see, it's two o'clock now, so even if Grundy keeps up a fair trot, we won't be there until getting on for three.'

'Well, we've nowt spoiling and the way we've worked we deserve a treat.'

'Ha! You never fail to surprise me. One minute it's "We've got to make savings" and the next it's "Let's gad off to Fleetwood!" . . . Come on then, we only live once!'

Laughing, Elisha had the feeling of being a child again.

They might be facing hard times, and having to work from dawn till dusk, but they still needed to enjoy life and make memories.

This thought froze inside her as she watched Jack walking towards where they'd tethered Grundy, and saw how thin he was and how his stride was no longer strong. Then another thought took its place and crowded her mind: *Will it be that, one day, memories are all I have? Please, God . . . No!*

The feel of the sea breeze on her face as they trotted along dispelled any doom and gloom Elisha had let in. Ted slept peacefully in her arms, fed and cosy now after a change of nappy done in his pram once they had the cart loaded.

'By, this is grand, lass. I'm glad you suggested it. I've been thinking that, though life dealt us a blow, we're very lucky to have all we have. And it set me wondering how Jan and Mick are doing.'

'Well, they've only had a short while to get used to things, but they must feel the wrench. Leaving all of this for a farm, when they know nowt about farming.'

'Knawing those two, they'll enjoy learning, and it ain't much different to market gardening, just on a bigger scale and with more animals than just chickens.'

'Aye, and you knaw, we could keep more. We ain't done much with the land at the back of the cottage, except put the chicken run there, but I was thinking about a goat. It would keep the grass down and give us milk an' all. I could make cheese for us then.'

'Cheese? You never cease to amaze me, love. What do you knaw about cheesemaking?'

'Nothing, but I can visit the library and read about it. It can't be that difficult.'

'You talking about the library makes me feel bad about how you had ambitions to be a teacher, and it was all taken from you.'

'It wasn't your fault, me darling.' A shudder went through Elisha as for the first time in a long time she remembered that disgusting episode of her life. That feeling of being dirty entered her. She pulled little Ted closer to her and gazed out at the passing sea. It was then that she felt the heat coming from Ted's body. Pulling back his shawl, she was shocked to see how red his cheeks were. They looked blotchy. Sweat beads covered his forehead.

'Pull over, Jack, quick, there's sommat wrong with Ted!'

'Naw! What? Eeh, naw!'

When Grundy came to a halt – at his own pace as usual – Jack jumped off the cart and came round to Elisha's side. 'Hand him to me, love.'

'He didn't wind after his feed, he just flopped off to sleep as if suckling had worn him out, and now he's hot and red-looking! Eeh, Jack, sommat's wrong!'

Taking off Ted's shawl, Jack lifted his gown. 'He's hot all

over. He must have a fever! We'll turn around and get to the doctors.'

As if to reassure himself as much as her, Jack said, 'Don't worry, I've heard that babbies can have these bouts and then recover just as quickly.' But, even so, he moved faster than she'd seen him do for a long time as he handed Ted back to her and scooted around the cart to take his seat again.

As soon as he could, he turned the cart around and urged Grundy on. And as if he knew the urgency, Grundy trotted faster than Elisha had ever known him to. But she took no heed of this – her head and heart were full of concern for her precious child.

'Measles! How?'

The doctor seemed unconcerned as he said, 'There's a lot going about. Someone infected could have sneezed near to him or touched him. You say you stand market? Well, I daresay many a customer looked over the pram to coo at little Ted. Blackpudlians love nothing more than a newborn. But we all carry germs, and if one of them was infected and touched his cheek – I don't mean today, as it can take two to three weeks to get to the stage Ted is at now, but what I am saying is that he could have caught this any time you have been around a crowd.'

'We were at a wedding and Ted had a lot of attention ... Doctor, he will be all right, won't he?'

'He does have a high temperature, so get him home and sponge him with cold water. Give him plenty of fluids. Do you have a feeder you can put water into – boiled water, mind. And then cooled.'

'Yes, he hasn't used it yet, but we have teats for it.'

'Well, sterilise it in boiling water, fill it with cold, boiled water and give it to him regularly. That and bathing him gently in cool water should bring his temperature down ... There's not much more that you can do, I'm afraid. But try not to worry, babies recover very quickly.'

As he said this last, the doctor didn't sound convincing. Fear gripped Elisha as she held Ted. This fear increased as Ted just flopped in her arms, his shallow breaths the only movement of his body.

The night was long and arduous as Elisha carried out the doctor's instructions. But nothing she did saw any improvement, only worsening of Ted's condition, giving her a terrifying moment when he convulsed. His body stiffened, his face turned blue and his eyes stared. Cooling him brought him out of it.

After a while he seemed to improve, looking into her eyes and clinging on to her finger.

'Ted, me little lad, fight. Beat this for Ma, 'cos I love you with all me heart, lad.'

Ted's lips formed a smile, warming Elisha's heart and relaxing her. Her Ted was going to be all right. Resting her head back in the chair, she let her eyes close, safe in the knowledge that Ted was on the mend, and that he was secure and comfortable as she had her feet up on a stool, providing a lap for him that he wouldn't slip from. She just needed to nod off for ten minutes.

★ ★ ★

'Elisha! Elisha! Naw ... Naw ... Naw!'

Startled out of sleep and filled with dread, Elisha let out a wail of agony. Ted lay as he had, with his face turned towards her. His little fingers, still curled around hers, were cold. His features were as if set in porcelain.

Gasping in a breath she didn't think she would ever release again, Elisha stared from Ted to Jack. Her head shook from side to side. Jack's groan, followed by the coughing fit that took him, brought reality to Elisha. Ted, her beautiful, darling son, had left them.

Releasing his fingers, Elisha hugged his little, still warm, body to her. 'Don't leave me, me little babby, don't leave me.'

Getting up, she paced up and down, gently rocking Ted. 'Come on, my babby, breathe for your ma, breathe, me little Ted, please, please, breathe.'

But seeing Ted couldn't do as she begged, her legs crumbled and she sank to the floor, her wails pitiful, her hold on Ted as if she'd never let him go – but still no sign of life came into his little body.

'He's gone ... me little Ted ... Help me! Hel ... help me!'

Jack's arms came around her. He was lying beside her, his sobs matching hers. Neither aware of the cold slab floor, just of their torment – their utter despair.

Elisha couldn't see light ever entering their lives again, only pain and the terrible suffering of loss. This was compounded when the doctor arrived and wrote out a certificate of death, as with that Elisha knew there was no going back now.

★   ★   ★

Three days later, Elisha walked by Jack's side as they left the cottage carrying the small white box that Jack had made and painted. Elisha had put little Ted's soft pillow inside. They'd lain him on this and put what had become his comfort blanket next to his cheek.

Both had kissed him, cried over him and clung to each other, before closing the lid and laying the tiny coffin on Grundy's cart, on which Elisha had spread a white sheet, wanting everything to be pure around her little son.

The service at St Cuthbert's in Lytham Road didn't take long. And now they had to take their little Ted to Layton Cemetery, where he was to be laid in the grave that held Elisha's ma, da and grandma.

As they walked out of the church, a voice said, 'Aw, Elisha, me Elisha.'

Elisha fell into the arms of Jan.

'I tried to get here in time, lass. Your letter arrived yesterday, and I made arrangements straight away.'

The tears that had burnt, but not spilt, tumbled from Elisha. But they were silent tears. She dared not give way to the terrible wailing again, or she'd never stop.

Turning, she saw her lovely Jack, sobbing in the arms of Mick. She wanted to go to him, but was like a statue being held tightly by Jan.

A cough from the priest brought their attention to him. 'We should go, Elisha. The groundsmen at the cemetery will be waiting.'

Aye, waiting to put me little Ted in the ground and shovel earth onto him . . . I can't bear it, I can't! This thought cut a pain to slice all the others she'd harboured in the last days, for now the moment was on her when it would be final – Ted wouldn't be there to gaze on, or to kiss his cold cheek and whisper her love for him as her lips were close to his ear. He'd be truly gone.

Jan held her the while that Elisha stared at the headstone lying nearby, ready to be put back into place.

Her eyes read the inscription over and over – 'Here lie the bodies of Millicent Finley, Alfred Finley and Alice Finley' – not taking in the dates of their birth and death under each name, just knowing the pain of their loss and how she'd love to feel their arms around her now, as below them she read the freshly carved inscription: 'Edward Alfred Randal, 25th December 1905 – 12th June 1906, great grandson of Millicent, and grandson of Alfred and Alice – May Heaven's Gate Welcome Them All'.

Her, 'I don't want it to ... Naw ... Naw!' was a whisper that carried on the breeze but seemed to sever her heart from her.

Jack's arm came around her. She leant into him, felt his ribs and knew a fresh fear as she glanced back at the stone and had a vision of seeing his name carved on it too.

At that moment, she wondered how she would carry on – go back to the cottage and do all she had to for them to survive – and found that she didn't want to, she just wanted to die too.

Stronger arms grabbed her as her body swayed and she gasped out, 'Naw!' Her protest wasn't hindered, but the arms weren't going to let her fall into the gaping hole with her beloved Ted.

'Don't do this, me lass. We'll help you. Come and live with us. There's another cottage you can have. We'll care for you both.'

Mick's whispered words didn't help, as the sound of earth hitting the coffin resounded in Elisha's ears. Jack had thrown it and was now putting out his hand to her. The priest held a platter towards her. She knew what was expected of her, she was to allow her son to go to dust and send his soul on its way! She couldn't do it.

Jack sprinkled another handful, letting it trickle gently this time. As he did, he said, 'This, son, is your ma and da letting you go to heaven. Be safe with them as have loved you from beyond the grave, and them here on earth who will never forget you. Go with me and Ma's love, little man, and rest in peace.'

The sobs of those around brought Elisha to take note of them – she saw lovely Hetty, and Mick's ma, and Mick, and then Jan. Behind them was Jean. Jean wiped a tear from her eye and gave her a sad smile. She would never now make it to her house to feed little Ted and have a cuppa and a natter, Elisha thought, but knew their friendship would grow as Jean visited their stall.

The priest was praying now, bringing Elisha's attention back to the little box deep in the hole in the ground, which held her heart.

With the prayers over, Elisha and Jack were held in the arms of Jan and Mick, while Hetty hovered close. She found Elisha's hand and squeezed it. Jean stepped forward and tapped Elisha on the back. Turning, Elisha saw Jean's face awash with tears. 'Me heart breaks for you, lass. I knaw your pain. Me three lads are buried in a pauper's grave over there by that tree.'

'Aw, Jean, I'm sorry.' On impulse Elisha took Jean in her arms. What she'd just told her had somehow connected them – Jean knew her pain.

'Come and see me when you recover, lass. We can still have that natter, and aye, cry together, and remember, and laugh an' all, eh?'

'I will. Ta, Jean.'

As Jean walked away, Hetty grabbed hold of Elisha. 'Aw, me lass, me lass . . .'

Feeling her love, but no comfort, Elisha glanced over Hetty's shoulder at the coffin and knew she was leaving her soul in that little box. And, at this moment, she couldn't see a time when she would do things like go for a cup of tea with Jean, or how she could carry on any life without her little Ted. His loss was too deep to surmount.

CHAPTER ELEVEN

Back home, Elisha was taken by surprise when she came out of the lavatory to find cakes laid out. And even more surprised to realise how hungry she was. She'd hardly eaten in days.

Finding Jan in the kitchen, she hugged her and thanked her.

'I bought them on the way. We had a delay in changing trains, and I ran out of the station and there was a cake shop! I kept thinking as you'd have nowt done in preparation of us being here.'

'Ta, Jan. Eeh, I've missed you.'

'As Mick says, you can come to us, love.'

'I can't, I've a lot of responsibility here ...' It was then, in contradiction to her thoughts at the graveside, that Elisha knew she had to carry on.

'We ... We owe money, Jan ... and some of the veg are ready to harvest. I must keep going to keep the payments up.'

'Eeh, naw, lass. You mean you owe money to the bank?'

'Aye.'

'Well, why not sell? That would solve everything.'

'By, Jan, I could never do that! I'd be letting me grandma and me da down, they had such dreams . . .'

'Aye, I knaw, you told me, lass, but you can't live your life around everyone else's dreams. If all of this had been left to you in the first place, as it should have been, then, aye, you may have stood a chance, but when you need to borrow money to keep going, that's not good. Send up a message to your grandma and da, tell them you did your best, but you can't go on. From what you've told me of them, they'd tell you the same as me.'

For a second, Elisha almost gave in, but then a picture of her grandma and da slaving through the daylight hours to reach da's dream came to her and she knew she couldn't.

'I can see you're not heeding me words, Elisha, so I won't keep nagging you, but just to say, you knaw where we are and that we'll allus welcome you, lass.'

Jan held out her arms and Elisha went into them. They clung together. 'Eeh, Elisha, I wish that everything had worked out differently, lass. I miss you every day. There's not another woman of me age anywhere around me. We had such giggles and could help each other through the bad times without the thing that older ones do – telling you to get on with it, like they had to! By, they make you feel inadequate somehow.'

'Not your ma, surely?'

'Not if she's on her own, but if with Ma-in-law, then even she gets this hard exterior.'

Elisha couldn't imagine this of Hetty, but didn't give attention to pursuing why Hetty did this as she'd picked up on Jan having troubles.

'So, what bad times are you having, Jan?'

'It's me monthlies. So painful and heavy, and going on a lot longer than they did ... I – I, well, I knew of a couple of cases in me nursing days, they had this condition that had a long name – endometriosis – and one of the symptoms was problems with their monthlies and, well, in one of them, it led to her not being able to have babbies.'

'Aw, naw ... I – I ...'

'I'm sorry, Elisha, I shouldn't be talking about ... Eeh, me lass, I shouldn't have said sommat like that at such a time. I'm so sorry.'

Jan's arms tightened around her and Elisha knew more comfort than she'd known from anyone.

'Naw, Jan, it's all right, love. I just had a moment when it seemed that I had that and lost it, and you may never ... I'll talk to your ma, make her understand and tell her to be there for you when you need her, naw matter what the views of Mick's ma.'

'Don't think bad of her, though, Elisha. She's only trying to build a good relationship with Ma-in-law. Both are having a hard time of it, Mick should never have persuaded them to give up their homes and follow him ... I understand why, he wants to care for them, but they aren't happy ... Me ma ain't the same somehow.'

''Cos she's cowing to Mick's ma and going against being her natural self by the sounds of things. I'll chat to her, love.'

Talking about Jan's problems had helped her own, Elisha found, as she told Jan, 'Go and see a doctor, Jan, there may be sommat they can do.'

'As far as I knaw, there's nowt can be done, if it is that.'

'Maybe it ain't, at least you can find out, it may be sommat different that they can help you with.'

'Aye, you're right as it's strange it's only happened since ... well, since I've been at it!'

This made Elisha laugh when she never thought she would again. Jan had such sayings that really tickled her, as they said what she meant in a humorous way and without being direct, which would be more embarrassing.

Hetty came through the door then. She had a grin on her face. 'By, that were a good sound, lass.'

'It's Jan, naw one can stay sad around her ... Eeh, I miss you both.'

With this they all hugged together. Elisha didn't know why, but this suddenly awoke her to Mick's girls not being there. But to her query, Jan told her they hadn't thought it suitable to bring them to the service and so they'd gone to spend the day with one of Mick's friends who had children of the same age, finishing with, 'Well, I'd better take the tea through, though knowing Mick and Jack they're probably in the garden talking men's talk.'

'I'll help ...'

'Naw, Hetty, stay here with me, Jan can cope, only we ain't had a moment together.'

'Aye, all right, lass ... By, Elisha, I miss you, and me cottage and ... I should have been here for you.'

'Naw, your place is with your daughter, and she needs you right now, Hetty.'

Hetty dropped her head.

'You knaw she's having problems, don't you?'

'Aye, and I'm worried sick about her.'

'Then show her that.'

'Has she said owt, then?'

'Aye, she has, she's missing the comfort you always gave. There's sommat not right, Hetty, and you should be there for her.'

'I will be, I've been a daft ha'peth trying to please others above me own daughter. I'll see that she gets to see a doctor. She's never been a complainer so I knaw there's sommat not right when she does ... I feel ashamed now.'

Elisha took Hetty into her arms, 'It's nowt that can't be mended, love.'

'Aw, I miss you, Elisha, I wish that Mick had never been left that farm, though he's as happy as a pig in muck – ha, he's often in the pig muck an' all. He loves the great fat, smelly things; he talks to them, and they oink back!'

Elisha felt another laugh coming as a picture of this came to her, but it strangled in her throat as she remembered her da talking of keeping pigs. An overwhelming feeling of letting him down took the place of anything funny Hetty said.

'Naw, lass, I didn't mean to make you cry ... Eeh, I'm sorry ... I'm getting it all wrong. I stand by the side of Mick's ma instead of me lovely Jan and now, when you're going through all you are, I'm laying me troubles at your door.'

'It's just me memories. At a time like this, I so need me ma and da, and me grandma who would've been a rock for me. It were you talking about pigs ... me lovely da wanted to keep pigs.'

'Then do it for him, lass.'

This was the opposite to what Jan had said, but it resonated more. 'I will, Hetty, I will.'

'Let's go and join the others, eh? We've both learnt a lesson – you to carry on with your dream and me to be a proper mum to Jan again. We can none of us go back and undo the bad bits, but we can take strength from them.'

To Elisha, the rest of the afternoon felt surreal. She chatted and laughed over memories, and ate heartily of the cakes, as did Jack. It seemed as if they were celebrating, not mourning, and yet she felt no guilt, just the comforting feeling that she would cope.

This all collapsed later when Jan, Mick and Hetty left to go to the B&B where they were staying, and she was in Jack's arms.

Jack's body heaved, undoing all the strength Elisha had thought she had. They held each other, sobbed together, remembered little things – Ted's loud burps, his waking in the night with a yell that would make the roof collapse if she didn't put him to her breast quickly, and his gaze at her as he suckled, his little fingers curled around hers.

'Me heart's broken, Jack.'

'I knaw, lass, mine is an' all.'

'How're we going to carry on?'

'We will . . . You knaw, Mick suggested selling . . .'

'Naw, Jack, I can't do that. I can't.'

Holding her closer, Jack snuggled into her neck. The kisses he planted rippled through her. They hadn't made love for weeks, and since Ted died Elisha had felt they never would again, as she had no inclination, and yet she was shocked to find that the familiar tickle of her tummy muscles and the clenching of those in her thighs was happening. Her throat tightened with anticipation as Jack's lips came onto hers and she hungrily sought his tongue – felt the tingle of finding it and touching it with her own.

What followed was a scramble of taking off clothes, kissing, declaring love, till at last they were both on the rug in front of the dying embers and Jack entered her.

Exquisite waves of ecstasy rippled through her and had her crying out with the sensations that gripped her and took her body to a place where she knew a release far greater than any she'd ever experienced.

Clinging on to Jack with her legs wrapped around him, his moan joined her cries as his body shuddered.

His words were of love for her. Words that quickly went into a sob that racked his body and jolted Elisha's own agony to the fore once more.

Without uncoupling, they held each other. Their cries now for their little lost son, as their joining had found a release for the sorrow that they'd been afraid to share so deeply, until now.

As their sobs calmed, Jack rolled off her, but still he held her.

'We have to help each other, Jack.'

'Aye. We must. When I lost me da, an old man who lived next door told me that there was healing in grieving, that I shouldn't fight it but let it run its course. That I should remember everything good and bad about me da, and that way I'd keep him alive. Not a fantasy figure of him, but the real him. Those words helped me.'

'I never let owt bad in about me ma, da and grandma, as I can't think of owt.'

'That's because you put them on a pedestal, love. That don't make them real.'

Jack was right. She'd made them into gods.

'If you remember the real them, it makes for better remembering – you can feel the whole of them. We can talk about Ted as if he was an angel heaven sent, but in truth he were a demanding little bugger. Ha, if our Ted wanted owt, he'd scream the place down till he got it. He was strong in his character. And yet, he could charm you with a smile, and I made him giggle that time, which showed he had a sense of humour.'

As Jack spoke, Elisha felt the surreal angel she had made Ted into strip away bit by bit, and Ted became real to her again. 'He had the smelliest poos.'

'Ha, he did. I had to stop meself heaving at times. And his burps! He could have won a burping competition!'

'He was a proper little man.'

'Aye, and that's how I'll remember him.'

'Me too ... but eeh, Jack, I wish it didn't have to be a memory. Me arms ache to hold him.'

They clung together once more, allowing their sobs, for Ted was alive now in their memory – the Ted they had known and loved had come back to them in his entirety. And Elisha knew this was the best way to keep him alive within her.

★   ★   ★

The nearness of them, and that need to seek something to help them, had them making love again. This time they explored new territory with their hands, their mouths and in their complete giving to each other. It was as if loss had stripped them of all inhibitions and they were to take all life had to offer them.

At this moment Elisha felt it was offering her the joys of love, a love that was complete. Not that anything could replace the joy she had from her little Ted, but this wasn't trying to. It was accepting. Giving her more than she dreamt there was for her in her love of her beloved Jack.

PART THREE

Hope Shattered
1907

CHAPTER TWELVE

Christmas had been a quiet time of reflection and planning, and of mourning and remembering, but somehow they had gotten through it.

Thanks to the autumn season's harvest of potatoes and root veg, along with Brussels sprouts and apples, and with the new chicks now matured into hens adding to the egg laying, their income had greatly improved.

But still the bank wanted more, pointing out that while they weren't paying the full payments the interest was mounting, making their debt higher than it had started out to be.

This led to them working their fingers to the bone and constantly worrying, to the point when Elisha had moments when she just wanted to give up and go to Jan.

But then her fighting spirit rose as she stepped out of the cottage on this, the eleventh day of March 1907, and pulled her cardigan around her, for despite the blustery cold wind, all around her spring was bursting into life.

Taking a deep breath, she told herself that, no, she wouldn't up sticks and run – she'd stay and fight, and besides, she wanted to stay near to her little Ted's resting place.

Already today Elisha had made pies, as she now had orders to fulfil from three cafés. And not just for pies, as a couple of her ma's recipes for scones and chocolate buns were good sellers too.

Turning from her contemplation, she saw Jack harnessing Grundy. He smiled and waved. He'd been in the greenhouse all morning, where most of the groundwork was at this time of year, nurturing the seedlings ready to plant out for next year's crop.

He called out to her now, 'Everything ready, love?'

'Aye, there's a crate full, so it'll take us both to lift it.'

Without warning, Elisha felt her stomach lurch. She was shocked to realise she was going to be sick! Turning away, she ran towards the outside lav, only just making it before her stomach emptied itself.

When the bout ended, she leant against the door.

To Jack's concerned cry of, 'Eeh, me little lass, what's to do? Are you ill?', she called out, 'Naw, I'll be out in a minute, love.'

The enormity of what could be wrong hit Elisha as if someone had slapped her face and suddenly woken her from a stupor. *Oh God! I ain't seen me monthly for a good while! What have I been thinking? I've been locked in a cloud of misery, not taking part in life – not really taking part ... just functioning, unless Jack was making love to me, then I came alive – now look where that's led me!*

Not wanting to feel the joy that vied with her worry, she tried to suppress it, but it was having none of that and her face creased in a grin – a babby. Another babby to hold and care for. *Not that it could ever replace me little Ted, but it would fill me empty arms and help the ache in me heart.*

Swallowing the sour taste in her mouth, Elisha opened the door of the lav, swilled her hands under the tap outside the door and then washed her mouth out.

Straightening, she looked at Jack. 'We have a babby on the way, love.'

Jack's eyes opened wide. His lips formed the word 'What?' but made no sound.

Elisha giggled, surprising herself at how happy she felt when the consequences were glaringly difficult – how would she work at the rate she did now? How would they manage?

But none of that mattered as Jack scooped her up and twirled her around, laughing his head off, and neither did it dampen her elation when he put her down and went into a coughing fit. She helped him by massaging him, but at the same time giggled and spoke of how wonderful it would be.

When the bout ended, Jack looked up at her. 'He'll never take the place of our Ted, though. You're not thinking that, are you, lass?'

'Naw, and you shouldn't ask such a thing!'

Without warning, the tears brimmed in her eyes. Jack took hold of her saying over and over that he was sorry, but nothing could soothe the pain that had risen and now threatened to strangle her.

'Elisha, me love, cry it out. Holding in your grief won't help you. We can wait an hour to deliver the goods.' With this, Jack steered her inside and sat down, pulling her onto his lap. She snuggled into him and gave her tears rein.

In the end she was crying for so many things, even their fight to continue existing in the cottage her grandma loved. *I can't lose it, I can't!*

This thought gave Elisha back the strength that had ebbed from her. Straightening, she smiled through her tears and, against how she truly felt, kissed Jack on the nose and told him, 'This won't make our fortune, love. I'm all right now. Let's get on with it, and by the time we've ridden down to the prom, I'll be fine.'

'Aye, there's nowt like a March wind to blow the cobwebs away.'

When he rose, he held her to him. 'You're the bravest person I've ever met, Elisha, me little lass, and I bless the day I walked through that gate. Me and you are a good team, and we'll weather owt they throw at us.'

This was tested as they urged Grundy on through a wind that was getting stronger.

'Eeh, I don't like the way the clouds are rolling, lass, I reckon we're in for a storm.'

'I hope not, Jack, I always fear for our sheds and greenhouse in a storm.'

'Ha, they're sturdy enough, it's us you need to worry about ... By, look at that!'

They had reached the seafront. A giant wave rose into the air – a spectacular sight, but when it heaved back and crashed onto the promenade, the water left behind flooded across the road.

A gust of wind followed, rocking the cart and scaring them both.

'We'll have to turn back, lass. This is bad.'

As the wind whipped her cheeks and threatened to take her bonnet from her head, Elisha tried to agree, but her words were taken into another gust that thrust her backwards.

Jack grabbed her, and once she was righted on the bench tried to steer Grundy to turn around, but the force was too strong for him. He jumped down, and as if he was fighting with something physically pushing him backwards, bent double.

Elisha held on tightly to the cart as she turned herself and then slid down to the ground. It was as if huge hands were pushing her body. Somehow, she managed to get to Jack, just as a boarding from one of the shops came crashing down. Caught in the wind, it twisted in the air and hit Grundy's head with such force that Grundy collapsed in a heap.

Helping each other, Jack and Elisha managed to get to their beloved donkey.

Grundy snorted in an indignant way, then rolled and tried to stand, but the weight of the upturned cart held him.

Relief at him still being alive filled Elisha. She cradled his head and tried to soothe him. His eyes flared with fear; his breath came in snorts.

Shouting to Jack, Elisha told him that they had to unharness the cart or Grundy may drown!

How Jack managed to do that, Elisha didn't know, but her fear was for him now, as Grundy rose to his feet and seemed none the worse for his ordeal but Jack collapsed in a heap and disappeared under the water!

Clinging on to the cart, which had remained intact, Elisha dodged the debris that crashed around them as she fought against the wind and waded through the thigh-deep water that swirled their ruined produce around her.

She dared not give thought to what this meant to them or she would sink into despair. She had to get to Jack. He lay face down!

Grabbing his hair, Elisha lifted Jack's head – taking no heed of the freezing cold ebbing, toing and froing water, she used all her strength to hold him up. Fear gripped her as she saw his nose and lips tinged with blue as he gasped for breath.

As if Grundy knew they needed help, he turned and came towards her. Grabbing his rein, Elisha clung on to it, her mind screaming at her that they were going to die!

But then, strong arms took hold of her from behind. 'I've got you, missus. I'll get your man to safety and come back for you. Keep hold of the donkey!'

Elisha looked up and recognised the man who made his money by performing on the promenade the amazing feat of lifting huge weights. Known only to her and many as the Strongman, he'd once lifted Grundy above his head, to cheers and applause from the gathering crowd in the market. Always the cap he'd lain on the ground filled with pennies.

'Is there somewhere I can take him?' the Strongman shouted.

'Round the corner. Number fourteen, Bank Street.'

'Aye, I knaws it, it's where Jean lives.'

Elisha hadn't known that Jean knew the Strongman – she hadn't ever mentioned him. But then, Elisha thought, she hadn't ever made it to Jean's house. With a heavy heart, the reason came to her, that Jean had invited her as somewhere to feed her little Ted . . . Even so, she knew she would always be welcome, but time was of the essence when she and Jack made their deliveries. Always they'd had to get home as soon as they were sold out, as Jack tired easily.

Grundy shifted about, turning his body and edging a little forward.

'It's all right, Grundy, lad. They'll come back for us.'

But Grundy was having none of it. He moved very slowly forward and followed the Strongman. Elisha didn't try to stop him; she realised that she, too, didn't want to wait for the Strongman to return.

Clinging on to Grundy's reins it seemed they were a team, as together they fought through the wind and rain and trudged through the swirling, filthy water until a crashing sound louder than any of the others made Grundy stop. His body trembled – always he'd been afraid of loud noises.

Elisha looked to where the sound had come from – saw the roof of one of the seafront cottages hurtling through the air. She held her breath, but as the wind swirled, it mercifully took the debris in the opposite direction.

'Go on, Grundy, lad. Gee up!'

Thankful that Grundy didn't have one of his stubborn moments, they resumed their slow progress.

It was with a sigh of relief that Elisha saw that the water hadn't flooded Bank Street but only lapped the beginning of the road – the waves weren't powerful enough to flood the incline.

The going was easier now, despite her exhaustion, as they left behind the drag of the tide. Grundy shook himself and looked back at her.

'I'm all right, Grundy. You saved me life, lad. Grandma would be proud of you. Aye and you've lost that stubborn streak you had in her day; she'd be shocked how compliant you are now.'

They'd reached Jean's house. Elisha tethered Grundy to the fence. She didn't have to knock, as Jean opened the door.

'Eeh, lass, come in. Jack's on the sofa. Bert's been helping him.'

Bert, Elisha assumed, was the Strongman, as he now stood behind Jean. 'Eeh, lass, you did well to get here. I'll go and get your cart afore it gets smashed to pieces.'

'Ta, Bert. Is Jack all right, Jean?'

'Aye, he is. I've kettle on to get him a hot drink and it looks like you could do with one an' all ...' Jean opened her arms. 'Eeh, lass, I've been at me wits' end that sommat might happen to you, but Bert saw from the window that you'd made it into the street.'

'I didn't knaw until now that the Strongman was named Bert.'

'Aye, one and the same. We've been friends for years.'

Bert turned on hearing this. 'Ha! I've wanted us to be more for years, an' all, but she ain't having none of it!'

Jean laughed a girlish laugh, and flapped the tea towel she held in his direction.

'Come on through, don't take any notice of him, he's nowt but a big daft ha'peth.'

Slipping off her soaking wet shoes, Elisha hurried to Jack's side and knelt beside him. He was wrapped in a blanket, his feet were bare and his hair was plastered to his head, but his grin told her he was fine.

'Aw, me Jack, me Jack.'

'Hey, you're soaked!' Jack laughed, a sound that brought normality back to Elisha but didn't stop her shaking all over as the shock of their ordeal hit her.

'Wrap this around you, love.'

A warm blanket came around her shoulders and a thick towel was put over her arm.

'Eeh, Jean, I've dripped all over your floor, I'm sorry, I didn't think.'

'It's nowt that won't mop up, so don't be worrying. You're safe and that's all that counts.'

As Elisha rubbed her hair with the towel, she looked around her. The room – Jean's front room – looked out on the street through a big window that gave plenty of natural light. The floor she'd worried about was covered in a brown linoleum and shone, showing how it had been lovingly polished. The mahogany furniture had obviously had the same treatment, as light reflected from the small table under the window and the dresser in the alcove of the fireplace, which had a rag rug in front of it not dissimilar to the one they had in front of theirs. A fire glowed in the hearth of a mahogany-surrounded fire pit.

Besides the sofa, there were two matching beige armchairs, their green heather pattern faded in places.

Umpteen ornaments of vases, birds and ladies in long frocks took every space there was on the mantel shelf and the dresser, and even the tabletop had a vase and a huge china horse and rider ornament standing on it. It was homely, a home that had stood the passing of time.

When Jean came back with the tea, Elisha felt more comfortable, though she'd have loved to have taken her soaking blouse and long skirt off.

'Get this down you both. It'll warm you up better than any fire can.'

'Ta, Jean, you're a pal.'

'It's nice to have you both here at last. They say it's an ill wind that blows nobody any good – this one blew you both to me!'

Elisha grinned. 'Well, I'd rather it hadn't in such a spectacular way!'

When Jack didn't respond, Elisha turned to see his eyes had closed. His pale face looked drawn.

Outside she could see Bert harnessing Grundy.

'I think I'd better get Jack home though, Jean. It's already getting dark, and I need to get him dry and warmed up.'

'Aye, I think that's best, lass. Keep the blankets around you, you can return them another time – that way, I knaw you'll come again.'

Elisha stood. 'We will. We should have done so afore now, but life got in the way ... I want to hug you, Jean, but I'd make you all wet.'

'Ha, hug me twice next time, eh?'

They both giggled at this.

Bert came in then and when told of their plan, lifted Jack as if he were a babby, took him outside, gently laid him in the cart and covered him with the blanket.

Elisha clung on to the side of the cart against the force of the wind.

'Will you help me up into the driving side of the bench seat, Bert?'

As he came to her side, the wind tore at them both.

'I'll help you to sit with your man, lass, and cover you with a blanket. You'll never manage to steer the donkey in this lot – I'll do that. Jean told me where you live, and I don't live far from you now. I took Hetty's cottage and at a cheap rent an' all in exchange for helping around the farm when I'm not entertaining on the prom. I was in me ma's old house before that, but the landlord wanted to sell it after she died.'

'Ta, Bert, and I'm sorry to hear about you losing your ma. Mind, it's grand that you live so near to us, pop in any time, you'll allus be welcome.'

Bert doffed his cap. 'I will, and if there's owt I can do for you, you just say, lass, as your man don't seem too well.'

The storm played havoc with them as they slowly made their way back to the cottage, threatening to upend the cart, but as they got further away from the coast it became easier, though still they had to dodge flying objects, and their pace was greatly slowed by the debris that littered the roads.

Elisha feared what she would find at home and prayed the damage wasn't too bad. But her worst fears hit her as they pulled up outside the gate.

'Naw! Oh God!'

Glass, splintered wood and the roof of one of their sheds littered every square inch of the garden. The greenhouse was no more, the potting shed door and windows were blown in, and boxes that had held their plants now lay strewn all over.

'By, lass, it's a mess.'

Elisha looked around her with despair in her heart. Yes, it was a mess, and one she didn't see them recovering from.

Jack hung on to the side of the cart and pulled himself up. His eyes filled with tears as he gazed at the painting he'd been working on every spare moment he had – now it lay in a puddle, its vibrant colours spread into each other, making it a mess of splashes.

With it, all hope seeped from Elisha as the carnage around her told that all their work had been for nothing.

Unable to take in the enormity of it all, Elisha just stared, her thoughts giving her the fear of how they were ever going to make the payments to the bank now. Why she even asked herself the question she didn't know, as the answer was laid out in front of her – it would be impossible to do.

'Eeh, I'm sorry, lass. I've seen this garden develop as I've passed by and admired the owners, not knowing who they were. It's heartbreaking ... but we can do nowt about it now, so let's get you both inside, eh?'

When she opened the door, Elisha bent to pick up a letter, which she knew was from Jan. As she put it on the sideboard, she hoped with all her heart that this storm wasn't hitting them in Surrey.

She couldn't give attention to this thought though, as when Bert laid Jack on the sofa his body began to tremble.

'Get another blanket, lass, and I'll stoke the fire up. We could do with getting him out of his wet attire an' all.'

Elisha's heart sank, but she pushed herself to do something to help her Jack. 'Bert, will you do that – help him to take his wet clothes off? I'll bring his pyjamas down.'

By the time she came back down, Jack was sitting in front of the now roaring fire with just a blanket around him, looking much better and with his shivers under control. He smiled at her as he took his nightshirt. 'Ta, love, but a bit early in the day for bed. I'm all right now, I'll go up and get some dry clothes on.'

Elisha released the deep breath she'd taken and smiled at him. 'Eeh, lad, you give me some scares!'

He grinned back at her. 'I've the nine lives of a cat, love. And while I have you, I knaw I'll survive them all.'

It was Bert who answered, 'Well, that's good to hear, lad, I'll leave you to your missus now, but I'll call in tomorrow if the storm's abated and give you both a hand to clear the mess outside.'

Jack shook Bert's hand. 'I reckon we'll have it done with your help, Bert, you could lift the lot in one go!'

'Ha, I could that, so don't the pair of you be worrying all night, get yourselves over your ordeal.' He'd reached the door. As he bent down to go through it, Elisha caught his hand and kissed his cheek. 'Ta, for everything, Bert.'

His grin lit his face. 'Well, lass, it was all worth it for that.'

Once the door was closed and Jack disappeared upstairs, Elisha picked up Jan's letter, went through to the kitchen and moved the kettle onto the hob, before going upstairs herself to change.

Throwing the letter on the bed, she asked, 'Are you sure you're all right, Jack, love?'

'Aye, I am, who's that from?'

'Jan. I'll get meself into dry clothes and then we'll have a read over a cuppa.'

'By, I feel full of tea, lass. I drank two at Jean's. But I'm starving hungry.'

'You allus are, Jack, you allus are!' Elisha laughed. Her happiness at seeing Jack was all right more than made up for all they had to face.

How enormous that was, she dared not give thought to.

CHAPTER THIRTEEN

Munching on a doorstep of her freshly baked bread covered with a thick slice of cheese, and seeing Jack enjoying his, Elisha ripped open the letter.

Her heart sank as she read the first line.

My dearest Elisha, tragedy has struck us. Our beautiful farmhouse and one of our barns have burnt to the ground!

'Oh, Naw!'
'What? What is it, love ... not bad news?'
'It is!'
Elisha told him of the fire, and then read out the rest of the letter:

It happened two days ago; we heard an explosion in the porch. When we opened the door, the flames almost engulfed us!

We're devastated, but though we have minor burns we're not seriously hurt as Mick closed the door in a flash.

We dared not stop to fight it. Our only thought was to get out and to alert our mas.

We think the hook holding the gas light to the ceiling must have come out and the gas lamp fell to the floor. Its cylinder was full.

By the time we were all at the front of the house it was a mass of flames, and the breeze took sparks to the barns nearest to the house. One caught alight. Luckily, not the one that our farmhand sleeps in. But he was woken by the noise and drove the tractor to the nearest town to alert the fire brigade as we couldn't access our telephone.

We carried bucket after bucket of water from the well to try to extinguish the flames, but it got the better of us and was too far gone by the time the fire brigade arrived, though they managed to stop it from spreading further.

The barn held the last of our winter feed for our cows, now it's all gone.

Me and Mick have moved into the cottage we offered you, love, so now, even if you change your mind, we've nowhere to put you. But by the sound of your last letter, you're both hopeful of righting your situation. I pray that is still so.

What we're going to do, we don't know yet, but though really upset to lose the house, we will pick ourselves up and get on with it. We have a new telephone on order but not sure when it will be fitted. They tell us it will be the same number, which is a blessing as everyone knows it — me friends from working at the hospital, and Mick's mates from the force, besides them as we deal with for our business. I'm always hoping you will find a way of giving me a call, I long to have a chat with you.

Miss you so much.

Take care, my lovely Elisha.

Jan x

'By, that's bad luck for them, lass. Not a good start at all. Though in one thing they are lucky – Mick was left some money along with the farm, so they'll get sorted.'

'I knaw, but to lose everything! And Jan doesn't say they have enough money to rebuild. I feel so sorry for them.'

'Aye, well, we've a lot to feel sorry about for ourselves an' all, lass. I didn't see all the destruction, as Bert whipped me in here so fast I couldn't take it in, but what I did see ... Eeh, Elisha, what's to be done?'

The despair that Elisha had quashed overwhelmed her, but she couldn't let it win.

'We'll have to go and see the bank manager again ... There's naw way we can meet this month's payment. We'll have to hope he says he'll wait.'

But the next day, their reception at the bank didn't go well. They'd been left with 'Your case will be discussed, and we will contact you.'

Six days later – days they'd lived in fear as they worked hard with the help of Bert to salvage what they could and clear as much debris as possible – the formal reply to their request for further time arrived.

The crisp printed paper held the ending of Elisha's world as she'd known it.

For the attention of Mr Jack Randal and Mrs Elisha Randal

This is to inform you that you no longer own the property known as 'Primula Cottage'. Ownership has transferred to the Radcliffe Bank.

A foreclosure notice is hereby issued for failure to repay a loan taken out with Radcliffe Bank secured on the above property.

Please vacate the premises within one week from today's date.

Sincerely,
A. Radcliffe

Attached to this was a document that spelled out the conditions of the loan and how they hadn't kept to them. Under this was a statement outlining the bank's right to take possession of their property.

With the words she had never wanted to read stark in her mind, Elisha sat down and wept.

Jack cried with her. His gasps saying over and over how he was sorry, how he didn't foresee this happening, until his breathing became laboured and he slid from her arms.

Panic had Elisha slapping his back, blowing into his face and screaming out his name, until at last, he came round.

Sitting on the floor next to him and cradling his head, Elisha stroked his hair. 'There's allus sommat we can do, Jack ... Look, I'll cycle to Nancy Barns' grocery shop and try to make a call to Jan. I knaw she'll help us somehow. We just have to pray her new telephone is installed, as her letter was posted three days ago.'

When Jack could breathe more easily and put his words together, he stammered out, 'It'll ... cost.'

'Well, I've tuppence in me purse and Nancy only charges a penny to use her phone.'

Jack's eyes showed the hope this had given him. 'Tell her we'll sleep anywhere, in the barn ... anywhere, and tell her we'll work for them, just for our food.'

With this, hope came into Elisha too. How she was going to leave the only home she'd ever known, she didn't know, but she had no choice. *Forgive me, Da and Grandma, I truly did me best.*

But the hope died when she dialled the number she had for Jan and nothing happened. Tears welled up and filled her eyes. They brimmed over when Nancy said, 'Aw, lass, what's to do, eh?'

Everything poured from her as if she was confiding in a friend, when she'd only ever dealt with Nancy as the shopkeeper – though always she'd been friendly and chatty.

'By, lass, misfortune knocks on your door. And it ain't fair! What will you do?'

'We'll go to Jan and Mick ... only I can't let her knaw, you see ...' Elisha explained the tragedy of the fire.

'Naw! Are they hurt? Have they lost the farm?'

'Naw, they're all right, and most of the farm was saved. It's just that I don't knaw how ... or if, they can help us now, as their telephone is out of action.'

'I don't knaw, it don't seem right that decent hardworking folk like the four of you should suffer like this. But I'm sure Jan and Mick will have sommat of a solution for you, so don't worry. But eeh, lass, how will you get there?'

'We've only got Grundy to transport us. It's a long way, so we'll have to rest him often. We'll camp in fields on the way.'

'Surely the train would be better?'

'I don't have the money, and besides, I want to take so much. There's stuff I just can't leave behind.'

'But you could sell what you don't need – Bernard Wall, the bloke who deals in second-hand furniture and stuff, would take it. He gives a fair price an' all.'

'Aye, there is that, ta, Nancy. In me panic, I hadn't thought. Maybe doing that will allow us to stay in a boarding house a few times on the way down, though it will have to have a stable for Grundy.'

'Well, there's plenty of them, and I hope you can, as sleeping rough in fields ain't going to help Jack, love. Is there nawhere nearer you can go?'

'I've a friend called Jean, she lives near to the prom, but she ain't got much room. And I've made friends with Bert, the Strongman who works the prom entertaining folk, but I couldn't put on either of them and ...' Elisha's body chilled, pebbling her arms with goosebumps and causing her to shiver, as her next words stuck in her throat. 'And ... Well, Th ... There's the workhouse!'

'Naw, lass, not that ...'

On an impulse, Nancy took hold of her and hugged her.

Not knowing why, Elisha blurted out, 'I'm having another babby an' all ...'

'Eeh, Elisha, I – I don't knaw what to say, except, well ... Take hope in that, make the babby a focus to keep you determined to get your life back on track, eh?'

With this, an inner strength built in Elisha.

'I will. We'll be all right. I'll do all I can to make it so.'

'I'll put together some canned foods for you for your journey, love, and I'll pray harder than I've ever prayed that you make it to Jan, and she can help you.'

'Ta, Nancy, that's kind of you. I'll call in afore we go, only I can't carry much now.'

'Well, it's only about six cans that I can spare, but each would contribute to you making a dinner each day – corned beef and the like. And with a bit of luck and a fair wind, you might make Surrey by then.'

Elisha didn't think so at Grundy's pace of around ten to fifteen miles a day. Mick had told them when he and Jan were first leaving that they had two hundred and fifty miles to travel from Blackpool to get to their farm, so it would take her and Jack at least a month to get there.

Dread filled every part of her. She couldn't imagine what such a journey would be like as still there were frosts to be expected at this time of year.

By the time she reached home, Elisha had convinced herself that they could do it and make it a travelling holiday. Thinking of all the good things about it that she could muster – no daily grind, the freedom of the journey, trotting along at Grundy's pace, and her and Jack going to be with lovely Jan, Mick and Hetty. Though Mick's ma would be a bit of a challenge, as she was inclined to be suspicious of everyone's motives, but they would win her round.

This optimism only lasted until she reached her gate. Dismounting from her bike, the devastation the wind had wrought hit her. Her eyes went to her beloved cottage, its thatched roof torn and scraggy and a window off its hinges rocking to and fro.

The sound it made seemed to be banging the drum of her doom.

But she wouldn't let it defeat her. She'd get on with what had to be done.

Jack was sitting up when she opened the door.

'Feeling better, love?'

'Aye. A bit . . . Any luck?'

'Naw. Sorry.' Going over, she knelt in front of him. 'But Jan is our only hope, so we'll set off anyroad, eh? Nancy suggested we contact Bernard Wall and let him give us a price for everything.'

'Aye, that's a good idea.'

It seemed to Elisha that Jack had given up. He offered no alternative as to what they should do but just went along with her.

'How much can I take with us, do you reckon? I'd like me grandma's clock and . . .'

'Eeh, lass, we can't take owt, other than clothes, and bedding and food. We'll need to make a bed in the cart, so that'll have to be practically empty.'

'But . . .' Elisha's protest died on her lips. Though it broke her heart to realise the truth of what Jack had said, she knew he was right.

A tear rolled down her face.

Jack wiped it away with his thumb. 'I've let you down, lass.'

'Naw, Jack! We've had bad luck. You meant well when

you took the loan, and we were winning. But ... Oh, Jack, it's unbearable ...'

Jack leant over and cradled her head in his arms. 'We'll rise again, lass. With Jan and Mick's help we'll survive, and I'll get stronger, then we can start to put our lives back together again. I promise.'

Latching on to this – the only optimism Jack had shown – Elisha smiled through her tears. 'That's the spirit, me grandma would say – "Never say die, lad!"'

Jack grinned. 'I'd have loved to have met your grandma. How she survived when left this place and very little money, I'll never knaw.'

'She had a very strong will. And a naughty side. She told me once under sworn secrecy that she trudged to the farm across the road during the night and stole seedlings once they showed their heads – "I only took what they would have hoed out, lass," she said, "It weren't stealing, but helping them." Grandma had giggled then, a crackling giggle that really meant she'd been naughty but crafty!'

'Well, I'll be blowed! But it wasn't a bad idea. Farmers scatter seeds all over the land they're planting and then when they show as seedlings, they hoe a lot of them out so that those they save can get enough nutrients to grow ... Ha! So, that's how she did it!'

'Partly. There was still the hard work she and me da had to put in to get the land ready, and he were only a lad at the time. And Grandma told me that she used to be up most of the night making jams and preserves to sell. They began to get on their feet by the time me da married me ma though. Then she took over the baking.'

'All from stealing, eh?'

'Aye, you could say that. Anyroad, we ain't going to do that. I'd fear being caught and put into prison!'

Jack was quiet for a moment. When he spoke, he asked, 'So, you knaw you have to leave practically everything, lass?'

'I do.' Elisha couldn't stop the sad sigh she released. 'I'll go and see this second-hand dealer tomorrow.'

'In that case, you need to pack what we can take with us today, so there's naw mix-up about what he can look at and bid for.'

Elisha couldn't stop her tears flowing as she began to sort out what was practical for them. How had it come to this? They'd tried so hard.

She rubbed her small mound of a tummy, and spoke to her unborn child: 'I wanted this to be yours one day. Yours and . . .' A huge sob took her then as she was about to say, 'yours and Ted's'.

Footsteps came up behind her, and a gentle touch of Jack's hand helped her.

'I knaw it's hard, lass, but we've naw choice . . . Look, make sure you take the things that are precious to you, eh? Your grandma's watch that you said she allus had pinned to her cardi, and your da's cap that you keep on the coat stand, and your ma's brooch.'

Elisha turned into his arms and found comfort in his hugging her. But how she wished she could find a way of them not having to leave.

★   ★   ★

The reality that there was no way hit Elisha hard the next day, as she stood in the empty living room. It hadn't taken long to clear it, and now two men were bringing down the beds from upstairs, whilst another packed boxes with the smaller items, and all for a measly two guineas. Though it cheered her to think that this was enough to stop at an inn each night, with a hearty breakfast and stabling for Grundy, as the thought of sleeping in the cart had terrified her.

Jean's arm came around her. 'Eeh, lass, me heart breaks for you.'

Turning into her hug, Elisha said, 'Ta for all your help, Jean. I'll write to you and let you knaw how we're going on.'

'Aye, that'll give me Jan's address, and make sure to let me knaw when the babby arrives, an' all. I want to knaw everything. I'm busy knitting you knaw, so I'll post off all I get done for the new babby – I'm using white and lemon as they suit a girl or a boy.'

'Aw, that's kind of you.'

Bert passed by carrying the crate Elisha had packed and left upstairs. 'This is the last of it, lass. The cart's ready for you. Jack's just tying a sack of straw to the back of it for Grundy.'

Jean held her tighter. 'It'll work out, you'll see. Jan and Mick'll soon help you onto your feet again. And when that happens, come and visit us, eh?'

'We will ... and, Jean, why don't you consider marrying Bert, eh? You'll be company for each other.'

'Aye, I might. Only, it's not an easy step to take.'

'I'd like to think of you two being together.'

'We'll see, lass ... One thing, you'll be the first to knaw.'

Bert came back in at that moment. 'First to knaw what? What are you two cooking up, eh?'

Elisha jumped in. 'Oh, only if you try your hand again, you might not get a naw this time, Bert.'

Bert looked at Jean. His eyes filled with tears. 'Aw, Jean, lass.'

Jean's eyes held Bert's.

Elisha didn't know how it happened, but suddenly she was no longer in Jean's arms, but watching as Jean went into Bert's.

'Will you marry me, Jean? You'd make me the happiest man alive if you did.'

'I will, Bert. I have me orders to say yes, and I don't knaw why I've been so daft about it.'

This time, Elisha's tears were happy ones, as Bert held Jean tighter and kissed her on the nose. Running to the door, she called out to Jack. 'Hey, you're missing out, love, it's happened, it's finally happened!'

'What . . . By, you look cheered up, me little lass, what's happened to cause that, then?'

Jack had walked towards her and she stepped back inside, 'Look, I give you the soon-to-be-wed Jean and Bert!'

'Well, I'll be blowed! How did that come about?'

'It were Miss Matchmaker here. She made me see I were daft to hold out. Me and Bert need each other, don't we, me darling?'

'We do, lass. And aye, there's a little thing called love motivating us an' all!'

Jean giggled. An almost girlie giggle that brought smiles all round.

Suddenly, Elisha didn't feel so bad about what was happening, as she thought of her grandma's saying: 'Good can come from bad, lass.'

Aye, and I'm going to make sure that good comes for me and Jack and our little one – I don't knaw how yet, but somehow, I'll do it.

CHAPTER FOURTEEN

This courage didn't last long as they trotted along at Grundy's slow pace, rested him often and only achieved getting as far as Penwortham, the other side of Preston.

Whilst Jack tethered Grundy outside the Farrington Arms inn, Elisha went inside to ask about lodgings and was relieved to find they had one double room left.

'Two bob'll get you and your husband a night's sleep, a pie for your dinner, fried tatties for your breakfast and a bath full of hot water, missus.'

'Ta, I'll take it.'

'Righto. And I see you have a donkey? Well, there's Crookings Moor, just across the road, so it'll be happy grazing there. You can unharness around the back and leave your belongings there on your cart, they'll be safe ... You travelling far?'

'Aye, to me friend's farm in Surrey.'

'By, that'll take you weeks, love. Rather you than me. But I wish you good luck.'

As she went outside to Jack, Elisha thought that they were going to need an abundance of that.

★ ★ ★

The pie was delicious, a thick crust of pastry on top of vegetables and meat in a tasty gravy. Both ate hungrily, hardly talking, as they swilled the pie down with a jug of beer.

For Elisha she was calculating how long it was going to take and how often they could stay at an inn. She could feel Jack worrying, and guessed he was thinking through the same problem.

It was when they were in the bedroom, bathed and ready for bed, that Jack sat down heavily on the side of the bed and asked, 'Are we doing the right thing, lass?'

Elisha went to him, anxious to allay the despair she heard in his voice.

Standing in front of him, she cradled his head in her arms. 'We have no alternative, Jack.'

Jack's arms came around her waist, making her feel safe, but only for a moment, as the enormity of their undertaking hit her when he put into words what she had been thinking: 'But at this rate, it's going to mean a lot of nights sleeping on the cart, and with you in your condition ... Eeh, me little lass, what have I done?'

'Naw, naw, don't think like that. It wasn't your fault, it was the storm ... Eeh, Jack, we've only been travelling for one day, and afore that all the hard work and stress of sorting things out. It'll get easier as we go along.'

He snuggled his head between her breasts, then looked up and grinned at her. 'Them's the best thing about you being pregnant, it gives you a good pair!'

'Jack!' But though she feigned outrage, inside her a trickle of excitement lit up.

This became a torrent of feelings as Jack pulled her down on the bed beside him and then gently manoeuvred her with him until they were both lying down.

'By, you're beautiful, lass.'

His lips sought hers, and she was lost in a world that held only pleasure for her, as Jack leant back, took off his nightshirt and lifted her nightie.

When it was over, Elisha lay and allowed the feeling of the exquisite pleasure that had taken her into a world where nothing mattered but their love for one another to remain with her.

Jack snuggled his face in her neck, his breathing shallow and wheezing, his tears wetting her skin.

Her tears joined his, until they came to a calm place and held each other.

'We'll be all right, Jack. We'll take one day at a time, eh?'

'Aye.' His humour came back as he said, 'And I hope every one of them ends like today.'

Getting onto her elbow, Elisha looked down at him, her smile cheeky as she retorted, 'Yes, please.'

Jack pulled her down until her head rested on his chest. They fell silent. Gradually, the fast beating of Jack's heart slowed, and his breathing became normal.

Three days later, they were travelling along Mill Lane having left Crewe when they passed by a small group of roadworkers.

Two young men stood watching them. One doffed his cap and called out, 'Top o' the morning to you. Where are you headed?'

Jack answered. 'Charlwood, in the county of Surrey.'

'It's a long journey you have.'

Jack waved and they trotted on, seemingly unconcerned, but Elisha had a feeling of fear in the pit of her stomach. There was something about the way the men had looked at her. A shiver trembled through her.

'Are you cold, love?'

Not wanting to worry Jack, Elisha pulled the rug that lay across her lap a little higher. 'Just a bit. I'll be all right now, though you'll have to stop so I can have a pee soon, you knaw what I'm like.'

'Aye, a leaking water bottle when you're carrying our babby. You were the same with little Ted.'

Their giggle died in the air at the mention of Ted, and Elisha thought, *Oh, how I long to hold you, my darling son*.

They hadn't gone far when Grundy began to show signs of weariness. His head drooped and his pace slowed to almost walking, no matter how much Jack urged him on.

'We need to rest him for a day, Elisha, we're wearing him out.'

'Aye, but I'd like to get further away from them workmen back there.'

'They'll do us no harm, lass. I joined a couple of groups and did casual labour as I travelled to Blackpool. At night after a hard day's graft, we camped in a nearby field and had the best time, singing and listening to tales of their life, and they cooked a good hearty meal. They're just hardworking men. You've nowt to be afraid of.'

'I knaw there's good and bad in all people, Jack, but them two as spoke to us ... well, they gave me the willies.'

'Ha! Don't be daft. You don't want to end up killing poor old Grundy off, do you? Let's find a sheltered spot and set up camp for the night. It's the sensible thing to do given the signs he's showing.'

Elisha had no more arguments to put forward, but she wished it was that they were miles away from the two lads. Their look had given her the creeps.

'Ahh, here's a gate, and the field it leads to isn't planted. Look, we could settle in that corner.'

Jack pointed towards an oasis of beauty – a fast-running stream glittered in the sun, flanked by a weeping willow dabbling some of its branches in the water.

Releasing a sigh, Elisha agreed, but had to quieten the unease she felt to truly appreciate such a lovely spot for them to spend the rest of the day and night.

Grundy was soon unharnessed. He looked from one to the other of them, almost questioning his freedom. Jack slapped him playfully on his rear. 'Go and enjoy some of that lush grass, and get a rest, lad. You deserve it. You've done well thus far.'

It didn't take them long to spread out a blanket and set up the cast-iron bowl they'd brought with them. This served as a cooker when filled with logs and lit.

Elisha balanced their kettle, filled with water from the stream – actions she did mechanically as her mind was disturbed by them stopping so close to the gypsy camp.

But with the peace of the early evening, a calm feeling came to her when they sat on the blanket sipping their hot tea, with nothing but the sounds of the ripples of the water and the singing of the birds.

'You knaw, for all the bad things that have happened to us, we're blessed in many ways.'

'Aye, Jack, it does feel like that at the moment. I'm glad we stopped now.'

'Good. We'll get there, I promise. It's just that like you said, we have to take it day by day, and today Grundy had had enough. Look at him, he's happy now.'

Grundy was lying close by, his eyes fixed on the water, his body slumped in the lush grass.

'Mmm, I think he'll be asleep at any moment and so will I, so stop talking now, Jack, I'm tired.'

The blissful slumber Elisha drifted into left her when a hand touched her breast. Thinking it was Jack, she rolled towards him, ready to accept his love, but when she opened her eyes, shock zinged through her. Jack wasn't beside her but sitting under the willow tree, bound hand and foot.

'Sure, there's no point in you objecting, young miss, for aren't I going to have me way with you, no matter what. But if it is you don't want to be hurt, then you'll do as we say!'

Realisation came to Elisha – the roadworkers!

Fear clutched her. 'Naw, naw, leave me alone!'

Struggling to get away from him, Elisha called over to Jack. 'Jack, what's happening?' Jack could only make a noise in his throat, but his tears spoke volumes.

A hand gripped Elisha's arm.

'Naw, please. Please don't.' Kicking out, she caught the man on his leg and he let go, yelping in pain, but then filled with anger and lashed out, knocking her back to the ground.

'Give it to her, Rory, lad. Isn't it that she was made for it. Look at those breasts, they're crying out to be released.'

This unleashed all hell for Elisha as her frock was torn open and her bodice ripped apart. Her world seemed to end with this exposure but then plummeted even further as the man attacking her grabbed at her.

For Elisha, she died at that moment. Tears tumbled down her face, caught in her throat and choked her as he violated her body.

At last her ordeal ended, marked by his guttural cries of agonising pleasure. His weight on her increased as he slumped down on her harder than before and then rolled off.

'Sure, it's my turn. Hasn't watching you given me the strongest urge.'

Elisha's 'Naw' came out as a whimper, she tried to roll away, but the second man held her in a grip that prevented her. Kicking out didn't help. His slap stung her face and rendered her unable to fight.

During his taking of her, she cried and begged him to stop.

'Aye, beg me, yes, beg me.' With this gasp, he stiffened and cried out in a holler that told her it was over.

Ashamed beyond anything she'd ever felt, Elisha glanced over at Jack. Sobs racked his body.

Anger seared through Elisha. She rolled over, saw one of the branches Jack had gathered and stripped of its twigs to light their fire, grabbed it and stood.

Wielding the branch, she lashed out. 'You pigs! You dirty, filthy scum.' A blow landed on the back of the man who'd just taken her. Still weakened by his rape of her, he couldn't get out of the way. His yell made the other one laugh. Turning on him, Elisha screamed, 'You animal! You filthy beast!'

A swing of the branch caught him on his shoulder. His face changed from amusement to pain and then to thunder as he lunged towards her. The blow he dealt her sent her reeling to the ground.

Pain stung every part of her, as he mercilessly beat her with the branch she'd dropped until the blessed relief of unconsciousness took her and she knew no more.

Darkness had fallen when Elisha roused. The agony of movement had her crying out.

'Elisha, oh me love, me little lass.'

Through swollen eyes, Elisha looked towards where the sound had come from. Saw a figure tied to the tree, but didn't know who it was, only that she needed to help him, that a part of her was him.

An agonising, inch-by-inch crawl took her to his side.

'Elisha, lass, untie me, help me to get free.'

Thinking that Elisha must be her name, she tried to do as he bid, but the pain in one arm made it impossible to move it.

'Can you get a knife, me darling?'

This man seemed to love her. He spoke in a gentle tone. But why did she hurt so much? Her back, her side and her arm?

Looking around her, she saw a donkey standing staring back at her. Then, to her left, a cart. Maybe there was a knife in there?

Her crawl was slow as she could only use one arm, but she reached the cart.

Standing seemed an impossible task, but the plight of the man spurred her on. Somehow, she turned and hitched herself up onto the cart. From there she had to roll, screaming out in pain when her bad arm was underneath her, but undeterred, as her need to free the nice man was greater than the hell of the pain.

There was nothing for her to find – no bags, no sacks, nothing that could contain a knife! The cart was empty.

'Have they taken it all?' the man tied to the tree asked.

Elisha didn't know who the man was referring to, or what it was they'd taken. She managed to call, 'There's nowt here, I'm sorry, sir.'

'Sir? I'm Jack ... Elisha, me little lass, it's Jack, your husband!'

Jack? Me husband! Confused, Elisha searched her fuzzy mind, trying to recall someone called Jack. But she couldn't take in that she was married to the nice man.

'Elisha ... Eeh, Elisha, me love, what have they done to you?'

Elisha didn't know what he meant. Had someone done something to her? But yes, they must have done. She hurt all over, didn't she?

'Aw, naw, naw.' The agonising cry coming from the man confused Elisha all the more. Why was he tied to a tree? Why was she hurt so badly? These questions she knew had visited her before, but her mind wouldn't give her any information.

'Elisha, try to get to the fire. See if there's a burning piece of wood that you can get hold of and bring it here. You can burn through the rope that's holding me ... Please, Elisha, but be careful ... don't hurt yourself any more than you are already.'

Somehow, Elisha managed to do this, though driven by orders not sense, she did try not to burn the man.

When his wrists were free he tried to hold her, but she shrank from him. There was something terrifying about a man holding you.

'Elisha ... Eeh, me Elisha, it's me, Jack, your Jack ... your husband ... !'

'Naw, don't touch me!'

A sob shook the man's body once more. But then he became in control of himself and rose. Taking off his shirt, he ripped it in two and went towards the water.

When he came back, his soothing ministrations calmed her. Though sore, the wiping with the cold, wet cloth, helped. It was when he tried to raise her left arm that she screamed out.

'I think they've broken your arm, lass. I'll bind it up, then we have to get you to a hospital.'

Elisha didn't understand, only that she had knowledge that hospitals cost money.

'I – I can't pay.'

'I knaw.'

Going back to the water, he wrung his piece of shirt out once more. When he was back by her side, he placed it on her head. 'I think you're concussed, me little lass, but don't worry, I'll bind your arm and then I'll get some of that devil's beard and boil it, there's plenty growing on the banks of the stream. That'll ease your pain and help you to sleep.'

The hot drink hurt her sore and cut lips, the bitter taste made her shudder, but she did as the man urged and sipped it until it was finished.

'There, that will help you, lass. Its real name is valerian. Me da used to take me to collect it so that he could help me Ma to sleep through her pain. He boiled it as I have done, and Ma slept for hours. It ...'

Whatever he was about to say went into a haze that gave Elisha relief from some of the pain her body was racked with. She didn't fight it, but let go of her confusion and rested in his gentle hold.

When she woke, she seemed to be in a cloud of white. Through the mist of her vision, she saw a nurse. Something in her mind made her feel safe. A nurse meant care, and love ... Why she knew that was a mystery to her, but she took the comfort and tried to speak. 'Whe ... where ... am I?'

'To be sure, you're in the Crewe Memorial Hospital, me darling.'

Terror shivered Elisha's body. Something about the voice frightened her. As the nurse approached, she shrank back. 'Naw, naw, don't hurt me.'

'Now why would I be doing that, eh? Unless it was pain that led to your healing. Don't you be afraid, no one is about to hurt you in here.'

The man who had helped her came to Elisha's mind. She wanted to ask where he was. Somehow, she knew he was important to her, but she didn't know his name.

The nurse said something strange then, 'Well, I think it is that we can let your husband in now, me wee darlin'. He's waiting anxiously to see how you're progressing, so he is. Maybe it is that you can manage a wee smile for him?'

Husband ... I – I have a husband! 'Naw ... who? I – I don't knaw ...'

'That'll be the concussion, don't you be worrying your head over that, all will come back to you, and that's a promise I'm making to you.'

The nurse went to the door and called, 'It is that you can come in now, Mr Randal.' Her voice lowered, 'You will find she is still for being confused, but it is how we would expect things to be.'

The man who had helped her came through the door. The nurse had said this was her husband! Why didn't she know him? All she knew was that he was nice – kindly – and she didn't feel afraid of him.

His face showed a split lip and black eye. 'Are you hurt?'

'Naw, me little lass ... well, a little. But don't worry about me, we need you to get better. The nurse told me that a doctor is expected to come and see you any minute now, so hopefully he'll tell us what's wrong ... Aw, Elisha, me Elisha ...'

The man broke down in tears.

He called me Elisha. Is that me name?

'Don't cry ... I – I'm ...' Elisha closed her eyes. She felt so sleepy. The man took her hand, but she didn't mind. It felt nice, and comforted her. All she wanted to do was to go to sleep.

CHAPTER FIFTEEN

Elisha woke to someone calling, 'Elisha, Elisha', over and over.

A man in a white coat stood at the end of the bed. The nice man who was still with her had tears running down his face. She wanted to tell him to not keep crying. That she liked him very much and didn't want him to leave her. She felt safe with him there ... safe from something, but she didn't know what.

The man in the white coat cleared his throat.

'I'm sorry, Mrs Randal, but you have lost the baby you were carrying.'

This hurt Elisha's heart. But still she felt confused. Had she been carrying a babby? Did she drop it somewhere? Then it dawned on her, he meant she'd been expecting a babby, but now she wasn't ... 'Naw ... Naw, I – I want me babby ... I want me Ted!'

'Ted?'

The doctor looked quizzically at the man holding her hand.

'He were our son ... he died of measles.'

'Oh dear, I am sorry ... They tell me you were travelling when you were attacked and the rape took place? Are you going to anywhere in particular or do you live on the road?'

'Aye, we're on our way to stay with our friends ... we – we lost everything we had ... We knew our friends would help us.'

'Can I contact them for you?'

'I – I don't knaw their telephone number or address – Elisha had it written down in her bag, but them men who did this took that, and Elisha maybe won't remember now.'

'So, you have nothing? Look, Elisha's memory will come back, and you can still get to your friends' house, as they tell me you have a donkey and cart tethered at the hospital gates. Elisha won't be fit to travel yet, but ... well, have you any money?'

'Naw. As I said, they took everything. I've nowt left but me donkey and cart.'

'There are charitable organisations that would help you. The Salvation Army do excellent work for the poor. Go along and see them and tell them your plight. The reception in the hallway will know the address and direct you.'

'Aye, I will, ta.' Elisha heard a sob in the nice man's throat. 'So, there's naw babby? Our babby has gone?'

'Yes. I'm so sorry, but your wife suffered a miscarriage just after you brought her in.'

The nice man lowered his head onto her hand. Elisha wanted to comfort him. She stroked his hair. He looked up in surprise. 'Do you knaw me, lass?'

'Naw, but I like you and I want you to stay with me.'

The doctor – a tall man, with a thin black moustache – coughed. His voice sounded a little hoarse as he said, 'Your husband can stay a little while longer, but visiting is over for today, he'll have to leave soon. We'll go now and let you have some time alone.'

When the door closed, Elisha tried to think of this nice man being her husband, but she had no recall of him. That didn't matter though, all she knew was she wanted him with her.

'Aw, Elisha, our babby . . . our babby!'

'Don't cry. Ted's safe, and at peace. He lives in me heart, you knaw.'

'Aye, in mine an' all. But our new babby . . . the one you were expecting . . . I – I, aw, Elisha, all I can see is the horror of what them men did to you, I'll never get it out of me mind, never.'

Not knowing what he was talking about, Elisha felt the urge to comfort him. 'Don't worry, I'm all right. I don't knaw what happened to me. Or who I am or where I come from, but I knaw you care about me, and I like that.'

'I love you with all me heart, me darling. You're me lass, me wife. We had a cottage that belonged to your grandma . . .'

His voice went on and on, telling her tales – some funny, some sad, about their little Ted and how they set off on the road to see some people called Jan and Mick.

Elisha cried when he talked of Ted. She knew there was a pain in her heart and that he had awakened it, but she laughed when he told of their donkey, and some of the tales of her grandma. But then cried when he told her of her da. She couldn't bring him to mind, but thought it sad that she'd made a promise as a daughter, to carry on his work and to achieve his dreams for him. What those dreams were, she didn't know, but still felt very sad when she asked, 'Did I do that? Did I make me da's dreams come true?'

'Almost, lass, almost, but then ... well, I did sommat silly ... I took a loan out to speed the process ... I caused our ruin.'

Seeing his distress, Elisha told him. 'None of it matters ... I want you to be me husband ... What's your name?'

Smiling through his tears, he told her, 'Jack. I'm your Jack, and I want allus to be your husband.'

This felt nice. Elisha felt a happiness deep inside her, but also sleep dragging her into its blessed release. 'I'm tired, Jack ... stay ...'

She knew no more then, until two men came into her dream.

Screaming out, 'Naw, naw, leave me alone', Elisha woke to the horror of what had happened.

The room was dark save for a light coming through a square window cut into the door of the room she was in.

Concentrating on this light as if it would be her salvation, she relived the moment her world crumbled into a hell of Jack being beaten, of herself being hurt and taken down to the ground ... 'Naw, naw, don't ... don't ...'

The door opened.

'What's going on? Ahh, bless you. You're having a nightmare. Well, you have been through a lot, but it's all right now, love, you're in hospital.'

Elisha gasped in a breath that hurt her chest. 'He ... He raped me ... he hurt ...'

'I know ... Oh, love, I'm so sorry.'

'Me babby, it's gone!'

The nurse, a different one to the first nurse she'd seen before, put her arm around her. 'Try to calm down, Mrs Randal. You'll only do yourself more harm.'

'I'm not having me Jack's babby now, am I?'

'No, love, you miscarried ... I don't know what to say. But you can get better and have other babies.'

'But I want me Ted, and I want me babby to be inside me ...'

The nurse just held her and rocked her to and fro.

'Where's me Jack? He was here, I knaw he were here!'

'He had to leave at the end of visiting, but he'll be back tomorrow. Lie back and I'll see if you can have something to help you to sleep.'

'I don't want to sleep ... I want ...' But the nurse had left, and everything Elisha wanted seemed to go into a haze once more ... 'Me ma and me da and me grandma ... and me Jack and me babbies ... I want ME BABBIES!'

The nurse came running back in. Elisha felt a cold, wet flannel slapped on her face ... With the sensation, she knew a calmer place.

'Sorry, love, you were going hysterical and that can lead to madness – God knows you've enough on your plate to drive you mad, but we don't want that for you. We want to help you, and we will. Now, take a drink and get this pill down you. It'll help you to sleep.'

'Stay with me ... please stay with me ... the room has pictures ... horror ... raping me ... hitting me and me Jack ...'

'Oh, Elisha, I'm so sorry. Yes, I'm your special nurse assigned to look after you, so I will sit in here and be with you. Now close your eyes.'

The haze gave the nurse Jan's face. 'I will, Jan, I knew you would help us.'

'Well, I don't know who Jan is, but if it helps you to call me that, that's fine, though me name's Dora.'

'Ta ... Dor ...'

Not able to complete the sentence, she felt herself drifting. Everything around her seemed to be floating – scenes, some nice, some frightening.

Elisha didn't know how long it was before the day came when Jack collected her from the hospital. She only knew that a part of her was sad to leave, as she'd been shown such love and kindness, and could somehow cope with all her returned memory gave her while she had such support.

But the happiness she felt at being with Jack once more and not confined to hours that he could visit, helped her to accept parting from them and to face the wide world once more.

That world that brought so much back to her – the past, the fear of being homeless, the loss of their children and the horror of what had happened to them.

And although Jack was Jack, there was a change in him. She knew there was one in her too – something had taken a part of them, violated it, and left them bereft and unable to reach out to each other in the same way they always had.

★ ★ ★

Jack was silent as he urged Grundy along by whipping the reins.

This wasn't her Jack, and she didn't like Grundy being treated like it.

'Jack, naw! Grundy will go along at his own pace, you knaw he allus does.'

Jack's face had the look of thunder as he turned to her. His shocking words left her stunned.

'Did you enjoy what them blokes did to you?'

'What! God, Jack, how can you even ask that?'

'I – I keep having an image of it, and I've heard tell that women like it rough.'

'That's an awful thing to say, and aye, most likely said by men like them two who hurt me so badly. Men who think of women as animals. I'm not an animal, Jack. And if you think I am, you can drop me off now, as I don't want to be with you!'

Elisha's heart hurt. Was this really her Jack asking such a thing? Was their happiness gone – their trust in each other? Could she trust Jack to love her as he always had – with kindness and respect?

'Eeh, lass, I'm sorry . . .'

'Sorry doesn't cut it, Jack. That was a despicable question, and naw doubt prompted by despicable thoughts that have gone around your head. With those words you hurt me more than anything them men did to me. You're not me Jack any more. Me Jack would never ask that of me . . . Never!'

'Woah, Grundy, woah, old boy.'

This command was said in the voice her Jack would use

– gentle and persuasive, as he always was with Grundy. But what about her ... didn't he still love her?

When Grundy came to a halt, Jack turned to her. He went to speak, but his sob stopped him. He leant forward with his elbows on his knees and put his head into his hands.

Elisha knew nothing but a coldness towards him. She looked around her at the fields, and remembered their garden and their plans to buy the field behind them. But most of all she thought of her da's dream to do just that. She would never achieve that now and it was Jack's fault! There! She'd admitted it to herself.

'Forgive me, Elisha, forgive me ... I don't knaw what I were thinking ... I keep having nightmares ... I see it all, over and over ... I'm sorry ... I'm so sorry ... I knaw that's not enough. I should never have voiced me thoughts ... I don't even knaw why I've been having them ... Please, Elisha, I'll never say owt like that again.'

'Naw, but you'll think it! The worst moment in me life and you ask me if I enjoyed it! Don't you knaw how it haunts me? Don't you knaw how filthy it was, how it hurt me, how I will never forget it? But I were willing to try. Willing to put it behind us so that our love could have a chance, but then you asked me such a question and me life left me – the life that I'd knawn with you, Jack. The life I thought we could get back! Now, I knaw we never can.'

Jack jumped from the cart and walked towards the gate that led to a field. His fist smashed into the gatepost. In obvious agony, he rubbed his knuckles and shook his hand.

'I have visions, lass. I can't get them out of me head. Them pounding you like naw one but me should, them hollering with the pleasure of it, and you lying there, taking it.'

'I was hurt, Jack . . . I couldn't do owt . . . I never thought after all I've been through – we've been through – that it would change you . . . I – I, hate you for what you're doing to us!'

'I ain't doing it – they did. They took everything from us.'

'Aye, they did, but it needn't have been like this. You've made it so. We could have supported each other through the nightmares. You supported me while I was in hospital . . . or was this festering inside you all the time and you never said owt?'

Jack kicked the gate, then came back to climb onto the cart. 'I've got some money that the Salvation Army gave me. I'm going to find the nearest pub and get drunk!'

Elisha looked at her Jack – he looked the same, but he wasn't. The pain in her heart deepened as realisation came to her that nothing would ever be the same again.

True to his word, Jack got back onto the cart and trotted Grundy along, pulling him to a halt outside the next inn they came across. Giving her a look that withered her, he jumped down from the cart and stormed inside.

Elisha gave way to her tears. After all the tears she'd cried since her memory had come back, she never thought to cry again when she left the hospital with her Jack. She'd thought it was behind them, but then, how could it be? For Jack to witness that happening to her must have been hell.

Part of her softened towards him. She should have understood his question, she should have helped him through his doubts. But instead, she'd added to his agony.

A feeling of guilt prompted her to climb down from the cart and go towards the pub door. Knowing women weren't allowed in the bar, she put her face against the window and peered through hoping to see Jack and to beckon him to come out. She'd say she was sorry. She'd tell him how she would help him as he had helped her. She'd reassure him that she did love him with all her heart and that together they could put the past behind them.

Not able to see him at first, she shielded her eyes and looked around the room – saw Jack with his back to her, standing at the bar. One of the dozen or so men sitting around supping ale spotted her. His grin made her feel that he was kindly. She waved to him, trying to indicate to him to tell Jack she wanted him to come out.

The man's grin widened. He turned and said something to the room of men. Elisha heard them all laugh and saw them look towards her. Jack turned and caught sight of her. His face took on an ugly mask, his movement swift as he grabbed the man. His fist came back. Elisha gasped, 'Naw!', but Jack's fist landed smack into the man's face.

'Jack, don't! Jack!' But then she witnessed what looked like a madman, thumping and kicking the man and anyone who tried to intervene.

Not able to stand watching any longer, Elisha ran into the porch and opened the door of the bar. Still Jack kicked the man now lying prostrate on the floor, and punched and hit out at anyone who tried to intervene.

'Jack, Jack, naw, naw ... I love you, Jack. We can start again, please, please stop!'

Standing still for a moment, his breath coming in deep gasps, his eyes red-rimmed and raw, Jack stared at her and then looked down at the man he'd assaulted. 'He was making fun of you saying there was a whore at the window who wanted him. Is that what you've become, Elisha – were you beckoning him to come out? Did you fancy him?'

'Naw ... What are you saying, Jack? Jack! It's me, your Elisha, I love you. I was trying to get your attention to tell you so. I want us to start again ...'

Elisha hadn't noticed that a couple of the men were attending to the man Jack had beaten. From encouraging him to get up and someone saying they should call for an ambulance, a silence fell.

Then a shocked voice made the blood in Elisha's veins run cold as she heard the words, 'He's a goner! He's dead!'

Jack's head swivelled on his neck from her to the staring faces around him and then back to her. His body slumped. 'What have I done ... God, what have I done?'

'You've killed a decent bloke that's what, you bastard!'

Another man spoke up then. 'Aye, and a father to five kids and a good husband, hard-working and good fun, and you've beaten him to death and for what, eh?'

Elisha's shock at these words held her still and staring as the mood turned ugly and the men in the room went towards Jack.

But then a commanding voice stilled the progress of the angry mob. 'Leave it! ... I said, leave it! I've called the police and they're on their way. They'll deal with this scum!'

Elisha's head went from side to side, her 'Naw!' coming out in a gasp as the full horror hit her – her Jack had murdered a man! How ... How did they get to such a place? Not her Jack ... How?

Her limbs began to shake, her stomach clenched with fear, as she saw Jack move towards her but then restrained from doing so by the hands of many men grabbing him.

Jack didn't resist. His face fell into an expression of fear, his eyes widening as she saw the realization of what he'd done dawn on him.

His breath laboured, he said, 'Elisha ... I ...'

As if someone had turned the light back on inside him, he became her Jack once more. 'I'm sorry. Eeh, me little lass, what happened to us? I love you, Elisha, never forget that ... I love you.'

Finding her voice, all Elisha could say was, 'Jack ... Aw, me Jack.'

The sound of bells clanging filled the space around her. The door behind her flung open. Four policemen barged in. One asked, 'Where is he?'

'We've got him, Cyril, he ain't going nowhere.'

'Well, he is now. Straight behind bars! What the hell has gone on here, eh?'

A dozen voices spoke at once, all condemning her Jack. Elisha wanted to shout that Jack wasn't the bad man they thought him to be, that the real bad men were further down the road – the men who had raped her and turned her Jack's mind, made him into a madman – but that now he was all right, he was her Jack again... Only, she couldn't as she caught sight of a stream of blood on the floor and the realisation came to her that she had witnessed her Jack taking another man's life in a brutal act of violence.

They were lost – she and her lovely Jack could be no more.

CHAPTER SIXTEEN

Jack didn't struggle as one of the policemen led him to his van. But as they got there, he turned his head towards her. 'I'm sorry, me little lass.' Turning his head back to the policeman, he said, 'What will happen to me wife? Who'll take care of her?'

'Have you no home she can go to? Family?'

'Naw, we've got nowt, only a donkey and cart. We lost our home. We were travelling to friends ... me wife were raped ... Oh, God ... I had to watch ... I ...'

'Save it all for the judge, mate. I can't do anything about anything, only take you to the cell in the station and file a report for the magistrate. You'll be up in front of our local one tomorrow, but then more than likely committed to Crown Court for their judgement ... But even with mitigating circumstances, what you've done ain't going to turn out well for you.'

'But me wife ain't done owt, she can't be just left!'

'Let's get you safely in me van and then I'll need to go back in and take details. I'll deal with everything, including what happens to your wife and whether she had any part in it all.'

'Naw, naw, she didn't, it was me ... I've been driven insane ... I ...'

'Just get in there and shut up. I ain't had time to caution you yet, and you need to know that everything you say will be taken down and used in evidence against you, so, keep quiet and let me do me job.'

As the doors of the Black Maria closed on Jack, they seemed to Elisha to close on their life together. She couldn't react, only stare at the van that held her beloved. Would she ever see him again?

'Now then, missus, is this your donkey tethered up here?'

Elisha nodded.

'Have you anywhere you can go?'

Elisha couldn't answer him. Her thoughts wouldn't give her a reason for being where she was.

'Right, you're in shock, as we all are. The local doctor is on his way. He's an old man and it takes him a while to react, but he should be here soon. Once he's seen to what's gone on inside, I'll get him to look at you. Go and sit on your cart while I get me statements.'

Elisha didn't move. She couldn't. The policeman shrugged his shoulders and went inside.

After a moment, the enormity of what was happening hit Elisha. She ran towards the Black Maria. Pounding with the palms of her hands, she called out, 'Jack, Jack, me darling, I love you, I forgive you, I – I, oh, Jack, Jack.'

'Elisha, go to the Salvation Army ... please, do sommat, me little lass. Don't let them decide what happens to you, you're still not well. I'm sorry ... I don't knaw what came over me ... That thing that those men did to you, it turned me head.'

'I knaw, Jack, I ain't blaming you, love. It all went wrong, but ... Aw, me Jack, what will happen now?'

'Please, just go, me darling. Get to Grundy and go to get help. If they give you money, sell Grundy to one of the farmers and get a train to Jan.'

'I can't remember where she lives ... I – I, don't knaw where I am ... I can't bear it, Jack.'

The sound of a sob came from behind the van doors. 'It's in Surrey – Charlwood – try to remember the exact address. You've written it down a few times to post letters.'

'I knaw, but it's gone ... Eeh, Jack, me Jack!'

'I'm sorry, Elisha ... Aw, lass, I've ruined your life ... I don't deserve you.' The sound of him coughing racked through her, then him taking a breath that rattled loudly as he cried, 'Our babbies were taken because I couldn't protect them, and our cottage because I was stupid in getting that loan. I deserve to hang for what I've done to you as much as for what I've done to that poor man.'

'Naw, naw, Jack. The loan you thought would help us get on our feet, and our babbies' deaths weren't down to you. Them workmen are the ones that should be in this van. Eeh, Jack, me Jack, we'll have to convince everyone that this ain't your fault.'

There was no response, only the sound of rasping breaths and desolate sobbing.

Elisha leant against the van, trying to get close to her Jack, trying to give him comfort and to have all of this go away. Her own tears wet her face and tore at her heart as the hopelessness of it all crowded her.

Life as she knew it was over. It had ended in a pub that she didn't even know – miles away from her beloved home, the lovely Primula Cottage . . .

A hand came onto her shoulder. A kindly voice said, 'Come on, Mrs Randal, let me help you. I'm Doctor Salter.'

Elisha put her hand onto the glass of the blacked-out van window. Her voice shook with emotion as she said, 'Me Jack.'

'There's nothing you can do for him, my dear. Now we must take care of you.'

Elisha didn't resist as he gently turned her. She looked into his face. His jowls hung each side of his small mouth, his moustache following the line of them. His blue eyes were kindly, framed by grey, bushy eyebrows. His hand holding her arm was bony and spotted with brown age spots.

'Let me help you, my dear. Come, we'll go inside.'

Though she went with him, her eyes never left the van. As they entered the pub, a huge gasp of breath hurt her throat and lungs. 'Me Jack, me Jack.'

They didn't go into the bar but turned to the right and went through the door that had a plaque on it that read 'Snug'. This she knew was where women were allowed, that there would be no bar. The menfolk would bring a drink of ale for their wives and then go back to the bar. It wasn't a life she'd ever known, only heard of. But her mind gave her the snug of the Shovels Inn, where her wedding breakfast had taken place, and her heart seemed to tear even more than it was already torn.

When she was sat down, the doctor began to examine her and to ask her questions, 'How did you get these bruises? Is your husband violent?'

Elisha stared at him.

'Talk to me, my dear. I'm trying to help you. Has your husband beaten you?'

Elisha shook her head; it was all her body and mind would let her do.

'Then, how?'

'I want me Jack.'

'You're in shock. But you aren't showing any worrying signs of the shock affecting you physically. Mentally you just cannot get your thoughts sorted, and that's not surprising. I'll get the landlord to make you a hot, sweet drink.'

'But ... me Jack ...'

'Your husband has committed a very serious offence. He's taken the life of a local man we all knew and liked – a joker, I know, but one who never meant any harm.'

'But he called me a whore ... Jack's mind wasn't in a good place ... The ... the rape of me that he witnessed and couldn't help me ... our babby gone ... He couldn't cope ...'

'You're not making a lot of sense, my dear. I'll get that tea, then you can tell me from the beginning.'

When he left the room, Elisha had never felt so alone in her life. She looked around her at the yellowing walls, the wooden benches and red tiled floor, and the thought came to her, *Why would any woman want to spend time in here?* But then she shook herself, unsure why her mind was going down that road. Why it was that she was wondering about others' lives when her own was in tatters!

The sound of the policeman's voice brought her out of her thoughts. 'Right, you can all get yourselves home now. I've got all your versions of events. The ambulance has arrived, so pay some respect and let them do their job.'

When the doctor came back with a steaming mug of tea, Elisha said, 'But the policeman didn't ask me owt! I knaw why Jack did it and it weren't his fault!'

'You can tell me, my dear, and I will make sure they know. But first, drink this, it's very sweet and will help you.'

Sipping the hot liquid brought reality back to her. Another deep gasp of air shuddered her body and hurt her throat. Her story tumbled from her.

When it came to an end, the doctor was holding her hand. His head shook from side to side. 'My dear, that's enough to drive any man to murder, but . . .'

'Why did that man call me a whore?'

The doctor sighed. 'You really aren't aware of the ways of the world, are you? You must have lived a sheltered life . . . You see, my dear, women aren't allowed in pubs without their husband, and any that do hang around pubs are not usually up to any good – they are after giving their bodies to any of the men who will take them on, in exchange for a payment – it's not always their fault, they are usually destitute, but they are known as whores.'

Elisha drew in her breath. 'Naw! I didn't knaw that . . . Eeh, Doctor, this is all my fault!'

'No. It is an accumulation of many things that have happened to you both. I'm so very sorry . . . Maybe, if you tell the judge all you have told me, then he will be lenient with Jack . . . But be prepared, as even if that happened, Jack would still be in prison for a very long time.'

'I can't bear it. How can our lives have come to this?'

'My dear, from what you have told me, you have been dealt a massive blow, and a poor hand of the cards of life, but you must try to be more like your grandma than you have been and take hold of your own destiny. You're young. Life may seem over, but it isn't, it is still what you make of it that counts.'

The door to the snug opened and one of the policemen came in. His expression told Elisha that there was more for her to face. Her heart raced; her eyes locked on the policeman. His face showed no sign of compassion, only condemnation. When he spoke, her blood ran cold.

'Right, missus, you're to come with me to the station. It appears from what the men were saying that you were partly to blame for what happened here. You were seen trying to get the men to notice you – they said you were whoring and—'

'Naw! I only wanted Jack's attention . . . I wanted to tell him—'

'That's not how it appeared to the witnesses. They hadn't seen either of you at the pub before. There was a man from the Salvation Army in there; he was taking his tin around collecting whatever bit of change the men could spare. He was appalled to see the suspect in there drinking, as he'd not long given him money to help the pair of you to carry on your journey. He says you were destitute and was shocked that the money was being used to buy ale. And even more shocked to see a woman, who at the time he didn't know was the suspect's wife, seeming to procure business at the window.'

'Naw . . . I just wanted to get the attention of me Jack . . . I – I . . .'

'Save it for the interview. But, as that won't happen tonight, you'll be spending the night in a cell.'

'Officer, is that necessary?'

'It is, sir. We cannot let someone we believe might be an accomplice to a murder be free to disappear.'

Elisha couldn't take this in. Her mind gave her terrifying pictures of being put into a women's prison – incarcerated for years, when all she'd done was try to tell her Jack that she loved him.

None of this came out as a protest. Something inside her died at that moment – hope. Not a trace of hope helped her. She was doomed. Life as she'd known it had ended.

The doctor's words didn't have any impact on her: 'Tell them what you have told me, my dear, tell them everything, from the beginning, they will believe you. Then go to the Salvation Army and they will help you. Use what they give you to get to your friend.'

None of that mattered now to Elisha. For her, her life was over.

As they reached the door, she thought of Grundy. 'Me donkey!'

'He'll be looked after. Which is more than he appears to have been. Poor sod's skin and bone.'

Shame washed over Elisha; she knew the long journey had taken its toll on poor Grundy. But she hadn't seen him as skin and bone, they would never have allowed that to happen! The policeman saying this just seemed to her as if he was using the condition of Grundy as another stick to beat her and Jack with.

But that shame was compounded when the policeman asked her to put her hands behind her back and clamped her wrists in handcuffs.

'Surely, they aren't necessary, Officer!'

'Oh, they are, Doctor. Women like this one can turn into screaming banshees when the chips are down. I ain't having me face clawed by a whore!'

'This appals me! You are behaving like a judge and jury! How dare you call this young lady such a name! It's assumptions like that that led to this whole tragedy! I will be speaking to your sergeant about this!'

'I apologise, I shouldn't have used that term, but you must realise, sir, I've had a lot of dealings with criminals, and from my experience, handling them this way is the proper way.'

The doctor looked at Elisha. His expression told that he was beaten.

She tried to appeal to the nature she'd seen he had, 'Help me, please help me.'

But he shrugged his shoulders in a helpless gesture. 'I – I cannot go against the law ... I'm sorry. Just tell them all you have told me, my dear. You see, this is my last day as a practising doctor, my wife and I are moving to her native France in just over a week for our retirement ... there's nothing I can do.'

Elisha saw him blink, and his Adam's apple bouncing told of how his emotions were high as he swallowed hard.

She wanted to let him off the hook, he was such a kind man. 'It's all right. I knaw you would help me if you could – you have already ... ta, for that.'

With this, she walked with all the dignity she could muster towards the Black Maria, trying to ignore the hissing and catcalls of the crowd that had gathered.

With words she had never thought to hear associated with herself flung at her – 'Slut!', 'Murderer!', 'Whore!' – Elisha knew terror she'd never known. It clutched at her and made her unable to control her bladder. To her shame, pee trickled down her leg and formed a pool at her feet.

'Ha, the dirty whore has wet her knickers!'

The crowd's laughter brought Elisha to the lowest point she'd never thought to reach. Silent tears ran down her cheeks. Her da came to her mind – *Help me, Da. I'm sorry I never realised your dream, but help me now, please, help me and me lovely Jack.*

As if he'd answered her, another policeman stepped forward. 'Leave the girl alone, or I'll arrest the lot of you for affray! Go back to your homes and show respect for the dead man you call your friend. In my world, people are innocent until proven guilty!'

The crowd dispersed without protest.

He then turned to the one who'd clamped the handcuffs on her.

'Are those necessary? She's just a young woman caught up in a nightmare, as I see it. Yes, we have to take her in as a witness, but handcuffs!' He shook his head from side to side.

'I ain't taking any chances. I've had me face scratched before and had to deal with a female flailing their fists. It's just a precaution.'

'One that's made her look partly to blame in the crowd's eyes. And we don't know if any of them will be called upon to be part of the jury. In my eyes, you're making things worse!'

'No, it's you that's doing that, objecting to my judgement in front of a suspect and a crowd of locals. I shall report this to the sergeant when we get back to the station!'

The policeman who'd tried to defend her turned on his heels and walked away.

Elisha was left to face the temper of her captor as he wrenched her hands forward in an angry gesture that cut the handcuffs into her wrists. She cried out in pain that tore through her recently mended arm, but her cries didn't deter him. He brutally shoved her body forward then almost threw her into the back of the van.

She landed on her face. The hard, cold metal floor smacked her cheek, causing her to bite her tongue. But the pain only served as a salve to the pain in her heart. Her world had collapsed. She was nothing. She had nothing. She could be raped, beaten, paraded in front of a braying crowd, and no one cared.

Loneliness crowded her. Despair soaked every ounce of her body and drained her of courage. There was nothing left to fight for. She'd lost everything and now was losing herself.

CHAPTER SEVENTEEN

Shivering with cold and shock, Elisha sat on the hard bench and stared at the bars of the cell.

She couldn't believe that she'd been brought so low. What had happened to the young girl that she'd been – the girl full of hope and dreams and surrounded by love?

The day that lorry took away her family marked the day that her life changed. And yet, she had recaptured some of the happiness she'd known, only to have it snatched away from her . . . Why? What had she ever done to deserve it?

Shock held her rigid as she distinctly heard her grandmother's voice: 'Take hold of your own destiny, my darling Elisha. Others have wronged you, but they are gone and must face their own destiny – you must be in charge of yours.'

The voice was so real that she found herself answering it. 'What should I do, Grandma?'

'Tell the truth, but tell your story too. Let the judge see how you came to this point. You love Jack, but he has done wrong. He lost control and took the life of an innocent man. You cannot save him, but you can save yourself.'

'But Jack . . .'

'I knaw you love him, and would fight for him, but you can't win. The only thing you can do for him is to hold yourself together. Don't end up in the madhouse, I couldn't bear that.'

'Can you still feel things? Is dead not being dead? Are you still there?'

No answer came. Nothing remained, only the feeling that she'd somehow had a dream while being awake, and the knowledge that the dream was reality. She had nothing that would help her to help Jack.

Tears streamed down her face.

'They won't help yer, luv.'

The voice accompanied the clanging of the chain that locked the bars to her cell as a policewoman undid the heavy padlock.

'I'm taking you to the bathroom to wash your face. You're up in front of the magistrate in half an hour – if you hurry yourself, you might have time for a sup of tea.'

Mechanically, Elisha obeyed, her thoughts a confusion of how this could happen, as she hadn't been given a chance to tell her story.

Within an hour, she stood in the dock. Her beloved Jack, looking broken and full of despair, stood beside her. The few inches between them seemed like a gulf so wide she couldn't reach out to him. Her emotions were locked – frozen, and as if they would never let her feel anything ever again.

The magistrate's voice echoed around the high-ceilinged

room, which smelt of polish, as witnessed in the shine of the many benches, as the sun glinted on them through a skylight. A room peopled with folk in formal suits, and the magistrate and his clerk in gowns.

'Jack Edward Randal, you have been brought before me accused of the murder by beating of one Graham Finch. How do you plead?'

'Guilty, sir.'

Elisha froze. She wanted to shout out a protest, but nothing came from her.

'Very well, you will be committed to the Crown Court for sentencing, but will now be taken to prison to await that time as no bail will be granted to you. Please take him down, officer.'

As if life had shot back into her, Elisha's head swivelled as she stared at Jack. 'Naw!'

'Silence in court. The prisoner will not speak unless spoken to!'

Fear gripped Elisha. She hadn't thought of herself as a prisoner!

Jack glanced at her. His heart was in his glance. It told her he was sorry, it told her this was goodbye, but most of all it told her he loved her.

'Elisha Millicent Randal, you are accused of being an accomplice to that murder. What have you to say for yourself?'

The voice of her grandma came back. 'Keep calm and tell him the truth.'

'I didn't mean to cause any trouble, sir. Me and me Jack were going through a bad time. Something really bad happened to me – to us. I felt I was losing him. He was never one to go to the pub, but he'd been badly hurt, and had said things to me that had made me angry. I wanted to call him out of the pub and tell him that all would be all right now, that I forgave him, and we could carry on as always, being happily in love. I knew I couldn't go inside, but I thought to tap on the window to get his attention. But that caused a fight. I've since learnt from the doctor who treated me for shock that women who tap on pub windows are thought to be whores. I truly didn't knaw that, sir. I never would have put me Jack in the position where he had to defend me.'

'What is this really bad thing that happened to you?'

Nerves kicked in again, but Grandma came back to help her: 'Tell him! Tell him everything! Go on, Elisha, lass. Stand up for yourself!'

The truth of how she'd been raped and Jack tied up and made to watch, and what followed, came tumbling out.

'It turned me Jack's mind, sir. He said things . . .'

'What things?'

Taking a deep breath and feeling the embarrassment of her next words, Elisha shook as she said, 'He asked me if I had enjoyed what they did to me, as he said he had heard that women liked it rough . . . It hurt me and I got cross, but then I understood and forgave him . . . I only wanted to tell him so, but it seems that made me a whore in the eyes of the man who died, and after all Jack had been through, it made him snap.'

'We're not trying the case here and we do not ask you for judgement on why Jack Randal committed murder.

That last statement shall be struck from the record and, unless your husband changes his plea, will never be heard or recorded. Have you anything else to say?'

'Yes, I want to tell all, sir.'

'Very well.'

Elisha told how she'd lost everything, was abused, and how Jack was her saviour. Tears streamed down her face as the story unfolded. But no one stopped her. Many discreetly wiped a tear from their own eyes, as she told of her lost children and the storm that took their livelihood.

When she finished there was a silence. The magistrate had his head down. When he lifted it, Elisha could see compassion in his face.

'I want it noted that I find you are innocent of being an accomplice to murder. You are free to go. But you must leave an address where you can be contacted as a possible witness in the event that Jack Edward Randal changes his plea.'

'I have nawhere to go, sir!'

The magistrate conferred with his clerk. When he looked up, he said, 'I'm sorry, but as the first hearing of your husband's case will take place in just a few days, we can only consign you to the cells. Not as a prisoner, but as a pauper and a possible witness, whose whereabouts must be known to us.'

He turned and spoke to the attending police officer: 'Elisha Millicent Randal is to be held in your care for the next twenty-four hours. At such time as the Crown Court sits, you will deliver her there as a possible witness in the event the plea is changed to not guilty.'

He banged his gavel. 'Court dismissed.'

A hand took hold of her arm. Elisha turned to face the policewoman who'd attended court with her. 'Come on, love. Don't be afraid, we'll take care of you. It'll only be for a couple of days as first hearings are done very quickly.'

Elisha could see the emotion the woman had been through at hearing her tale, and feel the kindness she now offered. This almost undid her, but she didn't let it, she just said, 'Ta. I feel very tired.'

'I'm not surprised, love. We'll get you a hot drink and a decent lunch. There's a café over the road that makes lovely meals, I'll go over there and get you something nice to eat.'

'Ta. I'm not sure I can eat owt, but I'll try.'

'You must stay strong. Your husband may well change his plea after speaking to a solicitor.'

'He hasn't got a solicitor, nor money to pay for one.'

'He'll be assigned one. He has to be, by law. And if he changes his plea, then he'll be committed for trial, but that will take a few months to happen as a case is prepared.'

'And if he doesn't?'

'Then he will be sentenced . . . I'm sorry, but you know what that will mean, don't you?'

Elisha gasped in air. She couldn't bear the thought.

'Anyway, love, don't give up hope. From what you've said in court today, there are mitigating circumstances and if your husband tells them to a solicitor, he will do all he can to persuade him to plead not guilty to murder, but guilty of manslaughter while diminished of responsibility.'

Hope trickled into Elisha. 'And if that is found to be the case?'

'Then he will serve a prison term – a long one, but he won't hang.'

Although this dampened the hope in her, it didn't diminish it, as to Elisha, it wouldn't matter how long her Jack was confined, she'd find a way to visit him and would wait however many years it took for him to be free. And then they could begin their lives again.

The cell seemed like a solace to Elisha as she willingly went back into it. Whereas the night before it had been full of doom for her, now it gave comfort. A second thin mattress had been added to the one she'd had to lie on the night before, and an extra blanket was folded at the bottom of it. There was a bar of soap on the small sink in the corner and a clean bucket for her to use as a lavatory. Small touches, but ones that showed she was being treated as a guest, not a prisoner. She understood and welcomed this detention. She so wanted to speak for her Jack and would pray that, after he had seen a solicitor, he would change his plea. With this thought, hope rose in her once more.

That hope was dashed two days later.

The policewoman accompanied Elisha to the Crown Court in Chester. Elisha had found out that her name was Jane, and that her father was a police officer and she'd followed in his footsteps.

'Well, almost. I ain't allowed to do the work I want to do – on the streets, protecting the public and catching criminals – I'm confined to the office typing up the other officers' reports and being on hand for any women or kids that are brought in!' This had ended in a deep sigh from Jane. And brought home to Elisha how often women were treated as second-class citizens, confined to domestic or office work.

For the first time, she began to understand those women who she'd read about, who did things like disrupting Parliament and holding rallies, as they fought for a woman's right to vote and to have a say in all matters that affected women.

As Elisha prepared for the court hearing, she realised that Jane had helped her so much. She'd talked to her for hours after her duty finished, and had made it possible for her to feel a confident young woman once more as she donned the grey frock that Jane had given her. Its pleated panel down the front of the bodice somehow gave the frock dignity. Held by a belt at the waist, the skirt fell to her ankles and went well with the elegant boots Jane had found for her. Clothing she told her she'd been given by the Salvation Army.

The confidence came and was helped by Jane's positive attitude towards Jack's case. She was convinced he would plead as she suspected.

That wasn't the case.

It broke Elisha's heart to see her Jack looking gaunt, with bags under his eyes – eyes that shot around the court, found her and gave her shivers as she saw only a vacant stare.

Elisha tried to smile encouragingly. But it was as if her Jack hadn't seen her. He seemed to her to be like an empty shell. The fear she'd lived with, but that had been lessened by Jane, now clutched at her stomach muscles. She wanted to cry out. To beg Jack not to plead guilty. But Jane had warned her that if she did, she would be removed from court.

The moment was on them.

'Jack Edward Randal, you have been brought to this court charged with murder. That on the third of April 1907 you did unlawfully beat one Graham Flinch to death. How do you plead: guilty, or not guilty?'

A sob could be heard; Elisha looked towards the front of the gallery. A woman had bent forward. She held her face in her hands. Elisha's heart went out to her, realising that she was the widow of Graham Flinch. A widow made so by her Jack.

The court hushed. Elisha held her breath. But then the words she'd prayed not to hear resounded around the court: 'Guilty, Your Honour.'

'Naw ... Naw!'

The banging of the gavel made Elisha jump.

'Silence in court! I will not have these proceedings disrupted!'

Jane's hand found hers and squeezed it.

Elisha stared at Jack, but he didn't glance in her direction again, as a fit of coughing took him.

'Take the prisoner down. Court will adjourn whilst I deliberate.'

None of the guards flanking Jack helped him. Elisha heard his hacking cough and his gasps for breath and so wanted to go to him, but had to watch as his head disappeared down the stairs.

'Is he ill, Elisha?'

Elisha swallowed hard. 'Aye, he's been so for a long time. He's ... he's been near to death a few times.'

Why am I talking like this of me Jack? I want to scream, but I can't ... Oh, God, help me ... help us!

'He sounds and looks terrible, love ... I'm so sorry, but listen to me. You have to prepare yourself for what will happen next ... It will be a terrible ordeal for you.'

'What? What's going to happen?'

'We talked about it, remember? Jack will be sentenced, and he has left the judge no alternative.'

'Naw, not that ... naw!'

'We'll have to go out if you're unable to control yourself, Elisha.'

Elisha swallowed hard. She glanced down at the weeping woman again, sure now that she was the widow of the murdered man, left with five children to care for.

Her arms ached to reach out to the woman to say she was sorry. With this thought, the enormity of what Jack had done hit Elisha hard. As did the horror that she was to face very soon. Jack would die for this crime. Her Jack would be no more.

Suddenly there was a sound coming from the steps Jack had been taken down.

And then he appeared. His haggard expression told of the coughing bout he must have had. He didn't look in Elisha's direction, though she willed him to.

The clerk of the court was the first of the officials to

return. He placed a black hat on the judge's desk. A murmur fluttered around Elisha.

'Pray silence in the court and all stand for His Honour, Judge Wilson.'

The shuffle that followed grated on her nerves. She stared at Jack – willed him to glance at her. But still he stared ahead.

When the judge sat, the clerk said. 'You may all be seated.'

Once more that shuffling sound, then once more silence – a silence that held Jack's doom, as the judge reached for the black hat and placed it on his head. Elisha hadn't heard of the significance of this, but the sight ran her blood cold in her veins.

Then the words resounded around the hushed court: 'Jack Edward Randal. By your own admission you are guilty of the murder of one Graham Finch. As a consequence of this crime, the sentence of this court is that you be taken hence to a lawful prison, and that you be there, one week from today, hanged by the neck until you are dead; and that your body be buried within the precincts of the prison in which you shall have been confined. May the Lord have mercy on your soul!'

A cheer broke the deathly silence.

Shocked, Elisha looked from Jack to the crowd now standing on their feet – men she recognised from the pub that night. Bringing her attention back to Jack, she saw he was looking at her – no, not just looking, but staring deep into her soul. Her head bobbed from side to side. Jack's mouth formed the words, 'I love you.'

Unable to contain herself, Elisha shouted, 'I love you, Jack, and will for ever ... Oh, God! Jack ... Jack!'

'Naw, Elisha. Live your life, me little lass. Be free. I'll allus look out for you, but I set you free, to live.'

Elisha's gasp hurt her throat. Her eyes, full of agony, fixed on Jack's back as they led him down. Just as he was about to disappear, he turned. His look told her of his love and of his resignation. His life was already leaving him. His body couldn't take much more than it had already from the sickness that rendered him weak.

Raising her hand, she shouted, 'I love you, my Jack.'

CHAPTER EIGHTEEN

The words 'hanged by the neck until you are dead' stuck in Elisha's mind, clouding her life and sending her to a dark place where she wanted nothing – not people, not friends, not life itself.

Squatting in a corner of the yard of the workhouse in Manchester, where she'd been confined by the same judge as a pauper of no means, Elisha closed her eyes but couldn't close her mind to the clang of doom sounded by the church clock as it boomed out its first dong to announce the hour of midday – on its twelfth stroke her Jack would die!

Gasping in a deep breath that hurt her chest and zinged a pain through her heart, Elisha saw her Jack in her mind's eye, walking towards the scaffold.

Her soul cracked with agony as she counted the strikes of the bell – *One, two* . . .

Her hands went to her neck, she pulled at the collar of her regulation grey frock.

. . . six . . . seven . . . eight . . .

'Naw, naw, please God, naw!'

An arm came around her. Elisha shook it off.

... eleven ... twelve ...

'Naw ... NAW ... NAW!'

The arm grabbed her and held her close. 'Hush, don't take on so, they'll mark you as a madwoman and put you in an asylum, lass.'

'I can't bear it, Harriet ... I can't!' The gasp Elisha took in hurt her throat. Tears stung her already sore eyes.

Harriet – the only person in this awful place who hadn't given up on her – snuggled her into her body. 'Eeh, let me help you, lass. You've not let anyone get near to you since you arrived. Most of us knaw what you're going through – we knaw what's happening – happened ... Tell me, what were your Jack like, eh? I mean, the rumours have him down as a thug, but the way you mourn him, he couldn't have been.'

Already me lovely Jack is spoken of as being in the past ... Naw, I don't want him to be!

'He's the loveliest man to walk this earth. Kind, gentle, loving, but things never went right for us, and we got into debt ...'

Elisha didn't know why, but the love story of her and Jack tumbled from her as she told Harriet, an almost stranger, everything she could about their life together at Primula Cottage. When she'd finished, she felt drained.

'It sounds like you had some bad luck. And circumstances brought you to this day ... but how? I mean, how did it get to who you say was such a lovely man committing murder?'

'I – I can't speak of it, but sommat turned Jack's mind.'

'Was it losing your babby?'

'You knaw about me babby?'

'We all do, love. You talk in your sleep – and weep. Some are fed up with you doing so as it disturbs their rest, but I lie listening and have tried to comfort and quieten you as a fellow former Blackpudlian – that's where you're from, ain't it?'

'Aye ... you said fellow, are you from Blackpool?'

'Born and bred a Sandgronian lass, but married a man from Manchester. I – I lost him ... he were killed in an accident. Me ma were coming for me, but she were knocked over whilst on her way and died from her injuries. She were in debt and there were nowt left to help me.'

'I'm sorry.'

'By, this shouldn't have become about me ... Look, from what you've said in the nights since you've been here, you were pregnant and something bad happened involving some roadside workmen, is that right?'

'I can't talk about it – It ... it took so much from me ... me babby ... and now, me Jack.'

'It's better to talk, lass, so work towards doing so, eh? Not now, but in the weeks ... well, years even, that we'll be here.'

'Years?'

'Yes, love, years ... unless you find a job and a home.'

'If I could get to Blackpool, I'd have both ... Or to Surrey. I've friends who'd help me, only I can't remember their address ... The men who caused all of this took everything we had. I had the address written down ...'

'You ain't got a cat in hell's chance of that, lass, so you'd better make the most of what you have, eh?'

'And that's nowt! Naw home, naw husband, naw family and naw money!'

'That's the way of it. But you've still got life and could have friends if you'd try a bit harder to mix and be civil.'

Through her tired and swollen eyes, Elisha looked at Harriet. 'Help me, lass. Please help me.'

Harriet's lovely freckled face, framed by soft, curly dark brown hair, beamed a smile. 'That's a good start – you, reaching out for help, and I will, love, I'll help you. I've tried to look out for you from the day you came, as I could see you were lost and alone, and knew from the little you spoke that we were kin in that we came from Blackpool.'

Desperate to keep her mind off her loss, Elisha asked Harriet, 'So, you losing your husband and your ma led you to this place?'

'Not straight away . . . I spent time in an asylum . . . You see, losing both me ma and me Harry tipped me over the edge. I set fire to the little cottage me and me Harry shared. I didn't mean to, I was in a haze of grief and fear of what would happen to me, and I wasn't thinking straight. I – I was to leave me home and I was packing what I could, not knowing where I was going to land up – me ma was me only relative. Anyroad, I'd put some fat on to fry off a slice of bread – the only food I had – and I forgot it. I was judged as having done it deliberate and, well, me hysterics swayed the judge to put me into an asylum.'

'Aw, Harriet . . . By, it's a wicked world when the chips are down for you.'

'It is. And Elisha . . . God knaws you've cause to go mad, but hold on for your Jack, and for your lost children. Live a good life for the life they can't live. That's what I try to do for me Harry and me ma, and that led to me coming here and escaping the horror of that madhouse.'

As if to give force to what she was saying, Harriet took hold of Elisha's hand and squeezed it. 'You can learn skills here if you put yourself to it, then one of the factories might take you on.'

'I knaw all about gardening, but me real ambition was allus to become a teacher.'

'My, you have to be clever to do that, have you got exams and things?'

'Naw, nowt official – well, except me school certificate, but I never stopped studying while me ma, da and grandma were alive.'

Without wanting to, or even knowing why, Elisha poured out the story of her grandma and ma and da.

At the end of her telling, she was sobbing again. 'I – I lost it all ... The dream I had ... the hard work done by me family ... It all went ...'

'It's not your fault, love.' These words of Harriet's came out hoarsely. A tear plopped onto her cheek. 'I'm sorry, lass ... Your story brought mine back to me. The pain of loss is too much to bear at times. But we've to be strong and find a way back to a life that we want to lead.'

'How can we, when we're confined to this place?' Elisha looked up at the grim building that housed so many desperate folk – over one thousand in total, with the inmates of the far building – the one they called 'the madhouse'. It was a place Elisha dreaded as, even in the state of mind she'd been in, she'd taken in the wails that came from there, and the sight of the inmates — their greasy hair and their rotten teeth, ground down by them gnashing them together — how they hissed at everyone and spat if you tried to greet them, their haunted look — hollow cheeks and staring eyes. She didn't want to become one of them ... but 'Eeh, Harriet, whilst I've been talking to you, me Jack's naw more — he ... HE'S GONE! HANGED BY THE NECK ... ME JACK ... I WANT ME JACK!'

'Stop, please stop, Elisha, ple-ease!'

Taking in a gasp of air that hurt her throat, Elisha pulled at her stray golden curls, wanting to pull her hair out, wanting to tear the badness of her life out of her body.

The while, Harriet begged her to stop.

A crowd gathered.

'Is she at it again? She's a pain in the arse. She wants a good smacking and that's what she'll get if she doesn't shut it!'

Another voice chipped in, 'She will too! We've been given an extra half hour recreation, but if there's any trouble, they'll call us back in!'

'Leave it, girls. Her hubby were hung at midday. Give the lass a chance, eh?'

'Hung! Christ! I knew there was a hanging today, it's been the talk of the workshops ... It were her husband, then?'

'It was. Try to have some compassion.'

'Sorry, Harriet. But she wants to watch out — they'll soon have her in the madhouse. There're rumours that we're overcrowded and some have to be shipped out.'

Elisha sobbed quietly in Harriet's arms, leaving her to sort out the mob that had descended, but how she was ever going to get to a quiet place in her mind, she just didn't know.

'I knaw, I heard the rumours,' Harriet was saying, 'but if any of you are chosen, then don't have expectations as all the workhouses are the same – work and little food, and naw freedom without permission, which is rarely granted.'

'Better than starving, I suppose.'

Elisha thought she'd rather starve to death than be cooped up here for the rest of her life. But she kept quiet, prompted by the squeeze of Harriet's hand.

The leader of the group spoke directly to her then. 'Well, we're sorry for your loss, but missus, you've to remember there's more than you in here, and all of us are suffering – even them as have their husbands and kids here, as they have the agony of not being in the same section as the rest of their family and having naw say in their kids' upbringing. All we ask is a bit of peace at the end of the day.'

Elisha couldn't answer. Harriet answered for her: 'Aye, she knaws. And it's what she needs an' all, besides some friendly folk willing to support her through this.'

Another voice, one Elisha hadn't heard before, piped up, 'I agree. It's just tiredness that makes us grumpy. Sorry, missus, we ain't been kind to yer, but we didn't understand your ramblings.'

Feeling she had to contribute, Elisha said, 'I'll try not to disturb you all, but me nightmares come without me bidding.'

'And that's all as lass can do, so leave her alone now. Just give her a chance, eh?'

The crowd dispersed, some muttering, 'You're right, Harriet', others nodding, but all agreeing, which greatly helped Elisha.

'Ta, Harriet, I'll do me best not to upset them. That one who spoke the most is right, they're all suffering.'

'Aye. It's rotten being in here, whether you've family or not. And trying is all you can do, but I hope you succeed. You're a lovely lass.'

Elisha pulled up her knees and hugged them to her. 'I need to think, Harriet. I need to sort out in me mind all that's happened.'

'Aye, it might help you to get it all into perspective. This break will be over soon, and it will be teatime and back to routines. We'll all be called to an evening service and that might help you – the vicar who visits is a kindly man.'

Elisha nodded. Her thoughts were already going back over the events that had led to her being in this awful place. Jack's mind being turned by the terrible rape of her, him losing control, his battering of the man who'd referred to her as a whore – why did he do that? Couldn't he see she'd only wanted Jack's attention?

But then, it was all so hopeless. Revisiting it all wouldn't help her.

Staring up at the sky, she imagined Jack's soul floating upwards. She knew an urge to put up her arms and try to grab him back to her, but then an acceptance came to her.

'Live your life,' Jack had said. But could she?'

'Come on, Elisha ... hurry. Didn't you hear the bell?'

Harriet tugged at the sleeve of Elisha's cardigan. But

Elisha was still seeing Jack floating. She wanted to stay with him – rise up and go to him.

'We must go, Elisha. I don't want to leave you, but if I don't, we'll both be on bread and water for a week!'

The fear in Harriet's voice jerked Elisha out of her dream. When she looked up again, Jack was gone.

'Please, Elisha!'

Rising as if in a stupor, she allowed Harriet to pull her along.

The stupor left her when a commanding voice told them to line up at the washroom door. 'Swill your faces and run a comb through your hair, then go to your locker and put on a clean apron. I want you all inside the chapel by four o'clock!'

The chapel stood at the entrance of the yard – an entrance that closed them off from the outside world, as huge padlocked gates formed a barrier to them leaving.

Inside the chapel felt cold and lifeless. Nothing about its stark white, bare walls told of this being God's house. No statues of Our Lady – but then this wasn't a Catholic church, as Harriet had said a vicar would take the service. But what did it matter? She didn't think she'd pray, not now, not ever again.

The altar was just a tall wooden bench. The man standing behind it, smiling a welcome, seemed strangely alien to his surroundings. Small in stature, he had a shock of ginger hair.

'That's The Reverend Myers. You should talk to him. Ask to have an appointment with him, lass, go on.'

'Ask, who? Won't I get into trouble if I go up to him now?'

'Aye, you will, but you can put your hand up and he'll come over to you . . . Look, a couple have already. He allus does his best to help.'

Elisha raised her hand.

The Reverend Myers acknowledged her with a nod of his head, then went over to one of the others.

When he came to her, Elisha swallowed hard. She didn't want to dissolve into tears.

'How can I help you, my dear – mind, I only have a minute as I must begin the service.'

Elisha burst out. 'Me Jack – me husband – was hung today!'

Reverend Myers' shocked expression compounded how Elisha felt – it was as if someone had at last taken in the enormity of what had happened, and not just accepted it and tried to console her.

'Good Lord! You poor girl! I – I won't ask for details, but I will pray for you and for Jack. And I will seek permission to come to see you and try to help you, my dear.'

'Ta, Reverend. I feel like me life's over. Jack was a good man, but circumstances . . .'

'I cannot talk now, my dear, but I promise that I'll come and see you.'

His smile changed his plain looks and transformed his face, so that you would call him good-looking. Elisha felt she'd found another friend.

She nodded. 'I'd like that.'

'My prayers will be with you, dear.'

When the service was over and they all rose, Elisha's face was awash with tears. It was as if the prayers she hadn't wanted to utter, but that had tumbled from her, had finally let Jack go, as now it was real to her – not just something she wailed about, but accepted.

This acceptance didn't ease the pain in her heart, but it helped her to see that there was no going back. It was done. Jack was gone for ever.

That life was truly over. All she had were her memories. Somehow, she had to save herself from going mad.

The days went into weeks. Summer arrived without a let-up in the drudgery of life. For Elisha, as she had gardening skills, that meant working long hours digging and planting, work she loved but had no heart to do.

Apart from a couple of visits from the vicar, which had helped a little, Harriet was Elisha's only lifeline. She listened. She talked of her own life and losses, and encouraged Elisha to do the same, until the day came when summer had faded into autumn and now there was the promise of winter in the chill of the wind, and they were both summoned to the matron's office.

No greeting, just a blank stare as the matron, a small woman with a pinched face, told them, 'You're both to leave here. You'll be taken back to where you come from . . . There's a new workhouse been built there with vacant places – Wesham Workhouse. You are both to go there on a date to be fixed in January next year.'

Just hearing the name lifted Elisha. Wesham was just on the edge of Kirkham, and only a few miles from Blackpool. Her home. The town she loved. She would be near to Jean and Bert, and Nancy the shopkeeper. Maybe they would find a way of helping her. She could try to get a leave day, saying she had folk who might be able to find her work.

Why she hadn't tried to contact them before, no matter how difficult this may have been to achieve, she didn't know, but then she hadn't done anything but exist. Nothing had touched her. No thoughts or ideas had given her anything to clutch on to. Her only comfort had been Harriet's friendship, but now a trickle of hope pierced that dead shell of hopelessness within which she'd lived for almost a year, as the move sank in. Blackpool! *Eeh, me Jack, I'm going home.*

PART FOUR

The Flickering of Hope
1908

CHAPTER NINETEEN

Their departure from the Manchester workhouse had been delayed many times, but at last, on a lovely bright day in February 1908, they arrived – though the sight of the newly built Wesham Workhouse sent shivers through Elisha, as she and Harriet walked hand in hand up to the open door. For all its fresh exterior, it was still nothing more than a prison to the inmates, and now would be to them too.

A portly man stood in the doorway. He looked at her and Harriet. 'Ahh, the two from Manchester. Come in, we've been expecting you.'

He then greeted the driver of the bus that had brought them, which had dropped off a few former Manchester inmates at various workhouses. 'Good journey, driver? Everyone behave themselves?'

'They did, sir. These two are the last. Here's their paperwork.'

'Thank you. If you go to the kitchen block over there, you'll be given refreshments. Good day.'

The driver, a nice man who'd chatted to them on the last leg of the journey, when only she and Harriet remained on the bus, turned to them. 'Good luck, ladies. I hope something turns up for you in the future.'

Harriet nodded, but Elisha felt the urge to thank him. 'Ta very much. And for your kindness.'

As the driver doffed his cap, the portly man took their attention once more. 'Come on in, we've a lot to do to get you admitted.'

The procedure was familiar to them both – their details were taken, and they were given the rules of the house and told their next step would be to have a bath and be kitted out with a uniform.

This last gave Elisha a sense of losing her identity once more, as on leaving Manchester they had been given the clothes they had turned up in when entering. For her, this had been the second set of clothes that Jane had acquired for her – a long brown skirt and a red-and-white checked blouse, covered by a brown cloak. Garments that brought memories of the sentencing of her Jack, and yet somehow brought a part of him back to her, as the last time they saw each other she was wearing them. Now, once more they were to be taken from her and stored – for how long, she didn't know.

The master, as the gentleman had told them he was, was now saying that his aim was to get inmates into work, to take some of their income for their keep and the rest to save for their future. 'However, you will be allowed a small allowance. But trips out of the building are restricted and strictly by permission only, and usually only granted to anyone seeking work. Now, for me to assign you to a useful placement here, I need to know your talents. Let us start with you ...' He looked at her application. 'Elisha Randal, well now, what are you good at?'

'Gardening and cooking, sir ...'

'Aye, and she's clever. She was once studying to be a teacher, sir.'

'Please don't speak unless you are spoken to, Miss ...' Again he looked down at the papers he'd just filled in, 'Harriet Wensley.'

'Sorry, sir. Only, it's missus.'

The master's eyes raised. He let out a sigh, then continued to speak to Elisha, 'Now that's interesting. Did you have any practical training, Elisha?'

'Naw, sir, I just had an ambition and studied in the hope of passing the exams needed. I studied maths, English and ways to teach children to read. I got me knowledge from books I got from the library. Me family were saving to pay for me to go to college one day ... but they were all killed.' The last word stuck in Elisha's throat; she had to swallow hard to stop the emotion triggered by it.

'Hum ... well, we do have a nursery block here, where children are kept until they are five and then go to an orphanage. The staff there could do with extra help with the toddlers, as the newborns take up a lot of their time. I will assign you to work there on a trial basis.'

The thought of this lifted Elisha's spirits. Though part of her had to school herself to be ready to be around little ones, as the losses of her own two hit her.

'Now, Mrs Wensley, your talents are?'

'I'm good at weaving, sir. I can make owt from some yarn and a loom, or some knitting needles.'

'Well, we don't have anything like that, but there is the laundry, where not only washing of clothes and bedding etc. goes on, but repairs too. I'll assign you to there.'

Though Elisha thought this drudgery, Harriet accepted it gratefully. 'Ta, sir, I'll do me best.'

'Good. Now, you are to report to the hospital wing, where you will both be examined and then handed over to the staff of the washing facilities. You will bathe and be given new uniforms. These you must care for and endeavour to look smart at all times – fresh, clean ones will be given after your next bath . . . that will be in one week. And as this is a Thursday, that will be your regular bath day.'

He went to the door. On opening it they saw a woman waiting outside in the corridor.

'Ahh, Mrs Katlin. Please take our new residents to the hospital wing and then wait for them and take them to the bathrooms. Hand them over to the attendants there, but when that's all done, take them to where they will sleep, and then to the dining room as it will then be supper time.'

Elisha's stomach thought it was supper time now as it growled out her hunger. Holding her tummy and hoping the noise hadn't been heard, she thanked the master politely, as did Harriet.

They both obediently went with Mrs Katlin, a tall, thin woman who looked as though her face had never smiled, it was so pinched and unreadable. Following her stiff back to the sound of her boots clomping on the stone floor made them giggle, but they did so silently. It was nerves as much as anything, Elisha thought, as this walk was like going into the unknown. Everything about this building was new and fresh – no peeling paint or doors that wouldn't shut. No grimy flagstones trodden by an army of the poor and outcasts. It was as if they had landed in heaven.

Both could remember there having been a workhouse here for many years, but didn't know it had been pulled down and replaced, and hadn't expected to be dealt with in a polite manner, as the master had done. Somehow, Elisha thought, this had given them back some of the dignity they'd lost.

But other feelings churned her stomach too. The sense of being home and yet not being, leaving her savouring the moment they'd entered Blackpool and she'd smelt the fresh sea air though the window of the bus. Her emotions at catching a glimpse of the tower, the memories that had assailed her, as she could see they had Harriet. How a longing had set up inside her to visit the churchyard at Layton and be near to the graves of her loved ones, especially her Ted.

At this thought, Elisha determined that if ever she got the chance to visit, she would put flowers there for her unborn and for Jack, as well as for those loved ones who lay there.

This thought tumbled the pain she'd warded off back into her.

'Right, this is the hospital wing.'

The words made Elisha jump.

'What's those tears for? The time for tears was when you could see yourself getting into this mess, so you could do sommat about it. It's too late now, so control yourself. If one starts, they all start, then we have a job on our hands!'

'Sorry, miss.' Elisha brushed the tears she hadn't been aware of from her face. Harriet's glance held pity, but she didn't reach out to her – they had both understood without being told that doing so wouldn't be acceptable to this woman.

With the examination over and both passed as fit for work, Elisha was really looking forward to her bath. They'd only ever had communal showers at Manchester and the first of those had been a time for jeers at her skinny body and the mocking of her bruises, until Harriet had stepped in.

But as she soaked in a tub next to Harriet, they both let go of their emotions. To Elisha, it was as if her whole body wept silently – partly for all she'd been through and partly through the joy of being home and there being hope on the horizon for her.

'Eeh, lass, are you all right?'

'Aye, I am really, Harriet. I'm just so full of relief.'

'I knaw. I feel the same. This place is like a palace to Manchester, ain't it?'

'It is, and we're so near to Blackpool . . . You've never said what part you were brought up in, was it near the centre?'

'Naw, it was near to the Gynn pub in Warbreck Hill Road. We had a house there when me da were alive. I used to listen to the trams rumbling by along the prom, just around the corner. And play in the street with the other kids.'

Harriet sighed heavily. 'Me da died of gangrene. He was allus ill and if he hurt himself, he didn't heal. He had too much glucose in his pee, the doctor said. It broke me ma's heart to lose him and we nearly landed in here – well, the old workhouse as was – but she kept working at different jobs and managed to keep our house on ... Eeh, I miss them both. It's having naw one to turn to. To call on for 'elp, as much as missing the cuddles, the understanding and the advice.'

'I knaw just what you mean, lass.'

A shout of 'Time's up. Get dry and dressed in the uniforms lain out for you, and hurry!' changed their mood as it set them giggling as they scrambled out of the tubs, grabbed a towel each and hurried to dress.

They each donned a liberty bodice, a petticoat and a long, brown calico dress, a white apron and brown sandals.

'Get as much of your hair as you can tied back with the scarf, please,' the disembodied voice instructed them.

They helped each other with this, and as Elisha tucked the last few strands of Harriet's hair into the scarf she said, 'There, lass, we both look good, but for how long, I don't knaw.'

'Well, at least for tonight, as it's too late for work to start, especially for you with the kids as they will be in bed by now!'

This wasn't the case though, as the warden in charge of the bathrooms told them, 'There's still plenty of time before supper, so get yourself to your workplaces and see if there's anything you can do to help with the end of the day.' She directed them where to go, then turned her back and called for a woman who was obviously an inmate: 'You, get the bathrooms cleaned, and hurry!'

Elisha's heart felt heavy in her chest – this place was different to the last in appearance only. How was she to bear it? Harriet squeezing her hand helped as she grinned and told her, 'See you at supper, eh, lass? And it can't come soon enough, as me belly thinks me throat's been cut!'

Elisha managed a smile she didn't feel. From the hostility they'd received so far from the staff, her hopes of getting out to see Jean seemed to be dashed. She could never imagine being given permission.

The nursery was in a separate block, which cheered her a little, as just to get some fresh air as she crossed the yard was a bonus. But then she thought of poor Harriet, who would be in a hot, steaming laundry.

When she reached the nursery, Elisha found mayhem. It seemed that all the children were crying and, in the case of the babies, screaming their heads off!

A smell of urine and excrement greeted her when she opened the door, knocking her back and turning her stomach. A hard-faced woman screeched, 'Shut that bloody door, it's cold enough as it is, and shut up the lot of you!' Her hand swiped the child nearest to her.

'Naw! Don't do that!'

The woman swivelled round to face Elisha. 'And who are you to tell me what not to do, eh? Scum!'

With her indignation driving her, Elisha spoke out. 'I'm not scum, I'm someone who can see that these little 'uns need cleaning up and feeding, and getting to bed, not punishing!'

'And you're the one to do that! Huh, I'd like to see you try. They're miserable little sods!'

Appalled, Elisha reached out to the nearest child and pulled him to her. The boy responded by clinging on to her legs. The contact bled her pain of longing to hold her little Ted, but she gained strength from going onto her haunches and comforting him.

'Let him go! I forbid you to mollycoddle these children. They need tough handling to prepare them for when they leave here and will no longer see their mothers!'

This didn't shock Elisha; she knew the practice of children of five and over being sent to a children's home, some never seeing their parents again, though some were lucky as their mum and dad managed to gain employment and get back on their feet. These were allowed to reclaim their children.

To her, the process for those who were adopted out, or sent to Canada or Australia, never to see their family again, was a cruel practice and one that must be even worse for the parents than what had happened to her. She couldn't imagine her Ted growing up somewhere across the world and having no contact with him. An agony without closure.

'But decent and human care ain't spoiling them, miss. They deserve that at least.'

'Don't backchat me, you scum! I'll see the master and have you taken off this duty, you ain't suitable for it!'

'Naw! I am, I will care for them, keep them clean, teach them their numbers and read to them ... Please, just give me a chance!'

'Huh, I'd like to see you try!' With this, she turned and went towards the door. 'I'll be back! And probably to chaos, unless you're some sort of magician or sommat.'

As the door slammed behind her, the wailing increased as the sound had frightened the little ones. Elisha stood, taking in the enormity of what needed doing, and for a moment didn't know where to start.

Another child – a little girl with blonde curly hair – came up to her and clung to her other leg. 'I want me ma . . . I want me ma!'

Shaking herself out of her fear and uncertainty, Elisha cuddled her to her. 'Later. I'm sure your ma will come to you. And that'll be grand, won't it? Now, let's get you all bathed and fed, eh?'

Releasing herself from their grip and closing her ears to the awful sound of distressed children, Elisha crossed the room and opened doors in her hunt for bathing facilities, clean nappies and nightclothes.

She found them all, though the bathroom, stacked high with small tin baths, left a lot to be desired. Its tiled walls and ceiling were filthy, and the bags hanging on the wall, containing dirty nappies and linen, stunk.

The sound of a sob coming from one of the cupboards had her running to it. Finding it locked, she turned the key, and then jumped back as a young girl sprang at her. Thin, with dainty features, she was around the same height as Elisha, though she judged the girl couldn't have been more than fifteen years old. Her large dark eyes filled with fear as they darted from Elisha, around the room and to the door.

From her clothes, Elisha knew this was a fellow inmate. Stepping back, she asked, 'Eeh, lass, what's to do? Why are you in the cupboard?'

'That witch locked me in there. I've been there for an hour. She's evil ... I only picked one of the babbies up ... By, she needs reporting, only naw one dare do it!'

'You're shaking. Look, she's gone. She was in a temper and said she'd go to the master, but let's not worry about that, let's get these young 'uns sorted, eh?'

'Aye, poor little mites. Though it's a big task. There's eleven of them and they all need seeing to.'

'We can do it. I'm Elisha, by the way. What's your name?'

'Edna. I ain't been here long. Me and me ma were made homeless, so we brought ourselves here. Are you new?'

'Aye, I arrived this afternoon.' Not wanting to tell her story or even listen to Edna's, in fear of it taking her back to her weeping state, Elisha took charge. 'Right, first thing is one of us take all the dirty nappies off the little ones while the other fills a couple of baths. We can put them close together, leaving a space in the middle for one of us, and get the older kids into them four at a time, two in each bath, and be able to see to them and keep them safe.'

'I'll do that as they knaw me and'll do as I say.'

'I'll work me way through the babbies then. I'll have a couple of them bowls and a pile of nappies. There looked to only be four little 'uns.'

'Aye, that's right – four under one, two of two years old and five almost five years olds.'

The process worked well, and soon the children were clean, the babies tucked into cots with feeding bottles

229

propped up and sucking away. Edna told her that the mothers expressed their milk. 'They ain't allowed to breastfeed their babby. It's part of the process of breaking the babby away from them, for when it's put up for adoption.'

'But they can see them, can't they?'

'Naw, though some try. But if caught, they get punished for it.'

'But that's cruel!'

'Aye, as is a lot as goes on, but them in charge look on it as a way of keeping order, so we've naw say in it all.'

Elisha had the feeling of being beaten, of never being able to get herself out of such a strict regime. Of having no future. Her hopes of getting to Jean and Nancy for help seemed impossible to achieve.

'Is anyone allowed out, you knaw, to go to Blackpool, or owt like that?'

'Naw. Some ask, but they're rarely given permission, unless it's genuinely to apply for a job. Some sneak out, but if they're caught they can end up in prison for stealing their uniform.'

'But I have a friend, she might help me . . .'

'Well, you ain't got much chance, unless you can convince the master that seeing her would lead to you getting a job and a home . . . Anyroad, we'd better see to getting the older ones fed, and shut them up, poor little mites.'

'How do we do that?'

'The kitchen'll send over some meals for them, they should be here at any moment, we just need to get them busy laying the table. They like to help out.'

Putting this into being cheered Elisha as the pyjama-clad little ones engaged enthusiastically with taking the spoons and bowls to the table. Elisha made a teaching game out of it.

'Right, each one of you tell me your name as you collect your spoon.'

'Betty, and I can sing.'

'By, that's a good talent, but can you count?'

'What's count?'

'It's telling me your numbers, one, two three ...'

'Naw, I ain't counted yet.'

'Well, Betty, let's start. How many babbies do we have?'

'I don't knaw, but Miss Wright says they sound like a field full of cattle when they start!'

'Right, all of you, put your spoons on the table and come with me.'

They followed her through to the room where the babies were. 'So, we have one, two, three, four! Four babbies!'

One of the boys, who'd said his name was Ernest, piped up. 'I knaw, I've got four fingers and a thumb, me ma taught me that.' But after this revelation, his face crumpled. 'I want me ma ... I want me ma ...'

Betty sidled over to Ernest's side. 'Ma'll come, she told us she would.'

Elisha, surprised at this, looked over at Edna.

'They're twins, Elisha.'

At this from Edna, Elisha's heart broke for their ma. How must it feel to have one child in here, let alone two!

Going over to them, she put her arms around them. 'Aw, Ernest, I knaw you do, but me and Edna are here, we'll be like mas to you, I promise. Come here, all of you gather around, let's have a hug like mas give, eh?'

This caused giggles and stopped the threatening deluge of tears and wails, as she and Edna hugged the little ones to them.

In doing so, Elisha vowed to do all she could for these little children. She'd do it in Ted's name and make it her mission to make them as happy as she could. Her Jack would expect no less of her, and nor would her ma, da and grandma.

CHAPTER TWENTY

By the time dinner arrived for the children, Elisha and Edna had swilled the excrement off the dirty nappies and had them bundled up to take to the laundry.

With opening the small windows, the smell began to improve. As she opened the third one, Elisha spied the nursery manager coming across the yard with the master. Her heart sank. She so wanted to stay in this job, but by the look on Mrs Parkin's face, as Edna had told her the manager was called, she didn't think that likely.

To distract herself, she turned to where the children were now eating the hot broth with chunks of bread that had been delivered.

'Now, listen all of you! When the door opens and the master comes in, I want you to stand and say, "Good evening, Master." Can you do that for me, me little lads and lasses?'

Betty, who was quite the spokesman, said, 'Aye, we can, miss.'

'Good. Now, get ready.'

There was a clatter of spoons being put down into the tin bowls the broth had been served in.

'Right, Edna. You stand at one end and I'll be at the other. Now stand straight, lass. Keep your dignity and don't look afraid. We've done nowt wrong, only right by these young 'uns and the babbies, so we must show that in our stance.'

'By, Elisha, I wish you were the manager here. Things'd change for the better.'

When the door opened, the children stood as one, and their 'Good evening, Master' was a sing-song chorus. Taken aback, the master half bowed. 'Good evening, children.'

Mrs Parkin stared in disbelief. Her eyes darted around. Taking in the orderly appearance of the nursery, she sniffed, but before she could say anything, Betty said, 'I can count to four, Master. Miss Elisha taught me. We have four babbies.'

'That's very good, my dear.' He looked around. 'Well, well, this is a difference, Mrs Parkin. Did you instigate it all?'

Mrs Parkin glared at Elisha as she said, 'Aye, well, with the extra hand so much more can be done. I'm grateful, Master.'

But Betty, the most intelligent of the four-year-olds, was having none of it. 'Miss Elisha and Miss Edna did it all, with our help, Master. And they cuddled us an' all . . .' Her bottom lip quivered. 'It were like me ma cuddling me . . .' A sob came into her voice as she said, 'I – I want me ma.'

'Shut up, child and speak when you're spoken to.' Mrs Parkin looked at Elisha. 'How dare you do such a thing and upset the children?'

'I – I . . . It didn't upset them; they were already pining for their mas. It comforted them . . .'

The master cleared his throat. 'Rules are rules, Mrs Randal, and here in this department, they are made by Mrs Parkin, though I do understand that their plight is sad, but it isn't of our making. We are only trying to make life better for them.'

Feeling brave now, as she felt strongly that things were not being handled right, Elisha spoke up: 'But, sir, keeping them dirty and living in a dirty environment, and punishing them, ain't making life better for them.'

'How dare you backchat the master! I told you, Master, she ain't suitable!'

'I'm sorry, Mrs Parkin, but I have to agree with Mrs Randal. The last time I visited, this place was chaos, and the children dirty and unhappy. Now I find them clean and polite, even if this little girl is outspoken, but then for the life ahead of them, they will need that confidence too. I want you to continue in this way. Mrs Randal has set a precedent for you. She has done the work needed, and so it should be easy for you to keep the standard up. Mrs Randal will be in charge of the children's education.'

'But—'

'I really don't see any "buts". Surely, it is a load off your back to have her. She's an asset to you. Things had slipped, as you couldn't manage, but they are back in order and with the help from Mrs Randal, they should stay that way. I'll be inspecting next week. Now, it is supper time. Release your helpers one at a time, and you and I will talk further when we dine with the rest of the staff later.'

This turn of events seemed to give Edna courage, as she blurted out, 'Sir ... Master, is it right as Mrs Parkin shuts me in the cupboard if I try to soothe the young 'uns? Only I'm terrified of closed-in spaces.'

'Shuts you in the cupboard! Good grief!'

He glared at Mrs Parkin, who came over all humble, wringing her hands and bending her frame, saying, 'She's a bad 'un, Master. Disobedient, and disruptive to the discipline I've brought to the nursery.'

Betty piped up, 'Miss Edna is nice.'

'Shut up, scum!'

'Mrs Parkin!'

'Sorry, Master, but you want to try dealing with them, they're uncouth, their habits are filthy!'

'Surely, it is our job to teach them to behave in a civilised manner and to keep them clean. I understand that you have been under pressure, but you should welcome the extra help Mrs Randal will be and the difference she has made already. And in the five minutes it took Mrs Parkin to fetch me is astonishing!'

'Eeh, it took longer than that, sir. Me and Edna have been working hard this hour or so, since,' Elisha told him.

The master turned a cold stare towards Mrs Parkin. 'I think we need to talk. We'll go back to my office, now!'

'Carry on here, Mrs Randal.' He addressed Edna then. 'You, Miss Fulham, can go for your supper on the first sitting.'

Edna bobbed her knee. The door slammed shut on the master and Mrs Parkin. Edna glanced at Elisha. 'Eeh, there's going to be trouble, if you ask me!'

'There needs to be. I ain't never seen owt like this place

was and how the young 'uns were kept. But I wonder where Mrs Parkin's been for all that time and why the master were so angry about it!'

'She'd have gone for a fag and a drop o' whisky – she likes both. She goes to the boiler house. Many a time she's left me on me own. And once, I came back from having me dinner and the kids were all on their own!'

'Naw! Did the master find out?'

'Aye, he called to ask her sommat and was furious. But it ain't stopped her.'

Elisha looked around at the vulnerable children, now sitting quietly as if they sensed trouble, and wondered at such cruel treatment as they'd been subjected to. Deciding to lighten the mood for them, she clapped her hands, but the gesture made them jump. Ernest, who Elisha realised was a timid soul, began to cry.

Edna went to his side to comfort him, but Betty already had her arm around him and was telling him that everything was all right now they had Miss Elisha.

Elisha chose to carry on and keep things normal for him. 'Now, now, children. When I clap my hands, it's to get your attention, not to frighten you. I've a game for you to play. It's called finding the colour. I say a colour and you have to put your hand up if you can spot it in the room. I'll start with brown.'

Rita, an overweight little girl – though how she managed to be on the rations they got Elisha didn't know – shot her hand up. 'Your frock!'

'Good girl.'

Rita beamed.

As the game progressed, even the shy Ernest joined in by pointing at the curtains when she asked for yellow.

The atmosphere soon changed from fear to laughter, and this continued as they each took their plates to the trolley ready for collection, and Elisha taught them how to stack them neatly and to put their spoon in the bowl provided.

When she went for her own longed-for supper, though she had shamed herself by finishing some of the scraps the children had left, Elisha was starving, and so hoped for Harriet to be on the same sitting.

Queuing for and collecting the plate of stew, which was more like a broth with a single dumpling floating in it, Elisha grabbed a chunk of bread then scanned the crowded room that stank of sweaty bodies. On spotting Harriet waving she knew her face to light up.

Set out with long tables, with wooden benches for them to sit on, the room was large and reverberated with chatter. Harriet had saved her a place. There was an air of expectation about her. 'Eeh, lass, I reckon I'm going to do all right here.'

'By, let me take the weight off me feet and then you can tell me.'

But that luxury was denied Elisha as the sound of a hammer hitting a table signalled a deathly silence and all rose to their feet.

The voice of Mrs Katlin shouting 'Quiet!' brought back the silence that had been disturbed by the movement of the wooden benches scraping on the floor.

'We will say grace!'

In unison, everyone bowed their heads.

'For what we are about to receive, may the Lord make us truly thankful.'

The 'Amen' that swirled around the room signalled the clatter once more of everyone taking their seats. As if the conversation hadn't been interrupted, Harriet said, 'I've learnt a few tricks already!'

'By, I'm pleased to hear it as I'm feeling the same, with one fly in the ointment, but tell me, what's got you all worked up and looking pleased?'

'I were put on mending – darning socks – and the laundry manager was very pleased with me effort. She said she'd keep me on that side of the operation and not put me on the dollying of the clothes – I can tell you, that was a relief and a half, you should see the size of the washing loads, and the steam ... eeh, them poor lasses are soaked through with it ... Anyroad, me and this other woman got talking and I told her how I can make owt with a loom and some cotton.'

As Harriet paused to take a breath, Elisha didn't interrupt her. Her interest was piqued.

'She said she was the same and she had one of the fellas in the other part of the house who was working in the woodshed to make her a loom, and she said she'd get him to make another one for me.'

'Won't he need paying? And where will you get the wool and cotton from that you need?'

Harriet lowered her eyes.

'Naw, Harriet, not ...' Then thinking her mind must have gone down the wrong path, as she'd heard tales in the Manchester workhouse of women letting the men have their way for sommat the men could get for them, Elisha stopped talking and just stared.

'I – I have nowt else to pay with, lass. And the wool and cotton I can get from unravelling the clothes – jumpers and such – that are binned. There's plenty of it.'

'But having a loom can't be that important! You never had one in Manchester!' The conversation was making Elisha see Harriet in a different light.

'Don't judge me, love. I knaw it ain't right, but, well, I can't spend the rest of me life in one workhouse or another, and if I can show the work I can do, the manager might let me out to seek work. I knaw of a shop that sells clothes, and most are made in the back room by a couple of women. I don't knaw if it's still there, but I could at least put it to the master to let me try applying for such a post.'

For a moment it felt as if Harriet was looking out for herself, but then it was a relief to hear her say, 'If I get out, I can then work towards helping you an' all. There're loads of market gardens in Marton Moss. I can see if any have vacancies that you could apply for. I could tell them of your experience.'

'Aye, I knaw, they were our biggest rivals, but where would you live?'

'I can stay here for a while, if I pay me board, but I can save up an' all. If we're both at earning, we could soon get enough to rent a flat.'

Hope that had died rose up in Elisha. *There could be a way for me and Harriet to get on our feet, there could!*

'By, that smile says I'm on the right track, lass.'

'Aw, but at what price? There must be another way. I don't want you acting like a prostitute ... I couldn't bear that.'

'There ain't. I've got naw money and neither have you. We've got nowt worth selling except ... Anyroad, as you knaw from Manchester, it's a way of bartering with the men. You see, they get out more often than us women do. They look for work – or say they do, to get a leave day. Most beg for the price of a pint once out of here, but they steal things the women need an' all. But I won't be asking that, I just want a chance to prove I have a skill.'

'But to lie with a stranger!'

Harriet blushed, and then a stubborn look crossed her face. 'It's needs must. And anyroad, it's a plan. Have you got one?'

'Naw.' Elisha didn't want to admit that she'd seen herself being happy if she could continue to work with the children, as now the longing to get out of here and to lead a free life had taken over once more.

Changing the subject, Harriet asked, 'So, how did you go on, then?'

Coming into her own, relating how wonderful it had all become once she'd sorted everything, Elisha could feel again that sense that she'd be all right here. Already she loved working in the nursery. But Harriet's 'You don't want to stay in this hole, do you?' brought her to reality.

'Naw, I'm just saying I could settle until we got out. After all, we don't knaw how long that will take.'

'Well, I'm glad you're happy, love. I hope that manager gets the sack, then you might get a chance of that job. I heard tell that the manager of the laundry was an inmate of the old workhouse who did a great job. She has a house that goes with her job and has her family back together, so you never knaw.'

With this, the trickle of hope that had entered Elisha grew. It filled her with anticipation for the future – a future she'd thought she would never have again.

She looked heavenwards. *Do this for me, me lovely Jack. You said you'd allus look out for me.*

Her name being called brought her back down to earth. Shoving the last of her bread into her mouth and chewing like mad, Elisha rose.

'You are to report to the master immediately!'

Harriet squeezed her hand. 'This could be it, love. Good luck.'

'Ta, Harriet, love. Don't do owt hasty, will yer, let's see how everything lies first, eh?'

Harriet nodded. Her eyes filled with tears. Elisha could tell that desperation was driving her lovely friend and hoped that the master's summons meant something had happened that may help her own prospects and alleviate some of Harriet's fears.

CHAPTER TWENTY-ONE

By the time she reached the master's office, Elisha was trembling. Partly with anticipation, but partly due to other thoughts that had occurred – *Maybe Mrs Parkin has convinced the master that I'm not suitable and I'll be removed from the nursery!*

Taking a deep breath, she knocked on the office door. Her nerves jangled as the command came for her to enter.

'Well, now, Mrs Randal, I didn't expect you so promptly. Did they allow you to finish your supper?'

Thinking it best not to try to put anyone in a bad light, Elisha answered, 'Yes, sir.'

'Good. And it's "Yes, Master, not sir."'

'Sorry, s . . . Master.'

'Never mind, just remember for the future. Now, I was very impressed with what you achieved in the nursery in such a short time. And I have had the occasion to retire Mrs Parkin as she isn't well. I'm going to appoint you as temporary manager. It will be a six-week trial, during which you will continue with the same regime as now regarding your accommodation and status. In the meantime, I will advertise the position and interview candidates, but if you prove you are up to the job, then you may be considered on merit along with any others who apply.'

'Aw, ta, Master, ta ever so much. I'll do me very best, I promise.'

'Well, it was worth offering you this chance, just to see that smile. But this is all down to you now, as all things in life are. You make of your chances what you will, and that's the only way to go forward. I like you, Mrs Randal, and I've read all about you today after one of the staff told me of your family background.'

Elisha wondered who could know about her, but had no time to ponder on this as the master continued, 'Though, I knew I'd seen your name before and dug out an old newspaper. It gave the story as you told it in court. Life has dealt you a few rotten blows. I'm giving you a chance here that I've only ever given to one inmate and that worked out well. So do your best to take it and make it so for you.'

'I will, Master. I promise.'

'Now, here are the keys to the nursery and to its office, you should find all the information you need in the office to take you forward. But if you have any questions, just ask. I'll keep a daily eye on things, which is something I should have done before now.'

Elisha almost skipped back to the nursery, the keys held tightly in her hand as if they were the keys to her future.

The moment she got there, she told Edna the news. 'Life's going to improve for you an' all, Edna. Between us, we'll have this place running like clockwork, and the children and babbies all as happy as sunshine.'

'Aw, that's grand. I could hug you.'

Elisha opened her arms. 'Always ready for a hug, love.'

Edna came into her arms, but soon jumped back.

'Are you all right, lass?'

'Aye, but physical contact between inmates is frowned upon. I don't want us caught hugging and lose you this opportunity when you've only just got it!'

'I guessed as much. Me and me friend Harriet have allus hugged each other, but in secret as it was a rule back in Manchester an' all, and not only that, but you could be ridiculed for liking women, not men, so we ain't since arriving here, just in case.'

With saying this, the thought occurred of what Harriet intended, and her blood ran cold. What if she were caught? Oh, God! She'd be the one to be sent away, not the man who did it to her. She prayed that the intended plan of Harriet's didn't happen before they met in the dormitory later that night and she could warn her off carrying it through – maybe give her hope with the prospects that she now had, as she'd never go forward without Harriet benefiting in some way.

In the office, Elisha found chaos. It was difficult for her to understand the bookkeeping or the timekeeping of staff, or to find anything relating to the children's health issues, diets, weight records or progress. Although, judging by the many ledgers she found, there was clearly a need for all of this to be recorded.

Calling out to Edna to come into the office, she asked her if she could fill any of the information in.

'Has there ever been any doctors visit? Are there things about any of the children I should knaw?'

'Aye. Mrs Parkin kept it all in her head. She didn't think much of sitting in the office, unless it was to have a sneaky fag with the window open. But just by working here, I can fill in a lot of the gaps.'

'Thanks, are all the children asleep now?'

'They are, even jack-in-the-box Betty has settled. I think it's the happiness they feel, bless them.'

Elisha felt herself cringe internally over the common saying of jack-in-the-box, but she swallowed hard and kept her train of thought, asking what time the night shift came on.

'I'm it. I sleep in the spare bed where the babbies are and tend to any who wake in the night.'

'What! After a full day's work! That can't be right. I'll see if we can take turns in that duty – a week about, or sommat.'

'Aw, that'd be grand, as I could see more of me ma then.'

'I'll have to pass it by the master, and it'll be most likely that we have to use the same bed in the dormitory. But mine is next to Harriet, so it'll be fine. You'll love Harriet and she'll look after you.'

This unsettled Elisha, as she so needed to get to Harriet to persuade her not to go through with her plan, but for now she had to get as much straight and organised as she could in this office.

By the time the bell went signifying everyone should go to their beds, Elisha felt a lot happier with everything. She had profiles of some of the children and babies, and knew the stage they were all at – which babies were teething and which were nearing weaning stage, how they were developing – and with the toddlers, how they were coping being away from their parents, and their behaviour patterns. None of it was good reading, but she determined to change all of that. She couldn't be a ma to her Ted or to her lost babby, but she could be to all the little ones in her care.

'Well, I'd better go. Ta for your help, lass. Try to get a good night's sleep. I'll be here as promptly as rules will allow. But I need to call on the master first thing in the morning to discuss us taking turns and one or two other issues we've found.'

With the windows now closed and shuttered, Elisha added, 'I reckon we could have a proper hug now, lass.'

She held Edna tightly to her. 'I ain't your ma, nor anywhere near old enough to be, but I'm here for you, lass. You can talk to me about owt you want to.'

'Ta, Elisha. I feel as though me life's changing now you've come into it.'

'I hope so, love. You don't deserve to be living in this place, and if I can in the future, I'll help you and your ma ... When will you see her next?'

'She sneaks to the back window of the babbies' room and blows me a kiss ... that's about now, afore she makes it to the dormitory in time, so I'd better get meself in there.'

'Aye, and I'd better hurry, an' all. See you in the morning.'

With this, a tired but elated Elisha ran across the yard, only just making the door to the dormitory as the warden was approaching with his keys at the ready.

As soon as she entered the dormitory, Harriet asked, 'Eeh, lass, where have you been? You didn't come to recreation and I daren't come to the nursery to find you.'

'So much has happened, Harriet, you wouldn't believe it!'

While they prepared for bed, Elisha told Harriet all that had transpired since they were together at dinner time.

'By, I must have had a premonition, as I said that, didn't I?'

'Aye, you did. I still can't believe it – we only arrived here today! But it could be the answer to our prayers.'

As they walked to the lav together, Elisha continued, 'So wait a while, eh? Don't go selling yourself for a loom. If this turns out for me, I'll no longer be an inmate. I'll be free to come and go, and I can look for a job for you an' all ... I might even have a place for us to live!'

Harriet's head bent low.

'Naw! Aw, Harriet, lass, you haven't!'

Harriet looked around her. They were in the lav now and others were coming and going. Seeing the coast wasn't clear, she nodded her head and then lowered her voice. 'I – I thought it would get us out of here ... me plan seemed our only way ... I never dreamt this would really happen for you. I mean, think about it! What are the chances in a million years that on your first day you'd be in line for a job and in the workhouse an' all. It's incredible!'

'I knaw. And it still might not happen, though I'm doing me best to make it so, as them young 'uns and babbies need someone in charge who loves them. But eeh, lass ...'

'It were all right. He were nice.'

'But what if he's made you pregnant ...? Oh, Harriet, they take your babbies from you, they put them out for adoption ... and the little ones who come in with their mothers are separated from them and they have to leave at age five ... It's unbearable.'

'I won't get up the duff, lass. He were careful ... I – I didn't mind it ... I told you, he were good to me.'

'Aw, love.'

Taking the now sobbing Harriet into her arms, Elisha held her tightly. But a sneering remark of 'Huh, I had you two down as being a bit too close' made Elisha jump away from Harriet.

The woman turned her gaze on Elisha. 'Like women, do you, love?'

'I – I was just comforting her, that's all.'

'Ha, you could call it that!'

Harriet turned and became someone that Elisha didn't know.

'Shut your mouth, slut! If you have them thoughts, then you must be one of them yourself!'

The woman pounced and grabbed Harriet's hair.

The moment turned into screaming, scratching and flaying of fists, as Harriet retaliated, got the woman on the floor and straddled her, held her head and banged it on the floor.

'Harriet, naw, naw, please stop!'

Turning a wild-looking face towards Elisha, Harriet spat out, 'I've had enough, I can't take any more!'

The door flung open and a warden stood there – a huge woman whose uniform struggled to contain her stomach.

'What the hell is going on! Gerrup, the pair of you!' She turned to Elisha. 'Are you involved in this?'

Harriet spoke up, 'Naw, she ain't, it was nowt to do with her.' She looked down at the woman she still straddled. Whatever she'd done to silence her Elisha didn't know, but the woman didn't object to Harriet's story.

'Well, you get to your dormitory, and you two come with me.'

Feeling like a traitor, but knowing that if she was judged as being involved she would lose everything, especially her chance of getting herself and Harriet out of here, Elisha turned and walked away.

Back in the dormitory, her whole body shook as she sat on her bed. Silent tears ran down her face. Was it all happening again? How could lovely Harriet have turned so quickly into this person who thought nothing of selling herself and who became violent at the least provocation?

Lying down and pulling the covers over her, Elisha sobbed into her pillow.

Someone shouted, 'Sherrup, will yer! We want to get some sleep!'

This brought the cold reality back into Elisha – life wasn't a bed of roses once more. She was here, in a stinking workhouse, surrounded by others whose lives were in tatters and had no prospects of them improving. The master wouldn't take her on – an inmate, a murderer's wife, a vagabond – why should he? He was just being kind to her – using her till he could get someone into the position of manager over the nursery. And what of the mothers of those children? Weren't they crying tears of sorrow, having their little ones so close and yet not able to hold them, feed them, take care of them, and probably never to see them again?

And Harriet. Poor, poor Harriet. She'd led this life for much longer and it had brought her low. Today she'd done something that Elisha was sure she'd never dreamt she would do, and it had affected her. Turned her mind. Made her into an animal. What would happen to her? *Oh, God, help us. Please, please, help us.*

After a fitful night, Elisha woke to the sun shining. It was early and yet she felt fully awake and turned to look at Harriet's bed.

Even through the darkness she could see it was empty.

Aw, naw! Me Harriet!

The ugly scene flooded her. What will have happened? Is there somewhere they lock inmates up if they're violent . . . ? The madhouse!

Hardly able to swallow, Elisha thought of what Harriet had told her when they first met of how she'd not long been out of the madhouse. And she asked herself once more, had what Harriet had stooped to turned her mind?

Naw, naw, please naw . . . Not me lovely Harriet . . .

Flinging the covers back, Elisha ran for the lavatory. There she threw up the small contents of her stomach, retching as acid burnt her throat.

Holding on to the pipe running from the cistern, she steadied herself. She had to keep strong. Her and Harriet's only hope lay on her shoulders. But if Harriet was in the madhouse, what hope had they then?

Forcing herself to behave as normal, as so much was at stake for her and her lovely friend, Elisha washed and dressed, then went up to where the warden sat at her desk.

'May I have permission to go to my post early, please? Only I've been put in charge of the nursery.'

'Aye, I heard. And I wish you good luck. And, love, don't worry about the scene last night. I knaw one of them were your friend, but don't get tarred with the same brush. You've got prospects from what I've been hearing.'

'She is me friend, and she's never been like that afore, is she all right?'

'I'm sorry, but she's in the asylum for now. Her record ... well, you probably knaw. She were judged as mad once before, and it seems the doctor says she's having a relapse, so she could be there for some time.'

'Naw! She ain't mad, she ain't. She's had a rough deal, but coming here to our home town, she had hope, she ... I mean, she wants to prove the skills she has as a weaver and with her knitting ... she just needs a chance.'

'Aye, we knaw about that, and the lengths she went to to get a loom. She should have asked. We try hard here to accommodate what talent everyone has – that's why the master put her to work on the mending.'

Feeling desperate, as this woman seemed to think Harriet was in the right place, Elisha pleaded, 'Can't you do owt? Can't you get her out of there? She's not mad, she just lost control.'

'That's what madness is, love – losing control ... Look, I've heard about your past, this has happened to you before. Don't let this drag you down. Sometimes you must think of yourself and your own future. You have a massive chance to make things better for yourself. Do that. Concentrate on you for once, and rise up ... I knew your grandma, by the way ... Aye, don't looked so shocked. Blackpool ain't that big.'

Elisha thought that this must be the member of staff who had told the master about her, but had no time to ask as she was now saying, 'Me ma used to take me to market and she'd allus stop and chat to your grandma and your da. Your grandma were kindly, and a hard worker, and from what I knaw of you, you are an' all. Your grandma was allus on about her granddaughter and how you were clever and would end up making sommat of yourself.'

Pointing the pencil she held at Elisha, she said, 'So do that. Do that for the lovely lady your grandma were, and the gentleman your da were. It's in your hands. Don't waste it on thinking you can make things better for your mate. She's just someone you met along the way. She's sick in her mind, and you can't do owt about that.'

Elisha had stood looking down at the warden's desk throughout this. Now she lifted her head. 'I can't abandon her. Please believe me, she ain't mad. Harriet's a lovely person. Life gets her down. It all seems so hopeless when your luck runs out. I need to give her hope. I need her to knaw I ain't abandoned her.'

The woman sighed. 'I'll get a message to her, but that's all I can do. She saw a doctor, and he judged her as insane. I can't do owt more than take her a message.'

'Ta, warden ...'

'Grace. Only don't call me that when anyone's listening ... well, not until you're one of us ... and you can be, lass. Think on. Think of what your grandma would want for you. She'd tell you to grab this chance with both hands and then sort your friend out.'

'Ta, I'll do me best, but will you tell Harriet that for me? Tell her I'm going to do me best at this job and work towards us both getting out of here. Tell her I love her ...'

Grace coughed, and a look of shock crossed her face.

'Naw ... I don't mean like that ... I never knew women could feel like that till I got to the Manchester workhouse ... it was a revelation to me. It ain't that kind of love I have for Harriet. I love her as a friend – well, like a sister. I have others I feel this kind of love for an' all, but it's just a sisterly love, nowt else.'

'Right, but I'd be careful if I was you. In here it can be misconstrued.'

'I knaw, that's what led to making Harriet angry last night.'

'I thought as much. Well, she did a very brave thing not telling on you or giving you as a reason for her outburst. It was judged as her having an episode. But she did that for you for a reason, so don't be throwing it back in her face. Go and do the job you've been given and, like I said, clutch this chance with the grip you knaw your grandma would. That's the only way you're going to ever help your friend in the long run.'

With her heart feeling like lead in her chest, Elisha nodded. 'But you will give her me message, won't you?'

'I will, except the bit about you loving her. I'll tell her that you're going to work hard to get you both out of here and that you are thinking of her every minute of the day. But that's as far as I'll go.'

'Ta, Grace ... and I love it that you knew me grandma and me da, it's brought them closer to me and made me realise that I'm truly back in me beloved Blackpool among me own. That'll help me.'

'All right, lass. And, remember. I'm here for you, but secretly. It won't go well for you with the other inmates if you're seen to have a warden on your side, so I'll treat you the same as the others. Though I'll try to seek you out when it won't be noticeable and watch out for you.'

Elisha smiled. She went to say thank you, but the sound of a yawn and then someone saying, 'By 'eck, it ain't morning already, is it?' stopped her, so she winked and went on her way to the nursery.

A good feeling came over her as she crossed the yard by the light of the gas lamps. It felt to her that she'd found another friend, someone who cared and would help her to keep her resolve. To do all she could to make a better life for herself and so for Harriet too.

CHAPTER TWENTY-TWO

All was quiet when Elisha unlocked the door to the nursery and entered. In the light of a new day, even though they'd done their best, she saw that there was still a lot more they needed to do to make it the clean environment she strove for.

Taking off her cloak, she went to the small scullery at the back of the building, donned a pinny she found hanging in there and filled a bowl. Putting her hands into the freezing cold water and squeezing the cloth she'd found, she set about washing the windowsills, the tabletops and the shelves that held the children's belongings in small boxes with their names written on the front. Each one held a folded apron of the kind that went over their head and tied at their waist, a cardigan, and a hat and gloves. This made her think that the children must be allowed outside.

Dropping the cloth back into the bowl, Elisha went back into the scullery. She'd seen a door leading to the outside. Pulling back the heavy bolt that felt as though it had never been opened, she stepped outside and was amazed to find a yard big enough for the children to play in. The high wall around it prevented her from seeing out onto the road, from which came the noise of a vehicle passing, but she knew they were at the back of the building, and though she didn't know the name of the road, it seemed to somehow be a link to the outside world. A place she would aim to get to one day.

But for now, this discovery excited her at the thought of letting the children out here to play. She pictured a place where she could paint a hopscotch pattern for them, and maybe the master would let them have a swing installed. It could be a haven. A chance for them to get some fresh air, and just to run around and scream their delight. She could almost hear the sound now and it filled with her own past and the feeling she remembered of being let out of the classroom!

But then she saw the yard for what it was – weeds growing around the foot of the walls, dead leaves and bits of rubbish littering the concrete, moss taking hold on the ground and the walls – and her spirits dampened. Shaking any negative thoughts away, she told herself that it was nothing that couldn't be sorted. Maybe the master would let her have some distemper and she could paint the walls white to cheer it all up.

The thought came to her that her lovely Jack could have done that, and then he could have used the walls as a canvas and painted animals to make them come alive – something to stimulate the children, to take their minds off not being with their parents.

Once more agony visited her – the agony of missing her Jack and of what had happened to him, and the fresh agony of knowing lovely Harriet was back in that awful place. This prompted her to ponder whether someone could have episodes of madness? And then to remember the look on Harriet's face as she'd banged the woman's head on the floor – wild, and as if she'd been possessed. Hadn't Jack had that same look as he'd said those awful things? And beaten that man to death?

Had what Harriet had done to cause the fire been a moment of madness, a moment of not being herself and forgetting the reality of having a pan on the hob? A shudder went through her. Madness was a terrifying state. A state of not being yourself. If ever they got out of here, how would she cope with Harriet if such an episode occurred again? Sighing, she told herself she'd find a way and that she wouldn't give up on her lovely friend. Not ever.

Going back inside, Elisha worked these feelings off with vigour and soon the nursery shone with cleanliness, and some order had been brought to it. But it lacked life – pictures on the wall, toys to play with, colour and joy.

That would be her mission today. She'd seen the brand new boxes of unopened crayons. And she'd tidied a pile of drawing paper. She couldn't wait for the moment she could put them out for the children and allow them to release their imaginations – the results she'd pin on the walls. But first, they would need the tables for their breakfast.

As she thought this, the first hungry cry of a baby came to her. The nursery day had begun.

It was just over six weeks later, a lovely warm day in late March, that the master came through to the yard where the children were playing. Now sporting the whitewashed walls Elisha had imagined when she first came out here, and echoing with the joy the children expressed at being free.

Seeing the beaming smile on the master's face, Elisha wondered if a verdict had been arrived at, but tried not to get her hopes too high, even though they had been heightened since the visit a few days previously when many of the committee who ran the workhouse had descended on her. She'd known she was being assessed for the job of manager of the nursery.

The master had pointed out all the improvements she'd made – how the play area was now utilised, and how she'd tapped into the children's creativity. The group of men and women, obviously from the upper classes, had admired the many drawings on the wall, those that were just scribbles of colour and others that showed people, looking like huge eggs with arms and legs and eyes, and had marvelled at the alphabet she'd drawn out in large black letters and pinned to one wall that she kept for displaying education aids.

Their words had been encouraging, leaving her full of hope and yet doubting they would agree to an inmate becoming a manager, as this was the reason they had gathered.

The master now asked, 'Can we go inside a moment, Elisha, dear?'

Getting up from the chair where she sat next to Edna, Elisha followed the master inside. As soon as the scullery door was closed behind them, muffling the noise from outside, the master said, 'Well, my dear, the board have agreed to give you the position of manager of the nursery! I'm so very pleased. You have done a marvellous job. Congratulations!'

'Eeh, ta, Master ... You've taken the wind out of me sails ... Really?'

'Yes, really and truly, and so deserved. Let's go into your office and discuss the terms.'

Hearing she would receive forty-eight pounds a year, paid in monthly increments of four pounds a month, along with a rent-free cottage, made all the hard work she'd put in worthwhile and filled her with anticipation for the future. But best of all was the feeling of being free, and the elation of being able to go and see Jean and Bert, and Nancy the shopkeeper – though a moment of emotion almost overwhelmed her as she thought of maybe going to her Primula Cottage and being able to visit Layton Cemetery and spend time with her family, especially her little Ted.

But she controlled herself as she heard her working hours were to be from seven in the morning until seven in the evening, with one day a week off, when one of the other managers would oversee the nursery, as this was a point she needed to negotiate.

'But, Master, that's not doable, unless I have more help. This is a twenty-four-hour job. Edna and I work around the clock taking turns to sleep in.'

'Yes, that has been noted and agreed that you should have another staff member, as there is no leeway with our employment regulations – all staff on day shift work these set hours. The problem is that there are very few inmates who are suitable, and paid help is out of the question.'

'There is someone ... Eeh, I just naw you're going to think me mad, but well, me friend who is in the asylum ...'

'What! Good Lord, that won't even be considered! Who is she?'

'Harriet ... Mrs Wensley.'

'The young woman you came in here with, you mean? Didn't she have a violent episode and a history of being in an asylum?'

'Yes, but she were provoked ... I can vouch for her. Please, Master, she just needs a chance. We all do. You gave me one ... What if she came on trial?'

'Well, I know she is ready to be discharged, as I read a report on her this morning, but ... Look, you're an employee now, not an inmate, so I can discuss another inmate with you. Only the report said that Mrs Wensley was well now but was to be monitored closely as she could still be prone to episodes of madness. Do you think you could handle that?'

'Aye, I can. And I reckon if she had a settled life, Harriet would never have another episode. Besides, she has skills that'll be useful to the nursery and the children.'

'Her weaving and knitting, you mean? How would they be useful?'

Elisha was lost for a moment. She couldn't think of a way and regretted saying it.

'I can see you're struggling on that point, but don't think I don't admire your loyalty. Though in this case, I cannot agree with you that Mrs Wensley is a suitable candidate to work for you.'

Sighing, Elisha tried one more tactic. 'Can I ask you, Master, if I found a job outside of the workhouse for Harriet, would she be allowed to live with me in the cottage?'

A look of shock crossed the master's face.

Elisha felt her throat tightening. Had she gone too far? It seemed there was a culture of being obsessed with the thought that two women being friends wasn't possible, that they must be engaging in sinful practices. But then she thought, why are they called sinful and vilified? Why shouldn't folk be allowed to love who they wanted to? She couldn't see anything wrong in it, not now she'd got over the shock of knowing such relationships existed.

'That wouldn't do at all!'

'I don't understand. We're good friends. I want to help Harriet.'

'Look, because I like you, and trust you, I will consent to Mrs Wensley working here with you, but I will closely monitor her progress. And as for your other suggestion, well, I can't stop you looking for work for her, but I won't consent to her being a lodger in your cottage, it would cause too many problems for you. So, I'd suggest that if you are going to seek outside employment for Mrs Wensley, you look for a position with accommodation.'

Feeling beaten but not without hope, Elisha accepted this. 'Ta, Master, ta ever so much.'

Releasing a sigh, the master said, 'So, now, can we get on with the rest of the business of you taking on the position of manager, please!'

★   ★   ★

Elisha learnt that she was to take the position on immediately, and couldn't believe it when the master handed her the keys to her cottage.

Her thoughts went from how she would manage to remembering that as staff, she would be fed, and it seemed there was an allowance of coal and wood. But how would she buy the clothes she would need? This concern disappeared at the master's next words.

'The board have recognised that you will need help towards the cost of clothes, as your first salary won't be until May. To this end, they have agreed on you receiving an advance on your first wage of two pounds, which will be deducted from your salary at ten shillings a month for the next four months. We suggest that you buy a jacket as part of your everyday wear when at work, as this sets you aside from the inmates. Also, you will have tomorrow off to move into your new home and to buy clothes. Moving in will only entail opening the door, as everything was prepared for the new tenant once Mrs Parkin vacated it.'

In the whirlwind of mixed feelings sweeping through her – the freedom, the sadness of not being able to immediately help Harriet, and the excitement of her own home once more – Elisha wondered what had happened to Mrs Parkin. This was answered in the master's next statement.

'We were all pleased to hear that Mrs Parkin has a home with her sister in Cleveleys.'

Though she'd only visited Cleveleys once, Elisha remembered it as a thriving small town on the same coast as Blackpool, and only a few miles away on the way to Fleetwood – a lovely place to retire to.

With this settling her mind, Elisha could enjoy the feelings assailing her of excitement, a promise of tomorrow, and yes, they were mixed with the sense of disappointment at moving on without Harriet, but she determined to do all she could to make her lovely friend's life better. This would be her mission.

As soon as she had a moment, Elisha dashed over to the asylum. Thinking she would be put off from visiting Harriet, she approached the gate with the determined air of a manager who wouldn't stand for being challenged. But she needn't have worried as Grace was on duty and sat just inside the gate.

'Eeh, Grace, I got it!'

'Aye, lass, I knaw. We all do. The master sounded us out before telling you and everyone was pleased. I'm over the moon. You deserve this chance, love, but what are you doing here?'

'I need to see Harriet. The master says that on her discharge she can come and work with me.'

'By, that's good news. Poor soul, she don't deserve to be in here. Aye, she went over the top but being in a workhouse can drive you to that. Let me get the keys and I'll let you through.'

'Could you bring Harriet to your reception office, Grace? Only it's difficult to talk amongst the others. Last time I was here one of them kept pulling my hair!'

'Ha, that'd be Peggy, she's allus doing that, no one knaws why. But, aye, I'll do that, love. You sit inside, I'll not be a moment.'

★ ★ ★

When Harriet arrived, they fell into each other's arms.

'Eeh, lass, I've missed you.'

'Help me, Elisha. I can't stand another day in here.'

'Haven't they told you you're to be discharged, love?'

'I am? Naw, I ain't heard that, when? Eeh, I hope it's soon.'

Grace interrupted then. 'I'll go and have a word with Matron now for you. She knaws that your papers are ready and when I tell her you have a position, you might be able to go now, love.'

Harriet's face registered shock, then curiosity, before breaking into a smile. 'Really? I have a position . . . Outside?'

'Naw. With me in the nursery. I got the job as manager. And, lass, you can sleep in the nursery every night if you want to.'

'Not with you in the cottage?'

'Naw, the master won't allow it . . . it's this thing . . . this culture that we women can't just be friends, they think we're up to being more than that if we get close and he don't want that suspicion on me or I could be forced out of me new job.'

Harriet nodded, her first reaction of joy turning to despondency.

'But life will be a million times better for you, love, I promise. And I'll find that man that . . . well, I'll see if he ever made you that loom. And I can make sure you get the jumpers that have been discarded so you can carry on your idea of unravelling them and using the wool. You can teach the children how to make pompoms as well, I can remember making them as a kid. Our four-year-olds would easily grasp it.'

Harriet's face brightened. 'Ta, lass. It sounds a good stepping stone for me ... And, well, Edwin, the man who I went with ... You'll be all right with him, won't you? He ... didn't take advantage of me, he was going to make the loom anyway, only, remember I said he was nice ... we ... Look, it weren't how I said, it was just ... I'm to blame, not him.'

'The men shouldn't be doing such things, Harriet. It's taking advantage and it made you low in your spirits and turned your head.'

'Please, Elisha, it weren't him. It was our situation, the hopelessness of it. It was meeting someone I liked and knowing nowt could come of it. It was hearing his plight an' all. His da had a carpentry shop, but they got into debt and ended up here, and his da died suddenly a week later. Edwin suffered depression, and that led him to not bother to do owt about his situation.'

This shocked Elisha. She hadn't taken it in that Harriet had liked the man she'd been with. Or was a willing partner, as it seemed she was from what she was saying. Although she still felt angry at Edwin, she didn't say so or act cross. 'Don't worry, I'll just ask for your loom.'

Changing the subject, Harriet said, 'Ta, love, but the penny's just dropped – you got the job! You're naw longer an inmate ... Eeh, lass, I'm right pleased for you. A teacher at last!'

'Aye, and this is just the start for us, I promise. As you will get out of here, Harriet, I'll see to that.'

'Out of the workhouse, you mean?'

'Aye, I do. I'll look for work for you and somewhere for you to live an' all.'

'By, that'd be grand. Ta, love.'

They hugged again, but pulled away when they heard Grace's footsteps.

'I have your discharge, Harriet, love! You're free to go with Elisha.'

'Eeh, lass!' Harriet burst into tears.

Not taking heed of the rule, Elisha cradled her to her. 'It's a new start, Harriet, lass. And we need to hurry back as I've left Edna too long as it is.'

'I'm ready, lass. I'm more than ready!'

They gave each other a squeeze and then separated. Grace smiled at them. 'I ain't telling any tales. Anyone can see the love you have for one another – sisterly love, that is. I like a hug meself now and then.'

Harriet turned towards her. 'I'd like to hug you, Grace. You've been kindness itself to me when you've been on duty.'

'Well, all right, but just a little one.'

Elisha didn't know why, but tears welled up in her eyes as she witnessed the hug, and they spilt over when Grace included her. 'I'm not leaving you out, lass.'

The hug Grace gave her had Elisha's emotions almost bubbling to the surface – with all that had happened and with finally getting lovely Harriet out of this, she wanted to cry with happiness mixed with sorrow. But she held herself together. Life looked to be picking up, didn't it? Not a time for tears, but for making this chance she'd been given work.

Crossing the recreation yard wasn't an easy experience, as glances came their way and snide remarks reached them.

'Ha, as soon as she got up the ladder, she fetched her lover to her!' was one that grated on Elisha. Without thinking, she replied, 'If you don't want to be on bread and water rations, I'd shut your mouth if I was you, Lilly Staining!'

The reply shocked her. 'Sorry, Warden, I didn't mean owt.'

So, they knew to give her some respect, but this saddened her too. She was only minutes out of the same status as they were, she knew their pain and their hopelessness, and didn't want to add to it. Her heart wanted to say it was all right, that she'd taken it as a joke, but she didn't want to set a precedent that could lead to problems for her in the future. Though her empathy for them hadn't changed, her status had. She was to be one of the disciplinarians, whether she liked it or not.

'I'll let it go this time, but I'll have naw more of it.'

'Sorry, miss.'

Elisha marched on. She could feel Harriet cringing beside her.

'Don't let that worry you, love, I've to keep it under control right from the start. They're bound to feel envious. It ain't every day that one of their own is elevated to warden.'

'I thought you were a manager?'

'Aye, I am, but I can act as a warden an' all, as Grace is doing today.'

'By, I'm glad about that, as it'll keep you safe. None of them like the threat of the bread and water days ... You knaw, I think I will sleep in with the babbies. I don't think I'd feel safe in the dormitory.'

'Good, I didn't like to think of you going back there. There's those who hold a grudge. And Edna'll be happy as she likes to go to be with her ma.'

When they arrived back at the nursery, Edna was in a flap.

'What's to do, lass?'

'I've had a bit of a job with Betty and Ernest. A woman came to the door after you left. When I opened it, she shouted to them and they went running, screaming, 'Ma . . . Ma!' I had a time of it trying to settle them. I just closed the door on the woman. I didn't knaw what else to do, though it broke me heart to do it. Poor soul.'

This was a part of the job that tore at Elisha, but she didn't see how she could change it. It was so cruel. But the powers that be, she'd learnt, looked on it as them giving the children the best possible chance in life, that they stood no chance with their parents but would thrive in places like Canada and Australia. She'd read about both during her days of studying and had to admit they did sound like paradise. And maybe the children would be better off once they'd broken their emotional ties. She just didn't know. Only that the rule was there and she had to abide by it in order to keep her job. Not that it was just a job, it was more than that. It was a means of changing hers and Harriet's life.

CHAPTER TWENTY-THREE

They spent the rest of the day settling Harriet in and teaching her all there was to know. She took to it as if born to be a nursery nurse, and the children loved her.

When the master called in, late in the afternoon, the children were sitting on their little chairs, which she and Harriet had carried out to the yard for them, listening to a story told by Harriet. They stood politely when he entered the yard, as did Harriet.

'Carry on ... Carry on. I heard a little of the story, and it was very interesting the way you were telling it, Mrs Wensley.'

'Ta, Master. I like being with children.'

'Good, good. Now, Mrs Randal, are you all set for tomorrow?'

'Aye, I am. I've nowt to take with me, so it's only a matter of opening me door.'

'Well, I've been having different thoughts. With you having Mrs Wensley here now, you might like to go a bit earlier. Edna sleeps in most nights anyway so she can tonight, as I'm not keen on you having to go back to the dormitory to be with the inmates – you should go to your own accommodation. And I have your advance here.'

As he handed her an envelope, Elisha's relief was enormous. She hadn't relished going back to her bed amongst the inmates, and hadn't wanted to send Harriet either so had already arranged that she would be the one sleeping in tonight.

An excitement mixed with trepidation took Elisha as she walked up the path to the cottage she'd been allocated. Each side of the path was a lawn, cut short and neat, with the one on the right belonging to her cottage as it extended under her small front window.

A smell of polish hit her as she turned the key and pushed the door open. The squeak of her sandals on the linoleum increased her sense of foreboding. There wasn't a good feeling about the place. Though neat and tidy, it was sparsely furnished – a hatstand in the entrance hall, a brown sofa and a side table in the living room, and two cupboards, a stove and a pot sink in the scullery.

The back door led to a small, concreted yard, with the outside lav and the coalhouse standing side by side attached to the scullery wall. This pleased her, as many were back to back with the neighbour, giving rise to embarrassing scenarios of folk carrying on a conversation whilst going about their business.

A loneliness clothed Elisha when she went back inside. Making herself busy, she opened cupboards and drawers, finding all she would need, including milk and bread on the cold slab and a small ham.

Suddenly feeling hungry, she filled the kettle and moved

it onto the hob, not questioning that the stove was lit, as the master would have seen to that, and made herself a doorstep sandwich.

The excitement had gone from the day, and the silence threatened to engulf her as she sat on the none too soft sofa. Not even looking forward to going to see Jean the next day made her feel better. All she could see ahead was a spinster existence, with no one to talk to or to turn to when she left work.

The prospect hung around her neck like a heavy millstone.

Not ten minutes later, a banging on her door made her jump.

'Can I come in, Elisha, only your door's open, lass?'

'Grace! Aye, you can come in and cheer me up.'

'Not sure I can do that, love, though I understand how you must feel being suddenly on your own. But I'm here because a tragedy has occurred.'

'Eeh, naw, what's happened?'

'Vera Longhouse, mother of the twins, has committed suicide! She slashed her wrists, poor soul. She was found behind the laundry. A mess she was.'

'Aw, naw. Have Betty and Ernest been told?'

'Aye, they were told their ma had gone to heaven, but they didn't really understand. It's sad but they would have been taken away soon, in any case. What are they, four and a half now?'

'Aye, poor little mites.'

'I knaw ... But, you've been crying, lass, are you, all right?'

Elisha felt she could confide in Grace. 'Naw. I can't see me living alone, year after year. I've never been alone.'

'I knaw how you feel. I couldn't think of doing it. I still live with me ma. You're welcome to come to ours whenever you want to, lass. Ma's been talking a lot lately about your grandma, since I told her about you.'

'Aw, ta, love.'

'Don't you have anyone apart from Harriet?'

'I have a couple of friends in Blackpool. I'm going to call in on them tomorrow . . . You might knaw one of them, the Strongman?'

'Oh, aye, I do. He got married recently. It was all in the *Gazette*.'

'So, they did it? Jean and him, I'm talking about. By, that makes me happy. I met Jean—'

'If this is going to be a long tale, I'll take the weight off me feet and put me bag down. There's room on that sofa for a little 'un!'

They both laughed at Grace poking fun at herself.

'I'll get you a cuppa. The kettle's on the side of the hob and won't take a mo to come back to the boil.'

Taking a sip of the hot tea a few minutes later, Grace asked, 'So, tell me about this Jean, then.'

Telling of how they'd met caused Elisha pain, as she could almost feel little Ted snuggled into her, suckling her breast. But Grace laughing at Jean sending the arrogant posh gentleman off with his tail between his legs lightened the moment and made it easier to carry on with her story.

'So, why didn't you contact this Jean and Bert, love? They sound like folk who would have helped you,' Grace asked once Elisha had finished her tale.

'I knaw, and they are nice, but it's never that easy, is it? I was distraught when everything happened, and because of me lovely Jack pleading guilty, it was all so fast. I found meself in the workhouse, me memory was very poor, I had naw money. It was just impossible.'

'I can see that. By, I've never met anyone who's been through as much as you have, lass. I'm sorry it all happened.'

'I'm still numb really. A couple of times I've broken, but never felt real release, it's like a knot in me chest that holds me as if in a vice. I reckon if it ever snaps, it'll be me in the madhouse. I nearly was once, but Harriet saved me.'

'Naw wonder you're close to each other.'

'We are, as I am to me friends Jan, Mick and Hetty, but they live in Surrey.'

'I read that you and your hubby were travelling there on a donkey when the mur – tragedy happened. Can't you write to them now that you're on your feet? We get leave once a year. You could maybe visit them. I'd like to think of you having folk in your life, lass.'

'I'm hoping that Jean has Jan's address, though I'm not sure she will have. I can't remember giving it to her, but I may have done – there's big gaps in my memory since . . .'

'Don't think about it, I didn't mean to drag it all up. Though I'm a great believer in talking rather than bottling things inside.'

'Aye, it's been good to talk.'

'So, now you've landed on your feet and you're off to the shops tomorrow? Well, to tide you over, me ma has sent one of her nighties. She ain't big like me, but more your size.' As she bent and pulled some garments out of her bag, Grace added, 'And a costume and blouse. They're a bit dowdy, being brown, though should suit you with your lovely golden locks. And the blouse, being cream, lightens the look.'

'Eeh, ta, Grace. And thank your ma for me. It's very thoughtful of her.'

'And at the bottom of the bag, separated by a newspaper, is a meat pie. You only have to put it into the oven when you're ready for it.'

The tears pricked Elisha's eyes at this. It had been a long time since she'd been shown any real kindness. And being in an emotional state meant that good things happening, as well as bad, could tip her over the edge.

Spontaneously, she hugged Grace. To her, Grace was another friend who she felt would always be there for her. Suddenly, all the lonely feelings left her. She had folk she could call on. She would start with Jean tomorrow and hope that led her to Jan and Hetty and Mick. Which might lead to other things in life for her, but she'd never move on without Harriet, and would always keep in touch with Grace and Edna.

Life wasn't so bad. She had prospects, and a lot to look forward to. She could almost hear her grandma saying, 'Never give up hope, lass, there's allus sommat around the corner.'

Aye, there is, Grandma, and it ain't allus good things for me. But I'll soldier on, I promise.

Not thinking she would, but after the meal of the delicious pie, a soak in the tin tub she'd found hanging in the yard, and a read of the newspaper, which gave her insight to the outer world and its happenings, Elisha slept peacefully all night in what proved to be a very cosy feather bed.

The morning brought excitement mixed with sadness, as the plight of Betty and Ernest came to her and marred a little what her day ahead held. Her mind went over and over what, if anything, she could do for them. Or what she'd be allowed to do. She wanted so much to adopt them and take care of them for ever, but that wasn't possible.

In the short time she'd known them, they had woven themselves into her heart. It consoled her that she would have them with her for at least another half year before they were taken away. How she would bear that though, she just didn't know.

All such thoughts left Elisha as she stood on the doorstep of Jean's house – somewhere she never dreamt she would ever stand again.

Dressed in the very smart costume, with its fitted jacket and straight skirt that just brushed her ankles, she must have looked very prosperous, when the reality was that she was wondering how she could afford to buy all she needed.

When Jean opened the door, she let out a wail that made Elisha jump, before enclosing her in her huge wobbly arms.

'Me Elisha, me lass ... Eeh, thank God, but where did you come from?'

'It's a long story, Jean, but, by, I'm so happy to be standing here.'

'Aw, lass, I heard some of what happened. It was all in the papers. Me heart's been breaking. I couldn't think how to get in touch with you ... Come in ... Eeh, Bert's going to be over the moon. He's been making enquiries you knaw, and so have others.'

When they got inside, Elisha had a sense of being home. Nothing had changed. She swallowed down the lump that came into her throat.

'You say others?'

'Aye, sit down. Kettle's on, so I'll tell you while it boils.'

Sinking into an armchair, Elisha waited.

'It was just yesterday. A solicitor he said he was. Name of Andrew Jackson, of Jackson & Jackson on Church Street. He said he had good news for you, and that he'd traced you as far as the court case but was waiting for papers to allow him to access the information about where you were sent after that. Then he said that his secretary – Wendy Baines, a woman I've known all me life – told him that I was a friend of yours, so he thought to try his luck here. But I couldn't help him.'

'Good news, you say? By, I could do with some of that. But I haven't an inkling what it could be.'

'It don't matter. In my books you're due some good things happening to you, though you don't look too bad. Has life treated you all right, since ... well, you knaw, lass?'

'Naw ... not until a few weeks ago ... I – I, aw, Jean ... I weren't going to cry ... but I – I've been to hell and back ...'

Huge sobs racked her body. It was as if all her defences came down. And there in the arms of the lovely Jean, Elisha emptied her soul.

When she calmed and sat drinking her tea, she was able to tell Jean all that had happened to her. Sometimes it seemed that's all she had – a horror story to tell, with a small bright light at the end of it with her now being the manager of the nursery.

'So, things might look up for you and this Harriet you've made friends with, lass? I really hope so ... Look, why don't you go into the kitchen and swill your face and then get off to that solicitor's and see what he has for you, eh?'

'Aye, I think I'd better, as I don't get another day off till next week. I don't think I can wait until then.'

The walk along the prom helped Elisha. She breathed in the sea air and enjoyed the calmness to be found with the season over, shutters down on the sideshows, and no hustle and bustle of traders and holidaymakers.

The breeze chilled her a little, but she didn't mind. It was a mild wind that lapped the sea onto the sand in a steady rhythmic way, soothing her turmoil.

In this, her own environment – a place she'd worked once a week running a market stall – she allowed memories. Smiled at some of them and felt pain at others. But, now drained of tears, she kept resolute in her quest to find this solicitor and hear his good news. What that could be, she had no idea, but prayed it was something that would change her and Harriet's life.

Turning into Church Street, she walked past the many shops with their pink and cream canopies, not stopping to window-shop, but gazing at each door hoping to see a plaque declaring it the office of Jackson & Jackson.

When at last she did, on an oak door between two shops, her nerves jangled with anticipation, but also a little fear. This news may not be what she wanted to hear – good news to one wasn't always so to another.

Ignoring these feelings, Elisha climbed the two steps and banged the shiny brass knocker. A few moments later, a thin woman with a pointed face opened the door. 'Yes?'

'I'm Elisha Randal. I've heard that one of the solicitors, Andrew Jackson, has been looking for me.'

'Aye, I knaw who you are, you're so like your ma, there's naw mistaking you. Come in, and I'll see if Mr Jackson can see you.'

Elisha followed who she assumed was the Wendy that Jean had told her of, her feet sinking into the thick red and gold carpet as they climbed the stairs, and her nose assailed by the smell of polish.

'This way.'

They went through a door that was half oak and half thick, bubbled glass. A plaque beneath the glass declared 'Andrew Jackson'.

Nerves now gripped Elisha's stomach.

'Don't look so scared, lass. Take a seat.' Wendy indicated a bench opposite another door. The cold leather covering of the bench sent a shiver through Elisha as she sat down.

Within seconds of Wendy knocking and entering Andrew Jackson's office, she came out smiling – an expression that softened her face and had the effect of relaxing Elisha.

'Mr Jackson will see you right away, Mrs Randal.'

Elisha didn't know why, but on seeing Andrew she felt immediately at home with him. When she took his outstretched hand, it was almost as if Jack had come alive and was reaching out to her. It was his eyes – they were the same as Jack's, dark and twinkly, with smile lines etched into the corners. His hair was fairer than Jack's and his face different – handsome, as Jack's was, but with more defined features.

He frowned and asked, 'Are you all right?'

Coming out of the daze she'd gone into, Elisha nodded. 'Aye, sorry. I'm just curious. Jean – me friend as you called on – told me that you had good news for me?'

'I do indeed. Please, take a seat.'

The chair he indicated was more like a dining chair than an office chair, with its curved mahogany back and red velvet seat pad. Realising how wobbly her legs felt, Elisha sank down, grateful for its support.

'Now, I need to run through a few details with you to verify you are who you say you are. And then I'll tell you the news you have come to hear.'

After checking her maiden name, and the address she'd lived at with her ma, da and grandma, he looked up. His eyes held hers.

'And where do you live now?'

'Until yesterday, I was registered at Wesham Workhouse, but—'

'Good Lord! I knew you had been committed to a workhouse, and felt dreadfully sorry about that, but to think you were just down the road and we could have saved you from that is distressing.'

'Saved me!'

'Yes. I have news for you of a legacy left by your grandma – Mrs Millicent Finley.'

At the gasp that came from Elisha, Andrew looked concerned. 'I see this is a shock to you. Can I get you anything ... A glass of water?'

'Naw, ta. But aye, it is a shock. I had naw idea Grandma had a solicitor, let alone left a will! Me uncle came and claimed everything ... there was naw bank account. Me grandma allus said that under the bed was a good enough bank for what she squirrelled away.'

'She didn't until about six weeks before she died. She came to see my father and he sorted one out for her. She deposited an amount and asked that it be written down that it was for her granddaughter, Elisha Finley, when she reached the age of twenty-one, whether her own demise had taken place by then or not. According to the birth date we have for you, 14th March 1887, I believe you reached that age this year.'

Not able to take in all he was saying, Elisha repeated in her mind ... *Me grandma left me some money!*

'Mrs Randal?'

'Sorry ... Aye, I did.'

'Well, I'm pleased to inform you that the sum of your legacy is three hundred pounds.'

Elisha could only stare. Her body began to shake. The past crowded her – the struggles, the concerns, the loss, and now this massive gift from her grandma.

'How . . . ? Why . . . ?'

'Well, the original amount was twenty pounds, a huge sum in late 1900 when it was deposited. My father persuaded your grandmother to let him invest it. He was a whizz at picking the stocks that would do well – though, as with every wager, they could do badly too – and, by a stroke of luck, not long before he died he cashed in the value. He had complete power of attorney to do so. He then banked the capital. If he hadn't done, you may have lost a great deal of it during last year when stocks and shares suffered. They are only just recovering now.'

'You mean, me grandma left me twenty pounds and your da increased that for me by gambling?'

'Quite safe gambling, as he knew the markets. He put it into gold and other precious metals.'

'Eeh, I wish he was here now so I could thank him. He's changed me life.'

'Your grandma did that – first, in putting this money aside for you, and second in agreeing to it being invested, as the risks would have been explained to her . . . May I ask if there's something you particularly want to do?'

'Aye, there is. I want me grandma's cottage back. It's called Primula Cottage and it has a market garden on Common Edge Road. By, I'd offer the owners the lot of this money if they'd sell to me.'

'You won't have to. I've always been interested in the story of your grandma, so much so that I visited the cottage to see where she lived and worked and amassed such a grand sum to invest for you. It's in a bit of a tumbledown state now and is still owned by the bank. They never did find a buyer for it. I think you could buy it for around one hundred pounds, but it would need a lot spending on it.'

Elisha burst into tears.

'Oh, my dear. I – I know this has been a lot to take in. Let me fetch Mrs Baines in, I'll get her to make you a cup of tea.'

'Naw, it's all right, honest. I was just overcome ... I've been through so much that this money could have saved me from, and now I have a chance of getting everything back and realising me da's dream.'

'Your father's dream?'

'Aye, me da allus dreamt of buying the field behind the cottage and having farm animals to expand their business, but I lost what they had built up and never stood a chance of making happen what me da so wanted.'

Andrew coughed again. 'Look, I read the court papers about your husband's case and know what happened to you both – to you in particular – and I cried when I read your testament ... I'm not one to do that. But you didn't lose your father's dream. The elements, the wickedness of others, the bad judgement of your husband – these are what caused the loss. Put it all behind you and begin again. And, if you want me to, I will guide you along the way.' He grinned then. A lovely cheeky grin. 'I'm not saying I can dig or plant, but I can make sure everything runs smoothly for you in the buying, the cost of renovations, and any planning permissions you may need – anything on the legal side you may encounter.'

'What does that kind of help cost?'

Andrew laughed out loud. 'Good question and shows me that, from what I know of your grandmother, you have her qualities. As regards my fees, there are set guidelines that give you the cost of different processes, and I will always factor the cost of my fee into whatever legal work I am called upon to sort out for you. But as regards general advice, that will come free of charge. I want to support you, Elisha . . . may I call you that?'

'Aye. And ta. I think with someone like you advising me, I can get back on me feet . . . There's sommat else though . . . Naw, it's all right, I'll leave it for now.'

'No. Tell me. If I have the full picture of what your ambitions or worries are, I shall be in a much better place to advise you.'

Elisha opened up on all her hopes and dreams – wanting to be a teacher, wanting to help Harriet, and Edna and her mum, even how she would like to adopt Betty and Ernest, and finishing with how she so wanted to find her friends, Jan, Mick and Hetty.

Andrew hadn't taken his eyes off her. Now he said, 'You're a remarkable person, Elisha. And, yes, I can help you to do those things.'

Elisha held his eyes, found in them a kindness and understanding, and yet with no demands made on her. She wanted to hug him. The feeling shocked her. Shame washed over her as she told herself she was betraying her lovely Jack. She cast her eyes downwards.

CHAPTER TWENTY-FOUR

As she left the building, Elisha had a moment of disorientation come over her. Had that really happened? Was she truly a rich woman? Standing on the pavement and looking around her at the people hustling and bustling, it seemed that she'd walked through a door as one person and come out as another.

Her thoughts raced. Primula Cottage was up for sale. Andrew was going to see to the purchase of it, and it would once more belong to her! It all seemed so incredible.

Her mind gave her a picture of her grandma, sitting with her hands in her lap, smiling and nodding her head.

Grandma couldn't have imagined what this moment would be like when she'd made this arrangement. That it would come to fruition just as her granddaughter was trying to crawl out of the gutter.

What were you thinking, Grandma? That the money would take me to college? Pay my fees, and give me independence? What an amazing woman you were, and I won't let you down again. I'll bring your cottage back to its former glory, I'll build a business you would be proud of, I'll extend into the back field as Da dreamt of doing.

But none of these thoughts solved her immediate problems. She needed to buy a couple of skirts, a blouse and a jacket, as she couldn't just leave her job, that wouldn't be fair after the master had put such faith in her. But maybe one of the others who'd applied for the job was a suitable candidate and could step in and allow her to be released very soon.

But, if so, that would bring other problems – where to live until the cottage was ready, and what to do about Harriet. She couldn't leave her in the workhouse. Oh, why hadn't she thought of all of this when she was talking to Andrew?

As if he knew her predicament, the door behind her opened. 'You haven't got far! Are you all right? You look a little lost.'

'I am. I feel as though there's a lot of weight on me shoulders, as I've so much to sort out.'

'Would talking a little longer, help? Only I'm just going across to the café for lunch. Have you time to join me? Maybe having a chat about the minor details whilst out of the office atmosphere will help.'

'Ta, I am hungry. And me head's in a spin.'

'I'm not surprised.'

After hearing her worries over a lovely bowl of vegetable soup and a doorstep of fresh bread, Andrew relaxed back in his chair.

'Well, there are a few mountains to climb by the sound of it, but like everything in life they are surmountable – especially by a lady of means. Let's take each problem at a time. You don't just have a couple of pounds, you have a small fortune, so we need to get access to it as soon as possible. This we can do by visiting the bank. That will be quicker than the conventional way of writing to them to set up an account in your name. We can do that now if you like, I have a couple of hours before another client is due.'

'Ta. It'd be good to have it to draw on.'

'As far as accommodation, you can go to an estate agent after the bank – Graham Michaels' is a good one, just over the road. I'm sure they have many properties to rent. They cover from Fleetwood to Lytham. You could go for a furnished one, or unfurnished and buy the furniture you would want to put into the cottage later.'

'Eeh, it all sounds so simple, but I ain't got the time until I leave me job, and if I leave me job, I have to leave the cottage that goes with it!'

'Right. Leave your job as soon as you can, then book yourself into a hotel whilst you organise everything.'

Nothing was a problem to Andrew. This solution seemed the ideal one, but to her – not used to having the money to do such things – it hadn't occurred.

'Now that's a lovely smile, and one that I hope will stay on your face – it changes you from someone downtrodden to someone very beautiful, and with all the hope in the world.'

Elisha blushed. He'd called her beautiful. She lowered her eyes. When she looked up, Andrew was staring at her. Once more she held his gaze.

What is happening to me? How is it I can have these feelings with me Jack not gone a year yet?

Telling herself she was being silly and disloyal, that suddenly coming into money and Andrew being the bearer of that news was making her confused between being grateful and other deeper feelings didn't help, it only increased her guilt.

As if nothing had happened, Andrew wiped his mouth with his napkin, grinned at her and asked, 'Shall we get to the bank then, or would you like to go to the estate agent first?'

This brought Elisha back down to earth.

'I'd like to go to the bank, then I need to buy some clothes and get back to the workhouse to begin working out me future.'

'That sounds like a good plan ... And Elisha, it will all work out. You will jump the hurdles and I'll be there every step of the way for you.'

Elisha relaxed, but then it occurred to her to wonder if she would even be believed when she told the master everything. She could hardly believe it herself!

'Would you do one more thing for me? Would you write me a letter to give to the master of the workhouse, telling him all that has gone on and how you will be helping me to get settled?'

'That's a good idea, and I will tell him that he needs to release you as soon as he can so that you can live the life you were meant to live. I'll even put in that your friend – what was her name?'

'Harriet Wensley.'

'Right, it seems to be apparent to me that you will need her to support you through this, so I'll request that her release is scheduled for the same time. Once we have that secured, I'll book you both into a hotel and then we can begin to sort out your future.'

'How long will it take to buy the cottage and have it back in my name? And how will you do that if the money is all in my bank account?'

'I can see you have so many questions. Well, we will deal with them all as they arise. As far as paying the bank for the cottage, you will be there when we sign the papers, and the deeds given to you, then you will pay the cheque for the amount we negotiate.'

Elisha felt a bit silly at this. Of course, she'd known how business works and the buying and selling of property, but all of it had crowded her and she hadn't been able to sort her thoughts out.

By the time Elisha arrived back at her cottage, having been back to see Jean and been hugged so hard by Bert that she'd lost her breath for a moment, she was laden down with shopping and just wanted to go and see Harriet. Though her feet hurt and she needed a cuppa, she dumped her bags and walked to the workhouse.

The master was just coming out of his office as she entered through the large front door. 'Now, this is dedication – coming in on your day off!'

'If it's all right, I'd like a word, Master.'

'Well, as long as it's quick. I was just going on my rounds before everyone finishes work for recreation.'

Following him back into his office, Elisha produced the letter. 'I need you to read this.'

The master's expression changed from utter surprise to a smile. 'Well, well! What a wonderful thing to happen! Congratulations, Elisha. I couldn't be happier for you. And of course I can release you very soon. There was another perfect candidate, and I know she will be more than ready to step in at almost a minute's notice. I will write to her this evening and have the letter delivered to her house. I would ask that you work with her for at least a week so that she can get to know the ropes that you have so excellently put into place.'

Elisha could have hugged him. 'Ta. Ta ever so much … And Mrs Wensley?'

'She can go with you, of course. I will discharge her into your care, just as soon as you can show me you have somewhere to stay, which seems highly likely with Mr Jackson seeing to every detail for you. Your future looks how it should – bright and full of promise.'

Elisha grinned. 'It don't seem possible, and I can't take it in, but aye, I'm on the up and up.'

As she left the office, elation gripped Elisha. It truly was going to happen! She and Harriet were getting out of here.

As she approached the nursery, Harriet must have spotted her through the window as the door flung open and she stood there aghast.

'Look at you! By, you look amazing! How did you afford that costume?'

'Eeh, Harriet, I've so much to tell you. We're getting out of here, me and you, lass. We're truly getting out of here!

But, eeh, I need a drop of tea afore I can even begin to tell you what's happened.'

'Well, you're in luck, Edna has just gone through to make us one. The young 'uns are all settled. And though Edna wants to get off in time for recreation with her ma, as you knaw, I've got all night.'

Calling through to the scullery to Edna to make an extra cup as the boss was here, Harriet let out a giggle. 'Seems funny calling you the boss, lass.'

'Aye, it does. But I won't be for much longer.'

Edna came through carrying a tray with a teapot, milk jug and three cups and saucers balancing on it. She in turn gaped at Elisha.

'It's a long story, sit down, lass, I'll tell the best bit as quick as I can and then you can go to be with your ma . . . But lass, tell your ma that it may take me a little time, but I will get you both out of here, and that's a promise.'

Neither spoke as Elisha told them about meeting her friend Jean and how that led to visiting the solicitor's. But when she mentioned the money, Edna put her hand over her open mouth and stared incredulously at her, and Harriet let out a little cry of joy.

After a moment, Edna said, 'Eeh, I'll have to go to me ma.'

'You will, but don't say owt to anyone other than her, and swear her to secrecy. Just give me time to put things in place afore it becomes common knowledge, lass.'

'I promise, but by, I feel sick with shock and the hope you've given us, Elisha. And I'm right pleased for you, I am.'

When she'd gone, Harriet, who had recovered from the shock, said, 'I can't take it in. So, you're rich?'

'Aye, and I'm going to buy back me cottage and start a business all over, with you by me side, but that's all to be sorted. First, we're getting out of here, in days maybe, or as fast as the master can arrange me replacement, and then going to stay in a hotel until the rest can be worked out – somewhere for us to rent until the cottage is ready for us. Aw, Harriet, life's going to change.'

As Harriet listened, Elisha outlined all that had been going through her head. Harriet had a smile glued to her face throughout, and she reached out her hands and took Elisha's. 'You've changed me life, lass. Eeh, I just can't believe it.'

'I knaw, I just wish me Jack was here to enjoy it an' all.'

'I knaw, but we can never go back, only forward. But we can do that for our lost loved ones, as they can't. So, no doldrums, not when there's so much to celebrate, eh?'

There didn't seem much time to celebrate, or to think of 'if only', over the next few days. Everything happened in a whirl.

Edith, as the new manager of the nursery was called, arrived and was, as described, the perfect candidate. Plump, with a lovely mumsy smile and dimpled cheeks, the children loved her. Though they cried when the time came and they learnt that Elisha and Harriet would be leaving.

In comforting them, Elisha so wanted to tell Betty and Ernest that she would one day come for them, but she couldn't. When she did, they would learn their ma was in heaven with their da, and that would be so much for them to take in. In the outside world, she could make it easier for them, but not here when she had to leave them. So, she gave them the same cuddles as she gave to all the children, and left them all in the care of Edith, reassured they would be loved as she had loved them.

'By, it's going to be hard stepping into your shoes, but I'll do me best, lass. You go and have a good life, as what I've heard it ain't been so since you were a young 'un.'

'Naw, that's not right. I did have bad times, but me Jack were a lovely man, and we were happy. He weren't what he did, that can't mark him as who he was. He was a good, kind man who was pushed into madness for a moment of his life.'

'Aye, well, lass. You don't have to justify him to me. Your love shines from you when you speak of him, and that's for you to hang on to. Your memories are yours.'

This sounded as if Edith was saying, 'but she knew better'. Elisha sighed. Unable to fight back in front of the children, she just accepted this and waved her goodbyes.

Saying goodbye to Edna wasn't nearly as painful, as Elisha had plans to come for her too and vowed to make it as soon as she could. Edna took no notice of the fear of being called names, she just hugged and hugged Elisha until they were both giggling. 'The time will soon pass, Edna. I'll write to you to keep you informed.'

Edna wiped a tear and gave a beaming smile. 'Me and Ma can't wait.'

When they turned to go, Harriet linked her arm in hers, 'Don't take on owt as Edith says, lass. It's just ignorance. They see the crime, not the man. It's the same with me, they see a madwoman, not someone pushed over the edge who can be comforted and helped.'

'Well, I hope you never have cause to feel you're being pushed over the edge again, love. I'm here for you, and together we'll be fine.'

They had a room in the Metropole Hotel, the only hotel on the seafront of Blackpool. A majestic building they'd both admired and never dreamt they would ever stay in. The huge, grand four-poster bed, draped in gold and red fabric, looked as though it would swallow them, and the ceramic bath was so deep they were afraid to get in it at first. When they did, they giggled together and drank from glasses of fizzy lemonade.

'Let's go for a walk along the prom afore dinner, eh?'

'Aye, that'd be grand.'

As they walked along the prom, arm in arm, Elisha remembered times past with Jan and Hetty, eating seafood on the wall, with the sounds of Blackpool ringing in their ears. She so wanted Andrew to find Jan for her. If only she could remember their address. Although Andrew had told her that there were means of tracing folk.

The sea was calm, just lapping the sand, though the tide would shortly start its rise to the sea walls. To Elisha, it was paradise, as the soft breeze played with her hair and tingled her cheeks.

A little ahead, a crowd had gathered. Something that often happened along the prom if some entertainer or other was vying for pennies to be dropped into his hat. When they reached the gathering, they saw it was Bert, lifting an iron bar. Jean sat to his left at a little table, selling tickets.

'Jean!'

'Eeh, lass. It's good to see you. Have you left that place now, then?'

'Aye, just today. I was coming to see you tomorrow, only it's been hectic, handing over and such like.'

'Well, you're seeing me now, me lass. Come and give us a cuddle.'

As always, Jean's cuddles were the best.

'I'm selling tickets for the circus in the tower. Bert has a job with them, and this is part of what the showmen do – perform on the streets to help to sell tickets.'

'Aw, I'd love some. Me ma and da took me once a long time ago and I've never forgotten it. What about you, Harriet?'

'Count me in, I ain't never been to a circus.'

After selling them the tickets, Jean said, 'We're having our supper at Roberts' Oyster Bar. What about you, can you eat with us?'

Elisha hesitated. So many memories had visited her, was this one too many?

Picking up on this, Jean said, 'Eeh, don't worry, lass, I knaw some things can hurt. And I remember you told me of having supper in Roberts' a while back.'

'Naw, I'd be glad to. I can't hide from all that hurts. I've to keep Jack's memory alive – the memories of the good times are important and that was one of them. Me, Jan and Hetty paddled in the sea. And we ate seafood out of newspaper. It was grand. And Jack enjoyed a pint ... Let's do it, eh? Let's have a paddle and then some seafood.'

'Don't be such a daft ha'peth, ha! Me, paddle? I'd wobble and fall over!'

This set them laughing.

The sound of clapping silenced them as Bert took his bow to the crowd. 'Just one more lift,' he said, 'then that's your lot ... Elisha, you sit on one of me arms and your friend on the other.'

'What? Naw! I ain't being lifted!'

But taking no heed of her protests, Bert grabbed her, wrapped her tightly in a blanket and lifted her high in the air.

Her laughter rang out, as did that of the crowd, as he began to twirl her around. The sensation was weird, being high above the crowd and twirling above them, but funny too, leaving her unable to control her giggling.

When finally he put her down and unwrapped her, she flailed him with her fists, much to the crowd's amusement. None of her blows had the least impact other than to have Bert put his head back and roar with laughter. He was a giant and she a butterfly, tickling him with her wings.

Giving up, she told him, 'You can buy the seafood now!'

He bent down and held her in a gentle hug. 'Eeh, me Elisha, it's good to have you back with us, lass.'

At this moment it felt good to be back on the promenade of her beloved Blackpool and with the friends she loved. The thought came that she wished she could turn back the clock, but then it could never happen, so she didn't dwell on this, just enjoyed the moment she was in. She was in her hometown – she was free and soon, she would be back in Primula Cottage, making her dream come true.

PART FIVE

Hope of a New Beginning
A WEEK LATER

CHAPTER TWENTY-FIVE

Awake early, Elisha lay staring at the ceiling, trying to piece her life together. How young she was when it had all changed. How Jack had been like a light beaming in a very sheltered life that had gone horribly wrong. How she'd been encouraged to remain insular and focused on her dream and, yes, how lonely that had made her, with no one to turn to when those who had closeted her were gone.

The shock of her uncle's vile treatment of her. Making her feel of no worth. And how the love she had inside her was so readily given to those who were kind to her. And how fragile life was. Not just the living and dying, but the breaking of one's mind, as had happened to Jack and to Harriet. And the losing of people as they moved on in their lives.

Did it all have a purpose? Did she? What of those little children in the workhouse and their mas whose hearts were torn in shreds? Why?

And why did she have this dream to continue her da's dream and achieve it for him? What of her own dreams to be a teacher and make a difference in the lives of each child she taught? Had she given up on that? Wasn't this what Grandma had in mind when she put the money aside for her – not for her to fulfil someone else's dream but to chase her own?

It was as if at this moment she was shedding the burdens of the past and opening a path to a future – her own future.

The very short time she'd spent with the children in the workhouse, teaching them, changing their lives in a small but significant way, had fulfilled her. This was the path she should tread, not the one her da had wanted to walk. They were his dreams to have; she had her own.

Suddenly, it was as if her da was releasing her of her promise. Shining a light on her future. Guiding her to the path she must take.

At this thought, Elisha filled with a joy she hadn't felt for a long time. A true freedom. Not just a freedom from confinement, but the freedom to live her own life and achieve her own dreams. But how?

She still had the dream to own Primula Cottage once more, but did she want to go back to market gardening? Couldn't she use the land to make a playground? And Jack's shed could be repaired and extended to become a schoolroom. The field at the back of the cottage, which Andrew was negotiating to buy for her, could still house animals, but of the kind that children loved and could help to look after – a dog and cat who would be house pets, but rabbits in a hutch with a good run, and chickens – she and Jack had loved keeping hens and Matty their cockerel. And they could have horses for the children to ride and groom.

She giggled then at the thought of this menagerie getting along together. But then thought of how the children would love being with the animals, and to do gardening too. They could have patches of the land in front of the house as vegetable gardens and others as flower gardens, but mostly it would be lush grass for them to play on, and a hard surface for their ball games – football for the boys and rounders for the girls.

An eager excitement filled Elisha at the thought of all this. This would be her new dream.

Sitting up, she looked over at Harriet. 'Come on, sleepyhead, wake up! I've a lot to tell you!'

Harriet stretched. 'What? What time is it?'

'I don't knaw, there's naw clock in here, but it's light so it must be getting on seven.'

'Seven! Why are you so flipping bright and breezy? I thought this being our first chance in almost for ever to have a lie-in, you'd be still in the Land of Nod!'

'Naw, I've dreams to fulfil, and so have you!'

'Well, you can't start to dig that field for your da until you own it, so go back to sleep.'

'I'm not going to. Me dreams have changed – well, not changed, but become me own, not me da's. I feel free to live me own life, Harriet, and I want to share your dreams with you.'

Harriet sat up, rubbed her eyes and said, 'Well, me dream afore you woke me was being in the arms of a handsome man who would take care of me.'

They both giggled. And this went into a girlish, playful laughter as Harriet threw her pillow at Elisha. And then squeals as they turned back the clock and became full of the joys of life in a full-blown pillow fight that had them releasing their past for just a few crazy moments.

'Stop! Stop, you win!' Elisha, beaten and helplessly floppy as her energy drained for a moment, gave in.

'Right, as the winner, I demand a hug!'

They fell into each other's arms.

'We'll allus look out for one another, won't we?'

'We will, Harriet. I promise. And as I realise me dreams, so will you.'

As they came out of the hug and faced each other, Harriet said, 'Well, you'd better tell me yours, I can see you're bursting to.'

'To own and run me own school for little children!'

'Now that's a surprise, lass!'

They giggled once more.

'So, naw market garden then?'

'Naw. I'm going to turn Jack's potting shed – or where it stood – into a schoolroom ...'

By the time she'd finished outlining all her plans, Harriet had a look of wonderment on her face. 'By, lass, you dream big, but you can achieve it all, I knaw you can.'

'Aye, but I can leave room for your dream an' all, love, and I knaw that's sommat to do with weaving.'

'Naw, not altogether. I – I fell in love, Elisha ... I want to marry again and have kids, and yes, I want to weave as a hobby – clothes for me kids, covers for me furniture, and even bits to sell – but mostly I want to be with the man I love.'

Elisha's mouth dropped open. This was the last thing she'd expected in all the world. 'What? Who?'

'Edwin, the man I went with.'

'The man who ... Oh, Harriet, I had naw idea. Have you seen him since? Was it an instant thing? Do you even knaw him?'

'Aye, I can answer yes to all of them questions. I knaw I went to him for the price of a loom, but I found not someone who would take a woman at a price, but a man who was kind. He wasn't the one who'd made a loom for the woman I told you about.'

Elisha could only stare, as Harriet continued. 'And, aye, I did feel dirty in a way and that I'd lowered meself because I'd offered meself to a man for payment. That marred what it turned out to be, a loving, giving to each other, but then that fight, and me going into the asylum ... But I saw Edwin. He came to the fence. We held hands. He told me he loved me ... It was just that our situation was hopeless ...'

'Aw, Harriet, I'm sorry ... Eeh, lass, why didn't you tell me all of this?'

Harriet lowered her head. 'I tried, but it all seemed ... Eeh, I don't knaw, lass.'

Elisha took Harriet into her arms once more. 'We'll get Edwin out, I promise. You said he was a carpenter, didn't you? By, I'm going to need one of them. I can give him plenty of work, and for a start he could convert one of the barns for him to live in while he carries out me plans for me schoolroom.'

Harriet clung to her. 'I bless the day I met you, Elisha. Ta, lass. But me and Edwin have spoken about getting out and one day having our own business. Him working with wood, making furniture, and me weaving the cloths for the chairs and sofas. Eeh, we did dream in the moments we had together.'

'I'll help you. I can. I have enough money to invest in you, Harriet.'

'Really? By, Elisha, you'll be broke at this rate!'

'Naw. Once I've bought back Primula Cottage, the possibilities are endless. It has land, and buildings – broken-down buildings, but they can be repaired and turned into workshops, and maybe another cottage could be built ... there's so much we could do together.'

Harriet lifted her head. 'By, it feels like we've landed on our feet, all of us – me, Edwin, Edna and her ma – and all because of you and your grandma.'

'We have, love, we have.'

'Trouble is, I want it to happen now! I want to go and get Edwin out of that hole and start me new life with him. And Edna and her ma, an' all.'

'That's how I feel. I want me dream now, I don't want it to be a dream but a reality, but eeh, we've a lot to do afore then, though as soon as I own the cottage, we can get Edwin out and he can begin work on the renovations I've mentioned.'

'But what of the meantime, where will we live? We can't stay in a hotel, it doesn't feel like a life!'

'That's our mission today. To go to an estate agent and find a place for us to live .... and, well, I want to visit the cemetery today an' all. I want to buy flowers and put them on the graves of me little Ted, me ma, me da and me grandma ... and for me lovely Jack an' all, though he ain't buried there.'

'I've not got any graves, me ma and me Harry had paupers' burials.'

'Well, you can do as I am for Jack and just put flowers at the churchyard for them.'

'Naw, me Harry allus talked of being a sailor. He dreamt of being in a boat on the sea. And he loved it if we visited me ma. And me ma loved to bring me down here to the seafront an' all. I'd like to put flowers in the sea and watch them float, and imagine it's me Harry floating as he allus wanted to.'

'That's lovely. We'll do that, eh? And I'll do it for Jack an' all, as he liked to be down here by the sea. He loved market days, though they were hard work for him with his bad breathing. He allus said that he improved the nearer to the sea he got. I'd like to think of him floating out to somewhere he could breathe and be happy.'

Harriet jumped up. 'Right, let's do it. We've a lot to get through ... Now, what shall we wear? By, it's a good job you had that shopping spree, lass. It were good to get out of that uniform.'

'I'm having the grey costume and pink blouse, so the choice is yours after that,' Elisha said.

'I'll go for the navy one and a white blouse ... eeh, lass, I never thought the day would come that I had a choice of such finery!'

'Naw, nor did I. Though I never wanted for owt as a youngster. Ma used to dress me in pretty clothes, and as I grew I had a choice of skirts and blouses.'

'Aye, I had me share – a lot were from jumbles, but they were good stuff. Me ma did well by me ... I feel I've let her down in a way.'

'Well, you can make her proud of you now, you can build your empire!' They gigged again, like two excited children as they washed and dress and both realised how hungry they were.

Over a breakfast of porridge followed by a boiled egg with bread and butter, they talked more about their plans for the future, making it all come alive and attainable.

The day was blustery and threatened showers as April always did, though in two days it would be May. Already as they passed the old houses in New Street, a tree in the garden of one of the cottages was full of blossom, which shed like snow in the breeze.

They held on to their hats – both large, with Elisha's matching her costume, only having a pink border to the brim, while Harriet had been left with the only other one Elisha had bought – a pale blue.

Linking into Harriet's arm, Elisha laughed at Harriet's antics with her hat. 'By, I ain't ever worn a hat like this, only a bonnet, but by 'eck, they were easier to keep on. And kept your ears warm an' all.'

'Ha, those were daft buys, but I felt like that on the day – flippant, and as if I were a different person.'

'Well, I suggest you buy a couple of bonnets and be the practical woman you've allus had to be. This is like a nightmare!'

At that moment the wind won, as both their hats left their heads and went on their own adventure, leaving Elisha and Harriet each nursing the place where the hatpin had been pulled roughly from their hair.

Watching the joyful hats twisting and turning in the wind, Harriet said, 'Eeh, I knaw just how they feel, lass ... As free as the wind, as free as the birds, as that's what I feel like. As if shackles have been taken off me.'

Elisha giggled and squeezed Harriet's arm. 'I knaw, but we can't present ourselves hatless, it ain't seemly. We'll have to buy a couple of bonnets.'

A few minutes later they walked out of a hattery with practical, smaller hats that had elastic bands that went under their chins. Still very smart and up to the minute, Elisha's was grey with a pink polka dot lining that showed under the high brim, and Harriet was happy and looking lovely in a navy bonnet to match her suit, which sported a fashionable bow in white satin on the side of its brim.

'That's better, I can take on any Blackpool wind in this!'

'Ha, you look like you can take on the world, Harriet, let alone Blackpool!'

The estate agent was able to show them a number of short-term lets. 'We specialise in them, madam,' he told Elisha. 'There's a few of the upper-class who prefer to rent rather than buy when they come to take the waters. I can recommend all the properties, they're all well kept. How long are you looking to rent for?'

'It could be at least two months, though I ain't altogether sure. It'll depend on how long it takes for me cottage to be ready for me.'

He didn't question her having money and yet speaking in her native accent, as a lot of Blackpudlians had made a packet out of the holidaymaking trade, so he was used to serving locals.

'Well, we do like a place to be taken for the season by rights.'

'That'll be fine. I'll look at sommat a bit away from the prom, though ... Maybe Lytham Road, or St Anne's Road? They are closer to where me cottage, which will be me permanent home, is.'

'Ahh, we have a nice property in St Anne's Road. A four-bedroomed house on the corner of Highfield Road.' He produced a photograph. Elisha recognised the house and jumped at the chance to live in it. 'Ta, I'll take it, but I need immediate possession. Is it furnished?'

'Aye, it's nicely furnished. And we can supply any household staff you may need.'

'I'll think about that. There may be a few of us live in the house, so we'll probably manage.'

'Family, you mean?'

'Aye, sort of ... Friends, who've become family.'

He didn't look so sure, but Elisha didn't give him time to object. 'So, what rent do you require?'

Hesitating for a moment, then making his mind up, the agent asked for two months' rent in advance, 'Three pounds six shillings, madam.'

Trying not to look like a novice as she wrote the cheque, Elisha kept her gloves on, not wanting to show her work-torn hands.

'Are you sure you don't want to inspect the property first, madam?'

'Naw, it'll be fine. Ta, for the offer though. I just need the key, and we'll move in.'

After signing an agreement to rent until the end of August, Elisha hoped with all her heart that she wasn't there until then, but it felt good to know that she had somewhere until her cottage was ready.

Once out on the pavement outside the shop, she had an urge to go to see the house, and without saying anything flagged down a passing carriage. As they climbed in and sat down on the leather bench, the driver put up the pram-type cover to protect them.

'That's better. I thought we'd have our heads blown off in an open carriage.'

'By, you've blown mine off! Eeh, Elisha, you're a quick mover, lass. How do you knaw this house is right for us? You've only seen the outside. And who's a few of us?'

'It's that feeling I get about a place. I've allus admired it. It has bay windows, and you can see a tree in the garden at the back. And just a small frontage that has shrubs growing, so takes naw looking after. It's in a sunny spot and is handy for the shops. And best of all, we can walk to the cottage, or we can buy a couple of bikes. Can you ride a bicycle?'

'Aye, I can, but you ain't answered me question as to who the rest are that are joining us.'

'Well, I keep thinking of Edna and her ma stuck in there, and if they're with us, as sort of chaperones, then why not Edwin?'

'Aw, lass, would you do that for me?'

'Of course. Anyroad, it's for me an' all, as the house will be a good base for him as he works on the cottage ... But, well, I don't want this to sound bad, only, well, I'd like to meet him first, and ... look, I'd want the pair of you to be ... Eeh, how do I say it?'

'You mean, we ain't to jump into each other's bed! Ha, you try and stop me!'

They both burst out laughing at this.

'Oh, but Harriet, you'll be discreet, won't you? I mean, if Edna and her ma are there ... It might upset them.'

'Not what I knaw of Polly it won't.'

'Polly?'

'Aye, that's Edna's ma. And she ain't a sourpuss, nor a killjoy, she loves a laugh. She's a woman of the world. She knew about women going to the men's quarters, but she never judged. You'll like her, I knaw you will.'

This relaxed Elisha a little, but she still didn't like the idea of such things going on in the house – not between unmarried folk.

As if she'd read her mind, Harriet said, 'I'm only joking about visiting Edwin's bed, love. He ain't like that. Aye, I knaw it comes across as if he is, and what we did that first time, well, it just happened – two lonely, sad and desperate people giving comfort. But he's said many a time that if ever we got out of there, we'd court proper and then marry afore it ever happened again.'

'Aw, that's lovely to hear, Harriet, it shows he has respect for you, and that's good. I'm liking him already.'

'I knaw you will. I'm still getting to knaw him. I mean, you can't knaw a fella from a quick rough and tumble and a few visits behind barbed wire, but I knaw he's the man I want to spend me life with. And he says the same. He feels he's met someone who understands his pain, who he feels comfortable being sad or happy with. He says he loves me.'

Elisha stretched her arm and put it around Harriet. 'I'm really happy for you, love. You deserve to find someone as good as your Harry.'

'It does feel a bit disloyal to Harry though ... I mean, I loved him with all me heart, so how can I give that same love to another?'

Elisha didn't answer this, she just made a gesture with her shoulders and showed with her expression that she didn't know. She didn't have the answer, as the question had come up for herself with her awakening feelings for Andrew. Something she never thought would happen or ever knew it could. But it was there, no matter how much she tried to deny it. And it filled her with shame and guilt, as well as the hopelessness of it. A gentleman of Andrew's standing wouldn't look at anyone from her class in a million years.

But then she shocked herself as she thought how she so wanted him to.

CHAPTER TWENTY-SIX

After asking the driver to wait for them outside, Elisha found the house was all she had thought it would be – from the entrance porch, with its polished, red-tiled floor, to the hall they walked through that had a door leading to a living room, furnished with a gold velvet winged sofa and two matching armchairs, which looked as though they would cuddle you when you sat in them.

They stood on a highly polished dark-wood floor, with a huge rug in golds and greens covering the centre. It looked elegant as well as inviting.

A round mahogany occasional table stood on the rug, and a matching china cabinet holding a beautiful tea set and glass ornaments stood against the wall. The long window drapes were in gold too.

As they walked through to the dining room and found that the furniture in there was also in highly polished mahogany wood and elegant, Harriet said, 'Eeh, lass, it's grand.'

'Aye, it is, Harriet. Just as I pictured it.'

To Elisha, though she thought it beautiful, it lacked the

feeling of being a home. That is until she entered the kitchen that led to the back garden. Here, she found a scrubbed table in the centre of the room with six chairs around it, and a fireplace that housed a tall black-leaded stove, with an open fire, ovens and hob. Each side of this were two well-used, comfy chairs.

The pot sink under the window had a curtain around it in red and white gingham that matched those at the window. A long dresser, filled with china, took up most of the back wall, and the red-flagstoned floor shone. A hearth-rug, made of rags, brought the one she used to have home to her, but also the thought that the thieving workmen hadn't even left that behind. They'd taken so much more from her than they knew.

'Are you all right, love? You've gone pale.'

'I don't suppose any of us will truly be all right ever again, Harriet, love.'

'I knaw. The past is allus with us. Is it the rag rug? Only, you went on about that when you used to scream out in your sleep, back in Manchester.'

'It was. But I'm all right now. Let's have a look upstairs, eh?'

The four bedrooms were of a good size; one had a big window that looked out over the garden and the fields behind. This gave Elisha another jolt, as she could see her cottage.

A longing came over her to go there.

'This'll be our bedroom, lass. We'll have to sleep together as we did at the hotel, but every day, I'll be able to look out over me real home.'

'Where ...? Eeh, can you see your cottage from here, then?'

Elisha pointed, 'There, we can almost touch it.'

'Aw, it looks lovely.'

'It is, or can be. I've seen it in its glory and as a wreck. We'll go to it after here and check out how much needs doing.'

'That's going to be hard for you to do, lass, especially with the cemetery visit an' all.'

'It is, but once I've done it, I'll have me mind settled.'

When the cab dropped them at the gate of the cottage, Elisha could hardly speak to ask the driver to wait for them, as her emotions were like a raging thunderstorm. So much hit her that she hadn't expected. She clutched her stomach, thinking she may be sick.

She saw herself hanging out washing. Saw her uncle at the window of the cottage that'd had looked as it did today, neglected and unloved – remembered his vile treatment of her.

The squeak of the hinges of the gate brought Jack to her. His grin, his twinkly eyes. She clung on to the gatepost as she surveyed the land. Still, it showed the signs of that terrible storm, but then she looked at it through the eyes of the child she'd been in happier days and saw its beauty – the lawn in front of the cottage, the tree that sheltered it, the rows of furrows with lush green vegetables sprouting, and others climbing neatly constructed frames. Grandma and Da working away, and Ma at the door carrying a tray – steaming hot tea for Grandma and Da, and homemade ginger beer for her.

And then with Jack again, sitting on the buckets – happy, in love, but oh, so young. Looking on him as her saviour, her hero – a best friend.

And Jan cycling from work, stopping for a cuppa and a chat, or if in a hurry, waving as she pedalled by. And Mick, smiling his kind smile. Hetty waddling up the path, bringing with her a pie she'd baked ... So many memories. A past, but no present with these folk who had meant so much and been such a huge part of her.

An arm came around her. 'It were bound to upset you, lass, but think on, it's going to be yours again. Think of the plans you have for it ... That shed over there, is that the one you have earmarked for the schoolroom?'

Elisha blinked the memories away. As she did, the tears that had pricked her eyes tumbled down her cheeks. She wiped them with her sleeve.

'I hope there were no snot with that. Eeh, some folk don't knaw how to treat good clothes!'

Looking blankly at Harriet and then seeing the funny side of what she'd said, Elisha burst out laughing.

'That's more like it, difficult things to face are better faced with a smile.'

'By, Harriet, sometimes I reckon as you're me grandma reincarnated!'

'Well, from what you've told me of your grandma, that's a compliment, lass. Now, this lot's a mess, and I don't doubt that Grandma would be rolling up her sleeves if she were faced with it, and that's what we've to do an' all.'

'You're right. And I've got what Grandma didn't have at first – the money to get it all sorted.'

'Exactly. Whatever your grandma intended you to do with the money she left, she'd be happy to see you put her cottage to rights.'

'And to get the school up and running, as becoming a teacher is what she so wanted for me.'

'Aye, and to realise your own dreams, not those of others. Naw matter how much you loved them, you don't owe them the achievement of what they wanted in life, only to do what they wanted for you.'

With this, the guilt Elisha hadn't known she was carrying left her. She took a deep breath. 'Let's pick some of those roses – they were planted by Jack when he made the bench and the small patch of garden for us to enjoy. I'd like to take them to put on the grave.'

'They're beautiful, like a sign of hope that naw matter what the winter throws at them, they'll bloom in the spring and give joy.'

'That's lovely, Harriet, love.'

As they tried to break off the stems of roses, Elisha changed her mind. 'I'm not so sure about joy! They give plenty of pain! I'm like a pin cushion with their prickles digging in me!'

'I knaw. Try twisting them, they break off easier . . .'

A loud squeak of the gate's hinges stopped Harriet in her tracks.

An angry young man stood glaring at them. Behind him a young woman with a haughty expression that demanded of them to explain what they were doing.

It was the man who spoke, 'How dare you steal roses from our garden!'

Shock held Elisha tongue-tied, but Harriet straightened

and, with hands on hips shouted, 'It ain't yours, it belongs to her.' She pointed in Elisha's direction.

'Since when? We had an offer accepted this morning! We have been organising the demolition company and the builders while we waited. Everything's in place to have this heap of rubbish knocked down and a new house built, so I'll thank you both to get off my land, or I'll go for the police and let them deal with you!'

Elisha didn't think she would ever close her mouth again, her shock was so deep, but Harriet was having none of it.

'It's us who'll fetch the police! Solicitors Jackson & Jackson are handling the purchase by the only person who will ever own this cottage as she were brought up in it. It's hers, so you two can sod off!'

'I beg your pardon. My solicitor is drawing up the papers as we speak. The deeds will be handed to me within the week. We are seeking planning permission. You are very much mistaken, and I would thank you not to use such language in front of my wife!'

'Huh, language! I'll knock both of your blocks off if you step a foot through that gate!'

This brought Elisha to her senses as she feared for Harriet's health if she was pushed too far.

'Naw, Harriet. Calm down, love. Everything can be sorted.' Turning back to the now red-faced young man, she said, 'I'm sorry, there does appear to be a problem. We had naw idea others were negotiating to buy me grandma's cottage. Me solicitor was going to make enquiries. I wanted to buy it back as it came into me possession when me uncle died. We'll go and see me solicitor now.'

'I should. And I would prepare yourself, miss, as I am the new owner. Though I'm sorry to dash your hopes as this place must mean a lot to you.'

Elisha bowed her head. 'It does, ta ... I have hopes and dreams for it. I wanted to bring it back to how me grandma knew it to be.'

'But it's all rotten and has naw proper foundations. Our survey showed that it can't be renovated, so even if you had bought it before us, you could only knock it down.'

They came further into the garden.

'I'm so sorry about this. I can see how this place means such a lot to you. But my wife and I are looking forward to building something similar to bring our family up in. We'll keep what we can of the grounds, but if there's anything you would really like for yourself, we'd be happy to let you have it.'

Feeling defeated and heartbroken, Elisha said, 'The bench. I'd like the bench, as me husband made it for me.'

The woman, who hadn't softened her stance, glared at Elisha. 'So, you're the murderer's wife! Well, you can have the bench as I'd not sit on it if you paid me.'

'Rita! Please, that's not called for.'

The woman hmphed. Her lips clamped together in defiance before she said, 'I didn't want to buy this place knowing such people had lived in it. I only agreed as you were having it pulled down!'

The man sighed. Then shrugged as he looked back at Elisha. 'Well, miss, if you've finished ... Oh, keep the roses. And I hope all turns out all right for you.'

Harriet, who'd kept quiet, now said, 'Aye, and for you an' all as this place ain't yours as you think!'

Elisha shot her a warning glance, but thank goodness neither the gentleman nor his wife responded.

In the carriage once more they held hands but didn't speak. Elisha's thoughts were a turmoil of shock and desperation to get to Andrew to clarify everything, but she wanted to go to the cemetery first.

Once there, she fell on her knees at the side of the grave containing four of her loved ones and lay a rose for each one as she spoke to them of how much she missed them, how the agony of their loss never lessened, and how she'd done her best but had failed.

Harriet didn't interrupt her but stood to one side and waited. When Elisha glanced at her she saw Harriet was weeping silently and was waiting to give comfort.

She stepped forward. They fell into each other's arms.

'Eeh, lass, life's cruel. One blow after another.'

Before Elisha could answer, she heard Andrew's voice. 'I thought I would find you here ... Oh, Elisha, I'm so sorry ...'

Looking up, she saw him striding towards her.

'I've only just heard. I put a bid in as soon as you left my office. It appears the couple you met had already made one and then upped it when they heard I had. I was certain I would get it for you. I've been to the hotel to find you and then to the cottage. I spoke to the gentleman ... Oh, Elisha, what can I say?'

'So, I've truly lost me grandma's cottage?'

Andrew nodded.

This confirmation was too much to bear. Elisha's legs gave way. Andrew caught her and held her to him.

No feelings of being disloyal came to Elisha; she just felt that Jack would know she needed the support Andrew offered and that he'd be happy for her.

'Eeh, don't take on, Elisha, lass. Nowt can be altered by you getting ill over all of this.'

Harriet seemed to have gained the strength Elisha needed as she said, 'I take it you're the solicitor fella? Well, this is a bad do. Is there nowt you can do?'

'No. I'm sorry.'

Elisha came out of his arms and looked up at him. 'Try again. Please try to do sommat!'

'I don't think there's much I can do. And, in any case, if I did try to buy it back from the new owners, you'll end up with nothing to carry your plans through. You'll need an income, or everything will happen all over again. Look, this isn't the place to talk. Let's go back to my office.'

Elisha paid the carriage driver off, then she and Harriet got into Andrew's car and waited while he cranked the engine. When it burst into life, he jumped into the driving seat.

Sitting back, Elisha watched parts of Blackpool pass by that she'd only seen from carriages taking her to and from funerals, and hoped as the houses whizzed by she never had to do that again, though she would visit the cemetery regularly.

'So, how are you enjoying your freedom, both of you? Well, I know this is a setback, but otherwise it must feel good.'

'Aye, it does. It were grand sleeping in a proper bed, I ain't known that for a long time, and we found a house to rent.'

Elisha left the conversation to Harriet and Andrew, while she tried to sort out her thoughts and feelings. How cruel that the new dream she had for her future, which would have seen her back in her home, had been snatched from her.

Could she lift herself yet again to look towards making different plans? At this moment, with the misery of knowing it was final that Primula Cottage would never be hers ever again, she didn't think she could.

CHAPTER TWENTY-SEVEN

Once they were sat in Andrew's office sipping hot sweet tea, with Harriet munching on a biscuit as if it was her first ever, Andrew leant back in his huge brown leather chair and sighed. 'I feel really bad to have raised your hopes only for you to have them dashed again, Elisha.'

'It isn't your fault, though it is a bitter pill to swallow and has added to me feeling of being a failure.'

'You're not that. Never that.' Harriet had an indignant tone to her voice. 'Look how on your first day in the workhouse here, you took charge of the nursery and look what you achieved, even being taken on as a staff member. Eeh, that's not failing, that's jumping a huge hurdle, lass.'

'I agree with Harriet, you've never failed. And you're not going to this time. I've a few things to discuss with you.'

Andrew shuffled some papers he'd taken from his in-tray. 'These are some properties that are for sale, and I think will suit your purpose. I visited the estate agents and picked up these leaflets showing what each has to offer. They're all affordable and have the outbuildings you need for the conversions you were thinking of.'

Taking the pile, Elisha shuffled through them. One caught her eye. A cottage not dissimilar to Grandma's.

'Where's this one, is it in Blackpool?'

'Yes, it's on a lane that leads to Weeton, just as you turn off Blackpool Road.'

Though the cottage looked right and had the outbuildings she needed, Elisha found she was out of her depth as to where it was. She'd been so closeted as a child, and even after marrying Jack, so knew very little of her hometown of Blackpool, other than the promenade and any roads leading to it from Primula Cottage.

She'd heard of Weeton, as some of the girls at school came from there, but where it was situated, or how you got to it, was beyond her.

'I could drive you there to see it, if you would like me to,' Andrew was saying. 'I cleared my desk once I heard about your cottage as I wanted to be available to support you.'

'Ta, I'd like that.'

The drive didn't take long. Elisha wished it could go on for ever – take her away from all the pain and guilt she harboured and the disappointment she felt like a lead ball for a heart.

But here she was, standing by the low wall that surrounded a cottage that cried out for love and attention. Its tiled roof seemed to sag in the middle with the weight of the chimney, its whole appearance telling of neglect.

Countryside surrounded her – green fields, with lush trees, now fully clothed with an abundance of leaves, swaying in the breeze. A little further in the distance, she could see cows grazing, and in another field horses and sheep. The whole scene spoke of peace.

But where were the people? Families with children who might join her school – everyone would have to travel here by carriage or car. This thought told her that this wasn't the right place for her. She turned to Andrew. He stood side by side with Harriet. She shook her head at them both.

'Eeh, lass, you haven't seen inside yet.'

'I like the look of the cottage, Harriet, but how will I ever build a school here? I need an area where there are families – children – or at least easy access for them.'

Andrew nodded. 'I didn't think of that, though the families that can pay for private education will have transport and be prepared to travel.'

'Yes, once I have a reputation, but I need to be in a convenient place to gain that, and then, as word spreads on me successes, people will travel to bring their children.'

'Nowt but your grandma's cottage is going to be right for you, love, is it?'

Elisha's misery was in the shaking of her head.

Andrew sighed. 'Do you really want me to try to buy the cottage from the new owners?'

'Aye, I do. And I don't see how a cottage that has stood for eighty or so years needs all that work. It's withstood many a Blackpool storm, it isn't damp, the roof doesn't leak! I don't understand. Yes, it needs tidying, but pulling down . . . I couldn't bear that.'

'It isn't going to be easy, that's if I can even achieve the sale. That couple must have had their hearts set on it to have upped their original offer.'

'It was unfair of the bank not to give you a chance to up our offer an' all.'

'Aye, I'm with you there, Elisha,' Harriet agreed. 'How come that was it, a done deal, when they had two interested parties?'

'I didn't think you could afford to pay what they did, or to offer more, once I heard about the surveyor's report, Elisha.'

'You didn't think to make a higher bid! You didn't even think to give me the choice!' Anger flared in Elisha. She'd have paid her last penny to get her cottage back. How dare Andrew make this decision for her?

Without stopping to think, she said, 'We'll find our own way back and I'll look for another solicitor to see to me affairs! One who ain't going to take actions without asking me opinion!'

Andrew's face registered shock. For a moment Elisha regretted her outburst, but then she thought of how much he'd lost her, and the feeling of mistrust increased – she never wanted to see him again.

This decision wasn't without pain. Something deep inside her wanted to run to him – to be held by him. Instead, she dissolved into tears.

Harriet was by her side in an instant. Andrew hovered, looking as if he didn't know what to do.

For Elisha it was as if the fragile world she'd built out of hope had crumbled once more. She sank down onto the wall. Felt the prickle of the brambles that had claimed it, but knew she couldn't stand so put up with it.

'Elisha, I'm sorry. I – I thought I was acting in your best interests, but I realise that wasn't so. I – I have no history to go on, I knew your grandma's cottage meant a lot to you, but didn't realise how much. I'll do my best, I promise. Let's go there now and see if the new owners are there still ... Please, Elisha, just give me a chance to put all of this right.'

Elisha lifted her head. 'Do you think there's a chance?'

'I don't know. Look, I'll drop you at the hotel and then do all I can to sort this out. I'll come to you once I know anything.'

'Naw, I want to be there.'

'I don't advise that as this may entail me going to the bank and seeing if everything is finalised and then if it is, trying to contact the new owners. It can take a while, and all you can do is sit in the car.'

'By, lass, I knaw it's a lot to contend with and the wait's going to be agony, but Andrew's right. You're tired now and distraught. Let's go back to the hotel for a rest, eh? Let's leave it to Andrew.'

Sighing, Elisha, now feeling weary to the bones of her, got up from the wall and went silently to the car. She didn't trust herself to speak, her emotions were a tangle of anger, renewed hope, frustration and, yes, others that wouldn't give her peace and yet gave her guilt.

How could she feel such an attachment to another man so soon after losing her beloved Jack? Besides, she was well beneath his class. He wouldn't look at her in that way. He'd be ridiculed for taking on a common Blackpool lass.

And yet, was she that? It was only her accent that marked her so. She had education, and money. Soon she would own property once more. And she could do something about how she spoke, couldn't she? She would need to if she was going to run a school for paying pupils.

Back in the hotel they sat drinking tea and munching on the biscuits served with it, when Harriet said, 'You've feelings for Andrew, ain't you, lass?'

Embarrassed that this had shown, Elisha blushed.

'I thought as much. Eeh, don't get your hopes up, someone like him will be spoken for and besides, wouldn't glance in the direction of the likes of us ... But, by, I knaw what it's like. I mean, I hadn't had any feelings for anyone since me loss, but I've felt the loneliness of not having a man and Edwin rekindled sommat in me.'

'I don't knaw why I feel like this, I don't want to, it feels like ...'

'Aye, I knaw, like you're betraying your Jack. But think on, lass. He betrayed you when he carried through with his feelings. I know it weren't easy for him, but he should have been a comfort to you after all you went through, not condemn you and accuse you of being a part of it. And then to take the money you'd been given and get drunk and end up taking a man's life! That's not standing by you, is it?'

For the first time, Elisha saw Jack's behaviour in a different light. Yes, he'd been traumatised, but not half as much as she had. She'd needed him. If he'd not allowed those thoughts to take hold of him, they would have been at Jan's now and getting on their feet – she would have recovered properly from what happened as well as from the loss of their babbies. *Oh, Jack, why? Why did you do this to me and hurt so many others?*

But then she looked at Harriet and knew. 'Harriet, love, you should understand more than anyone what happened to me Jack to make him act how he did.'

'Aye, I do. I'm sorry, lass. I've known the feeling of losing control. I shouldn't have said that about your Jack.'

'It's not that you're altogether wrong. Jack should have been stronger. For me as well as for himself. Naw one has to lose control. We all get pushed to our limits. I don't want that to happen to you again, Harriet. We've to find a way to help you.'

'There was a young man came to visit us and talk to us back in the asylum. He was studying to be a psychiatrist. He said we needed to develop a way of coping. He made sense an' all. He said it can be as simple as counting to ten before we react, or taking deep breaths. I tried it, as there were a few in there that got at me. And it worked. Though I had to do both – deep breaths and count to ten – with Nellie.'

'Who's Nellie?'

'She were in the asylum. She'd keep picking at me clothes. I'd be minding me own business and suddenly feel me blouse being pulled from behind. I smacked her one around the face once, then felt awful as she cried like a babby. So, I started to take me deep breaths and counting, and found I calmed, and didn't even mind. I chatted to her. She liked that.'

'Eeh, that's good to hear, not the plight of poor Nellie, but you calming yourself. That'll stand you in good stead.'

'Aye. Anyroad, talking about me problems seems to have helped you, lass, and that's good.'

'It has. Ta, Harriet . . . I tell you what, this hanging around will drive me mad. Let's go and splash our faces and tidy our hair and then go to the circus, eh?'

'By, you couldn't say owt better! The tickets say there's a performance at five. Well, it's four thirty now. Come on, let's hurry!'

It didn't take them long to freshen their faces, apply a smidgen of rouge and a thin layer of lipstick, so they were soon hurrying towards the tower.

'Eeh, I feel like a kid again, Elisha. I can't imagine what it will be like!'

'I can't remember it all. I remember the huge elephant. And the lion with a roar that scared me. Oh, and the clowns, they were so funny.'

'I saw a picture of one once when I was a kid. It was advertising the circus, and it scared the wits out of me! Me ma said she'd take me one day and I peed meself at the thought!'

This had them laughing.

'Well, don't do that today! The clowns are lovely, funny and look amazing.'

They were soon caught up in the wonder of the big ring – the music, the dancing horses dressed in red and gold blankets and wearing huge red plumes. The fear at the roaring lions as they performed tricks. The bearded lady, and the giant elephants dancing in a dainty fashion you wouldn't expect from such huge animals. And they screamed and cringed from the water the elephants sprayed from their trunks. Marvelled at the tightrope walker and the trapeze artist, and laughed till tears ran down their faces at the antics of the clowns. Squirmed at the snake charmer and cried out when a huge snake was brought towards them.

But despite these moments of fear and repulsion, Elisha loved it, and she could tell Harriet did too.

When they came out of the tower, the breeze had become a wind that swirled their skirts around their legs. Juggling with holding hers around her, Elisha cried, 'Oooh, look, candyfloss! I love it, shall we have some?'

'Ugh, it's sickly!'

'Naw. It's like eating the clouds, me ma said. And that's how I imagined it – sweet clouds, but not sickly ... I'm having some anyroad!'

'Ha! I'll have a toffee apple then, seeing as we're reliving our childhood.'

Elisha pushed Harriet playfully.

Once they had bought their treats, Elisha said, 'I do feel like a kid after the circus and eating this candyfloss! ... Ha! I can imagine me walking that tightrope.' Elisha stepped on her toes on the edge of the pavement. At that moment, the wind whipped the candyfloss into her face, causing her to lose her balance. She heard a car skid to a halt, couldn't see for the sticky sugar cloud stuck to her, but then heard the concerned voice of Andrew and felt her heart thump in her chest.

'Oh, God, Elisha, darling, are you hurt?'

He'd called her darling!

But then, with seeing she wasn't hurt, she heard him

giggle. Harriet joined him, letting out a belly laugh that resounded around Elisha.

Wanting to crawl into a hole, she scraped the pink mess from her eyes and looked up into the faces of a laughing crowd. Giggling with them to hide her embarrassment, she took Andrew's hand and allowed him to haul her up. But then felt even sillier as he mopped her face with his hanky!

'Stop! I'll do it. You'll be spitting on your hanky next!'

'Ha! My mother used to do that!'

They laughed together, as the memory came to Elisha of her ma cleaning her face in that way.

Andrew sobered first. 'Oh, Elisha, are you sure you're not hurt? I almost hit you when you fell.'

'Only me pride is burning me with shame.'

'Well, lass, you shouldn't have acted like a kid, having candyfloss at your age!'

Elisha turned to see Harriet with toffee all around her mouth and was undone. She bent double, holding her sides against the pain the laughter was giving her.

Andrew looked from one to the other, and his laughter joined hers. 'Now, I *will* need to spit on my hanky to get that toffee of your nose, Harriet! What on earth have the pair of you been up to? No, don't tell me. Let's dive into here and have tea. I have something to tell you.'

He pointed towards Elizabeth's tea rooms.

'Naw, I can't go in there looking like this! And Harriet ain't being successful getting that toffee off her face either!'

'Well, we could go back to your hotel, you can go to your room and clean up and then come into the lounge for tea – though it might be sherry when you hear my news!'

Elisha gasped. 'You've got the cottage back for me?'

'Let's not jump the gun. I'll tell you all about it when I have a cup of tea in my hand. I need it after making a big mistake, being fired, and then worming myself back in favour!'

He smiled his lovely smile that made his eyes sparkle.

Elisha's heart flipped over. And it came to her that despite the feelings of guilt, she was in love with Andrew. Where that would lead her to in the future, she just didn't know, but she did know she wanted that to be by his side for ever.

This thought stayed with her, making her feel his presence in a way that brought her body feelings of warmth and longing as they sat together in the lounge of the hotel.

Harriet had cried off saying she needed to rest, that the pace of life outside the workhouse was tiring her more than it did being inside!

They sat at a table for two surrounded by the sumptuous décor of elaborate arches, stone carvings and deep blues contrasting with light blues, after treading the royal blue and gold carpet.

A shyness came over Elisha as she remembered Andrew's endearment and the feelings she'd acknowledged. But this soon lifted as she listened to what he said, between sips of his tea and crumbly bites of the scone and jam he'd ordered, and wondered at how he used a fork to eat it! This was something new to her. But what he was saying lifted her so high in spirits that she wanted to call out with joy.

'It appears that the papers aren't finalised and signed, that an acceptance has been agreed verbally but holds no water legally. Therefore, a higher offer can still be considered.'

'Eeh, Andrew ... we still have a chance you mean?'

'We do. Though I would still caution you.'

'Naw, there's naw caution to be considered. I want me cottage back. It should belong to me. It was taken from me ...'

'Don't think of it like that. The cottage had debt attached to it. The debt couldn't be paid and so it was repossessed by the bank, which had a legal right to take ownership.'

'I don't care about any of that. I just knaw it was passed down to me and I lost it!'

The reason for the loss hit her afresh. She hung her head as it came to her that she had a lot to forgive Jack for. And with the thought, some of her grieving healed. She'd held a rosy picture of Jack as her saviour, her lover, her friend, but would any of those do to her what he had? Actions that left her destitute and brought low – put her in a position where those men could do as they liked to her, took her body for their own pleasure and caused the tearing of her babby from her womb. Actions that saw her placed in a workhouse, filled with shame, and having lost everything. *Oh, Jack, Jack, were you the man I painted you as being – or was I just desperate to be saved from the depravity my uncle had taken me to? Did you just appear at the right moment and became like a God to me?*

'Elisha?'

'I – I'm sorry. Aye, I knaw there were reasons, but they weren't of my doing, and so it hurt badly to lose everything.'

'I'm sorry. Sometimes people do make bad decisions, I'm truly sorry that Jack's affected you in such a way.'

'I did love him, but now, in the light of everything, I'm wondering if that love was gratefulness.'

'You had reason to be grateful? I thought you had the cottage and Jack came along and moved in.'

'Naw. It wasn't like that ... I ...'

His hand came across the table and covered hers. 'You don't have to tell me.'

The touch shivered through her. She looked up. Saw what she was feeling mirrored in his eyes.

'Would you like to go for a walk? The wind has dropped. Like all Blackpool winds it can blow you over one moment and then brush your cheek lightly the next.'

These words weren't profound, but Elisha found them beautiful. She nodded.

Taking her bonnet from the back of the chair, she placed it on her head. She wasn't sure why she'd brought it down from her room, or her shawl, but she donned that too.

As they walked along the promenade, they talked. Elisha found herself unfolding her life story to him and ended with her revelation about Jack. 'I think now, I mistook love for the security and friendship that I felt, and the warm feeling of being loved again – of having someone of my own.'

This statement didn't give her shame. It just presented as fact, for now, here with Andrew, she knew what falling in love really was. This was compounded when they reached the area called the gyn – a sort of crossroads that ended North Shore and took you along to Bispham.

Above them folk walked on the high prom, but they were on the lower prom with the sea so close that it occasionally lapped the shore and sprayed tingling drops onto their feet. Andrew halted his steps and looked down at her. She held his eyes. Felt herself become part of him as he swayed closer to her and pulled her into his arms. Without referring to anything she'd told him, he asked, 'May I kiss you?' And in that was all the comfort she needed, as his acceptance of all that had happened to her, without condemnation, meant the world to her.

The kiss was light at first but deepened, until a loud cough had them jumping apart. And then the mutter of 'Disgraceful!' shamed them.

It was a shame that turned to giggles as soon as the stranger had passed by. And then to overwhelming feelings rippling through Elisha as Andrew leant over her again. 'I've fallen in love with you, Elisha . . . I don't know how, or even knew that such a thing could happen so quickly, but it's something I can't deny. I love you.'

She couldn't speak. Everything around her hushed – the swishing of the sea, the whistling of the breeze, the squawks of the warring seagulls and chatter of others, for at this moment a happiness filled her – made her want to burst with the joy that bubbled inside her and shout out to the world that Andrew loved her!

CHAPTER TWENTY-EIGHT

With no one else on this lower prom now, Andrew held her body close with one arm and her head to his chest with his other hand. 'I want to protect you. To make everything right for you and heal the hurt you've been through.'

Elisha couldn't speak, it was all too much, but after a moment she said, 'And I love you, Andrew. Above all others. This feeling I have now, I knaw I haven't ever experienced before.'

That's a lovely thing to say, but I don't want you to deny your love for Jack. I want it to stay with you, and for you to remember him.'

'Ta. And aye. For a moment, as me thoughts gave me all the bad things Jack did, and me feelings for you overwhelmed me, what I felt for Jack paled into not being love. But I did love him. And will remember him with love.'

He pulled away from her and held her hand. 'That's good. Now, what we need to do is to sort out how everything will work. I want us to be married . . . Will you marry me, Elisha?'

'Aye. It's what I want more than owt else.'

'More than the cottage?'

'Aw, that's a hard question.'

'Oh? It shouldn't be.'

'Ha! I were only having you on. But, aye, more than me cottage.'

'That's good to hear. Because ... what we could do ... Look, let's go and sit on that bench. We've such a lot to talk about.'

Once they were sat down, Andrew said, 'So much is occurring to me that I can't keep up with my own thoughts. You come with so many hopes and dreams, and quite a package – the cottage, the school, the mother and daughter, and the two children, besides Harriet, oh, and her carpenter boyfriend – I just don't know how it will all work.'

She told him of her plans for them initially to all live in the house she'd agreed to rent. 'Will you be able to help me apply for their release, Andrew?'

'Yes, of course. Though, you'll have to have jobs in place for them.'

'I can say that Edna and her ma will be me cook and cleaner, and of course Edwin will be me carpenter and odd job man.'

'And the children?'

For a moment, Elisha felt unsure, but then she said, 'Would you mind if we adopted Betty and Ernest? They are so lovely and have been through such a lot ... Besides, I came to love them.' Elisha told how they had lost their mother.

'That's a huge undertaking. Look, I'll arrange to meet them. Get permission to have them out of the workhouse for a day and we'll take it from there.'

This worried Elisha, and yet she understood. No one could be expected to agree to take on two children without even meeting them. 'Can you do that – get them out for a day I mean?'

'Yes. I'm sure there will be a way to have them on a visit, with a view to us adopting them. And I promise you, if they take to me and me to them, I'll prepare myself to be an instant father.'

His smile softened the concerns she had. She recognised that his approach was the best one for him and for the children.

'As for the others, they just need a chance,' she told him. 'Somewhere to live and the means to earn their living. Once out of there, I'm sure they'll find sommat. But they'll need help with their housing, and far as Harriet and Edwin go, a shop or sommat ... Well, she and Edwin are in love. Harriet has the idea of them setting up in business together.' She told him what Harriet had told her. 'They're both very talented and have talked of making furniture and Harriet making the covers and cushions. She can make owt with her weaving, knitting and crochet.'

'Has she had any formal training?'

'Naw, her ma were talented and taught her. I haven't even seen owt she's made, but I believe her. She even hoped to get us out of the workhouse by proving her talent to the master and being allowed out to find work.'

She didn't tell him the lengths Harriet had gone to to

get a loom. She didn't want him thinking badly of her or Edwin.

'Well, well, I didn't know male and female mixed in the workhouse, but I suppose love always finds a way. But now I have some idea of the scale of what comes with you, and it's quite a lot, though you have formed part of a plan and I think we could work it all out between us.'

'I'm sorry to burden you, but they all mean a lot to me.'

'No! Please don't be sorry. It shows me what a lovely, kind person I've fallen in love with. And I haven't forgotten you want to find your friend . . . Jan.'

'Aye, and Mick, her husband, and Hetty, Jan's ma.'

'They were the ones you were trying to get to, weren't they? And you can only recall that they live in Surrey, is that right?'

'Aye, though bits keep coming back to me. A place called Charlwood, or sommat like that.'

She didn't want to be talking about all of this, though it was important to her life. She just wanted Andrew to hold her again, to tell her of his love for her.

'That's a massive help. Finding them will be so much easier now . . . So, we just need to concentrate on the cottage, as the rest is in the future . . . Tell me honestly, what are your true wishes for it?'

'Just to make it beautiful again. To fill it with the love it used to house, and fulfil me dream, aye, and part of me da's dream – to buy the field at the back and keep animals. I see me pupils helping to feed them . . . By, I wish I could find out what happened to Grundy, me donkey, an' all. The young 'uns would love him.'

'That might be possible. But there's quite a lot to be going on with, though I'm sure it can be achieved, I promise you I'm going to try. And to that end, I have an appointment at the bank first thing tomorrow, by which time I'll need an offer to put into place. What are you thinking about that?'

'Eeh, I knaw I said I didn't want you to make choices for me, but in this you'll have to, as I haven't a clue what it all takes.'

Everything crowded Elisha at that moment. Her new dream for herself, and everyone, seemed so out of reach. But she had Andrew by her side, and he would help. He hadn't denied one of her hopes, only picked up on the difficulties of them. For the first time, she began to believe that all her dreams would come true, even down to Da's animal farm becoming a reality.

'That's a lovely smile, Elisha. If I can make that smile appear every day of our lives, I'll be the happiest man alive.'

'Eeh, lad, you're a charmer with your words.'

Andrew burst out laughing. 'I love that you called me lad.'

He took hold of her hand. Shivers went down Elisha's spine with the contact, and increased with him looking into her eyes. But she swallowed hard to dispel them as there was something she needed to ask him. 'I knaw me calling you lad made you laugh, but I shouldn't really speak with me accent. It won't go down well with the parents of the children. Will you help me to speak proper English, like you do, Andrew?'

'Oh, Elisha, you are you. I love your local dialect, and would hate it to be different, but yes, I can see what you mean ... If I do help you, you're only to use your posh voice for work. Otherwise, you won't be you ... The you I've fallen in love with.'

For Elisha, this hit her as something she'd never dreamt would happen – Andrew, a solicitor, falling in love with her, Elisha Randal, née Finley, a girl from a broken-down cottage, with a ma, da and grandma who had made life better for her than those in a similar boat.

'I'll try, though I might slip up sometimes. Jan as we've been talking about did. You see, afore she was married she was a nurse, and she had to use her posh voice for when she was nursing, but her Blackpool one when she was out of the hospital amongst her own, as she feared them thinking she was above herself.'

She related the incident at the hospital to him of Jan being reprimanded by the ward sister. Andrew grinned. 'Well, I bet she doesn't have to think about that now as a farmer ... Anyway, we'd better get back, it's getting late. We've covered a lot considering I only wanted to talk to you about plans for the cottage – I've ended up blooming promising to marry you!'

They both laughed at this. And continued to giggle about it as they walked back to the hotel hand in hand. It all seemed so natural, as if they'd been a couple for ever.

They received a few sideways disapproving glances, but they didn't care. They had just found love and were cocooned in the wonder and joy of it.

As they chatted, Elisha found out such a lot about Andrew. How he lived in a flat above his office, but often visited his mother, who lived in Wrea Green, a village on the way to Preston, and how, when he did, she stuffed him full of food.

She'd asked if his mother was lonely and found that she was too busy to be. She attended church activities and ran charitable organisations to help the poor.

'My flat's a pokey, two-roomed place with one half of the larger room being my kitchen,' Andrew told her. 'And my toilet is outside, and I have a tin bath to lug up the stairs when I want to bath.'

'Naw! I can't imagine that! I thought you'd live in a big house with bathrooms and everything.'

'Mother's house is like that, and it's what I would want for you.'

This made Elisha blush. It was the thought of them living together and all that entailed. Was this really happening? Was she the same Elisha who'd left the hotel just an hour ago? The answer was no; she would never be that Elisha ever again.

'So, is the cottage big enough for us and the ready-made family you're thinking of?'

'Aye, it is. And there's room to make it bigger.'

'And you wouldn't consider demolishing it and building a bigger and better home?'

'Not yet, maybe in the future. But, eeh, we have to make sure it's mine first.'

'I'll do my best for you, darling.'

They had reached the hotel. When they entered there was no sign of Harriet. 'By, she can sleep that one. I've seen her snore her head off when there's been a fight going on in the dormitory in Manchester with all the occupants shouting and screaming – mind, it were different if I woke in one of me nightmares, then she'd be by me side, but sleep through whatever the others fought over, not like me, hiding wherever I could when they started.'

'Oh, Elisha, I hate that you've been through all of that.'

'I knaw. I do an' all. It was an awful experience. But it's over now and I have a lot to look forward to ... I'll see you tomorrow and will keep my fingers crossed all night.'

As she waved him goodbye, Elisha felt bereft. And yet, full of hope and excitement.

As soon as Elisha entered the bedroom she and Harriet shared, Harriet said, 'Eeh, lass, I thought you were never coming back. I'm that hungry!'

There was a pause, then Harriet continued, 'Sommat's happened, ain't it? Have you got the cottage?'

'Naw. Well, not yet, I'll knaw tomorrow.'

'So, what? I can tell by the look on your face, sommat's going on.'

Telling Harriet made it all real to Elisha.

'Aw, lass. That's grand. I'm so happy for you.'

'Ta, Harriet.'

'Naw, I mean it. Naw one deserves the happiness that's coming to you more than you do.'

'That's a lovely thing to say. But you ain't going to be left out. We've plans for you and Edwin, and Edna and her ma, and Betty and Ernest an' all.'

They spent the next half an hour chatting about everything, until Harriet said, 'By, we've gotta go for sommat to eat, before I fade away.'

As they sat at the table in the dining room, eating heartily of the meat pie that was on the menu for that evening, Harriet said, 'So, a shop for me and Edwin! ... Our own shop ... I can't believe it. I'll work hard, lass, and I knaw Edwin will too. We'll make a success of our furniture business.'

'Aye, I knaw you will.'

'But how will it work?'

'I've been thinking about that. And everything hangs on me getting the cottage. If I do, then I'll offer Edwin the job of fixing it up and being in charge of overseeing any building work that's needed. In the meantime, we'll all stay at the house I'm going to rent.'

'Aye, and I can help around the place and maybe start looking for the right shop for me and Edwin.'

They talked for an hour or more, until the waiter came and asked them to move as he had to clear away and close the dining room. By this time, they had a plan. It just needed everything to be in place with the bank.

Elisha couldn't sleep that night. Come morning though, she didn't feel tired, but ready to face the excitement of the new life ahead of her.

She was surprised when Andrew called just as they finished breakfast. Going to where he stood in reception, she was further surprised when he told her that he wanted her to go to the bank with him.

'I've managed to move it to eleven thirty, so we haven't got long before the appointment. Will Harriet be all right?'

'I'll pop back and tell her.'

Harriet was fine with the idea of spending time alone. 'I'd love to go to me old street and see if there's any of me ma's neighbours still there, so don't worry about me. And I might look in a few estate agents' windows for a shop premises up for rent that might suit me and Edwin's needs.'

'That's a grand idea.' Elisha kissed Harriet's cheek. 'Do I look all right, lass? I just thought, I've to go into a bank and they can be a toffee-nosed lot.'

'You look lovely . . . Eeh, you chose well with the clothes you bought, and I love how you share them with me an' all.'

'You're welcome, love.'

Elisha looked down at her navy skirt – liked the shape given by her bell petticoat and how she could just see her navy shoes peeping out from under it. She'd teamed this with a white blouse with billowing sleeves and flared cuffs. To top it off she'd donned the bonnet in navy, which she'd brought down from their room ready for their planned walk, and to provide a contrast she'd chosen her pale-green shawl.

Satisfied after wrapping this around her shoulders, Elisha turned, gave a wave and said, 'Wish me luck.'

Harriet followed her into reception where Andrew was waiting. 'I'm praying it all comes right for you, lass. Give us a hug.'

As she came out of Harriet's arms and turned to go towards Andrew, Elisha had a sense of a being someone different. Someone with real hope.

★ ★ ★

At the bank, Andrew did most of the talking. The bank manager was a man who gave the impression of pushing his importance to make up for his small stature, as everything about him was thin – his strands of ginger hair, his nose and his bony fingers, which he now linked in front of him as he looked at her.

'So, you are asking the bank to give you another chance?'

Stung and embarrassed, Elisha's temper rose. She drew in her breath and stared back at him. 'Naw, I'm here to bid for a property you have for sale.'

Andrew shifted in his seat, making Elisha feel he was cross at her retort. But instead, he stood up for her. 'My client is a lady of means, Mr Peal. She hasn't come here to have her past flaunted in her face, but to partake in a business transaction.'

Mr Peal coughed. His embarrassment obvious from how he shifted in his seat. It was clear to Elisha that this was a man with no respect for folk like herself. There were many like him, who thought those in the lower class shouldn't cross over to their paths unless it was to be a servant to them.

'Well, as I see it an agreement on the property has already been made.'

'But nothing is sealed until the deeds are handed over. You only have an offer you have accepted. I understood that you would be open to a better one.'

Elisha bit her lower lip. Prayed Andrew was correct in all he said, as this didn't seem to be going well. Had Andrew's judgement in bringing her along been a bad decision? Was her presence annoying this obviously prejudiced man?

'Quite so.'

There was a world of disapproval in his answer and his look of disdain. Elisha's hope began to wither.

Mr Peal shuffled the papers in front of him. 'And what is your offer?'

What Andrew offered shocked Elisha, it was over half of all she'd been left, and she had already spent a good sum on the hotel and the shopping she'd done, not to mention the advance rent she'd to pay for the house. Her nerves jangled as she looked at the surprised expression on Mr Peal's face.

'Good gracious, that's quite a jump from what we have been offered. Of course we will take it, but it is subject to the other interested party having a chance to bid further.' He stood and extended his hand to Andrew. 'I'll be in touch. I'll need to contact them as they have a verbal agreement and have consulted a solicitor to draw up the papers and apply for the title deeds.'

He suddenly smiled, but to Elisha it was a sickly smile. 'I can't see them bettering this offer, so with you being able to put everything in motion yourself, I don't think that if you're successful with this bid, there'll be any problems. The bank needs this to be finalised.'

He shook Andrew's hand and bowed a stiff nod of his head towards her. 'Good day. I'll be in contact, Andrew.'

The use of Andrew's first name surprised Elisha. She hoped he wasn't a friend, other than a business one, as she didn't relish having him or anyone like him in her life.

Once outside, Andrew took hold of Elisha's hand. 'Don't worry about people like him. At the end of the day, they are your servants and cannot function without your money.'

Elisha smiled and relaxed, and then wanted to giggle as a picture of Mr Peal sweeping the yard with her witch's broom came to her – though for a moment she wondered if she still had that! And with that realisation came the thought that she'd visit the second-hand shop tomorrow and see if there was a chance Bernard still had any of the pieces of furniture she'd sold to him. She hoped so. Rebuilding her life was going to be easier with treasured items around her, bringing to her future the happiness of the past.

CHAPTER TWENTY-NINE

Two days later, Elisha was signing a bill of sale that finalised her ownership of the cottage. No more bids would be accepted, and she learnt that no new offer had been made. There was a fleeting moment of guilt — almost as if she'd stolen it from under the noses of the couple she'd met, but then she thought of the attitude of the woman and let them slip from her mind.

'There, it's yours once more, Elisha, darling.'

Mr Peal's look of astonishment at this endearment made the happy giggle bubbling inside her spill over to a sort of childish sound, which in turn made Andrew laugh a boyish, pleased-with-himself laugh.

Once outside, he took her hand. 'Let's walk to the seafront. I want to talk about a few things.'

They strolled to the promenade, a place Elisha didn't want to be right now. She wanted to go to her cottage, to check it over and take stock of what needed to be done, but she didn't object as this walk was also a need in her.

It wasn't far, and soon she could hear the familiar sound of the waves splashing on the shore.

They sat on a bench in the warm sunshine, held hands and stared out at the sight of the endless water ebbing and flowing.

'Happy?' Andrew asked.

'Aye. I feel as though I'm back to being me. Though I need to go to me cottage soon to make all of this feel real.'

'We will. But it is the cottage I want to talk to you about. I want to fund half the purchase and half the cost of the work that needs doing ... No, hear me out.'

After making a small gasp that must have held disapproval, Elisha sat quietly by his side, aware of every sinew of him and wanting to hold him, not talk about money matters.

'You see, if it is to be our marital home, then I should have part ownership, and if we are to repair it and extend it, then funds will be needed for that. Yours are running low and I don't want that for you. I want you always to have money of your own. You need to get your school up and running, and that should be just yours as it is your dream.'

'Aye, I can see that and want it that way. So, you're saying that you will own half the cottage and the land?'

'Yes and no. We will own it jointly. All of it.'

'Aw, Andrew, that sounds lovely, like I'm not parting with owt, but gaining a great deal.'

'And that's how I always want you to think. Now, I have news for you. I've been in touch with Jan and Mick this morning by telephone. It was easy to get their number from the exchange once I had their location.'

'What! Eeh, how are they? Were they worried about me ...? Did they knaw ...?'

'About Jack? Yes, they read it in the papers and have been shocked to the core and frantic with worry about you. They wrote to a lady called Jean, but the letter was returned "address unknown". Jan said she'd only an inkling of where Jean lived, not her full address, and had got it wrong. But then Mick's mother took ill, and their lives were in a turmoil as sadly ... I'm very sorry to tell you, darling, but Mick's mother passed away a few weeks ago.'

'Naw!'

Andrew nodded his head, then Elisha felt his arm come around her as she asked, 'Is Hetty all right?'

'She is. Jan says she misses Blackpool. They all do and want to come back.'

'Eeh, that'd be grand, but how can they?'

'Well, firstly, they're coming to see you. And while here they will look around. They want another farm, as they love the life, it's just the place that isn't right for them. They'll be here in the next few weeks.'

'Naw! That soon! Eeh, Andrew, it's as if all me wishes are coming to me ... And you've made that possible. You've done so much for me ... I love you. By, I love you so much.'

'And that's all the thanks I need ... Your love.'

His hand pulled her closer. And as had happened before, the sounds around them faded and her world became just him and her. A world full of love and hope.

When they reached the cottage, the sun shining down on it gave it a happy appearance, almost as if it was smiling with happiness and welcoming her back.

Elisha ran up the garden path with the key she'd held so many times now feeling like the key to the rest of her life.

The door creaked open. The air smelt musty, but the feeling she'd always had rushed into her. A feeling of being home.

She turned a happy grin towards Andrew. 'It's so wonderful ... It's our home.'

He beamed at her as he entered. 'And one day soon, I will carry you over the threshold ... Oh, Elisha, I don't know how this all happened so quickly, but you've made me the happiest man alive.'

She went into his arms and received his kiss as if it was the nectar of her life, clinging to him, expressing her love in the brief moments their lips parted, felt the stirring of desire deep inside her, and his need as he pressed closely to her body.

'I love you, my Elisha ... I want to make you mine.'

How it happened that they were on the cold, hard floor, Elisha didn't know or care, she only knew that she wanted to give all she was to her Andrew. And as his kiss deepened, she yielded to him, drank of his kisses, his touches, allowed the stripping of her clothes, rolled with him till she straddled him, not feeling the harshness of their bed being stone slabs.

And then he was on top of her. She cried out as she took him deep inside her. His cries joined hers as they sought to give and to receive a love that was almost too huge for them both, but found the fullness of it in the waves of the exquisite pleasure they shared.

When it was over, they clung to one another, kissed, cried tears of joy, and spoke of their love being stronger than either of them – wondered at how soon it had come to them and consumed them. And knew they were one.

This then went into giggling out their joy as they rose and dressed, hugged and found a wonderment that Elisha had never experienced. For her, it put Jack to rest in a corner of her heart that she would keep for him, but she had given herself to Andrew and that, she knew, would be for ever.

More kisses followed, and declarations of love, and plans to marry within weeks were made as they went hand in hand around the cottage.

Memories assailed Elisha and she related them to Andrew, making him laugh at some but hold her close on hearing others.

All in all, Andrew agreed with her that the cottage was sound, and didn't even have any of the subsidence often seen in properties in Blackpool. They both wondered at the surveyor's report, with Andrew saying he would look into it. 'There's something fishy here. I'm suspicious that bribes have been given to help further planning permissions. We need another survey doing to make sure, but it feels as though illegal and false statements have been made.'

'So, they could pull it down, you mean?'

'Yes. You see, you can't just demolish property and build what you like in its place, there need to be reasons. Anyway, let's go and have a look at the grounds.'

'Aye. Though they're the saddest part as they're in ruin to what they were in the past, both in me grandma's time and me and Jack's time.'

'Anything can be restored, darling.'

'It can, and you've proven that by rebuilding me, as I were in ruins an' all.'

Andrew loved everything he saw and had the same visions that Elisha had for it all – for where the schoolroom should be, the animal farm, even down to Jack's bench.

'We'll keep it in memory of him. And we'll enjoy many a happy hour sitting there under the tree, planning our future and, hopefully, with our own family of children – Betty and Ernest, and those we're going to make too.'

'Eeh, Andrew, I do love you ... And by, we may have started making them of our own already!'

'Ha! I hope so, though I would worry that would interfere with your plans, so we won't hope for that, and I'll be careful in future until you're ready.'

Elisha felt so ready now. The thought of holding her and Andrew's babby filled her with wonder. She'd never forget or seek to replace her little Ted, or her lost unborn babby, but give the same love to her and Andrew's child as she had to them.

The next few weeks passed in a whirl of moving into the house, and getting the right permissions in place for Edwin, Edna and Polly to be released into her care. But best of all having the permission to have Betty and Ernest out for day visits, as was happening today.

'Eeh, calm down, lass, or you'll explode!'

Everyone around the breakfast table laughed at Harriet saying this as they munched the delicious fried eggs with fried bread prepared by Polly. Elisha had found that she and

Polly took to each other as if they'd known one another all their lives.

Polly had the funniest sense of humour, which had them all laughing at the silliest things. Edna was the happiest that Elisha had ever seen her, to be back with her ma and at having prospects of helping Elisha with her school. They'd even planned that she should study to one day become a qualified teacher herself. Something she could never have dreamt of in the past.

'By, it's a grand day though,' Polly said now, 'Them two young 'uns deserve the chance you're giving them, lass. I hope today goes well for them, and for you and Andrew.'

'Ta, Polly.' Elisha sighed. 'I wish I could get all the kids out of there, but it ain't possible. And though naw teacher should ever think this, Betty and Ernest touched a special place in me heart.'

Elisha caught a glance between Edwin and Harriet. Knew their love for each other had deepened and that they couldn't wait for the day they had a home of their own and were married. As it was, she often woke in the night to find the bed next to her empty. She prayed they took care, but couldn't condemn them as she and Andrew were lovers out of wedlock too, only their love nest was his flat, which she visited as often as she could without raising suspicion.

The love they had first expressed on the floor of the cottage had grown into something Elisha never imagined could be between two people. A colliding of souls, a desperate taking and giving of the love they had for one another. A sating of the desire that consumed them. Both longed for the cottage to be ready so they could arrange their wedding day.

For her, it was ready now. The inside had all been painted, doors repaired and a thatcher was coming soon to repair the roof. It was the extension they'd agreed upon that was taking the time. Planning permissions, engaging architects and builders, and then a landscape firm to put the garden how she wanted it. Everything took time. Though both were so in awe of Edwin, and his knowledge and skill at what he did, and how he was overseeing the work needed, they had agreed that her schoolroom should wait until after all was completed and they were married.

As Elisha entered the workhouse to collect Betty and Ernest later that morning, Andrew squeezed her hand. In tune with every part of her, he knew her feelings at having to go through these gates once more.

The shudders of her time here rippled through her, bringing a fear of not knowing what the future held. How could it have happened to her – the her she'd been? But it was still a reality for all the poor souls she saw wandering about – lost, and bewildered. How she wished she could make their world right as her own had become.

All these sad thoughts left her as she heard Betty's squeal of delight, 'You came back! By, I thought we'd lost you an' all, miss.'

'Naw, you'll never lose me, lass . . . Hey! Watch out!' This last was said on letting out a loud laugh as Betty jumped at her and she only just caught her whilst she struggled not to overbalance.

Hugging Betty to her, she said, 'By, it's good to see you... And you, Ernest. You're a sight for sore eyes.'

Ernest looked up at her. 'Have you got sore eyes, then, miss?'

They all laughed, and Andrew put out his hand to Ernest. 'Come on, Ernest, we're taking you and your sister out for the day.'

Ernest looked unsure, so Andrew went down on his haunches. 'I'm Andrew. Pleased to meet you, Ernest. And I love you already.'

'You love me? I don't knaw you.'

'Ha, you may not, but you're more like me than you know.' Then, referring to the query about the sore eyes, Andrew told Ernest, 'We're alike because we deal in facts. You and I see everything as it is until we can get to the bottom of it. And we speak in a direct manner. We're going to get on well, I can tell.'

Ernest smiled but didn't say anything. Elisha had thought that what Andrew had said would have gone over his head, but it didn't seem to. And as Ernest took Andrew's hand it was as if he was accepting Andrew and ready to make friends with him. Andrew beamed at her.

With the paperwork completed they walked back out of the gates. To Elisha, it was like shedding the last of the invisible chains that held her to this place, as a freedom to come and go was truly how it was. And the thought came to her that she'd never again have to stay in the confines of the workhouse walls.

Grateful that the day was a sunny one, as they'd been having a lot of late-summer showers, Elisha's happiness seemed complete as they headed for the beach, making a stop at one of the many street kiosks on the promenade that sold buckets and spades.

Ernest stared out at the water, his face showing his wonderment as they got out of Andrew's car and walked across the road towards it.

'Where does it come from, Andrew?'

What followed Ernest's question turned into a deep discussion, as they found a good place for the deckchairs they'd hired from the man with stacks of them on the approach to the beach, and spread towels for Ernest and Betty to sit on.

'I don't knaw why you want to knaw all that stuff, Ernie. It's just there, ain't it?'

'Naw, it has to come from somewhere.'

'Ernest is right, it did.' With this, Andrew carried on his explanations that, though Elisha found them interesting, she had to let go over her head as Betty vied for her attention.

'I've never heard you call Ernest "Ernie" before Betty.'

'Naw, I weren't allowed to, Mrs Parkin told us we were to use proper names only.'

Thinking this strange, as Betty was short for Elizabeth and that had been allowed, Elisha just said, 'I see, well I like it. Shall we call him that today?'

'Aye, I want to.'

Turning to where Andrew and Ernie were still deep in conversation, Elisha called over, 'Hey, this is supposed to be a fun day, come and build sandcastles with your sister, Ernie.'

Andrew grinned. 'I think Ernest suits him better, but I like the informality of Ernie. What do you think, young man?'

'Ernie is what me ma called me, and I like it.' Then something happened that didn't very often – Ernie grinned. As he did, he ran over to Elisha and flung his arms around her. 'And I like you, and don't want ever to go back.'

Elisha's eyes filled with tears. But then with joy as it appeared Andrew didn't need a few days with the children to make his mind up, as he said, 'Come here, both of you.'

Ernie ran to him, but a shyness had come over Betty.

'Come on, I want to tell you something, Betty.'

His endearing smile took Betty's shyness away as she got up and ran to him too.

'How would you like it if you could stay with us for ever?'

Betty answered, as was usual when they were together in a conversation. 'By, I'd love that, wouldn't you, Ernie, lad?'

Andrew threw back his head and laughed out loud. Then cuddled Betty to him and became serious. 'Well, that's what we are working towards, becoming your mummy and daddy.'

'Like a ma and pa, you mean?'

'Yes, Betty, like a ma and pa.'

Both children were silent for a moment and Elisha's heart dropped. Quickly qualifying what Andrew had said, she added, 'Only if you want to that is, and it will take time – a few weeks or more.'

'I want to, miss.'

'Aw, Ernie, come here.'

As she cuddled Ernie to her, Elisha thought the longing for her little Ted would overwhelm her, but then Betty flung herself at her saying, 'I want to an' all, and I don't want to go back, I don't!'

Elisha realised with this that they had spoken too soon. A promise of a future wasn't good enough for a child, especially those suffering as these two were.

'We can't stop that happening, Betty,' Andrew said, but we can make your time in there as short as possible – a few weeks maybe, maybe less as Elisha can offer you a home. But in the meantime, we'll come for you as often as we are allowed to and have you for visits.'

This cheered Betty, but mystified Elisha. Was he saying they would be married sooner than they planned?

'Now, go and play. Elisha and I have things to discuss.'

'What's discuss?'

This from Betty shocked Andrew.

'It's to talk about things – having a discussion about them, Betty,' Elisha told her. 'Now do as Andrew says and go and play with your brother. Build sandcastles and paddle, only don't go too far into the water, just on the edge and let the sea lap over your feet.'

With the children happily competing over sandcastles, Elisha looked at Andrew. 'By, it's grand that you already feel like you could be a da to them, but I wish you hadn't said owt, they have their hopes up now.'

'That's fine, darling, as I already have things in place.'

'What?'

'Yes. I knew how much all of this meant to you and had made my mind up that even if the children hated me, I was going to go through with it. I can't finalise everything until we're married as it isn't allowed for a single person to adopt a child, so I think we need to set our date, and soon.'

Elisha's heart lifted and skipped a beat. 'But the cottage isn't ready!'

'Well, you have a lovely house on rent. And I have my eye on a couple of places. One for Polly and Edna – they should have a place of their own. And I know of a job that Polly could take over and will pay enough for them to cope with the rent, etc.' He told then of how Gertrude, his cleaner, who also cleaned other offices, besides a school in the evening, and earnt a good wage, was retiring and he thought Polly could take over from her.

'Eeh, that'd be grand for her – for both of them. And I'll be employing Edna soon to help sort out and set up the schoolroom.'

'So, that leaves Harriet and Edwin. I went to the cottage yesterday and had a chat with Edwin. I think his dream of making bespoke furniture could really work. His carpentry skills are excellent. Anyway, we talked of me finding a premises and making him a loan to get him started.'

'You'd do that for them! Aw, Andrew, I do love you, you're the best thing that's ever happened to me.'

'And you to me. You've brought out something in me I never knew was there – the need to help those less fortunate than I have been ... Anyway, the rest of my plan is also in place – well, in part, I've to get your approval first.'

'Mine? Is it owt to do with the cottage?'

'No, and don't look so worried. The cottage, though it will grow over time into being a beautiful house, is our forever home ... It's to have a double wedding with Harriet and Edwin!'

'A double wedding! Eeh, I'd love that, but ...'

'Well, Edwin spoke of wanting to marry Harriet so she could move in with him if we find the right place for their work and as a home, and I thought this would help them both as they wouldn't afford a proper wedding without our help – sharing ours would give them that help.'

'It all sounds grand. Ta ever so much for everything, Andrew. You've given me so much by helping me and me friends, I don't knaw how to thank you.'

'You already are. You've brought happiness to my dull existence. You've saved me from the stuck-up young ladies my mother is always parading in front of me, and you've given me love.'

Elisha looked into his eyes. He was the most loving and kind person she'd ever met. Everything he did, he did for others and to make her happy. He reminded her of her grandma, for she'd been the same; look how she always put her barrow of veg and fruit outside the gate for the poor to take from, and how she had one mission – to fight for her family.

Andrew tightened his grip on her hand. 'Everything will come right, Elisha, I promise.'

To Elisha, it already had. Her dreams were in place and achievable, those who meant so much to her had a future, and soon she was to marry the man of her dreams.

EPILOGUE

1909

Elisha stood in the refurbished barn and looked around her. The little tables and chairs that Edwin had made cried out for children. The blackboard, blank for now, would soon have the sound of chalk scratching over it, and happy children would fill her life. For in the near future, she was to open the doors to her first pupils – seven including her own children, Betty and Ernie.

What a wonderful day that had been, when the twins' official adoption was finalised!

And that had been followed by many a happy day – her own and Harriet's wedding day, when the twins had been bridesmaid and pageboy. Jan and Mick returning, and Harriet and Edwin opening the doors to their business, which already showed signs of thriving, with orders going as far as London, won from the many visitors who came early in the season.

But the cottage being completed was the highlight.

Elisha closed her eyes and giggled, as she was back in time when she and Andrew had walked up the path together. 'Now, my day has come,' Andrew had said. And with this he'd picked her up and done as he'd promised he would and carried her over the threshold.

Her giggle increased as she remembered him getting stuck in the new porch they'd had built on the front of the cottage, but determinedly making it into their living room.

'The first thing I am going to do, Mrs Jackson, is dispel the memory of that cold, hard floor.'

With this, he'd lowered her onto the huge, soft rug, joined her and, between kisses and declarations of love, stripped her of her clothes.

What happened between them was special, something she would treasure as a homecoming to remember. A new beginning. Nothing that had happened between these walls in the past mattered, as they were in the present, they had love to give and to take.

A sudden opening of the door to the schoolroom jolted Elisha out of the wonderful dream.

'Eeh, lass! Everyone is waiting on you – the endless dreamer – and you stand in here, as if you'd have everything materialise for you this moment!'

'Jan! Aw, Jan, can you believe all that has happened?'

'Naw. It's a whirlwind and one carrying everyone forward on a happy tide.'

'You knaw, here we are, just six months in from me and Harriet's wedding day, and you, Mick and Hetty are back living across the road – it all beggars belief.'

'I knaw. When I was a little lass helping me da on the farm, I never dreamt I would one day own it, or that I would have such lovely tenants as Edna and her ma living in the cottage I was brought up in. Everything has worked out perfectly.'

'It has. They weren't happy in that flat, but now, with Polly working and earning good money, they have a good life. And Edna only has to come across the road when she works for me.'

'It's all grand. Now, come on, love. It's the day of your dream coming true – the day your school is licensed! Jean, me ma and your ma-in-law are vying with each other over the cakes they've baked, Harriet and Edwin are here, and Bert is entertaining the kids!'

'Where's Polly and Edna?'

'They've just arrived, and naw hostess to greet them.'

'Aye, and I've come on the same mission as Jan, lass.'

Elisha turned to see Harriet entering the schoolroom. 'We need our hostess out here with us.'

'Eeh, Harriet, we've made it, me and you, lass. We're on our feet.'

'You have,' Jan agreed. 'Both of you are set for life and I reckon that calls for a group hug.'

Elisha and Harriet went willingly into Jan's arms, giggling like schoolchildren. The hug seemed to seal the happiness they all felt, as well as marking the three of them as friends for life.

Going into the kitchen cemented for Elisha how much her fortunes had changed, as instead of the small, ill-equipped scullery-type she'd grown up with, it was now huge, thanks to the extension at the side of the cottage. But for all its modern appearance – a full range on one wall, a lovely dresser that went the length of another, and the deep pot sink with the shiny, brass pump on the side, enabling them to have a supply of rainwater for bathing, and the large central table with eight chairs around it, made by Edwin – it was cosy.

The walls were cream, and this was offset by the lovely spring-like fabric of blues and yellows that covered the fireside chairs, the seats of the dining chairs and the matching curtains, all made by Harriet.

Elisha loved it.

'Ahh, there you are!' Alice, her ma-in-law, looked flustered. I've been setting out the cakes and couldn't find enough cake stands for them.'

'Oh, Alice, I'm sorry. I have a couple in the sideboard in the living room. I'll get them.'

As she said this, Elisha thought it a fitting place for her new china – her grandma's lovely old sideboard. The only piece of her furniture left in the second-hand shop, that had been in her life for ever.

'No, dear, this is your day. Jean will do that.'

Jean looked up, exasperated, but grinned at Elisha as she obediently went into the living room.

For all Alice's bossy ways, they all loved her. Elisha thought the world of her for accepting her into the family with loving arms and being a wise counsellor. A tall woman, she carried herself in a stately way that had everyone doing her wishes and almost bowing to her. But for all that, she was a kindly woman at heart.

★ ★ ★

'Eeh, lass, there you are. I ain't had me cuddle yet.'

'Mick! Where have you been hiding?'

'Ha, in the garden. I knaw when to keep out of the way of the ladies when they're in the kitchen.'

Alice giggled. She'd really taken to Mick and Jan – especially Mick! – and hung on his every word. With Harriet and Edwin, she had a kind of admiration of their talents, and treated them kindly, but that's as far as it went. Jean, Edna and Polly she treated as though they were her servants, but none of them minded. They tolerated her and showed her respect. It seemed, though, that Alice was one for the gentlemen, as she always chatted with Bert too.

Sadly, Nancy hadn't been able to come today, as she hadn't anyone to take over from her in her shop, but she'd sent along a card wishing Elisha luck and had also sent some of her best home-cooked ham for the buffet.

As Elisha went out into the garden, she sighed happily.

Looking at all those she loved gathered there, and hearing the sound of the pigs snorting in what they called 'Pa's field', joined by the clucking of the hens, and the odd laughing sound from their donkey, Grundy the Second, made her think that, all in all, they were a family – a joyful family.

The afternoon was a mixture of chatter, munching on delicious food and enjoying the playful laughter of Betty and Ernie. It was when Elisha got up to go to bring out the huge pot full of tea, that Andrew followed her into the cottage.

'So, how is the new schoolmarm feeling?' he asked.

'Eeh, I'm as happy as a pig in muck, ta, love.'

Andrew characteristically laughed out loud, with his head back, before recovering and retorting, 'Eeh, lass, that's good to hear.'

They both giggled. But when they reached the kitchen, Andrew opened the back door and gently pulled her outside. There, in the privacy of only having the animals watching them, he took her in his arms and kissed her.

As the kiss deepened, Elisha was lost in a world of love and the promise of a wonderful life ahead. And not just for her but for all those she loved. They were all beginning again. And all were on a path that meant she could never see the day when their destiny was taken from them.

Her beloved Andrew would see to that.

He'd taken her and her shattered life and put her back together again. He'd helped her to realise her dreams. The one she had as a daughter, and the one she'd harboured for herself. And in doing so, he'd given her the knowledge that her grandma could now truly rest in peace.

A LETTER FROM MAGGIE

Dear Readers,

Thank you for choosing my book. I hope you have enjoyed reading it as much as I loved writing it.

When I set out a story as a draft, it is then a journey of ups and downs as the characters become alive and dictate their story to me. My own emotions are a rollercoaster as I travel through their lives and become part of them. I hope I have achieved that for you. There is no greater compliment to an author than a reader saying they felt everything was happening to them, that they knew the characters as if they were alive and they were part of their stories.

And then, if as a reader you leave a review on whatever media site you follow, you are hugging the author. I hope I get a hug from you all.

As we take our own journey through life, we are often wobbled from our normal path as something is thrown at us that we didn't expect. That has happened to me this year. My secure, happy, full-of-love life has been thrown into a direction that has taken my stuffing from me and changed everything. I have gone from having all the time in the world to write as everything was supported and coped with by my darling husband, to now being his carer and supporting him with all my love, time and effort – a labour of pure love, which I am happy to dedicate myself to.

But adjustments have to be made. One of these is that I have to retire from traditional publishing, and there will now only be one more book by me as Maggie Mason. I am drafting it out as we speak and loving the process, hoping to make it my best yet.

I am continuing to write my books, and they will be published by myself on Amazon as Kindle downloads, paperbacks and ebooks. I am also looking into audio too as I know many of you enjoy this format.

I have loved my journey writing as Maggie Mason, setting my stories in my lovely hometown of Blackpool, a place of warmth, welcome and fun. And I've loved working with the wonderful team at Sphere. It will be sad for me to write my last one for them, but I will try to make it my best for you. So, look out in the springtime of 2027 for it appearing on the shelves.

In the meantime, thank you for all your support and the understanding I know you will have for me, and I hope you will continue to enjoy my work, and spread the word for my Maggie Mason books which will always be available on Amazon.

Take care, all of you, and remember, when trouble comes to your door, reach out as I have done and you will find friends in caring people who have their arms open to you. For me that has been at the wonderful Forget Me Not Café for Dementia sufferers and their carers. They have taken me and my darling husband from despair to a place of hope and adjustment. I cannot thank them enough.

Much love to you all,
Maggie
xxx

I love interacting with my readers. You can find me at:
www.authormarywood.com
From here you can email me and sign up for my three-monthly email.
I'm also at:
Facebook: www.facebook.com/MaryWoodAuthor
Instagram: mary.wood.7796420
TikTok: marywood616

ACKNOWLEDGEMENTS

So many people are involved in getting a book published and my heartfelt thanks go to all those who worked so hard to make this happen for *A Daughter's Dream*, and took time to involve me in every process - the wonderful team at Sphere:

My editor, the kind, caring, and always on hand for me Elisha Lundin. Who helps and advises me from synopsis to completion. Thank you, I am so grateful for your insight and knowledge. I hope you like that my main character is named after you as a tribute to you.

The editorial team headed by Frances Rooney, who scrutinise my work and make it shine from the page with their suggested tweaks and checking on my research. Thank you. I'm sorry that there is always a lot for you to do as my fingers rush away writing the story that is pouring from me, and I make mistakes in the process – always I know you have my back and that of my book.

All those who work away in the background – the team who take care of publicity, the cover designers, typesetters, and formatters, and many more. All play a valuable part in the production of my books, and my heartfelt thanks go to you all.

My thanks go too to a valued member of my personal team – James Wood, my beloved son. James scrutinises the proof copy – this is the stage when the book is formatted, and ready for publication, but needs a final check. James finds so many tweaks that need adding, or correcting, and helps, along with the editorial team, to ensure a clean manuscript is ready to go to press. Thank you, James, you are my rock.

Many others are a rock to me and help me to climb my mountains – my darling husband, Roy, my adored children, Christine, Julie, Rachel and James, and my much-loved grandchildren and great-grandchildren. You are all the light of my life. Thank you - always you are by my side, encouraging me and giving me support. My love knows no bounds for you all.

And finally, my thanks to such a huge part of my writing world – my valued and lovely readers. I cannot thank you enough for your support, your encouragement, and for those of you who follow me on social media or take the time to find my email through my website - your lovely comments and interaction with me mean such a lot to me. I strive to bring my imaginary world to you in a way that you feel involved with my characters. It warms my heart when you tell me I have succeeded. As does the way you are always there for me if I am flagging. You are an extension of my family to me. Thank you.

More from Maggie Mason

Blackpool, 1914

Seventeen-year-old Maddie has grown up in a boarding house on one of Blackpool's poorest streets. Life is busy, but happy, as she works alongside her mother taking care of their visitors. But when war breaks out, her happiness is shattered as her fiancé is called up to fight for his country, and suddenly Maddie's future is filled with uncertainty.

As Blackpool becomes a training ground for the army, the guesthouse is used as a billet for soldiers, and Maddie soon finds herself drawn to one in particular: Arnie. As the pair grow close and his departure date nears, their feelings for one another intensify. Little does she know, the short six weeks she's known and loved Arnie will impact the rest of her life . . .

As Maddie comes to terms with a future she couldn't have ever imagined, her best friend Daisy, working in her mother's café on Blackpool promenade, promises to help any way she can.

With so much change and uncertainty on the horizon, can Maddie protect her growing family from the hardships of war?